JAGGER

STEELE SHADOWS INVESTIGATIONS

AMANDA MCKINNEY

HH TISEVICH

Paperback ISBN 978-1-7340133–99
eBook ISBN 978-1-7340133–7-5

Editor(s): Nancy Brown
Cover Design: Steamy Reads Designs

AUTHOR OF SEXY MURDER MYSTERIES

https://www.amandamckinneyauthor.com

DEDICATION

For Mama

A note from the author:

Welcome to the small, southern town of Berry Springs! If you're looking for sizzling-hot alpha males, smart, independent females, and page-turning mystery, you've come to the right place. As you might have guessed, STEELE SHADOWS is a spin-off series from the Berry

Springs Series. But don't worry, you don't need to read Berry Springs first. Think of Steele Shadows as Berry Springs' darker, grittier, bad boy brother. That said, grab a tall glass of sweet tea (or vodka if you're feeling saucy), and settle in for a fun adventure that—I hope—gives you a little escape from the day to day... (and maybe a new book boyfriend).

Enjoy!

ALSO BY AMANDA MCKINNEY

★*The Viper, coming Fall 2021* ★

And many more to come...

AWARDS AND RECOGNITION

AUTHOR OF SEXY MURDER MYSTERIES

JAGGER (STEELE SHADOWS INVESTIGATIONS)
*2021 Daphne du Maurier Award for Excellence in
Mystery/Suspense 2nd Place Winner*

THE STORM
*Winner of the 2018 Golden Leaf for Romantic Suspense
2018 Maggie Award for Excellence Finalist
2018 Silver Falchion Finalist
2018 Beverley Finalist
2018 Passionate Plume Honorable Mention Recipient*

THE FOG
*Winner of the 2019 Golden Quill for Romantic Suspense
Winner of the 2019 I Heart Indie Award for Romantic Suspense*

2019 Maggie Award of Excellence Finalist
2019 Stiletto Award Finalist

CABIN 1 (STEELE SHADOWS SECURITY)
2020 National Readers Choice Award Finalist
2020 HOLT Medallion Finalist

THE CAVE
2020 Book Buyers Best Finalist
2020 Carla Crown Jewel Finalist

DIRTY BLONDE
2017 2nd Place Winner for It's a Mystery Contest

RATTLESNAKE ROAD
Named one of POPSUGAR's 12 Best Romance Books to Have a Spring Fling With

Steele Shadows Reviews:
"Holy crap! What a book!" -5 STAR Goodreads Review

"Riveting mystery romance." -5 STAR Amazon Review

"A page-turning blend of suspense, steam, and heartbreaking angst." -5 STAR Amazon Review

"My mind is BLOWN." -Book Blogger, Books and Beauty by Cassie

"A brilliant, compelling, raw, breathtaking story. Cabin 1

should be read by every romantic suspense lover." -5 STAR Goodreads Review

"Wonderful, amusing, absolutely addictive." -5 STAR Amazon Review

"Scorching." -5 STAR Bookbub Review

"My mouth literally hung open when I finished this book. You do not want to miss this one." -5 STAR NetGalley Review

Praise for the Berry Springs Series:
"One of my favorite novels of 2018." -Confessions of an Avid Reader, **The Fog**

"**The Woods** is a sexy, small-town murder mystery that's guaranteed to resonate with fans of Nora Roberts and Karin Slaughter." -Best Thrillers

"Danger, mystery, and sizzling-hot romance right down to the last page." -Amazon Review, **The Creek**

"Amanda McKinney wrote a dark, ominous thrilling tale spiked with a dash of romance and mystery that captivated me from start to finish..." -The Coffeeholic Bookworm, **The Lake**

"**The Storm** is a beautifully written whodunnit, packed with suspense, danger, and hot romance. Kept me guessing who the murderer was. I couldn't put it down!" -Amazon Review

"I devoured **The Cave** in one sitting. Best one yet." -Amazon Review

"**The Shadow** is a suspense-filled, sexy as hell book." - Bookbub Review

∼

Fair Warning: Jagger contains adult language, content, and steamy love scenes.

LET'S CONNECT!

Text **AMANDABOOKS to 66866** to sign up
for Amanda's Newsletter and get the latest
on new releases, promos, and freebies! Or, sign up below.

https://www.amandamckinneyauthor.com

JAGGER

He found her covered in blood.
She promises she's innocent.
The question is... Can he trust her?

Feared just as much on the streets as at a crime scene, Homicide Detective Max Jagger has dedicated his life to one thing—speaking for the dead. Everyone and everything else be damned, including his own demons. During one of the most oppressive heat waves to hit the small, southern town of Berry Springs, the former Navy SEAL is called to a scene where a real estate heiress is found standing over a dead body, holding the murder weapon. The local cops immediately dub it a slam-dunk case, but if Jagg has learned anything from his days running special ops, it's that nothing is as it seems... including this suspect.

Despite her name, Sunny Harper is as beguiling as a fallen angel. Mysterious, clever, completely unwilling to cooperate, and, perhaps his least favorite quality—mind-numbingly intoxicating. When evidence from the scene suggests an accomplice, Jagg begins to believe that Sunny is both innocent and in danger, despite the towns' uproar to lock her up. Torn between his growing feelings for his suspect, he takes Sunny to a secluded lake house where he discovers there's much more behind those enchanting green eyes... including secrets that could take them both under.

With his career on the line and the clock ticking, Jagg must decide if he can trust Sunny... before they both get burned.

2021 Daphne du Maurier Award for Excellence in Mystery/Suspense 2nd Place Winner

1

JAGG

a thin fog slithered around the headstones like a snake searching for its prey. Or perhaps more fitting for this story, like a virus, spreading, spreading, spreading, slowly consuming everything in its path. But it was too late. The crowd was gone. I was the only one left.

Come and get me, I thought. I'd spent my entire life tempting the devil and always won. Little did I know what the horned fucker had in store for me next.

I tilted my head to the moon. Glowing iridescent clouds crowded the spotlight, waiting for the perfect time to steal its light.

A full moon was coming.

I did not like full moons.

I refocused on the swaying milky mist, my back against a tree, my feet planted in front of me. Uneven rows of head-stones—most tilted and unreadable—speckled the rolling hills, once a vibrant green now brown with dying, wilted grass. Even the trees seemed to sag. Berry Springs was in the middle of the hottest heatwave on record, according to the weatherman. The night had ushered in cooler temperatures

—cooler, as in low-*eighties*—but no reprieve from the suffocating humidity. It had been six days of three-digit temperatures, and feels-like temps of your-balls-are-guaranteed-to-stick-to-your-leg-all-day. Brutal, if you're unfamiliar. Or neutered.

I shifted, the root poking into my tailbone finally making my ass numb. I was hoping that numbness would climb to my lower back.

No luck.

I popped another pain pill then hurled a rock into a nearby bush in an effort to silence the screaming cicadas, a million maracas shaking between my temples.

Despite the bugs and the ball-plastering heat, I couldn't leave. I stared at that damn trident, etched on the headstone in front of me, until the thing began to blur.

It had been eight hours since the small, southern town had gathered in their black best, weeping, grieving, trying to understand. Colleagues, friends, family, trying to wrap their heads around a new life suddenly derailed by the finality of death.

Cheated life.

Too early.

Way too fucking early.

Shadow Hill was a typical small-town graveyard where everyone born and raised within a thirty-mile radius was buried. Located in the center of town, the cemetery was nestled in a clearing outside of City Park, which consisted of twenty acres of manicured woods and jogging trails just behind Main Street.

I suppose this is where I'm supposed to say I hate cemeteries, like any normal human being. Truth is, I've been to so many over the years that they've lost that haunting luster. Death is the only thing certain in life. I know that better than anyone. Some deaths you accept, a normal course of immortality stolen by time, but others were stolen by six rounds to the chest.

That night was the latter.

I scanned the tree line past the clearing for the hundredth time. The chatter of the town had died down, as most small towns did after eight pm. Trucks, cars, horses had disappeared from the roads with the exception of a few logging trucks passing by. Three, to be exact.

I smashed a mosquito the size of a Volkswagen against my forearm, this one double the size of the last. The blood-sucking bastards were swarming and getting ballsier by the minute, probably attracted to the seventeen layers of sweat that had settled under my white dress shirt. Always white, by the way. I don't do print. Print button-ups are for pussies and men who manscaped.

Although I tossed the suit jacket and loosened the necktie I'd gotten at the thrift shop earlier that morning, my Hanes had been in a constant state of damp since taking my place among the mourners.

It had been a hell of a day.

Not unlike so many before.

I tipped up my whiskey, my throat numb to the burn of the tepid liquid by that point.

A whisper of a breeze swept over my skin, on it, that familiar earthy scent of a freshly dug grave. A scent that never failed at triggering memories to loop in my brain like a black and white horror movie. One dead body, two, three, four... spinning, spinning, spinning, their eyes locked on mine begging for answers.

I swiped the fresh sheen of sweat from my brow.

I was so damn sick of the heat.

My hand drifted to the tie around my neck, giving it a

few more tugs. Polyester, best I could tell. Silk was also for pussies.

I hated ties. A noose invented by some overindulgent silver-spoon prick in the seventeenth century had now become a symbol of status in our society—you know, with the printed-shirt people. A man wearing a necktie was considered to have an importance of sorts, always busy, always on the go. Rushing from one very important meeting to the next, with a quick stop off in the company bathroom to rub one out because his barbie stay-at-home-wife never let him stick a finger in anything other than her wallet. Always in his shiny sports car or slick SUV, a weak attempt to prove a masculinity that ironically dissolved the moment he'd asked his nanny to Plattsburgh-knot his tie after pulling his dick from her mouth. Yes, I'm important, the tie told society, despite being bound and gagged at the jugular.

Ties were like dog collars, in my humble opinion. I hated dogs, too, for that matter. Pitied them, having to always wear their version of a tie—the ultimate noose— slowly tightening over years, going unnoticed by their neglectful owners. The only thing that reminded the dog of years gone by was the deep ache in his back and that damn collar growing too tight.

Hell, I was that dog.

A tissue tumbled across the grass, dancing along the mound of dirt like an evil fairy taunting the dead to rise again. For one last chance. One last fight. One last night in a world that had released them to their fates.

I leaned my head against the tree and contemplated heaven and hell, and good and evil, as I had done so many times before. After years being on the front lines of fighting a concept that has ripped nations apart for centuries, I came to one conclusion: Good is a fluid concept and evil is a guarantee. While good is easily overlooked, our society has turned evil into a separate entity, a faceless label given in an attempt to understand the atrocities that happen on a daily basis. Because something has to be responsible, right? Something, or someone, has to be blamed and held accountable. Evil gives us something tangible to focus our anger on, and therefore, we accept its place on earth.

Genocide, terrorists' attacks, rape, murder, torture, all caused by evil.

Is it?

Or is it simply a passive acceptance, a way to turn a cheek and dismiss a responsibility that society is too scared to address. Too scared to attack head on.

Too scared to look in the face.

That was *my* job. To face the evil and expose it for what it truly was.

I didn't allow myself the luxury of believing in good or evil, simply because they don't come in black and white facts. Declaring someone evil isn't enough to get them locked behind bars. Evil doesn't give grieving families closure.

My job was to speak for the dead.

To bring them justice.

And never, in my career, was that resolve stronger than it was at that moment.

On that note, I decided to get moving. Hunting, probably a better word for it.

I pushed myself off the dirt floor, freezing mid-way like Bigfoot caught on camera. Searing pain shot up my back, waves of nausea following seconds later.

Always the nausea.

Goddamn the nausea.

As always, this pain was followed by a rush of fury.

Anger at the realization that I wasn't the invincible man I used to be. Anger that my life had changed in an instant, leaving me with a constant reminder of what had now become the good 'ol days. Anger that I couldn't fight the heavy hand of time. A bitch, time was.

Unlike good and evil, old was one concept I never thought about. I never assumed I'd reach the age to be considered *old*. Records are old, aversion to anal is old, the Karate Kid is old. I'm not old. If I'm being totally honest, I expected to go out years ago in a blaze of glory—in my vision, I'm wearing a sweatband in a mid-air Kung Fu leap with a ball of fire at my back. You know, like Rambo but without the quirked lip... ... who is *also* now old, come to think of it—with one hand flashing the middle finger and the other wrapped around my nuts.

Unfortunately, the universe had other plans for me.

My pain finally dulled to what I imagine a severed organ would feel like. My hand mindlessly drifted to the bottle of pills in my pocket.

Wait until you get home, a little voice in my head whispered.

I straightened fully, cursing my bones, then took off down the graveled drive that cut between the headstones, the blue-glow of the moon lighting my way. I decided to avoid Main Street and cut through the woods of City Park.

The night dimmed around me the second I stepped under the thick canopy of trees. My only light was from the dim lampposts that line the jogging trails. I knew every inch of those woods, that park, by heart. Not only from running the trails every morning, but from responding to countless noise complaints during my beat cop days before becoming a detective. It was a favorite spot among the local teens, their own little Hookah lounge right there in the middle of town.

The clouds drifted over the moon and darkness engulfed me, my senses shifting to hearing and smell only. For a moment, I felt like I was back in my twenties, slipping from shadow to shadow on a black op that usually ended in more than one dead body. It felt good.

God, I missed it.

I stepped onto the jogging trail under the yellow spotlight of a lamppost, and that's when I got that good ol' feeling that I wasn't alone. I paused, scanning from left to right when a soft chiming caught my attention. A distant song, carrying through the midnight breeze like a siren's call. My brow furrowed as I looked in the direction of the sound, trying to figure out where it was coming from. It wasn't music, in the traditional sense anyway, just random creepy-ass chimes, growing louder in the wind. Soft, tinkles of a song.

The clouds parted, moonlight washing over me again as I stepped off the trail and into the woods, following the sound. More chimes, this time followed by a sparkle of lights flashing through the trees overhead. My hand instinctively slid to the gun on my hip as I picked my way through the brush, each flash of light increasing in speed as I approached. Like a freaking discotheque, or maybe a late-night fiesta of dancing cicadas wearing little red hats and shaking their maracas.

The music grew louder. My senses piqued. My hand squeezed the hilt of my gun as I stepped into a clearing.

A massive oak tree sat in the middle of the clearing with long, low branches, snarling around each other like arthritic fingers. A perfect climbing tree—aside from the fact that someone had turned it into a shrine.

Dozens of wind chimes, crystals and strings of broken mirrors dangled from the branches, catching the slivers of moonlight and reflecting in a kaleidoscope of colors on the surrounding trees. I half-expected Cinderella to jump out of a pumpkin—something I would not have minded, by the way. The compliant, blonde maid was my first childhood crush. I mean, the woman could really clean a floor. The difference here, though, was that Cinderella didn't carve Wiccan symbols into tree trunks.

A rotted branch had been positioned at the base of the oak, a circle of candles flickering on top. And hidden among the branches sat dozens of voodoo dolls, their black, beady eyes staring directly into my soul.

2

JAGG

I pulled the gun from my belt and did a three-sixty scan, the shadows from the candles taunting me, playing tricks on my vision. A less experienced man might have emptied a few rounds into the shadows, or perhaps dropped to his knees to repent.

Not this man.

Once I was certain I was alone—in the human form, at least—I slid my Glock into the holster and used my cell phone flashlight to scan the tree. One particular doll caught my eye, stringy, black spirals of hair fanning across a carved face. A flash of light lit the doll's eyes.

The hair on the back of my neck prickled.

My gaze shifted to the slashes of moon through the leaves, spotlighting each doll, their beady gazes fixed on me.

I was familiar with witchcraft. Even dated a few women who'd promised special powers. One of which required a number change and two doses of antibiotics to vanish. But it had been years since I'd come across a Wiccan shrine in the middle of the woods... Yards from the cemetery... Days before a *full moon*.

I'm not too proud to say I was a bit of a nerd in school, as most highly intelligent people are. I took an interest in astronomy, particularly cosmology, where I learned about the highly debated theory that a full moon affects human behavior. "The Lunar Effect," or "The Transylvania Effect," suggests the full moon causes changes in behavior and exaggerates mental illness. Theories are just that, though. I prefer science:

Every thirty days—twenty-nine point five, to be exact—the earth aligns between the sun and the moon, causing a gravitational pull called tidal force. Ocean water is pulled to the closest side of the moon, known as high tides. Cycles of mammals and marine life are linked to this phenomena. No one can deny its effect on earth. Here's where the theory comes to play. The human body is made up of seventy-five percent water. That's a lot of water. Many people believe this epic gravitational pull affects not only ocean water, but the water in our bodies as well, causing our system to go awry.

And that's when the crazies come out.

You've heard the rumors that people and animals sleep less during a full moon, and crime is more common on those blessed nights. Here's what I can attest to: I've delivered five babies, three in the back of a car and two in bath tubs, rescued a group of campers from two tigers who'd escaped their cages from a nearby zoo, and slapped cuffs on a group of nuns who'd decided to rob a liquor store while wearing nothing but titty tassels and Playboy bunny ears—each of these incidences happening on a full moon. Some of the wildest nights of my life have happened during full moons, most of which will remain locked in a vault, along with a pair of diamond handcuffs that I'm pretty sure once belonged to Tommy Lee. Now, also old, by the way.

I pocketed my phone and secured my gun. Taking care

not to touch any of the dolls, I pulled myself onto the lowest branch of the tree, then onto to the next, then the next, testing each before releasing my weight. Being a six-four, two-thirty one-time badass had taught me both the brittleness of branches and bones.

"'Scuse me, Chucky," I muttered, passing a doll that I swear had changed positions since I'd started climbing.

Once at the top, I gripped the branch above me for stability and peered down at the cemetery in the distance, at the *exact* spot I'd been sitting not ten minutes earlier. A beam of moonlight highlighted the fresh grave. It was a perfect view of the gravesite, and of the funeral hours earlier.

Coincidence?

I didn't believe in coincidences.

Swatting a cloud of gnats, I climbed down the tree, this time with faster, swift movements reflecting my racing thoughts. My loafers hit the ground with a feminine whisper while I pulled my phone from the pocket.

"Nine-one-one, what's your emergency?"

"Tanya, it's Jagg."

I heard a rustle on the other end of the phone, followed by something clamoring against the floor, then a distant, *'shit.'*

Finally, "Ah... Detective, good to—how can I help you?" Her octave increased with each stutter. She'd probably been painting her nails or scrolling through Pinterest.

"Send someone out to the city park. I've got a fire hazard and some sort of Wiccan shrine I want to get eyes on."

"I'm sorry... a shrine?"

"Yes. Shrine. A sacred place."

"Okay, where would you—"

"Six yards east of the cemetery. Tell them to follow the music."

"Music?"

"Is there some sort of connection issue here, Tanya?"

"No. Sorry. Shrine, music, got it. I'll have someone there right away. Can you please tell me—"

I clicked off and swept my light along the forest floor, kneeling beside a patch of bent grass that was next to another, then another. I followed the boot prints past the Voodoo Tree into the thicket, where they disappeared. Weeks of no rain and sweltering temperatures would make it impossible to pull a cast from the prints, or discern the length, width, or tread of the shoes worn. Assuming shoes were worn, of course. Did witches even wear shoes? Are clogs considered shoes?

I sat back on my haunches, surveying the ground. No cigarette butts, chewed gum, match sticks, vials of potion, pixie dust, or little green frogs with little golden crowns. Just a pile of deer scat and a few acorns.

I was photographing the shrine when a twig cracked behind me.

"Holy *sh*—"

"Watch your step."

In full uniform, Tommy Darby, a recent high school graduate and even more recent academy graduate froze mid-stride, his big brown eyes wide, his mouth squeezed into a little "O." Rumor was, the only reason Darby had been hired four months earlier was that he'd been the only person who applied for the position at BSPD. Doesn't get more quality than that. Darby was as green as the stains that colored his tube socks, and to this day, I wondered if he either only had one pair, or simply never washed them. The kid was long and lean, with a pair of spaghetti arms sure to intimidate no one. To top that off, Darby had a smattering of freckles over pale skin, colored with a constant flush from either heat or nerves, I wasn't sure which. His uniform was always wrinkled, stained with something I assumed to be jelly or Hershey's syrup, and a size too big. He was the modern day Barney Fife. The kid had the high and tight, though, I had to give him that. His hair was always freshly cut and combed to the side, not a strand out of place. It was the only thing about him that ever seemed to be on point. He reminded me of a puppy— and we all know how I feel about dogs. Darby was eager, which I appreciated, but absolutely clueless. I did not do clueless well.

Hell, I didn't do eager well, either.

"What is this, sir?"

Sir. It was always *sir.*

"You tell me, Darby."

"Looks like a shrine." He didn't move beyond the bush he'd froze behind.

"Did you deduct that from Tanya telling you to respond to my call about a shrine in the woods, or from Tanya telling you to respond to my call about a shrine in the woods?"

His eyeballs shifted to mine.

Snap back at me, I wanted to say. *Grow some fucking balls.* But he didn't. Snap back, I mean. Not sure about the balls. My guess was that the damn things hadn't dropped yet.

"Yes sir. Stupid question." A bead of sweat rolled down his temple as a moment passed.

"You waiting for a fucking invitation, boy?"

"Sorry sir."

Darby stepped over the thicket, his eyes skirting between the voodoo dolls. This *kid.* I shuddered to think what would happen when he saw his first real-life homicide.

I returned my focus to photographing the surrounding trees.

"What's the code for unlawful burning, Darby?"

"5-38-310, sir. Is that right?"—How the fuck should I know?—"A class A misdemeanor and a five hundred dollar fine."

"Incorrect."

He looked over his shoulder at me. I waited, waited, waited...

"Pretty damn *hot* out here isn't it, Darby?"

"Oh! The burn ban. We're under a burn ban."

Christ. "That's right and this triples the penalty." Whatever that was. I picked up a handful of brown pine needles. "We're smack dab in the middle of wildfire season. Wind is supposed to increase to fifteen miles per hour tonight. Those candles would've been on their side within the next hour." I tossed the needles at his feet. "These pines would've gone up quicker than a trucker's dick at Juicy Lucy's."

He laughed at this. A girly cackle, really.

"This ring a bell?" I asked.

"Uh, well, yeah. I've been to Lucy's a few times, I guess. Quarter drafts on Tuesdays. Your picture is still on the wall, by the way."

"That plaque was from two decades ago and the number relates to shots, not women. Just so we're clear." I deadpanned.

"Of course..." He cleared his throat. "Anyway, yes sir, I'm familiar."

"Good to know, but I was talking about wildfires, not how many fingers Lucy can slide between her legs, you perverted son of a bitch."

His cheeks hit a new shade of red.

I shook my head, then continued the good fight. "Eighty

percent of forest fires are caused by human neglect. An ember can travel hundreds of feet. What's hundreds of feet from here, Darby?"

"Main Street."

"Exactly. Your little fire just turned into a mass evacuation, and probably a search and rescue, too, which cuts the manpower to fight the thing in half. With dry weather like we've been having, this fire could travel eight miles an hour —a mile an hour faster than your sprint, according to what I saw when Jenkins delivered a dozen jelly donuts yesterday. And double that in valleys and gorges. Got any valleys around here, Darby?"

"More than I can count."

"Think close. Closer."

"Devil's Cove, a few miles west of here."

"That's right. That cove connects us to miles of forest. This town is surrounded by steep mountains, a ticking time bomb for wildfire season. Now, tell me again, what's the charge for unlawful burning in *this* case?"

"Uh, okay, let's see. The penalty for leaving a fire unattended, like these candles, while violating a fire restriction, such as a burn ban, can lead to six months in jail and fines exceeding five thousand dollars. But..."

"... But what?"

"This particular incident didn't cause a forest fire. So, it's still a class A misdemeanor."

"Look around. What else do you see?"

His gaze lifted to the carvings on the tree trunk.

"Defacing of public property, because this is a city park. So, vandalism."

I nodded. "What else you, got, Inspector Maggot?"

He ignored that one and took a few minutes to survey

the shrine. Finally, he turned to me, a line of confusion squeezing his brows. "Do you know who did this?"

"No, but I want you to find out."

Darby pulled a notebook from his pocket and scribbled something as I watched his little wheels turning. He finally looked up, inquisitive brown eyes narrowed.

"This just doesn't seem like that big of a deal to me, or worth our time to pursue, Detective. Forgive me, sir, but you're notorious for letting misdemeanors slide. I heard about the time you caught a group of football players fighting a bunch of band kids in the park, and instead of arresting them, you laid out each one on their asses in what you called a self-defense lesson. And about the time you chased down a man who kicked a woman out at a stoplight, ran him off the road and slit his tires, only after stopping to pick up the woman. And then, there's the story about the two women you caught soliciting prostitution on Main Street. You ordered them to clean the bathrooms of the women's shelter for six months, only after someone called in a noise complaint behind Donny's Diner, citing, I quote, two woman groaning, gasping, and multiple rounds of screams."

I cleared my throat.

"So, Detective, my question is, what's so different about this one? So, what? Some witches decided to have a little party. Who cares? Nothing serious came of it. Why not let this one slide?"

I stared at him.

Ten grueling seconds of self-restraint later, his puppy-dog eyes rounded.

"... Unless you think this has something to do with Lieutenant Seagrave's murder."

3

JAGG

I picked my way through the park, pausing at the tree line to check both ways before stepping onto Main Street. Not because I was worried I'd get hit by one of the three cars that had passed in as many hours, but because I didn't want the insomniacs to see me emerging from the woods in the middle of the night. Berry Springs had plenty of insomniacs, or busybodies, if you will. They were the first at the diner every morning, eager to spread the evening's comings and goings, or whatever conspiracy theory they'd drummed up in their heads the night before.

Donny's Diner was the hub of Berry Springs, the birth of all gossip, and the first place I went to catch a lead. That was the thing about smalls towns. Gossip was as valuable and heavily traded as gold. Donny's was a stereotypical small-town eatery, inviting busybodies both young and old with cozy red leather booths, blue and white checkered curtains, and a soda fountain in the back. Damn good food, though. All southern, all day.

I'd left Darby to his spinning thoughts at the Voodoo Tree where he ensured me he would search every inch of the area—not that I asked him to. I'd already searched and was confident I'd missed nothing, but hell, if that's how the kid wanted to spend his evening, have at it. I didn't know much about his home life, but assumed there wasn't exactly a line of blondes outside his front door. Or brunettes. Or even red-heads.

I made my way down the alley that cut between Donny's and Tad's Tool Shop, otherwise known as second church. My living quarters were on the backside of the diner's brick building. The apartment was on the second floor, over-looking Main Street and the town's square, which was the entire reason I'd rented it. No better place for a detective to live than right in the middle of the action.

The rickety wooden staircase creaked and groaned as I made my way up it, mimicking the thoughts of my lower back. I unlocked the deadbolt, pushed open the door and was greeted by a humid wall of rotted trash. Nice. The place was dark, except for a pool of light on the brown carpet from the streetlamp outside. I flicked on the fluorescent lights, the room illuminating like a high school cafeteria. I tossed my suit jacket on the floor and hung my shoulder holster on the coatrack I'd dug out of the dumpster a month earlier. I grabbed the hunting knife I kept on the windowsill next to the front door, lifted it to my jugular and sliced the noose from my neck. The tie tumbled to the top of my loafers, where one of the tassels had fallen off at some point over the evening. Yeah, the shoes had tassels—well, only one now. I bent over and ripped off the other tassel. I wasn't much into fashion but I knew to have only one tassel where there should be two was a major *faux pas*. The pleather wonders had been five dollars at a suspect's garage sale. I got them for three, along with a shovel containing enough trace evidence to indict him for murdering his babysitter. I considered them my lucky shoes. Tassels be damned.

After peeling off my button-up—six dollars at the same sale—I made my way across the living room, to the kitchen.

12.06 a.m.

The beginning of another long, sleepless night. I yanked open the fridge and squinted at the contents. My choices included a Ziplock bag of bacon that had taken on a green shimmer over the last twelve hours, a block of moldy cheese, something else in a grease-stained paper bag, and twenty-three long necks. Not even enough to make my trademark breakfast burrito, otherwise known as the only thing I cooked.

Also otherwise known as the best damn food on the planet.

I slammed shut the fridge door, grabbed a loaf of bread, and after tossing the ones that felt like cardboard, I stuffed a slice in my mouth and set the coffee to brew. A friendly note of advice: Never eat plain bread when all you've had to drink is a pint of whiskey.

After washing the playdough down with a drink from the faucet, I poured a cup of coffee and walked to the center-piece of my place, my desk. I'd set it up in front of the living room window that overlooked the town's square.

A lump caught my throat, more dense than the bread.

Although I'd already seen them a hundred times, the crime scene photos still made my stomach roll.

They'd had an open casket at Lieutenant Seagrave's

funeral but no amount of makeup or fancy clothes could replace the image of his bloodied torso obliterated like a slice of swiss cheese. Or the grimaced expression his face had frozen into, as if to remind us that his death was no accident.

No accident.

Coffee in one hand, I picked up a photo in the other and scanned it from top to bottom, corner to corner. Not that I needed to. The images would be burned into my brain for the rest of my life. My pulse kicked, a rush of energy suddenly flooding my system. Nothing sobers you up like white-hot rage. I set my cup next to the multiple coffee rings that already speckled the papers. Coffee rings were my personal mark, the entire station knew. Clichés be damned.

I lifted the second image that had been burned into my brain, but not because of the blood and gore. This one was a grainy, black and white image caught from a street cam. I tilted my head to the side, tracing the lines of the blurred silhouette frozen mid-jog, passing by a window in the art shop next to the alley where Seagrave's body had been found. The image was captured at one-thirteen in the morning. The thief was carrying a black bag that would have faded into the silhouette if not for the corners sticking out. Black, black, black. Hat, mask, clothes, shoes. All black.

"Mother fucker," I seethed, my hand beginning to tremble, from either rage or the caffeine. Probably both.

I set down the second photo and shifted my attention to my laptop. After logging in several security screens, I hit play on the video I'd watched countless times since that morning. I memorized the flashes of the silhouette moving back and forth past the window, smooth, quick, calculated.

Planned.

Sipping my coffee, I settled behind the desk and

watched the video over and over, as I had done every night since my friend's death. I wasn't sure how long had passed when my senses suddenly switched to the front door behind me. A distant creak told me I had company, and I never had company.

Then, a *rap, rap, rap* of knuckles against the paper-thin door.

I grabbed the gun I kept secured under the desk, and in nothing but my suit slacks and socks, I padded to the front door.

"Don't do it," the voice called out from the other end.

I yanked open the door.

"Detective." Lieutenant Quinn Colson shifted out of the shadows in a way that reminded me of his military days before accepting a position with BSPD.

"Another second and you'd've been on your back." I holstered the gun in my waist band.

"Already told you, you're not my type."

"Everyone's your type. What's got you slummin' in the back alleys of Berry Springs at midnight?"

"Thought I'd come by and say hi."

"I've known you for three years and you've never come by to say hi."

"Guess today's your lucky day."

My eyes narrowed. "Aren't you supposed to be practicing Lamaze or something?"

"I did." He blew out a breath. "A hundred fucking times already today."

I grinned. Colson's new bride, Bobbi, was in her third trimester, although you'd think it was her fifth talking to the guy. Quinn Colson was a few years younger than myself, with the same build and grit that came from spending years in the military. Except he and I had gone very different paths after getting out. The obvious being a white picket fence and family. Pending family, anyway.

"Seriously. Cut the bullshit. What's up?" I asked wanting to get back to Seagrave's case.

"Fine. I couldn't sleep, took a drive to get some of this stifling fresh air, and came by to check on you. Don't make a big girly thing about it. God knows I've dealt with enough emotional shit today. Anyway, I noticed you were still at the cemetery when I'd left earlier. Went by just now but you weren't there. You alright, bro?"

"Fine."

He jerked his chin past me. "That empty pint you've got on the floor says otherwise."

I turned, picked up the empty bottle of Jack and hurled it over his head with nothing short of a Jordan follow-through. Two seconds of dead air went by until, *bam,* the glass shattered in the empty dumpster at the bottom of the staircase.

"Dammit, dude. *Thanks.* Now we're gonna get a call from old lady Doris Dill about a noise complaint."

"Dill passes out cold at six-thirty every day. The woman could sleep through world war three."

"I don't want to know how you know that, man."

"Probably for the best."

"Anyway, recycle next time, will ya?" Colson craned his neck to see into my apartment. "Not that you have *anything* to recycle. *Jesus* dude, do you sleep on the floor?" He shoved past me. "What are you? A college kid? You've got one ratted couch that I don't even want to know where the stains came from, and a—" He looked at me, gaping in utter shock as if I had three human heads nailed to the wall—"a *box* television? You have a fucking *box* television? You know they have flat screens now, right? Your TV is from the freaking *nineties.*" He continued his visual ass-rape of my place. "And kitchen the size of—you don't even have a dishwasher—and one desk. And a *window* air-conditioning unit..." He leaned down and sniffed. "That smells like burnt cheese."

I kind of liked that scent, if I'm being honest.

Colson breezed past me, checking out the bedroom, where I kept a Queen—mattress, not woman—and an alarm clock on the floor, not that I needed one. I don't even think the alarm function worked. Thank God I'd removed the antennas from the top or the guy might have had a coronary.

"You've been in Berry Springs three years, dude." He turned and fisted his hands on his hips. "I mean, I get the minimal lifestyle thing but you don't even have a single picture on the wall." He scowled. "Unless you consider that nasty-ass peeling wallpaper some sort of hippie art. Is there some sort of gambling addiction I'm not aware of, because I can loan you some money if you—"

"You come here to check on me or give me decorating tips? Because one of those is gonna get you kicked out on your ass."

"Fine." He raised his palms to surrender. "Just... unexpected, I guess. Anyway, come on. We know you're not going to sleep, so come on."

Another few drinks and passing out might have been more accurate.

"Come on," he said again. "We're going to Frank's, not Lucy's, so get a damn shirt on."

Human beings—even strippers—were the last things I wanted to be around at that moment, but the bar part didn't sound so bad. It was my second home, after all. Franks, *not* Lucy's.

Frank's Bar was a hole-in-the-wall pub on the outskirts

of town. A retired officer, aptly named Frank, had purchased the old log cabin and turned it into a hub for first responders needing a moment of reprieve. For cowboys seeking the best barbecue across three states, and for cowgirls seeking the best meat across three states. It was a southern, small-town bar at its finest with antlers and flickering road signs along shaded walls, and buckets of ice water on tap to extinguish the routine bar fights.

Especially during full moons. That was a fact.

"I'll buy the drinks." Colson said.

And, sold.

I plucked a grey T-shirt off the back of my *"ratted"* couch, gave it a sniff then pulled it on. I swapped out my slacks for a pair of jeans and cowboy boots, then followed Colson down the staircase.

"My Jeep's around the corner," I said.

"Is your air conditioner still broke?"

"Yep."

"Then we're taking my truck."

We stepped onto the sidewalk.

"I don't want to talk to anyone." I said.

"You never do, and no offense, no one ever wants to talk to you either."

We hit the asphalt, still warm from the day before.

"But I will say..." Colson continued. "I'm curious as hell to hear why you've got Darby casing a voodoo tree in the park."

JAGG

*C*olson parked his truck on the edge of the gravel lot next to Frank's Bar. The clouds had faded, the moonlight so bright we could have driven without headlights. The night had cooled to a chilling seventy-six degrees.

A trio of cowgirls eyed us as we walked to the front door.

"Evenin' officers," one winked.

While Colson politely dipped his chin as he passed, I yanked the cigarette from the blonde's red-tipped fingers, tossed it on the ground and stomped it out.

"Burn ban." I informed her as I grabbed her Miller Lite and emptied it on the glowing tip. The girls squealed as the beer splashed onto their fancy boots. They gaped at me, speechless—my favorite reaction from a woman, by the way.

Colson rolled his eyes and pulled me inside.

"Can you cool it for a bit? *Shit.*"

I yanked my arm from his hold, my focus immediately shifting to the scent of stale beer, cedar, and barbecue sauce. My three favorite smells. We saddled up at the end of the bar, ignoring the glances and whispering that followed.

Typically, Frank's Bar was a flurry of drunken energy. Not that night. That night, the low moan of a Willie Nelson song hung in humid air as thick as the mood beneath it. I'd seen almost every face at the funeral hours earlier.

"Howdy do, boys?" Frank walked up, wiping his hands on an apron that read, *Eat my Meat.*

Colson and I grunted.

Frank nodded, looked down. "It's a tough day for everyone. I've been there multiple times. The Lieutenant was a good man. Whiskeys?"

"Coffee," I said.

"I'll take a Shiner," Colson said.

We sat in silence until Frank delivered our drinks.

I sipped the coffee, hot, strong, black. Just the way I liked it.

"Okay," Colson said finally. "What's Darby still doing at the Voodoo Tree? Aside from muttering half-sentences about witches and strings of garlic?"

"Spinning his damn wheels."

"Ah, come on. Give the kid a break. We were all new once. I'm glad you're letting him work with you and I hope you continue to pull him along. Bet he's jumping up and down to get to work with the infamous *Dog.*"

"Kid needs more training."

"Kid needs to get laid."

"Agreed. I've got him searching the park. I did all the important stuff like bagging up the candles, dolls, chimes and shit. What'd he say about it?"

"I want to know what *you* say about it."

"Ah, the truth comes out. You didn't come by my place to check on my well-being. You want to know what I found."

"True, but I did also want to check on you, Jagg, because you're an introverted son of a bitch who's idea of grieving involves a handle of whiskey and a few broken knuckles. And based on what I've seen now, I'm glad I dragged you out." He paused, sipped. "I think you should take a few days off."

"Fuck you."

"Listen. I understand being a workaholic. I understand getting personally invested in cases. But in your case, in *this* case, it's not healthy for you—"

"What the fuck do you mean *my* case? This is Seagrave's case."

"That's exactly my point. You know the victim, Jagg. You take it personally—"

"Bullshit."

"Let me finish. I know you don't talk about it, but everyone knows. After your dad died, you slept on Seagrave's couch for six months. I know he was the entire reason you applied to become detective. Hell, the guy gave you a personal recommendation." He paused. "I knew he meant a lot to you and... under your current circumstance, I really think you need to hand this case off. Give it to someone else."

"What's my current circumstance?"

"You know exactly what I'm talking about. You're one bad decision away from being fired, Jagg."

My hand squeezed around the coffee cup, the ceramic cooler than the heat that just rolled up my neck.

"Just think about it. All I'm sayin'."

I forced myself to take another sip of coffee instead of what I really wanted to do, which was throw it against the wall.

Truth was, Colson was right. I shouldn't have been on the case. But the moment I got the call that Seagrave had been shot, there was no thinking, no questioning. I drove straight to the crime scene knowing I was going to handle the case one way or another. On—*or off*—the books. My boss didn't care that I knew Seagrave. He only cared about getting the job done. If I fucked up? Well, he'd fire me and make the Governor happy. Win/win for him. Bottom line, no amount of whispers or red tape was going to keep me from getting justice for the man who'd taken me in at my darkest time.

I'll never forget it. It was one month after I'd been discharged from the Navy after being labeled unfit for active duty. Fucking back. I thought I was at my lowest low, but then, one month later, my dad keeled over from a heart attack. Rock bottom, officially hit. My brother wasn't around, so Colson had dragged my ass to the funeral. My mother had watched from across the street, standing next to a dumpster. Where she belonged. That's all I'll say about her.

Jack Seagrave had literally caught me stumbling out of Frank's Bar six days after Dad's funeral. I don't remember the five before.

Jack took me in, sobered me up and gave me the kick in the ass I needed. He was quite possibly the reason I wasn't dead in a ditch somewhere with a bottle of whiskey glued to my hand. I owed him my life.

I owed him justice.

"I'm getting the vibe you think this Voodoo Tree is connected to Seagrave's death." Colson asked finally, knowing there was no way in hell I was going to drop the case.

"Everything needs to be considered at this point."

"Any viable reason to assume it?"

"Any reason you're immediately doubting it?"

"I'm not challenging you. Just asking the questions."

I stared at him for a moment not liking what I was seeing. One of his own had been slain, but I didn't see that fight, that hunt to find the killer, behind his eyes. Was it because his thoughts were at home with his pregnant wife and pending family? Regardless, Colson didn't seem focused and I didn't like that. Baby on the way or not, Seagrave's investigation deserved the full backing of the BSPD, and I felt like I was only getting half from Colson.

"God, I hate this fucking case." He scrubbed his hands over his face. "Okay. Let's go over this again. Start from the beginning of the night Seagrave was murdered. The Black Bandit breaks into Mystic Maven's Art Shop to steal the third Cedonia Scroll—"

"Fourth."

"Fourth?"

"Fourth. There are four scrolls total. All four were stolen together, a year ago, then sold off. The first three were recovered within days of being stolen. Two in New Orleans, one in Houston. The fourth just turned up here in Berry Springs."

"The initial report said there were only three Cedonia scrolls."

"The initial report was wrong. There are four."

"Does the fourth show a picture of a location around here, like the others?"

I nodded and took a quick sip of coffee. It felt good to be talking about the case with someone other than the mice in my apartment.

"The image of Otter Lake is on one, Shadow River on another, White Rock cliff on the third, and brace yourself my friend"—I shot him a look—"The fourth shows the Voodoo Tree in the park. Sans the voodoo shit, of course."

Colson's eyebrows popped. "No shit?"

"No shit."

"Okay, now I know why you're interested in the tree. But how'd you find out about the fourth scroll? I had, like, three people looking into it."

"Investigating, Colson. You should try it. *Yourself.*"

He ignored the jab. "Was the fourth scroll sold after it was stolen, like the others?"

"Yep. For six figures."

"*Six* figures?"

"Yep. It sold for the most of the group. All four scrolls sold for about four-hundred thousand total. The underground black market for stolen art is a world-wide, billion dollar industry. In case you didn't know."

"I'm in the wrong industry."

"You're on the right side of the law." I sipped again. "The FBI has an entire unit of agents trained to recover high-value art, not to mention dozens of agencies in the private sector. Art investigators, they're called. Thing is, stolen art moves quickly, which makes it tough to trace. The Cedonia Scrolls have been stolen and recovered three separate times over the last few decades, making them even more valuable in the black market."

"That, and the fact that they're said to be cursed. What idiots would *want* to be cursed? Let alone kill a cop for one?"

Colson obviously hadn't spent the last seventy-two hours of his life researching the dark underworld of supernatural powers. The moment I began researching the infamous Cedonia Scrolls, two things surprised me. One was how little information there was on them, and two, was the massive cult that worshiped them.

The legend went something like this: In 1968, a group of hikers found four scrolls locked in a chest, hidden deep in a cave just outside Berry Springs. The scrolls were constructed of leather sheets sewn together and wound on two wooden rollers. Using punched designs in the leather, each scroll depicted a different location around Berry Springs. Although there's no record of the scrolls being professionally appraised, they're assumed to be from the seventeenth century. According to the Wiccan websites I'd perused, the location on each scroll signifies a monumental ceremony held by the famous witch, Cedonia, where she raised demons from the earth.

The hikers who found the scrolls died two weeks later, one from a rare virus, and the other, a tumble off a cliff. And so began the rumor that the scrolls were cursed and all those who touched them were doomed to face eternity in hell. I wish I could say I was surprised at the demand to own one of these scrolls, but the truth was, I knew far too well about the obsession to tempt fate. To own it, to control it. To be a part of something bigger than yourself, for better or worse.

As decades went on, the gossip of the Cedonia Scrolls slowly faded away, until a year ago when whispers said the scrolls had been stolen from an art lover named Charles Nicholson, who was in hospice, now dead. Over the following weeks, three of the four popped up at various private art auctions, where each was stolen sometime in the night. An anonymous witness to one of the heists dubbed the thief the "Black Bandit," a nod to the black suit, hat, and mask it wore. The story quickly became sensationalized, gossip colored with stories of witchcraft, curses and supernatural power.

The fourth scroll was MIA until it turned up at a local art shop named Mystic Maven's. According to the shop owner, Hazel De Ville, she'd purchased the scroll at a thrift store for two dollars, the infamous piece of art finding its way out of the black market and into the hands of someone who had no clue what they had. After bragging about her find to everyone in Donny's Diner, Hazel locked the scroll in her art shop, where it was stolen that same night. During the robbery, the station received a call about a "suspicious person," wearing head-to-toe black, lurking around the building. Lieutenant Jack Seagrave was the first one on the scene—where he was shot to death moments after the Black Bandit escaped with the fourth scroll.

"It's all connected, Colson. A cursed Wiccan scroll was stolen. Then, Seagrave gets shot while responding to the heist. *Then,* on the day of his funeral, a voodoo shrine is assembled ten yards away."

He slowly nodded, then asked, "Anything on the car?"

Earlier that day, I received the surrounding street camera feeds from the scene and hit my first lead. My first in three days.

Three fucking days.

"Nothing worth anything." I said. "I ran the description through the system. No blue, four-door sedan associated with any recent crimes. I reached out to a few of my counterparts across the state, see if it rang any bells for them."

"No luck?"

"No luck."

Colson blew out a breath. "Could've been anyone, you know."

"Or, it could be Seagrave's killer. A piece-of-shit car with no license plate was caught on camera outside the art shop, moments after Seagrave was shot six times. Why wouldn't you think it was the shooter?"

"But there were also two other vehicles that passed by within thirty minutes, right?"

"Sandra Nickels, on her way home from the nightshift at

the processing plant, and Carlos Muniz, on his way home from a gig at a bar in Eureka."

"You talked to them both already?"

I grunted.

"Verify Muniz's story?"

"With the bar and his roommate."

"Humph." Colson chewed his lower lip.

"The unmarked blue sedan is our guy. Just have to find him."

"I'm assuming you've been to Ron's lot?"

I nodded. "His, and two other used car lots in town. Still need to hit up the surrounding towns. There was one blue sedan sold to an old lady name Ingrid, two years ago. She still owns it today."

"You talk to her?"

"Went to her house before the funeral."

"Of course you did. See any pentagrams on her front door?"

"No."

Colson took a swig of his beer, then blew out a breath. "So we're assuming the blue sedan belongs to the Black Bandit..."

"And that the Black Bandit killed Seagrave."

A moment slid between us as we contemplated that assumption.

"What about the dumpster diving?" I asked. "Anything turn up?"

"No murder weapon."

Searching the surrounding trashcans and dumpsters for the gun used to kill Seagrave had been a stretch, too. The Black Bandit wasn't that stupid. Obviously.

"We'll have the dolls and candles you bagged up from the Voodoo Tree scanned for prints. If the Bandit was the one who built the shrine, maybe we'll get a hit. Maybe that'll give us a legit lead. I'll start the paperwork first thing tomorrow morning."

I scoffed.

"Takes time. You know that."

"We don't have goddamn time, Colson. We're already three damn days into this."

He didn't respond because he knew just as much as I did that after the first forty-eight hours of a homicide, every hour that passed made it less likely the culprit would be caught.

"Have any other of the Cedonia Scroll heists been associated with homicides?" He asked.

"No."

"So, the Black Bandit stole the scroll, got busted by Seagrave on his way out, put a round of bullets in Seagrave's chest, then disappeared in a blue four-door sedan?"

"Wouldn't be the first time a B&E ended in a homicide."

"We've got no murder weapon, no prints, not a single piece of trace evidence. Only a random car and a blurred side-shot of the Black Bandit."

"And this."

I pulled out my phone and hit play on the video I'd watched a hundred times since that morning.

DARBY

I waited until Colson's flashlight had faded into the distance to resume my search of the woods around the Voodoo Tree. I assumed he was on his way to track down Jagg, and I only hoped he'd tell him I was still searching the scene. Two points for the new kid.

I kept my flashlight up and my head on a swivel. Never could be too careful when it came to witchcraft. Being born and raised in Berry Springs, I knew that all too well.

The town was made up of three types of people. Your traditional cowboys—the majority of the population—who's idea of dressing down was wearing their leather cowboy boots instead of their ostrich ones, their wool cowboy hats instead of their felts. Acknowledging anyone by anything other than sir or ma'am was unacceptable, and very likely to get you a swift slap in the jaw. Southern women were serious about their discipline. I still can't look at a wooden spoon without a shudder. The folks that inhabited Berry Springs were the real deal. True southern cowboys and cowgirls, the kind that rode horses and shit. I rode a horse once on a class field trip. Fell face first into a mound of horse dung, fracturing my shoulder and busting out my two front teeth. I was called Dingleberry Darby until the day I graduated high school. I was also laughed out of anything that involved any kind of athleticism whatsoever.

Kicked ass at Dungeons and Dragons though.

Anyway, a smaller part of Berry Springs was made up of hippies, as the rednecks so lovingly called them. They were nature lovers who'd migrated to the town for its hiking trails, campsites, creeks, caves, and some of the best rivers for kayaking.

Thirdly, there was a small group of misfits—as they'd been labeled—who practiced Wiccan, claiming half the land as their own, their annual protests always falling on deaf ears. I remember first hearing about the Berry Springs witches on the playground at school, then, my grandpa would tell me the stories at bedtime after he'd fall off the wagon. Many moons ago, he always started out, a small group of witches escaped the Salem Witch Trials and fled to the mountains of Berry Springs. They lived deep in the shadows of the caves and cursed anyone who crossed their paths. Normally, that's where the story would end, but on nights that he overindulged, he'd tell me the most tantalizing part of the tale, leaving me with visions of twitching noses and my hand between my legs. Aside from the curses, the witches used their beauty to seduce the men of the villages with one goal in mind—to avenge their dead sisters by reproducing and re-populating the world with more witches. The Berry Springs rednecks hated the story and tried, unsuccessfully, to bury it for decades. Bad blood for our small town, they'd say.

As I stared up the Voodoo Tree, I was afraid the age-old feud was about to fire up again.

Starting with Detective Max Jagger of the state police.

It took me a minute to figure out, but suddenly every-thing clicked into place. From the detective's sudden obses-sion to prevent forest fires, to the reason he was wandering the woods with whiskey in his back pocket in the middle of the night—not that the latter was abnormal. The detective's superhuman ability to consume alcohol while remaining coherent was also legendary in Berry Springs.

Under normal circumstances, Detective Max Jagger, known as Jagg, would have probably taken a piss on the shrine and sauntered away, but not this one. Why? Because Jagg believed this one had something to do with Police Lieu-tenant Jack Seagrave's murder, three days earlier.

I'd stood behind Jagg at the funeral where he'd posi-tioned himself just far enough away from the crowd to let everyone know he didn't care to be addressed. As was Jagg, in every social setting he crossed. It was just him and I, in the background, although I assume he didn't notice I was there. Not many people noticed I was anywhere. Pretty much the opposite of Jagg. *Everyone* took notice of that guy, no matter where he was, what he was doing, or who he was insulting.

He stood like a statue during the benediction, behind dark Ray-Bans and a faded grey suit. While everyone else hovered under shade trees, Jagg stood in the blazing sun, as if welcoming the punishment of the heat.

Tears were shed, prayers whispered, none of which by Jagg. And while everyone exchanged hugs and kisses after the casket was lowered, the detective still didn't move. Didn't speak. Nothing. The funeral goers passed him by, a few wary glances by the men, a few lingering ones from the women.

I didn't receive a single glance, men or women.

As was my life.

I was always that kid that no one noticed. Always hiding in the shadows, ducking behind other kids, praying that the teacher wouldn't call on me in class. The curse of being shy. I learned quickly that shy meant nerdy, meant no one wanted to hang out with you. And then the whole Dingleberry Darby thing kind of sealed the deal.

Confidence was something I never had. *Ever.* I doubted every decision I made, every move I made, every breath I took. I floated through life on fear, nothing else. I graduated high school with nothing—no friends, no money, no job, no idea what I wanted to be. Then, I heard that BSPD was hiring. I'd almost pissed myself when I hit the submit button, adding my name to the list of badasses who surely applied for the job. I passed each test by the hair of my chin —three to be exact—and was floored when I received the offer. To this day, I don't know how or why I'd been chosen over someone else. Anyone else. Regardless, with a bottle of Pepto in the glovebox and Saint Christopher hanging from the rearview mirror, I'd shown up to my new job pretending to be ready to tackle whatever they could throw at me. I threw up twice that first week.

Jack Seagrave's murder was the biggest thing to happen since I'd started.

I hadn't worked the scene but heard about it. Everybody had. The Lieutenant had been shot six times in the chest in an alley downtown and left to rot in a puddle of his own blood. I heard Jagg lost it at the scene. Not crying, but going completely ape shit. A prequel of what was to come, no doubt about that.

Lieutenant Seagrave had spent over a decade in the Navy, like Jagg, before deciding to walk away from the military after knocking up his new bride during one of his leaves. Definitely unlike Jagg. Seagrave had accepted a job as a beat cop at BSPD and worked his way up to Lieutenant where he remained before someone shot him to death.

The man was two months from retirement.

The connection between Jagg and Seagrave was cloudy at best, as was most of Jagg's life, but I got the impression the two men had been close.

Jagg was the type of detective to go to the ends of the earth to solve a case. Add in a personal connection and the devil himself couldn't stop the man.

Forget about witches, Jagg was a true legend in Berry Springs. Someone talked about, whispered about. Wondered about, fantasized about. Hell, Tanya, our receptionist/dispatcher couldn't even form a full sentence around the guy. I couldn't imagine having that kind of power over the opposite sex. Jagg was said to have plenty of lovers, but was always single, if you catch my drift. Women dropped to their knees for him, and if I'm being honest, this phenomena was a bit of a mystery to me. Sure, the guy was the walking stereotype of a bad boy biker, covered in tattoos with dark eyes, and a six-foot-four frame that I'm not ashamed to admit that I'd kill for. But the guy seemed to live every day in a constant state of pissed. He was an asshole. Cynical. Assume the worst, there was no best. The guy never smiled, but maybe women liked that. I sure as hell wouldn't know considering my last sexual experience had been with a jar of jelly and a banana peel. Two birds with one stone. Delicious.

They said Jagg was so good at his job because he didn't believe a word out of anyone's mouth. Didn't take a thing at face value. While most people believed a stranger would do good given the opportunity, Jagger believed that person would cut off your balls and wrap your dick around your throat given the opportunity—something I heard he'd done, by the way. Innocent until proven guilty? No, not in Jagg's delusional world. Guilty until proven innocent, every time.

I'll never forget my first experience with the detective. It was my first week at BSPD. I'd been given the graveyard shift and was somewhere between watching a tutorial about evidence collection and contemplating how to remedy my boredom woody when Jagg burst through the door to the bullpen, singlehandedly dragging a man twice his size who had a bloodied lip, two swollen eyes, and a swastika on his neck. I recognized him instantly. The infamous Pistol Pete, one of the most notorious gang members in the tri-state area. Pete was loosely connected to several homicides but the cops couldn't link enough evidence to ever arrest the man—until Max Jagger took the case. Rumor was the detective spent days, weeks, stalking the gangster. I mean, literally *stalking* the guy. From his car, a drone, the woods surrounding the gangster's house. Rumor was Jagg spent thirty-one hours perched in a ninety-foot hickory tree in Pete's backyard with nothing but his camera, his gun, a pack of beef jerky and a flask, before capturing the moment Pistol Pete tried to sell a handful a jewelry he'd stolen from an old woman who'd been beaten to death during a home invasion. Those pictures had been enough to get a warrant to search Pete's home and, within six hours, Jagg had arrested a man who later confessed to killing six people over three states. Confessed, because, rumor was, Jagger had threatened Pete with photos of him on his hands and knees accepting an unconventional kind of payment from a fellow gang member. Decades in federal prison, a pile of dead bodies and evidence to match had nothing on Pete's sexual orientation, apparently. Jagg had found the man's weakness and exploited it, saving years of trials, thousands of tax payers' dollars, and perhaps most importantly, providing closure to the victim's families.

After getting the confession, Jagg breezed out of the station with a cup of coffee in one hand and a stack of files in the other, like it had been just another day at the office. While most cops would be gloating and celebrating, Jagger went back to his house, wherever that was. Not many people knew where Jagg hung his shoulder holster. I imagined a cave, or a dungeon of sorts.

A day didn't go by that I didn't see Jagg either in the station or working a case somewhere in town. He was the definition of a workaholic. People said he didn't sleep, rarely ate. The man put everything he had into his cases, cutting through red tape, legally and illegally, to get things done. He was a dog with a bone when it came to solving a case, hence the nickname *Dog*.

Stories of his days as a ruthless, merciless Navy SEAL proceeded him, as well as the number of bodies he'd left in his wake. It was still debated why he'd left the military. Some said it was because he was dishonorably discharged after kicking his CO's ass. Some say he just simply walked out one day because there were no more terrorists to kill. Others even suggested he'd turned, hated the very country he'd spent decades defending. No one really knew. He'd just shown up in Berry Springs three years ago and applied to be a beat cop. I heard that when he accepted his job at BSPD, crime in our small town immediately went down by seventeen percent. Six months into the job, that number dropped to twenty-seven percent. Two years after that, Jagg accepted a position with the state police, as a detective. His territory covered multiple counties around Berry Springs and had the same effect on surrounding crime rates. Detective Max Jagger was a feared man.

You see, Jagg had his own Wild West way of doling out punishment beyond what the courts offered. The stories were always spun, either by Lieutenant Colson, or "witnesses," to Jagg's outbursts—more often than not, blondes with a pair of double D's and a dazed, satisfied look behind their eyes. There were even a couple times where the infamous Steele brothers, of Steele Shadows Security, took the rap for one of his "disciplinary actions." Everyone would simply look the other way... until he cracked the wrong man's jaw.

Max Jagger might have been like an immortal God around town but everyone has their secrets, and thanks to my ability to flutter from room to room without being noticed, I knew his.

And it was a big one.

I was there. He didn't know that, though, of course. It was a typical, small-town Saturday night, my third night on the job. Berry Springs was having their annual bluegrass festival to kick off tourist season. Main Street was closed, cars and trucks replaced by tents and food carts. A band played on a makeshift stage in the center of the square. It was one of those rare times that the town's cowboys and hippies came together in a blur of spiked coffee and glaucoma medicine. Jagg slinked through the crowd, not speaking, not drinking, not laughing, certainly not dancing. Working a case, I knew, so I followed him. I watched him, his gaze skittering from belt buckle to belt buckle, taking inventory on each person with a gun hidden on their hip. Then, he slipped out of the crowd and into the shadows where I followed. I lost him for a moment, until I heard a scream. I took off on the direction of the single shout and that's when I saw a pair of silhouettes behind the maintenance building of the city park. Drawing my gun, I sprinted across the footbridge but came to a halt when the faces came into view. Why? Shock, really. I jumped behind a tree and watched Detective Max Jagger beat the living snot out of a kid at least two decades younger than his rumored-to-be forty years. Jagg didn't fight like a normal, rough and tumble redneck. The man was like a feral cat, with lightning quick speed and accuracy that involved some sort of martial arts. MMA, more like. The kid didn't stand a chance and was on his stomach with both arms twisted behind his back in seconds flat. Jagg said something in the guy's ear, then pushed off him, and I remember grinning when the kid took off like he'd seen a ghost, stumbling and tumbling down a hill.

Then, I realized why.

I watched Jagg help a younger boy off the ground, using a piece of ripped fabric from the kid's T-shirt to dab the blood from his face. The kid was skinnier than me, and based on the confused, sluggish movements, had been beaten pretty badly. I watched Jagg guide the battered boy across the park and fade into the darkness. The next day, I learned that boy was an autistic junior high kid who played the violin, only when his flute hadn't been busted in half. Rumor was, after the fight, Jagg had taken the kid to Steele Shadows Security to be taught self-defense. It was also rumored that he'd been gifted a priceless, vintage car for all his troubles. Two weeks later, the kid rolled up to high school in a gleaming, six-figure mustang and was never bullied again.

Sounds like everyone won, right?

Wrong.

The bully? Received a new set of front teeth, courtesy of

his father, the governor. That's right, Max Jagger had beaten the living shit out of the *governor's* son. Normally, this would've been enough to remove the detective's badge and gun, but good 'ol Jagger marched himself into the state capitol building and bribed the governor with a video of the beating, proving his spoiled rich-ass son was a guilty asshole. Very bad press. The validity of video is still heavily debated today. Anyway, Jagger walked out of there with his badge and gun still on his hip because he'd exploited the governor's weakness—his need for a smooth reelection.

But it wasn't over. It never was.

Jagg was on his last leg with the state police, with the CID Commander, Governor, and Chief of Police watching him like a hawk, just waiting for a reason to fire him.

The legendary Max Jagger had fallen from grace.

When dispatch had summoned me to the Voodoo Tree, I'll admit, I sped to the park. It wasn't often that anyone got to work with Jagg. The guy was a loner and rarely pulled anyone into his cases. And when he'd asked me to help? I hadn't been that excited since I discovered I had Cinemax for free.

I had a chance to learn from the man himself.

Dammit, I wanted to *be him.* I wanted to have that kind of innate authority that came so easily to the man. I wanted to have that kind of *presence.*

I wanted people to fear me the way everyone feared him. Hell, the way *I* feared him.

I wanted to leave ol' Dingleberry Darby in the dust, or dung, I should say.

I decided right then and there, I would *not* let him down. I would soak in everything I could so that when Jagg was fired, as he inevitably was going to be, I would have a chance at becoming the next Detective Max Jagger. I just had to prove myself first and it was going to start with that case. If Jagg really believed the Wiccan shrine in the woods had something to do with Seagrave's death, I was going to find out.

... Evil witches and hexes, or not.

JAGG

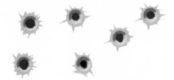

$\mathcal{C}$olson grabbed the cell phone from my hand.

"Where the hell did you get this video?" He demanded.

"Lady across the street."

His gaze shot to mine. "Cora Hofmann?"

I dipped my chin.

"What the?... We already interviewed her. Hell, *I* personally interviewed her. She said she didn't see or hear a thing that night. Until we showed up, anyway, which, by the way, I was informed kept her cats up all night. Woman hates the police, that much was obvious."

I shrugged.

"No way. Tell me now. How did you get this?"

"Doesn't matter."

"Oh yes it does. I've got a half a mind to drive over there right now and charge the old lady with obstruction of justice." His eyes narrowed. "What did you have to do to get this?"

"I've got an actual *video* of the Black Bandit and this is what you want to talk about? Who cares how I got it?"

"You agreed to go on a date with her daughter, didn't you?"

I lifted my cup to my lips.

"You sly son a of a bitch. Just remember how that worked out for you last time with... what's her name again? Oh yeah, Susan. I remember because I was the one who booked her into jail for breaking into your house and stealing your underwear. Susan Stalker. People still call her that, you know."

"Her last name is Smith and that was my priciest pair of Hanes, by the way."

"Yeah, they really upped the ante when they went tagless. God, you're cheap."

I snatched the phone from his hands. "Listen, if you're not—"

Colson grabbed the phone back and hit play. We watched the green-tinted feed from a night-cam that Ms. Hofmann had set up in her back yard to capture activity around her bird house. A widow of twenty years, the woman was a nature fanatic, with multiple cameras set up to record deer, raccoons, and a feral cat that kept getting into her, quote, damn trash.

I'd watched the video so many times I could recite the exact second the oak tree swayed in the breeze, the moment three leaves tumbled down two seconds later, and the reflective eyes of a raccoon in the corner of the frame a second past that. And in the distance, through a break in the trees, a blurred silhouette emerging from the shadows, slipping through the back door of Mystic Maven's Art Shop, after taking only three seconds to pop the lock. Exactly one minute and six seconds passed before the Black Bandit emerged through the back door again, holding a black bag, and slipped into the woods. Ninety seconds after that, lights from Lieutenant Seagrave's patrol car bounced off the trees. And the grand finale, one minute and fourteen seconds later, his foot flops onto the ground in the bottom of the frame.

Colson watched it two more times before speaking.

"This leaves a lot of questions. Timing, for one."

He didn't need to say it. It was the one thing that didn't add up for me either. If the Black Bandit had already gotten what it came for—the fourth Cedonia Scroll—and exited the building in a clean getaway, why had the bandit circled back and killed Seagrave?

Had the Bandit gone back for something? Then ran into Seagrave, where an altercation took place? If so, why wasn't that caught on camera?

"It's impossible to make out the height or weight of the Bandit, too. Other than 'not obese,' and 'relatively normal height.'" Colson hit replay for the third time. "It does, however, confirm three things. One, the images from the street cam, two, the fact that Ms. De Ville needs to get better locks, and three, the timing that the heist occurred."

"Not just that, Colson. Look closer. *Investigate.*"

The lieutenant rolled his eyes, then focused back at the phone. A minute ticked by. My patience cashed out as the video played for the fourth time. I yanked the phone from his hand. "Jesus dude, stay with your day job."

I fast-forwarded to the spot I'd replayed more than a hundred times. "Our Black Bandit has a limp."

Colson's brows pulled together. "What?"

"He has a limp. Watch as the Bandit jumps off the back steps as he's leaving the building. He favors his left hip."

Colson leaned inches from the screen as I replayed it again. "Holy shit. I'll be damned. You're right. You can see it right there—" he pointed to the screen. "After he jumps, he drags his left hip and there's even a limp as he disappears into the woods." Colson shook his head and leaned back. "I'd ask how you noticed that, but based on the bags under your eyes, I'm assuming you haven't slept more than ten hours in the last three days."

Two, but he didn't need to know that.

"Nice work, Detective. Alright, what's your profile so far? Because I know you've already built one."

I tossed my phone on the bar and leaned back. "I think the Black Bandit has a strong interest in art, or appreciates it at least. I think he practices witchcraft, is a Wiccan, or at the very least, drawn to it. I think it's someone smart, crafty, who enjoys beating the system. As for age, I'm torn. Coupling the fact that most thieves range from teens to mid-twenties and the speed of the Bandit, I'm leaning toward young. No older than thirty for sure."

"But the limp? Old people limp."

"My gut tells me it's an injury, not from age."

"It's a good lead. Motive?"

"Could be greed—they want the scrolls for either money or bragging rights. Or, it's something to do with Seagrave."

"Personal, then? You think the Bandit lured him there? It was a setup?"

I shrugged. I had no reason to assume it was personal other than the nagging feeling in my gut.

Colson sipped his beer. "I'll have Tanya see what she can dig up from Buckley at the hospital. See if anyone has come in recently with a left hip injury."

Our attention was pulled to shouting from the pool tables in the back.

"You hit my fucking stick."

"Kinda like I hit your mom last—"

I grabbed Colson's beer bottle and sent it shattering

inches from the drunk cowboys' heads. The bar went silent. Gaping, the rednecks turned toward me and Colson. Colson's hand rested on the hilt of his gun.

I turned back to the bar. "Another coffee and another beer, Frank."

Frank winked, a subtle 'thank you,' for not having to spend his next hour dealing with a bar fight.

"It's on the house," he said.

The bar remained hushed, eyes boring into my back. Fuck, I was ready to go. Where, I wasn't sure, but I wanted to get the hell out. Be alone. Figure out who the hell was the Black Bandit.

Our drinks were delivered, three chocolate chip cookies with mine.

I eyed Frank.

"The wife made them."

Colson snatched one up.

"Don't forget to eat," Frank said, eyeing me back. "That's what she'd always tell me when I was working a case. A drop in blood sugar can make anyone crazy." He nodded toward the cowboys, now busy picking up shards of broken bottle, then he tapped the cookie plate. "Eat. Don't insult my wife now, son."

I took a damn cookie and set it on my napkin. Frank nodded in approval, then pushed the plate to Colson who devoured the third cookie faster than the first.

"Not bad, Frank, but I know a chocolate chip cookie when I try one and this ain't it."

Frank grinned. "They're gluten free. And they got carrot and flax-something in them."

Colson's eyes widened as if the man had just announced they were mixed with arsenic. "What's *flax-something?*"

"Some sort of seed. I think."

"What the hell is so wrong with gluten?" I asked, a question that plagued me ever since the gluten-free section had replaced my beef jerky section in the grocery store.

"What the fuck even is gluten?" Frank answered back with a question of his own.

We all shrugged simultaneously.

Colson studied the cookie on my napkin, shaking his head. "Seeds in gluten-less chocolate chip cookies, Seagrave shot to death. What the hell is the world coming to?"

"Stick around here a few more hours and they'll be plenty of theories."

"Don't doubt that."

"On that note." Frank tapped the bar. "Better get back to work stocking the shelves for the crazy weekend coming up. Damn hippies. Enjoy the flax."

Colson groaned as Frank walked away. "The damn Moon Magic Festival. Hotels are already booked solid. Supposed to have double the attendance as last year. And with the freaking burn ban right now..." he shook his head. "Chief McCord is rounding up extra volunteers to monitor the grounds."

"It's being held at Devil's Cove, right?"

He nodded.

Devil's Cove was a secluded cove off Otter Lake. Beyond the steep cliff that encircled the cove was a clearing where local concerts and festivals were occasionally held. Miles and miles of forest surrounded the clearing, making it ideal for avoiding noise complaints and for setting up road blocks to catch drunk drivers. That year, though, it made it an ideal place for a wildfire. But a wildfire wasn't my concern.

"You ever heard of Lammas?" I asked.

"Yeah, a South American camelid. Stinky as fuck." A

crumble of cookie fell out of Colson's mouth. He flicked it on the floor and grabbed mine.

"Not a llama; *Lammas.*"

"No then. What's *Lammas?*"

"It's a Wiccan holiday. One of the four Greater Sabbats, or some shit. Happens once a year. It's a festival honoring the end of the summer."

His brow cocked. "And when exactly does llama take place?"

*"Lammas, you idiot, a*nd, August first."

"This Saturday?" He eyes rounded. "The day of the Moon Magic festival? You've got to be kidding me."

"And the day of the next full moon. By the way, guess what else is called Moon Magic?"

"I don't think I want to know. But I get the feeling you're about to tell me."

"Wiccan covens meet under full moons to perform rituals that supposedly bring psychological and physical transformations. They pull energy from the moon, which they think increases their powers for whatever spell they're doing that evening. This tradition is called Moon Magic."

"Christ. It's like the stars are aligning for trouble."

"Yeah. Too many coincidences here. This could also be linked to the Voodoo Tree. I don't know."

"Listen, Jagg, unless you find a viable link to the Black Bandit and the Voodoo Tree, let it go. Witchcraft, Wiccans, whatever, have been around these parts for decades, and let's just say those who have barked up the witches' trees have stumbled onto their own bad luck."

I turned fully to him. "You're fucking kidding me. You seriously believe in curses, Colson?"

He shook his head. "I just know what I know."

"Which is what, exactly?"

"A few years ago, an officer took a witch into custody to question her about a kidnapping case. After he had nothing to hold her on, he let her go. The woman was bullied out of town, and a week later, the guy dropped dead of a heart attack. Never had a single health issue in his life. And remember ol' Sanchez? Went after another rumored-witch about a bunch of cows being poisoned. Dude's side-business went under a month later and he had to file bankruptcy. And, you remember that guy—"

"You're unbelievable."

"Just sayin,' don't spend all your time on the Voodoo Tree, bro. Hell, give most of that part to Darby. Focus on Seagrave."

A moment slid by as I actually considered working alongside the kid.

Colson downed his beer, then leaned back, deep in thought. "What the hell? So we've got a bunch of witches all riled up about cursed scrolls and the llama's holiday, going around constructing shrines and shooting police officers? You've got to be kidding—"

His phone went off. He pulled it from his pocket and clicked it on.

"*Shit.*" Colson shoved out of his seat and dropped a few tens on the bar. "Are you sure there're only four scrolls?"

I pushed my empty coffee cup to the edge of the bar and stood. "Yeah, why?"

"Because there's been another shooting."

7

JAGG

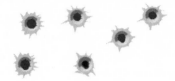

I pulled my gun as Colson's truck skidded to a stop at the wooded edge of City Park. The treetops were washed in moonlight, the ground, shaded in shadows. Two lampposts, around fifteen feet apart, barely illuminated the trail and the two silhouettes standing just past it.

"Jesus *Christ,*" Colson shoved the truck into park and pulled his gun, but I was already out the door. He was calling in for reinforcements as I sprinted ahead.

Fuck was all I could think.

My brain raced to assess the immediate threat in what appeared to be an active homicide/shooter situation. Always act on the immediate threat first, then next, then next. Take 'em down one by one. As a solider, you're trained how to adjust to an op when things go south and leaves you with multiple moving parts. And this scene definitely had multiple moving parts. I'd seen entire missions crumble because one man focused on the wrong threat.

Double grip, barrel up, I jogged across the grass, tunnel-visioned on the pistol shaking in old man Erickson's grip.

"Gun down, Erickson."

The man didn't hear me. Jacked up on adrenaline, I assumed. His gaze was fixed on the two bodies at the edge of the woods. One standing, one motionless on the ground.

"I said put the gun *down*, Erickson." I moved closer, my voice calm but loud. "This is Detective Max Jagger and Lieutenant Colson. We've got this, buddy. Put the gun down."

My peripheral caught Colson just past the tree line, skirting the edge of the trail, coming up on the side of the scene. I edged closer, my eyes locked on that arthritic finger starting to squeeze the trigger.

Shit.

Like a flash of lightning, Colson lunged out of the woods, tackling the old man. The gun went flying along with an impressive amount of expletives considering the man was a regular at church. With that threat neutralized, I shifted my focus to the other players of this blessed event.

Erickson's shouts and Colson's grunts drowned out as I rushed threat number two, my gun pointed directly at the dark silhouette's head.

"Get on your knees." I yelled.

Just then, a siren sliced the air and blue and red lights bounced off the trees, brief flashes illuminating my target. My brows pulled together in what felt like stepping into a crazy dream after an evening of tequila shots. I blinked, my steps wavering. No way was I seeing clearly. Headlights moved along trees, stopping perfectly on the scene ahead of me, illuminating it as if it were on stage.

I froze, confusion—*shock*—momentarily clouding the focus I was known for. The sounds around me, the shouts, the flashing lights, everything faded as I looked at her.

Looking back, that was the moment.

The beginning of my fall.

A gust of wind blew a mane of long, curly, black hair

across a pale, blood-spattered face. Her eyes, an emerald green reflecting in the headlights like a cat. Feral, based on the fury behind them. Wearing a pink tank top, grey leggings and jogging shoes, the woman stood tall and strong, motionless except for the heavy rise and fall of her chest. A line of red slashed across her top like morbid spray paint, up her neck, coloring the bottom of her chin. Blood speckled her milky-white arms. In her hand, a gun, pointed directly at the dead man at her feet.

Assess, assess, assess.

I refocused on my sights and repositioned the barrel of my gun, realizing that sometime during my hypnotic gaze, I'd dropped off the target. Something I never did.

Ever.

Like I said... the beginning...

"Ma'am," I said. "I'm going to need you to toss your gun to the left. Now. Right now. Release the gun from your hands."

She said nothing, but I knew this thing could go either way. I'd seen the look before. Wild, unbridled emotion. Crazy. Fitting, I know that now.

"Drop the gun, lady. I will *not* say it again."

I crept closer, keeping my eyes locked on that damn pistol she wouldn't let go of. I caught movement behind her and risked a glance at Officer Darby emerging from the trees at her back. His eyes were fixed on her, bulging with adrenaline. His knuckles white around the gun in his hands, pointed directly at that mane of wild hair. The kid stumbled on a tree root, but caught himself. A flicker of awareness flashed in the woman's eyes, my first indication to suggest she was coherent, at least.

"Drop the gun." Darby's pitched voice sounded like a pre-teen at a Bieber concert. Typically, I'd laugh, but not then. That shaky, squeaky voice was a sign of lack of control. Not good.

And then it hit me. This was the kid's first dead body.

So then, my focus was split between him, his gun, and the woman, and her gun.

It was the shitshow of all shitshows.

And my patience dissolved.

"Ma'am—"

Everything went into slow motion at that point. The pistol slowly slipping from her red fingertips, the burst of energy in her eyes, the shift of her hips, the spin of her heel.

Shit.

As she took off, I snapped to action.

"Don't shoot, Darby!" I lunged forward, shoving my gun into the holster on my belt and sprinted after her. Three steps later, I leapt through the air and tackled her. I pinned her arms as we hit the dirt, pain exploding up my back. My grip wavered with the blow, this moment of weakness opening the door for another as her forehead connected with my chin. A flash of pain burst behind my eyes. The *woman* had just *head-butted* me. The chick was *fighting* me. This one-hundred pound spitfire lunatic was actually engaging in a physical fight with an armed man more than double her size. Bucking, twisting, writhing under my hold.

I can say, with one-hundred percent confidence, that in my two decades of military and law enforcement, not a single man or woman had ever fought me after I tackled them. It was instant surrender, every time.

Not with this one.

This *woman.*

Her curls whipped around my face as she fought like a rabid dog. Or cat, I should say, with those damn claws dragging down my back. The heat radiated off the woman in waves, our sweat sliding together as we wrestled on the dirt floor.

She smelled like coconuts. Sweet, vanilla coconuts.

Frantic shuffles beside me sent my awareness skyrocketing.

"Don't shoot, Darby," I ground out.

At this point, the wild beast and I had resorted to a school-girl like swatting match that I wasn't particularly proud of. What the *fuck* was happening here? I caught her hand mid-air, twisted. Her body jerked, followed by a quick whimper, then, submission. Thank fuck. Every inch of my skin stung from her scratches as I straddled her, pinning her arms above her head.

"Jesus, woman," I exhaled, getting my bearings.

Her hair, speckled with grass and twigs, fanned out around a face that I guessed was no older than mid-twenties. Her emerald eyes shimmered in waves of different colors against the blue and red lights flashing across her face. Magical, almost.

Unnerving.

We stared at each other for a moment, chests heaving, sucking in breath that had escaped us. That was the first time I got a real look at her. And that was the first time I felt... *something.*

Her skin was a flawless, snow-white, almost glowing under the moonlight. Not a freckle, not a single flaw on it. Her lips were full and deep red, with a little indent in the bottom one. A smattering of blood speckled the corner of her mouth and I found myself wanting to wipe it away. It didn't belong on that skin, that face. Her forehead shimmered in sweat, her hair wet at the temples, little kinky curls framing her face. Despite the fact I had her pinned, her body tensed beneath me, as if waiting for an opportunity to strike. Those eyes daring me with a wild kind of defiance that told me she still hadn't given up.

Fearless. That was the one word that materialized through the fog of my brain.

The woman was fearless.

"You got her?" Darby's voice yanked me back to the present moment.

Keeping my eyes locked on hers, I addressed the rookie.

"I need you to check the man on the ground for a pulse. Call an ambulance. Then secure the scene and call in all available units. Have Tanya wake up whoever's on call. This place will be crawling with joggers at the first crack of dawn. Check on Colson, get the medical examiner, and turn off your damn flashers. And for God's sake, Darby, tie your goddamn shoe."

"Yes sir. On all counts."

"What's Colson doing?" I asked.

"Interviewing the witness. Something Erickson, I believe. Want me to take that over?"

"I want you to do exactly what I just told you to do. And watch where you step. Don't contaminate the scene." More than this woman had, anyway, with her brazen attempt to flee.

As Darby stepped away, I spared a quick glance at Colson, who met my gaze immediately. I dipped my chin —*good?* He nodded, dipped his, returning the question. I dipped back—*good.*

I refocused on the woman between my groin.

"What's your name?"

Her lips pressed into a thin line and it was the first time I noticed the blood on her mouth was her own. A deep split slashed the corner of her lower lip. I raised up and scanned her body, noting scrapes down her neck, her chest, the beginning of bruising underneath the spray of blood on her arms. A nasty gash sliced her bicep. The woman was hurt. My hands loosened around her wrists immediately. Her fingers flexed in response, but she didn't move as I continued to look her over. It was the first moment her eyes left mine, hooded eyelids lowering, feathered lashes hiding the flash of embarrassment I caught in those green irises.

I lifted off of her slightly, relieving her of some of the two-hundred-plus pounds pressing against her.

"Are you hurt? Anywhere other than the obvious?" I asked.

She continued to avoid eye contact. A deep swallow moved the muscles of her neck, followed by the slightest head shake.

"Okay. So that's a no. What's your name?"

No response. I considered that she might be deaf, or a mute. Nothing would surprise me at that moment.

"Name." I repeated again.

Normally, at this point, I'd either man-handle or threaten someone who wouldn't talk, but not her. Why? Because my instincts were screaming at me. Something was just *off*. I wasn't quite sure what or why, but nothing about it felt normal, including the dead man inches away that neither one of us were addressing.

Something about *her* was off.

Different.

The scene, everything. Everything felt off.

And, *fuck,* my back hurt.

"Alright, listen, it's up to you how smoothly this goes from here. You continue to fight me, that's your choice. Because I can go all night. You got that, lady?"

A moment passed before I felt her arms go weak beneath my hold. A subtle submission, but a start. I felt like

I was addressing a toddler. A very smart toddler. The moment felt like a delicate dance that I wasn't sure how to navigate.

"Good girl. Now. Here's what's going to happen. I'm going to release you and you're going to raise onto your knees and put your hands behind your back. You try to run again, I'll have your ass back on the ground and in cuffs in under ten seconds flat. Got it?"

Her jaw twitched.

"First, you're going to tell me your name."

Her head twisted to the side, as if searching for something on the ground. When she didn't answer, I lost all remaining patience. I'd responded to countless calls where people, whether it be victims, witnesses, or the criminals themselves, were in psychological shock. Unable to speak, sometimes barely even able to walk. I knew psychological shock, and this wasn't it. This woman's eyes were too clear, too aware, too alert. And I was done with the bullshit.

"Jane Doe it is, then."

I shifted off of her, gritting my teeth at the lightning shooting up my back. I yanked her torso up by her wrists. She didn't like this.

"Sunny." The single word spat out in a low, husky voice. She jerked out of my hold. "My name is Sunny."

Sunny? *Seriously?* A woman with hair as dark as midnight, skin as porcelain as vanilla, and crimson lips as seductive as sin was named... *Sunny?*

"Got a last name, Sunny?"

"Harper."

Sunny Harper.

"Okay, Miss Harper. On your knees. Let's go." I reached for her armpit.

"Don't touch me."

"Don't make me."

She lifted herself from the ground and shifted onto her knees.

"Hands behind your back."

She kneeled strong, shoulders back, her chin held high despite the tremble that had started the moment our bodies left contact.

"Wrists together, please." It was the first time I'd ever used the word 'please' while cuffing someone.

"Jesus." Colson walked up, gaping at the victim on the ground feet away from us. Then, his narrowed eyes pinned the woman named Sunny Harper.

"You interview her yet?"

"No. Tried to run." Emphasis on *tried.*

He looked back down at the dead body, then at the gun she'd dropped to the ground. "You mirandize her yet?" He asked me, leading me to believe that Erickson's statement had suggested nothing innocent had happened there. Hell, I had no reason to believe otherwise at that moment.

"No," I nodded to her arm. "She needs to be looked at by a medic before anything."

"I don't need to go to the—"

"We're legally obligated."

Colson snorted at this response. Not sure what he thought was so funny. The guy knew I didn't do kid gloves. Then, he said, "I already called it in. Ambulance should be here any minute."

Just then, sirens cut through the air and the meat wagon pulled into the lot, followed by backup.

It was an instant circus.

"I'll take her over," Colson said. "You start on the scene."

I hesitated—this shocking the hell out of me. I stepped back while Colson jerked her up with more force than necessary, inciting a blow of protectiveness to my system. Another first, ever.

"You have the right to remain silent..." He pulled her away from me. *"If you give up the right to remain silent, anything you say can and will be used against you in a court of law..."*

I watched him drag Sunny by his side, her head held high. Her steps strong, unwavering.

"You have the right to speak to an attorney and to have an attorney present during any questioning. If you cannot afford a lawyer, one will be provided for you..."

The headlights outlined their bodies, two long, black shadows stretching eerily across the grass behind them. Sunny's head turned, but her eyes didn't land on mine, they focused on the body that lay at my feet. There was another flash in that green before she turned back, then disappeared in the chaos.

I looked down at the dead man at my boots.

Half of his face had been blown off, leaving nothing but open flesh and bone. It was the first time I noticed more than just blood specking the grass. That gore was nothing, though, compared to the bullet hole where his left eyeball had once been.

8

JAGG

*D*espite being three in the morning, the station was abuzz with activity and as hot as an Iranian brothel. Smelled about the same, too.

Something about a second dead body in less than a week added a sick level of excitement to the anxiety in the air. I paused by the air-conditioner panel on the wall and clicked it down to sixty-five. Instead of a kick of a fan, I got a series of beeps, followed by a *thud* and blinking red light. Of course. I popped my fist against the panel, leaving heads turning and a crack down the middle.

"AC's broke," I shouted as I passed the bullpen.

It had been two hours since we first responded to the park and we knew not much more than when we'd arrived. Thanks to a pesky little thing called non-custodial interviews, law forebade us to interview Sunny until after she'd received medical care. Sunny had yet to give her statement. My patience was gone.

While the medics tended to Sunny and Colson continued his interview with old man Erickson, Darby and I secured and searched the scene. The medical examiner and "additional resources" had shown up twenty minutes later. By additional resources I mean, Officer Haddix, a part-time patrolman who'd been dragged out of bed. That was another thing about small town departments, lack of funding. Undertrained patrolmen did everything from evidence collection to interviewing the witnesses. Being overworked and underpaid tended to lend itself to shoddy investigation work. It was a vicious cycle and shoddy anything was unacceptable in my mind. It was one of the many reasons I was called in to assist in most homicides in the area.

This one just so happened to fall right into my lap.

The body was zipped up and taken to the morgue where it would sit until its autopsy the following day—if we were lucky.

Jessica Heathrow was the county medical examiner, another overworked, underpaid invaluable asset in a community with as many meth labs as churches. The difference in Jessica was that this overworked asset was always on her toes, always giving each case her full, undivided attention, whether it was ten at night or five in the morning. I don't think she thought too much of me, but I'd grown to respect her, regardless. A lot more than I could say for most women.

According to the medic, Sunny was banged up with cuts and bruises and a pair of bruised ribs. It took eight stitches and sixty damn minutes to close the gash on her arm.

I wondered if any of those injuries had happened when I'd tackled her. Then, I promptly forced away an emotion I didn't feel often—guilt—and reminded myself it was part of my job. What the hell was she thinking trying to run?

Her fault.

Not mine.

The medic said she'd denied any pain pills. Idiot.

After searching the scene with my new shadow, Officer Pukes-A-Lot, Darby and I went back to the station with Colson and Sunny behind us.

Darby was on his third handful of antacids trying to ease the stomach he'd emptied in the park earlier. Never knew a man could puke that loud, and that's coming from someone who shut down bars for ten years of his life. Sounded like a pair of walruses mating. I looked the other way, though, because I knew that seeing your first dead body was never easy, especially when half the face had been blown off.

Not pretty.

Definitely not accidental.

I'd instructed Darby to dig up everything he could on the star of the evening, Miss Harper. The woman had already received more attention than a normal suspect in what was being whispered as a murder case. The men stared, slack-jawed like sex-deprived preteens, the women, like gum-popping mean-girls, scoffing and gossiping. I'd already heard the word "witch" being thrown around.

I combined the last dregs of the station's coffee with a pain pill, a combination surely to have me gripping my own bottle of antacids before bed. Assuming I even made it home, because, as my churning gut had indicated, the "Slaying in the Park"—as it had already been dubbed—was becoming more unusual with each passing moment.

"I put her in interview room one."

Mid-stride down the hall, I glanced over my shoulder at Colson coming down the hallway behind me. "Interview Room One" was the bullshit name given to the conference room when a situation called for it. Small town budgets, small town buildings.

"She needs to be interviewed immediately. I already don't like this thing."

"Agreed. What did Jessica say?" Colson asked.

Colson and I had divided and conquered everything that needed to be done at the scene. He'd updated me on old man Erickson's statement, I'd updated him on what I'd found at the scene, but other than that, we'd yet to compare notes, or thoughts for that matter.

"COD is gunshot wound to the head, perforation of the brain. The shot that blew off half his face passed through. The one through the eye did him in."

"The bullet didn't lodge in his brain?"

"Nope. Blew out the back of his head."

"You find the other casing?"

"Only the one. Bagged it up. Will get it logged and sent to ballistics at sun up, and we'll search again for the other."

"Probably in the woods under a pile of deer shit. Is her gun bagged up?"

I nodded.

Colson shook his head. "The chick was carrying a *gun* with her at midnight in the city park. A freaking *nine millimeter. Ruger, right?*"

I nodded.

"What the hell is a woman doing carrying that thing around?"

I reminded him that almost everyone in Berry Springs carried a weapon of sorts. Hell, everyone in the South did, for that matter. A concealed carry license was as common as a driver's license. To his point, though, a nine millimeter was a significant weapon, especially for a "woman."

"I meant," Colson corrected, "who the hell carries a gun with them during a jog?"

"Someone who takes security very personally and knows their shit. The fire power alone suggests a fair amount of knowledge about guns."

Colson's brows squeezed together. "The most common Ruger pocket pistol for concealed carry is a 380, not a nine millimeter. I understand carrying one in her purse or something, but *jogging* with one in her waistband? Why not carry a taser or a shiv like a normal person?"

It was something I filed away as interesting, too. Very interesting.

"What about the knife?"

"Bagged up, too."

"And it was next to the victim's body?"

"Seven inches from his head."

"No blood on it?"

"No."

"No knife wounds anywhere?"

"Not on him. Medic said her wound wasn't from a knife."

"Need to figure out if it's hers or the vics, then verify the prints."

I nodded. "You started trying to track down his next of kin yet?"

"Not yet. That's next on my to-do list."

We didn't know much about the victim other than what I'd pulled from the wallet in his back pocket. His name was Julian Griggs. A five-foot-eleven, brown-eyed, organ-donating twenty-two year old Berry Springs resident. His wallet contained two credit cards, a debit card, a coupon for a free ice-cream at Donny's, two sticks of wintergreen gum, and six dollars cash. According to the fast-food receipt in his pocket, he'd had a double-cheese burger, large fries with extra ketchup, and a large soda two hours before Sunny Harper blew off his face in the park. A ring of keys were in his right pocket, along with some lint. He'd been wearing a black T-shirt, navy blue shorts and white joggers, now speckled with blood. A password-restricted cell phone from his other pocket and one private social media account gave us nothing. A black Chevy was parked at the trailhead, which was assumed to be his considering the keys found in his pocket unlocked it. I told Darby to run the truck plates to confirm, and if so, gather a list of his previous addresses so we could begin the arduous task of finding the next of kin to contact. If that failed, I instructed him to check Julian's birth certificate or check for marriage licenses. All that *after* he found out everything he could on Sunny Harper, of course.

"Erickson was positive he saw her shoot the guy in the face?" I asked.

"What he said. Said he was driving home from the hospital—"

"What was he doing at the hospital?"

"His niece just had her first baby—"

"You verify that?"

"Yep. Said he saw someone in the woods, verbatim 'lurking under a lamppost.' Struck him as odd considering it was midnight, so he turned into the park. That's when he saw Sunny Harper with Julian in a bear hold, with a gun to his head. According to his statement, he then pulled into a parking spot, called us and heard two gunshots. He grabbed his gun—*idiot*—and approached the scene. Said there was a dead body at Harper's feet when he walked up. He pulled his gun on Sunny and threatened her until we got there minutes later."

I shook my head. It was unbelievable how many times well-meaning assholes inserted themselves into dangerous situations in an effort to help when what they should have done was haul ass out and leave it to us.

The fact that Sunny Harper had overpowered Julian Griggs, almost double her weight, was nothing less than shocking. I'd been on the receiving end of her strength and while it was nothing short of impressive, combining that with the fact she'd been carrying a nine millimeter and her refusal to talk, and something just wasn't adding up.

"Wanna take a bet on self-defense or murder?" Colson asked.

"A hundred bucks on self-defense."

"I'll take that bet. The woman was in the park with a gun at midnight, got the drop on the vic, then shot him twice in the head... and she's just weird on top of that. I'm going with murder, with jilted ex-girlfriend."

We shook on it.

Colson gazed at the closed door of the conference room. "Would be interesting to know if either Julian or Sunny Harper believed in voodoo."

It was one of the first thoughts that crossed my mind while processing the scene. What were the odds that a man had been shot yards from the newly-discovered "Voodoo Tree," and the evening of Lieutenant Seagrave's funeral? Coincidence?

Just then—

"Hope you brought a string of garlic."

Colson and I turned to see Officer Haddix striding down the hall.

"Huh?"

"Wards off evil spirits, 'cording to the wife, anyway." Haddix jerked his chin to the conference room. "Chick's notorious around here. Y'all don't know?"

"What are you talking about?"

"Sunny Harper. Been pulled over seven times in the last six months for traffic violations. Speeding, running red lights. Got out of every ticket. Every *single* one. Not even a warning."

"How?"

"Shows a tit, hell, I don't know. Proud to say I wrote Miss Harper her first ticket a few weeks ago. Know what happened next? The woman convinced Judge Carter to throw it out. Chick's got some sort of power over men. Saw her at Frank's a few times. Never pays for a single drink or food, but always leaves alone. Dick tease."

"She ever with anyone?" I asked.

"Don't think so. Rumor is she's some sort of loner. A hermit. Lives in a cabin in the middle of the woods." He snorted. "That she probably got for free. Same goes at the coffee shop she frequents, by the way. Dax, the owner, told me she hasn't paid for a single coffee. Gets one of those nasty skim milk drinks every time."

"Sound like you sure keep tabs on the woman." I said.

"Naw. Not me. Can't stand women like that. Breezes through life on nothing more than a wink." He scowled. "And what's with those eyes, anyway? Gold specks in green eyes so bright they look like they're plugged into an electrical socket. Has to be contacts. She always wears those low cut shirts too. Anyway." He shrugged.

Colson and I exchanged a glance.

"How do I not know about this? The tickets?" Colson asked.

"You think anyone wants to admit to having their balls handed to them?"

Someone yelled Colson's name from the end of the hall. He shook his head. "Whatever, dude." He glanced at the clock. "I've got to figure out who the hell to call to verify Julian Griggs' body."

"Darby's on research work now." I said. "Go find him."

He grunted, turned, and started down the hall. Haddix followed suit.

"Colson," I hollered after him. "What are you going to do with her?"

Without looking over his shoulder, he threw his hands up. "She needs to be interviewed right now. You're best around. Go see what you can get out of her."

9

JAGG

I slipped into the eight-by-five room the chief had built onto the conference room, or "interview room one." The small space had two chairs, a speaker with a feed that led into the room, a notebook and pen, and a two-way mirror that overlooked the conference table.

It's no secret I wasn't a fan of the chief, but adding an observation room to the station had given BSPD a huge leg up in interviews. Well, for me, anyway. While I'd never seen anyone use it for anything other than a nap, I'd used it at least a dozen times. I always took time to observe whoever I was about to interview.

There's a lot of debate surrounding the validity of nonverbal behavior when it comes to distinguishing lies from truth. I happen to believe you can learn a hell of a lot more about someone by paying attention to their nonverbal, rather than listening to the words that come out of their mouths. Unfortunately, nonverbal cues don't hold up in court. Damn shame, in my opinion.

During my door kicking days, I was trained in multiple interrogation tactics. Not only with me as the interrogator, but how to resist an interrogation in the event I found myself on the receiving end of a cloth and bucket of water. SERE training, it was called. Survival, evasion, resistance and escape. Most SEALs excelled at survival and escape, mainly because if you were one of the twenty percent who made it through BUD/S and actually became a SEAL, chances were you had that God-given grit and instinct when it came to survival. Resistance training was challenging because it targeted the most powerful part of any man, his mind.

Torture and interrogations have evolved over the years, but one thing remains true—your goal is to find the person's weakness and exploit it. We all have weaknesses. Good soldiers, good interrogators, good detectives each have their own unique ways of finding whatever that weakness is and not letting up until one of two things is obtained: Enough actionable intel to advance whatever the end goal of the interview was, or two, to get that rare, coveted confession. Some detectives went their entire careers without hearing those three sweet little words. I'd already heard them six times in my life. How I got there, though, was questionable at best and I wondered if all my red-tape cutting was finally catching up to me. Times were changing. I wasn't. I still used tactics behind closed doors, behind prying eyes, behind the law. I would until they kicked me out, which according to Colson, wouldn't be too far away.

At the end of the day, though, I believed in my gut instinct. Educate, educate, educate, then fall back on your gut. Know your facts, the intel, but ultimately trust your gut.

And my gut was screaming at me about this case.

I closed the door to the observation room behind me, kicked a chair to the side and crossed my arms over my chest as I looked through the two-way mirror.

Someone had offered Sunny Harper a BSPD sweatshirt —undoubtedly, a dude—but based on its location at her feet, she'd declined the offer. Sunny was apparently still considered a loose-cannon flight risk because her hands were still cuffed. Someone had been thoughtful enough to reposition her cuffs to the front, though—also, undoubtedly a dude. The blood had been wiped from her face and neck, revealing that milky-white skin that glowed against her inky curls, which were still speckled with grass and dried leaves. I was surprised at the lack of tattoos. I figured a woman with fight like she had would've been covered in some sort of feminist propaganda. Chalk it up to another thing that surprised me about her. My gaze drifted away from her face, noticing her body for the first time. Even sitting in a chair, I could see the curves of her waist, the round ass, and, Lord help me, a pair of erect nipples poking from under the thin fabric of her tank top.

A wave of heat ran over my skin, the temperature in the room suddenly sweltering. I yanked at the tie I didn't have on, almost ripping the collar of my T-shirt. Damn laser beams those things were. Her breasts were perky, a handful at best—smaller than my usual preference—but in perfect proportion to her toned, fit body. And why the hell was I spending so much time on her tits? I gave myself a mental slap in the face and focused on the baseball-sized lump swelling around the stitches on her arm.

That guilt, again. Had I done that?

There was no shifting in her seat, no frantic eyes skirting around the room, no twitches, no tears, just those feline eyes staring straight ahead. My head titled to the side as I assessed the woman, trying to get a baseline on her nonverbal before the interview. I wasn't getting shit.

She was different.

Something was different.

My body pulled like a magnet to her, my weight shifting to my toes until I was inches from the window.

Nothing.

No tells.

No emotions to read.

Nothing.

I wasn't sure how long had passed while I stared at her, waiting for something—*anything*—until her head turned and met my gaze through the two-way mirror as if she could see right through it. I pulled back, a weird quiver in my stomach as our eyes locked.

Must be the coffee, I convinced myself.

We stared at each other for a minute in a way that had me questioning the quality of the secret window, and I filed away the whisper of unease that settled around me.

What the hell was wrong with me?

I was off my game. I needed food, sleep.

So, I said to myself with another inward slap to the jaw, *let's get this shit done and end this Godforsaken night.*

I stepped into the hall where the chatter in the station had doubled. Colson's voice boomed from his office. The case was already growing legs.

I pushed through the door to the conference room and was met with the same piercing gaze I'd received from behind the mirror. I had no question Sunny had known she was being watched, and by the spite in her eyes, she knew I was the one doing the watching.

I tossed a notebook and pen on the table, passed by the open chair and stopped at her side, standing over her.

Her brows lifted with her eyes, leveled, controlled, but *loaded* with defiance.

But *why?*

It made no sense at this point. I'd had my fair share of cantankerous suspects before, but none of them—not a single one—had been found standing over a dead body literally holding the weapon that killed the victim. Why wasn't she talking?

Scared?

Arrogant?

Fearless?

Idiot.

"Miss Harper I've got a lot of questions for you, but first, I'd like to know how you overpowered a man double your size."

She blinked, the only indication that I'd thrown her off with an unexpected question. My specialty. Thanks, Columbo. Not all my training came from the teams.

"Krav Maga." she responded, simply. With that *voice.* Deep, sultry. Sinful.

"And where did you learn martial arts?" I forced myself to keep my eyes from sliding down to those nipples that I swear had doubled in size since I walked in the room. Cold? Turned on, perhaps? Was there any other time a woman's nipples got hard? When was the last time I'd seen a pair of erect nipples?

"I taught myself," she said, pulling me out of my pubescent thoughts. I was beginning to understand the lack of traffic tickets.

"Online classes?"

"A few."

"Well, Miss Harper, I hope those classes offer a full refund because you apparently missed the most important part of Krav Maga. Rule number one is that the best way to win a fight is not to get into a fight, at all. De-escalate the situation and win through avoidance of conflict."

"Some conflict is unavoidable."

"That's correct, but in your case, with me, it was avoidable. I asked you to put down the gun. What did you do? Tried to flee, causing me to tackle you, where you proceeded to fight me like a rabid raccoon, making me disable and cuff you."

Her nostrils flared, her wrists twitching against the cuff. Yeah, I didn't like that wrestling match either, Ronda Rousey.

"Why did you try to flee? You appear to be a smart woman. Why—"

"I had three guns pulled on me in under five minutes, Detective. When I heard the old man call me a murderer..." Her voice trailed off.

"Are you a murderer?"

"No."

"So you ran because..."

She looked away.

"You panicked?"

Her eyes drifted closed as if embarrassed. Or annoyed, I wasn't totally sure which.

"Okay, we'll call it panic. Well, Miss Harper, are you going to panic and attempt to flee and kick my ass again right now?"

"No."

"I'm sorry, I couldn't—"

"*No.*" She said, louder.

"Fantastic." I pulled the keys from my pocket, unlocked her cuffs and tossed them across the room, sending them clamoring against the chipped tile.

She didn't flinch.

I turned my back to her and walked to the chair on the opposite end of the conference table.

"Would you like some coffee?" I settled into the chair. "Water? Cigarette?"

A quick shake of her head told me no, so I hit the call button on the phone and asked for two waters, two coffees, and a pack of cigarettes.

Her eyelids fluttered in the closest thing to an eye roll without actually being an eye roll. I let the minute linger like lead weight while we waited for the drinks and pack of COPD. The door opened. I kept my eyes on her as Officer Darby set two coffees, a pack of Virginia Slims—*Virginia Slims*—followed by two waters on the table. Based on the way mine tumbled to the floor, the rookie also had his eyes only on hers.

This woman.

"Whoops. Sorry." He grabbed the water from the floor and set it in front of me. "Uh, you know you can't smoke in—"

"Thanks."

"... Anything else?"

"Get some ibuprofen from Tanya."

"Okay."

Sunny lifted her hands onto the table. Composed, controlled. Odd. I couldn't tear my eyes away from her. I watched every flicker of her eye, every move of muscle as we sat silently in the room.

The door clicked open again and a small bottle was placed on the table—carefully this time.

"Anything else?" Darby asked.

"Go get that donut Colson just heated up."

"I don't think... he didn't—"

I shot him a look.

He retreated.

I leaned forward on my elbows, closing a few of the

inches between us. Sunny looked away and begun rubbing her thumb over her clasped hands as we waited for Darby to return. It was a tick. Sunny didn't like people in her space. Good to know, and it was a weakness I could definitely exploit. Especially with a smokeshow like her.

The door opened and a glistening, pink iced donut with rainbow sprinkles was placed at the center of the table. I made a mental note to chastise Colson on the way out.

"That it?" Darby asked.

"Yep."

I waited until the door clicked closed, then picked up the bottle of pills. I shook two out, pushed them in front of her.

"Take the ibuprofen."

"No. Thank you." The last two words an obvious effort.

"Take it. It will help with the swelling."

"My arm's fine."

"Agreed. I'm talking about your ribs. Ever had bruised ribs before?"

Something flickered behind her eyes. It was my first red flag.

"Hurts like a bitch," I continued. "'Scuse the language. Take the pills and eat the donut if you'd like. I'll wait."

"I'm gluten free."

I paused, leaned back. "What's the thing about gluten, Miss Harper?"

Her lips parted, considering her answer. Then, with a heaved breath, she rolled her eyes and grabbed the two pills on the table. "Fine. I'll take the pills."

"You'll thank me in the morning. Now, let's get down to business. It's my understanding you've waived your right to have an attorney present, correct?"

"That's correct."

"It's not smart."

She stared back.

"Why? Why waive the right?"

"Because I have the utmost faith in Berry Springs PD's ability to determine innocence."

I grunted. "I don't. Let's begin, then." I hit the red button on the recorder and recited all the mandatory bullshit, reminding her of her rights, then got into the questions.

"Can you please state your full name for the record?"

"Sunny Anise Harper." Her voice still held that controlled confidence but less of the punch. A rasp that I hadn't heard earlier suggested the beginning of an adrenaline crash from killing someone. I knew that feeling all too well myself.

"Age?"

"Twenty-eight."

I cringed. A baby. Compared to me, anyway.

"Tell me what happened tonight, Miss Harper."

"I was attacked."

"Are you saying what happened was done in self-defense?" I needed that one on the record. A hundred bucks would buy my beer for the month.

"Yes," she said.

"Do you know your attacker?"

"No."

"Not a friend? An acquaintance? A boyfriend?"

"I've never seen the guy before in my life."

"Okay. Tell me exactly what happened."

Her shoulders squared and she licked her lips, drawing my attention to the swollen split at the end. Did I do that?

She began. "I was out for a jog—"

"At midnight?"

"Yes."

"Why?"

"Why what?"

"Why jog at midnight?"

"Why not?"

"Security. Safety. ... Common sense."

"Would you say the same to a man?"

"I'd say it to Imi Lichtenfeld himself. Answer the question. Why were you jogging in the city park at midnight?"

"I'd just gotten off work."

"What do you do for a living?"

"I'm a dog trainer."

This time, I blinked. Of all the jobs I expected this woman to have, a dog trainer was not one of them. Supermodel, actress, WWE ring girl, jazzercise instructor, Playboy bunny, mime...

"You train dogs for a living?"

"Yes." Her tone a bit attitudinal. This telling me two things: Sunny took pride in her job, and also, it wasn't the first time she'd defended her choice in occupation.

"What kind of dogs?"

"The furry ones."

"Ah. So for comedy acts, then?"

Her lip twitched. "I train security dogs."

Now *that* made sense. *That* fit her personality.

"How'd you get into that line of work?"

Her shoulder lifted, gaze shifted.

"Why didn't you have one of these security dogs with you on your midnight jog?"

"Because I don't like to take them on long trips in the car."

"So you'd left town today?"

"Yes."

"Where to?"

"A kennel in Missouri."

"You breed?"

Her brow cocked.

"Dogs." I said quickly. "You breed the dogs?"

"No."

"Why were you going to a kennel then?"

"To purchase a few to train. I'm a dog trainer," she reminded me, impatiently. "I get dogs, train them, then sell them."

"This still doesn't explain why you decided to go on a jog in the park at midnight."

"Have you ever been in a car for eleven hours in one day?"

"I've been in a car for twenty-four hours in one day."

"Then you understand the need to stretch your legs."

My gaze dropped to her legs before quickly shifting back up.

"I prefer the public trails. I've jogged that trail more times than I can count, day and night." She continued. "The concrete's easier on me. The lights."

"The security the light provides?"

She nodded.

"Your gun isn't enough?"

She sat up straighter, her chin lifting, this telling me her job wasn't the only thing she'd defended before.

"I carry it when I don't have one of my dogs with me."

"You got a license?"

"Yep, and a hell of an aim."

I thought about the bullet to the eyeball.

"You carry it all the time?"

"Mostly."

"Why?"

"Why not?"

"Meaty gun. Where'd you get it?"

"I can't remember."

"Who taught you to use it?"

"Why do you assume I need to be taught?"

"Meaty gun."

"A gun is a gun. I'm not the only one who carries one on their hip."

"Not when they're jogging."

She didn't respond to this.

"A can of mace, a shiv, coin knife, zip blade knife. Those are normal self-defense jogging weapons. I've been in this business a long time, Sunny Harper, and never once have I met someone who jogs with a loaded gun, especially with that kind of firepower. A 380 is the most common type of concealed carry weapon. Not good enough for you, though. A nine millimeter pistol suggests more thought. More reasons behind the carry."

"Who says?"

"I say."

"That's your opinion."

"Tell me about the attack."

She squinted with anger, not fear, then began.

"I was about a mile in when something caught my eye."

"Where?"

"In the woods. To my left."

"What caught your eye?"

"Someone. Movement."

"So your attacker came out of the woods?"

"Yes."

"Which direction were you running?"

"South, a mile from the parking lot at the trailhead."

I made a mental note to check the area at sun up. "Continue."

"Thanks. I stopped running and that's when I was attacked."

"Why'd you stop running?"

"Because I don't have eyes in the back of my head."

It made sense, but went against most people's instinct. If a jogger thought they saw someone lurking in the woods during an after-dark jog, nine out of ten runners would pick up speed and haul ass back to their car. Not this one. This one stood her ground. This one was willing to get into a physical altercation rather than run scared. Sunny was the one percent and I got the feeling it wasn't the first time she'd been odd man out.

"So you stopped, then what?"

"He jumped out of the woods and attacked me from behind."

"Did you see his face?"

"No. Not, initially. It was dark. He attacked me between light posts. The city needs to put up more lights."

"Agreed. So you didn't actually see him jump out of the woods?"

"No."

"What is your first memory of that moment?"

"That it was a man."

"You knew your attacker was a male?"

"Yes. Based on the size, weight, movement. The smell."

"The smell?"

"Yes."

"You can tell if someone is a man or a woman based on smell?"

"You're clearly not a woman."

"And you're clearly not a bloodhound."

"That's correct, I do not have three hundred million scent receptors like a bloodhound, but I do have more hormones than men—most, anyway—which gives me a superior sense of smell compared to my male counterparts. Men have a scent, trust me on this."

I wondered what my own had been when I'd tackled her.

"Okay. Fine. What did your attacker smell like, then?"

"A man."

"So, tacos and Old Spice?"

She didn't laugh at this.

"At what point did you see his face?"

"After the attack. After..." She looked down.

"After he was dead on the ground."

"Yes."

"And you didn't recognize him?"

"No."

"Not at all? Even a little bit?"

"No."

"Continue. He grabbed you from behind..."

"I..." She bit her lip, the first show of nerves since she'd started the story. "I fought back. I fought him back." There was strength behind the words. Pride.

"When did you pull your gun?"

"I don't remember."

"Where do you keep it on you?"

"I slide the holster along a hidden pocket at the small of my back."

"What else did you have in these hidden pockets?"

"My car key and my gun, that's it."

"No knife?"

"No."

"No four-inch switchblade knife?"

"No."

"Do you recall seeing a switchblade during the attack?"

"No."

"Okay. So during the tussle you managed to pull out the gun, get your attacker in a bear hug and shoot him through the eye?"

"No."

"No?"

"I didn't kill him."

I paused, squinted, and leaned forward. "You didn't kill the man you were standing over while holding a gun?"

"No."

"No?"

"... No."

"Who did?"

"I don't know."

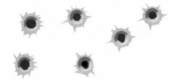

*W*hat. The. *Fuck?*

Did I mention my gut instincts were never wrong? I knew something was off from the get go, but this case already had more curve balls than a urology clinic. I didn't even know what to call the woman anymore. A suspect? A witness? A victim?

"What do you mean, you don't know *who* killed the man that was dead as a doornail, lying at your feet?"

She cringed at my crass choice of words. I didn't care. I didn't like curve balls. Or urology clinics for that matter.

"Someone else came up while my attacker and I were fighting. Tried to pull him off me. I was thrown to the ground, two shots rang out, and the next thing I know, my attacker was at my feet. Dead as a doornail as you so eloquently put it. And the other person was gone."

I stared at her, processing this *insane* new information.

"You mean to tell me that there is a *third* person involved in this attack?"

"Yes."

"And that person is the one who killed your attacker?"

"Yes."

"Not you. To reiterate, Miss Harper, you are saying that you did *not* kill your attacker?"

"Yes. That's correct."

"You had a gun in your hand, Sunny, pointing at your attacker's head when our witness walked up. How do you explain that?"

"I dropped the gun sometime during the fight. I picked it up after I was pushed to the ground. I kept the gun down, the aim not intended at his head—or at the old man pointing his at mine, for that matter."

"Did the mystery person use your gun to shoot your attacker, or do you think he used his own gun?"

"There's no way mine was used. It was on the ground next to me when I heard the shots."

So there was also a gun missing from the scene now. I scrubbed my hands over my face. Damn, I needed a drink.

"Okay, so you're pushed down, your attacker is shot by this mystery third person, the mystery person flees, then you grab your gun from the ground, stand up—"

"And see an old man pointing a pistol to my head, telling me that if I move, he'll kill me."

"Did you notice a vehicle pull up while you were being attacked?"

"No."

"What about headlights on the trees? The sound of a truck? Anything?"

"No."

A moment slid by while my mind raced with a dozen incoherent possibilities.

"Did you see this third person?"

"No. Nothing. I was engaged with the attacker and I remember seeing something in my peripheral. The third person, I guess. Then, I was shoved to the ground."

"Do you know if this third person was a man or a woman?"

"No."

"Didn't catch the scent?"

"No. Smartass."

My brow cocked. Good for her. I was being a dick. I respected her standing up to me. Not many people did. Especially women.

"I need to make sure I am one-thousand percent clear. There is someone else involved in this attack. You are saying three people. You, your attacker, and a mystery person who pulled the trigger of a gun that is not yours."

"You don't believe me."

"It doesn't align with the witness account."

"Well, it's the truth."

"So is guilt after shooting a dude through the eye."

"You think I'm making this up so I won't have to be responsible for a man's death?"

I shrugged.

Pissed now, her controlled armor began to chip. With narrowed eyes and a twitching jaw, she pinned me to my seat with a look as cold as ice.

"I understand that blaming me for my attacker's death is the easiest way to go detective. Call it self-defense, call me a liar, and forget about the third person. Close the case and get back to your pink sprinkle-donuts. I get it, but I'd appreciate a little more respect than the snide remarks you consider professional."

"Had that bottled up, didn't you, Miss Harper?"

"Call me Sunny. Easier on your vocabulary."

Alright. So we had a spitfire on our hands.

"Let's recap here, then, Sunny. After a long day driving to visit a kennel in Missouri—where you don't breed, you buy —you decided to take a jog in the park on your way home. Stretch your legs. Midway through your jog, you noticed a man in the woods, who attacked you when you stopped running. Mid-attack, another person came to your rescue, shot your attacker, killing him, then ran away, leaving you holding a gun over the dead body. Am I leaving *anything* out?"

"No."

"So you're confirming that there are two victims here, then."

"Two?"

"The man who was just unloaded at the morgue, and you."

"I'm not a victim."

"I suggest you reconsider that for the sake of this incident."

"I defended myself." Venom shot from her eyes. "I am not a victim."

That instinct in my gut? Damn thing tingled. There was more to this story, I was sure of it.

"Let's go back to your attacker. Did he say anything to you?"

"No."

"Not even mutter something during the attack?"

"No."

"*Think,* Sunny."

"*No.* Nothing was said."

"What about anything on him? You said you didn't see a knife, but did he have anything else in his hands? Any kind of weapon? A stick? A gun? A cell phone? Did you notice anything at all?"

"No."

"No, as in, he didn't have a weapon, or you didn't notice one?"

"I didn't see a weapon." For the first time, she paused, looking up in deep thought. "That's weird, right? That he didn't have a weapon?"

"You're only assuming he didn't."

"Why wouldn't he have used it, then?" Her eyes rounded. "Do you think he intended to abduct me?"

"You tell me."

Her back straightened, this new line of thinking obviously spinning her wheels. "I don't know..."

I sat back, contemplating my next question.

"Did you notice if your attacker had a limp?"

"A limp?"

"Yes."

"No, not that I noticed."

"Are you sure? Maybe you subconsciously noticed while he was running up? Or maybe he favored a right or left leg during the attack?"

She shook her head.

"Okay. Same questions for this third mystery person now. The person who threw you to the ground and killed your attacker. You're sure you didn't get a look at him or her?"

"I'm positive. Trust me, I'd be drawing you a picture if I did."

"Did you notice anything about the person? Clothes, hat or no hat, weapon, tattoos, skin color, hair color, anything?"

"No. I'm sorry."

"Limp?"

"No."

"Like a ghost, then."

Her gaze leveled mine. "Yes."

"The bare finger on your left hand suggests you're not married, is that correct?"

"Yes."

"Boyfriend?"

"No."

"Since when?"

"Since a long time."

"Friends with benefits?"

"That's none of your business."

"Everything's my business right now. Take some time thinking about your former lovers and let me know if you think any of them might fit this bill. Assuming there are some, of course."

Those eyes squinted.

"Are you an only child?"

"Yes."

"Parents?"

"My dad lives in Dallas. My mom is no longer with us."

"I'd appreciate his contact information and the contact info for the dog breeder you visited earlier today."

"Why? To determine if I'm telling the truth?"

"Your attack ended in a man's death. It's my job to gather everything I can surrounding the incident, including the whereabouts of everyone involved."

"Fine."

"Thank you for your cooperation."

"Thank you for toning down your smartassery."

I pulled my card from my pocket and tossed it across the table. "If you think of anything else, give me a call. Day or night."

She slid the card into one of the many hidden pockets in those leggings. "When do I get my gun back?"

"It'll be awhile." I stood. "Do you have a ride back to your car?"

"I'll take care of it."

"I'll take you." I turned and made my way to the door. "Stay here. I'll be right back."

Colson slid out of the observation room as I stepped into the hall and pulled the door closed. He jerked his chin and I followed him into his office, where he closed the door behind us.

"How much did you catch?" I asked.

He drug his fingers through his hair. "Everything, and not damn enough."

"Agreed."

His phone rang. He silenced it, lingering on the blinking red light a moment before shaking his head. "Shit never sleeps. Never fucking sleeps. What are your initial thoughts?"

"Do you have old man Erickson's interview notes?"

"Yeah." Colson picked up his notebook and tossed it into my hands.

I flipped through the pages. "Jesus, dude, did you sleep through handwriting in school? How the fuck is anyone supposed to read this shit?"

He snatched it back. "What do you need to know? You're such an asshole."

"Did Erickson mention anything about seeing a third person?"

"No."

"He said he only saw Sunny and Julian?"

"Right."

"Did he say *specifically* that he saw Sunny Harper shoot Julian in the head?"

Colson skimmed his notes. "Yes."

"Impossible."

"Why?"

"The attack happened between lampposts. I couldn't even make out her face, or hell, the fact that she was a woman, when I rushed the scene. There's no way in hell he actually saw her face, or anything more than two dark silhouettes. He's just assuming."

"Then you're assuming that when Erickson said he saw Sunny with Julian in a bear hold before shooting him, that it wasn't Sunny. It was the third person?"

"According to Sunny, she was on the ground at that moment."

"If she's telling the truth."

"We need to follow up with Erickson. Ask him specifically. We also need to have ballistics check the pin markings on the casing I found to see if it matches Sunny's gun. If the markings do match then that means Julian was shot by her gun and that she's lying. If the markings don't match, it confirms a third player."

Colson nodded, scribbled on the pad.

I began pacing. "This wasn't a mugging gone bad. Her attacker didn't ask for any personal items, didn't take the key from her pocket, nothing. She said he didn't even speak."

"Personal, then?"

"Possibly, but she says she doesn't know him. Or it could be some cracked out drug addict tripping his balls off."

"What about the abduction theory?"

"Eighty percent of women who are abducted are taken by someone they know."

"Good point. What else do we know about her right now? Other than her ability to get out of speeding tickets."

"I've got Darby looking into her now, Google, social media, any records, anything. And I'm going to sync up with the dog breeder she said she visited. Try to get some more insight on her and confirm she was where she said she was, and ask if they noticed anyone following her."

Colson fisted his hands on his hips. "Okay. Two scenarios as of right now, then. One: this woman—what do you think she is? A buck ten?—is able to hold off an attacker twice her size until her guardian angel shows up and kills the guy for her. Or, two, the crazy bitch is lying and she killed the guy, and there is no third guy. She could know Griggs and is lying. He could be an ex-lover or some shit."

"Okay, going with your option one, then, Sunny Harper is an innocent victim in a shitty attack. She's banged up, which can confirm that story. Check that box. It is also plausible that a woman of her size could hold off an attacker if it's true that she's skilled in Krav Maga, which I'll verify. Considering the physicality of it, it is also plausible that in the scuffle she dropped her gun, leaving her defenseless and allowing this third mystery person to shoot. The smoke clears and she's staring down the barrel of Erickson's pistol, and freezes. Then we show up."

"Hell of a woman, Jagg." It wasn't a compliment. "Ever met a woman who checks all those boxes?"

No, was the undeniable answer to that question. Assault victims rarely fought back, and it was even rarer for them to overpower their attacker. And none carried a gun like that.

"Something just doesn't feel right." Colson picked up a stress ball from his desk. "The only thing we have to go on right now is her story and Erickson's eye witness account, which are different." He began pacing. "Self-defense is understandable and forgivable. So if she is making up this third mystery person, why? She has to know we'd write it off as self-defense and be done with it. Why make that up?"

"Killing a man fucks with your head. If she is lying, it's

probably because she's scared she'd get pinned with murder or something."

"Then someone needs to convince her that's not the case so she'll admit to lying about the third person and we can close the book before the entire town goes apeshit about this. God, I hate this already." Colson ran his fingers through his hair again. "I'll call old man Erickson at dawn and verify his statement. And I'll also have Darby pull the street cams for the hours surrounding the attack. See what vehicles passed by the park."

"Have him look for a blue, four door sedan."

"Wait." Colson turned to me. "You think Sunny's attacker could be the Black Bandit? The same guy you think killed Seagrave?"

"It's a possibility. Too much violence in such a short amount of time. We have to consider that it could all be connected."

Colson paused, blinking, assessing. "Did I mention I hate this already?"

A knock sounded at the door.

"What?" Colson snapped.

Darby walked in, his skin an almost iridescent pale. The kid needed food and water to replace the amount he'd vomited at the scene, and maybe a valium to go with it.

"Got more information on the victim." His eyes were wide, way too hyper for the moment. My senses went on alert.

"Julian Griggs is the pastor's son."

"*What?*" Colson's voice raised an octave.

"Yep. Works full-time at the local Baptist church. Runs the kid program and the soup kitchen."

Colson's neck snapped to me. "Did you recognize him?"

I shook my head. Half the kid's face had been blown off... and I wasn't exactly a regular at church.

"Me, either. *Shit.* I didn't even put it together when we read his name from his driver's license. *Shit, fuck, shit.*"

Darby handed Colson a photo of a smiling kid surrounded by a bunch of gleeful children. "That's Julian on his mission trip to South America last month. He just got back. Printed it from a newspaper article."

Colson's mouth dropped. "The *pastor's son* was just shot in the head in the park. This is going to hit the fucking fan."

Darby nodded, but the rookie had no idea how bad it was going to get. Pastor Griggs had been the lead pastor in Berry Springs since the seventies. Smart, respected, and had dunked more local citizens than the city pool.

"Does Julian have a rap sheet?" I asked.

Darby shook his head.

Of course he didn't. Of course the kid was going to be a model citizen who would never attack a woman jogging in the middle of the night.

Yeah, shit was going to hit the fan, alright. Not just because the town angel had just been shot through the eye, but because Berry Springs was going to want someone's head for it.

And I had feeling that head came with long, dark curls.

11

JAGG

"*I*'ve got to call the chief." Colson said. "He'll want to make this call personally. He knows the pastor. Hell, I think Pastor Griggs baptized the chief's kids. He'll probably come up here. *Dammit.*" He reached for his phone.

"Darby." I jerked my chin to the door.

Colson was already dialing the chief when Darby and I stepped into the hallway.

"I got everything else you asked—"

"Not here, kid."

The station was a flurry of chatter and whispers, sudden overachievers swinging by the station at five in the morning. I had no doubt everyone in town would know about the "Slaying in the Park," by daybreak.

I led Darby down to the hallway, past the conference room, glancing in to make sure Sunny Harper hadn't popped the window locks and escaped, because, for some reason, I knew she was capable of it.

The woman hadn't moved a muscle. Same spot, same alert, rod-straight posture, same sharp, controlled expression on her face. To any bystander, Sunny looked calm, complacent almost. But the extra frizz in her hair suggested she'd run her hands through her curls many times since I'd left. Nervous energy.

Our eyes met.

Her head didn't move, neck didn't move, she just watched me pass by like one of those creepy paintings you were sure were staring into your soul.

Jesus, this woman.

I led Darby into the observation room, then clicked the door closed.

"Go." I crossed my arms over my chest and faced him, keeping Sunny in my peripheral.

He fumbled with the papers he was carrying, a slight tremble in his hands.

"Uh. Yes. Okay—"

"Darby."

He looked up.

"Take a deep breath. Calm yourself. You are stressing me the fuck out."

He took a shaky deep breath, then another. "Sorry."

"It's okay. I know you just saw your first dead guy. Accept it, get over it, and focus. It happens. Control yourself. Now. Go."

"Okay." Another breath. "So I dug up everything I could on Miss Harper."

"Yes. Go."

Fuck.

"Do you want her background first or—"

"Background."

"Okay. Miss Harper is a twenty-eight year old—"

"Dog trainer who's social media is comprised primarily of work-related posts. It appears that Miss Harper is an introvert, has no friends or social life, and is a hermit on all counts..."

"You got all that from one ten minute interview?"

"Comes with experience. Deeper, I need deeper, Darby."

"Okay, so yes, you're right on all counts. The woman appears to be a hermit. She started an LLC for her dog training company a few months ago. Runs it by herself. Other than social media posts about that, there are a few posts about wine and that's it. She likes wine."

"What kind?"

"Uh, reds. Bordeauxs."

"Okay, go on."

"No obvious men, or women, for that matter, in her life"—my brain momentarily short circuited. Did Darby think she was gay? Was she a lesbian? No. No way. ... What the hell did I care, anyway?—"and, like I said, no besties or book club pics. By all accounts, Sunny appears to be a dog-loving homebody who likes good wine, which isn't surprising considering who her dad is."

"Who's her dad?"

Darby's eyes flashed with victory. "Ah, so you don't know *everything* about Sunny Harper. Interesting..."

"Darby," I growled between my teeth.

"Sunny is the daughter of the one and only Arlo Harper, multi-millionaire real estate mogul born and raised in good ol' Berry Springs."

My brows arched. I knew the name. Everyone in the tri-state area knew the name Arlo Harper. The man started his own construction business when he was just nineteen, and in two decades, owned half of the surrounding counties. Years later, he moved to Dallas where he tripled his net worth. There wasn't a county line you could cross without going onto one of his properties.

Sunny Harper was a rich girl.

A *very* rich girl.

I had a thing about rich people. Call it a chip on my shoulder from growing up dirt poor but I never got along with them, their type. Not much set me off more than entitlement. Spoiled brats who had doors open for them simply because of their last names, not because of busting through it with grit and determination. Brats who thought they owned the world and everyone in it. I'd broken my fair share of rich kids' noses and didn't regret a single one.

Darby continued, "Appears Arlo's had some run ins with the law over the last few years in Dallas."

"Yeah?"

He handed me a police report with DPD stamped on the letterhead—Dallas Police Department—for a DUI. "There's another DUI after that one, and one drunk and disorderly."

I hmphed.

"Guy got off, of course."

Of course he did. Rich fuckers. Money always talked, but not from Sunny's lips, apparently.

I kicked myself for not connecting the dots, but nothing about this woman screamed heiress to a real estate fortune. I was pretty good at pegging rich girls but the thought hadn't even popped into my head with Sunny. Not only were her jogging clothes faded and mis-matched, they didn't appear to be designer, either. You know, like Nike or Adidas. Her right running shoe had a hole at the tip, her nail polish chipped on each finger. No diamond studs in her ears, no jewelry, no perfectly quaffed mane of highlighted hair— quite the contrary there, in fact. Her hair was long, wild, a horse's mane blowing in the wind. Nothing—not a single thing—about her suggested she had more than a few hundos sitting in the bank.

Considering her daddy's obvious business acumen,

you'd figure she would have had the wits to demand a lawyer. Or at least throw her daddy's name around while I was pinning her to the ground. Why hadn't the woman mentioned him? Or demanded one of her daddy's lawyers?

Nothing about Sunny Harper made sense.

... Until it suddenly did.

"And then there's this." Darby handed me another DPD police report.

I had a slow, gradual reaction as I read the report. First, shock, then a clenching gut, then heat prickling my skin all the way from my toes to the tops of my ears, then finally, a rush of white-hot rage.

That *protectiveness.*

"She almost died."

His words barely registered through the thudding of my heart.

I held up the single piece of paper. "Is this all you got on it?" My voice was sharp, clipped. No way to hide that.

He nodded. "I spoke with someone at the department. They just sent that over."

"At Dallas PD? When? Now?"

"Yeah. I got ahold of a fellow rookie working the night-shift. Turns out we both like video games. Anyway, he pulled the full file, which has the medical report and everything. The responding officer to the attack is his mentor. They'd even discussed the case as a training exercise."

"What did he say?"

"Basically, Sunny's cracked-out boyfriend almost beat her to death in some sort of jealous rage after her twenty-first birthday party. Beat her with a baseball bat, slammed her head against a bathroom mirror then threw her down the stairs."

Darby handed me a collage of the crime scene photos.

It was horrific.

I had a visceral reaction when I looked at the blood splatters on the cracked mirror. *Her* blood. A fresh sheen of sweat broke out under my T-shirt.

I've responded to plenty of domestic disturbances during my career, some of which contained a dead body, but *these* pictures, I couldn't even look at. It was like a switch was flipped inside me. I handed it back as he continued.

"Miss Harper was in ICU for forty-eight hours. Broken arm, collar bone, swelling of the brain. She got one-hundred and sixty-seven stitches across her body. Doctor noted the dude had ripped clumps of hair from her head."

I looked through the two-way mirror at the silky mane cascading down her slender shoulders. Long tresses marking victory over a story, a nightmare, she'd likely never forget. Her eyes flickered with awareness, her face turning slightly in my direction, but not all the way. She knew I was there. She knew I was watching.

I ripped my eyes away. "What's his name?"

"Kenzo Rees."

I didn't need to write it down because it burned into my brain like a branding iron, or baseball bat if you will.

"What did he get?"

"Assault with a deadly weapon. First degree felony. Got him a four year sentence in prison but the guy was already on probation for two DUIs and possession with intent to sell, so the judge threw the book at him and gave him another two years. Rees was rumored to be one of the biggest cocaine dealers in the area, but cops could never pin him for it. Rumored gang affiliations, too."

"And this happened when she was twenty-one?"

"Right."

"She's twenty-eight now. That was seven years ago. His sentence was six years. Is he out?"

"No according to my DPD rookie."

"He should be. Find out why he isn't."

"Yes, sir."

The door flung open. Colson stormed inside and slammed it behind him, a tornado of energy that had Darby inching closer to me.

"Let's fucking recap, shall we?" Colson interrupted.

I glanced at Darby, who muttered, "I set a copy of all this on his desk."

Colson ignored Darby and turned to the two-way mirror, staring at Sunny as he addressed me. "We've got an emotionally scarred rich girl who dated a gang member who almost beat her to death, and a dead pastor's kid who just got back from a fucking mission trip. Who, according to our guest of the evening, attacked her and was killed by a phantom ninja who came out of nowhere and then disappeared into thin air. *Despite* the fact that she was found holding a gun over Julian's dead body."

"You don't believe her." Darby said.

"No I don't. There's something about her. About this whole thing. My gut is screaming at me. There's something about her I don't like."

"That's not going to stand up in court." I said.

"Like you're so politically correct? Give me a break." Colson turned to me. "Why the hell didn't she lawyer up? Why didn't she tell us everything at the scene? Blabbering like a normal panic-stricken person would be? What's with the fucking attitude and nine millimeter? Who the hell jogs at midnight? Why is she being so... *not normal* about this whole thing? Chick's not normal."

"Is this your first assault victim, Colson?"

"Why are you so sure she's telling the truth?"

"Why are you so fucking sure she's not?"

"Why are you so fucking defensive about this? She's hot and all, but shit, Jagg, I thought you had better contr—"

"You finish the rest of that sentence, you'll be slurring it through a hole in your mouth."

Colson squared his shoulders. "You threatening me, Jagger?"

"Whoa." Darby shifted between us. "Guys. Stop."

"Get out." I said to the rookie, my eyes never leaving Colson as Darby slinked out and shut the door.

Colson threw up his hands, heaved out a breath, and took a step back. "I know you're messed up about Seagrave's death, but you need to reset, Jagger. Check yourself. Because we both know you're hanging onto your job by a thread right now and the last thing you need is to stick your neck out for some random chick. There's emotions already involved here, bro. The Chief knows the pastor. He knew Julian. He hates you. My opinion, you either need to pass off Seagrave's investigation or this one. Leave the cursed Cedonia scrolls and this Sunny Harper shit alone."

"I'm already involved in this Sunny Harper *shit.*"

"Exactly."

"I don't mean emotionally you, asswipe. I was one of the first responders with you. Hell, I just interviewed her for you."

"That's not why you want to stay on. You think Sunny Harper, Julian Griggs, and the freaking Voodoo Tree are all connected to Seagrave's death."

"You're goddamn right I do."

Colson shook his head, placed his hand on the door-knob. "I hope you know what you're doing, bro. All eyes are on you, just waiting for you to screw up." He glanced over his shoulder and gave me the once-over. "Speaking of, maybe now's the time to start dressing like you give a damn. Button-up, slacks, shoes that don't have beer stains on them. Walk the line, at least until everything blows over. That's my advice."

I looked down at my T-shirt, jeans and boots.

He turned the knob. "Go home and get a solid night's sleep. This'll all be here tomorrow."

I jerked my chin to the two-way mirror. "What about Harper?"

"I've got nothing to hold her on. I'm going to let her go, strongly suggesting not to leave the area for the next few days."

In case he got something to bring her back in for, he meant.

"You can't take the easy way out here, Colson."

He spun around. "You mean by signing the report that says Julian Griggs was simply killed in self-defense? Then filing it away so everyone can move on with their lives? No. I can't do that. Why? Because the pastor is going to want answers. The town is going to want answers. Because it makes no sense that the God-fearing kid of a pastor would hide in the woods and attack a woman in the park. And don't even get me started on this mysterious third person." He pushed open the door. "Forgive me, dude, but you're fucking crazy to take on a case so high profile right now."

The door slammed followed by Colson's heavy footsteps and Darby's tip toes down the hall.

Colson was right. I was crazy to stay on the case.

Good thing crazy never stopped me before.

12

JAGG

*J*hung back until Colson's and Darby's voices faded down the hallway. I didn't know how much Darby had heard but I guessed most of it. Just as well. Assuming Darby hadn't slept through his human behavior class at the academy, the kid had probably already picked up on the fact that the Chief wasn't too keen on me, as everyone in town had.

Not that I gave a shit. I learned long ago to only give shits about what I could control, and a balding, brash sixty-something divorcee with one foot in retirement and the other in a box of jelly-filled donuts was something I couldn't. He wasn't technically my boss, although he liked to think he was. I answered to the state's attorney general, who didn't give a shit what I did as long as I got him results and kept him in the voter's favors. Did I mention I hate politics?

I turned and braced myself on the small ledge below the two-way mirror, looking at Sunny Harper in an entirely new light. Suddenly, the scattered dots started to connect, painting a picture of a woman who'd been to hell and back.

Sunny Harper was a victim.

A survivor.

A fighter.

Colson was dead wrong when he'd labeled her response to the Slaying in the Park as "not normal." If he truly knew anything about assault victims it was that their entire world became "not normal" after an attack as vicious as Sunny's. I'd seen it dozens of times over the course of my career, not only as a detective, but in war zones overseas. Women thought they had it bad here? Shit, the things I'd seen done to women overseas would make your balls shrink to your throat and give you nightmares for years. It had me.

PTSD was a very real thing, and in my opinion, too big of an umbrella for conditions with so many symptoms and repercussions. PTSD effects almost ten percent of people over a lifetime, with women twice as likely to experience it than men. Most cases are short-lived, with symptoms easing with time. Some, though, experience chronic effects including legit personality changes. New studies have shown that chronic PTSD creates an "amped up" nervous system—think constant 'fight or flight' mode—causing actual chemical changes in the brain.

After an attack as brutal as the Dallas police report claimed Sunny's to be, it's not far-fetched to imagine her life taking on an entirely new normal. Shaping, adapting, changing.

Yet somehow, after the attack, Sunny had picked herself up, gotten her conceal carry license, enrolled in Krav Maga, bought herself some badass dogs, and dedicated her life to training guard dogs for others in need. Sunny had found a way to adapt, weird behavior be damned.

But now, seven years later, another attack.

Coincidence?

Coincidence that it happened right after Seagrave was shot to death?

Was I crazy?

As I stared at Sunny through the two-way mirror, I clicked off the things I knew to be true, willing the pieces of the puzzle to magically fall into place.

One, I had four ancient Wiccan scrolls, rumored to be cursed, that had suddenly risen from the dead days before the annual Moon Magic Festival.

Two, I had the "Black Bandit," the name given to the thief rumored to be responsible for stealing said scrolls.

Three, I had Lieutenant Seagrave, responding to one of those heists where he was shot six times in the chest, moments before a blue sedan was caught on camera driving away.

Four, I had a creepy-ass voodoo shrine resurrected yards from his funeral, and hours after that, I meet Sunny Harper, gun in hand, standing over the pastor's son's dead body.

Lastly, I had Sunny's story of a third mystery person who supposedly shot the pastor's son, then vanished without a trace.

If I'm being honest here, I was still trying to figure if that last part was true. Colson didn't think so, but he was right about one thing, nothing added up, although my gut was screaming at me that it was all connected. That Seagrave's murder and Sunny's attack were linked, and that every piece of the puzzle added up.

I just had to figure out how—starting with finding the damn Black Bandit.

I watched Sunny's head jerk up as the door to the conference room opened and Colson stepped inside. I clicked on the speaker and listened as he told her she could leave for the night, but not from Berry Springs until he gave her the okay.

Colson was already on his phone and halfway down the hall as I stepped into the conference room where Sunny was slowly pushing herself to a stance.

"Here," I rushed forward.

"Don't." She jerked away. "Please."

I took a step back and had to restrain myself from helping her out of the chair. The woman was in obvious pain and I wondered if she had more than just a bruised rib.

"Is there something you need?" She snapped, her cheeks flushing with both pain and embarrassment. I tore my eyes away and pretended to busy myself with repositioning the phone to a perfect ninety degree angle.

"You have my card, Miss Harper." I chanced a look at her once she'd fully straightened. "Call me if you think of anything else."

She kicked the BSPD sweatshirt to the side of the room and stepped past me.

"Thanks."

I followed her out.

A hush fell over the station and heads turned as she walked down the hallway, her shoulders back, head held high. It was remarkable to watch, really.

I shoved ahead of her and opened the door that led to the lobby, then the door to outside.

The early morning was as black as midnight. A cool breeze carried through the air, a brief reprieve until the blazing sun came up.

Sunny's long curls whipped around her face as her pace quickened down the steps. The woman was practically running away from the station—or away from me. Either way, Sunny was beelining it somewhere.

"Do you have a ride to your car?" I asked from the steps.

"Yes," she hollered back, her focus staying ahead.

I looked around the parking lot. Only a few cars, and none were running. I glanced over my shoulder at no one coming outside, keys in hand. It was then that I realized Colson had either *not* offered her a ride, or she'd declined. Based on the way she shot out of the interview room, I assumed the latter.

"Is your driver on his way?" I promise I hadn't intended the condescending rich-girl implication. She didn't respond.

I jogged to catch up with her abnormally long strides, making me wonder exactly how long they were, and how they would feel wrapped around my waist. This led me to wonder what time it was and how long since I'd eaten or slept.

I was losing my mind. I was literally chasing after a woman, a first for me.

I wish I could say it was the last.

Sunny stepped onto the sidewalk that led to Main Street. The streets were bare, store fronts black. It was that unsettling time of night, or early morning I should say, when darkness seemed to envelop everything, including sound.

The street light short-circuited above her as I finally caught up.

"Take it easy, Flo-Jo. Where's your ride?"

She ignored me, laser focused on her destination, wherever the hell that was.

"Didn't doc tell you to take it easy until your body heals?"

Still, no response. Not even a glance.

"Something happen to your ears during the attack, Miss Harper?"

"What are you doing?"

"Trying to keep up with those stilts you call legs."

"I mean, why are you following me?"

"You've never had a gentlemen walk you to your car?"

"I told you I had a ride."

"I wasn't asking if you owned a motor vehicle. I was asking if you had someone to drive you to your 'ride?'"

"I'd rather walk."

"Would you?"

A crack in the sidewalk caught her toe and she stumbled forward. The groan of pain that escaped her lips sounded like a dying dog.

"Alright. That's it." I stepped in front of her, cutting her off. "I'm going to touch you, Miss Harper. Don't go all Krav Maga on my ass."

She didn't smartass back, suggesting she was in a load of pain.

I touched her with my fingertips first, as one might an injured bear, then slowly wrapped my hand around her forearm, then my arm around her back.

"This is what's going to happen here. I'm going to slowly pick you up."

"No." The low, gruffness of her voice and the fact she didn't fight me confirmed her pain.

"Yes. On three."

"No."

One..."

"No."

"Two..."

"Detective—"

"Three."

I expected a backhand as I swooped down, but instead, her body stilled. Slowly, I lifted her into my arms, my own back screaming at me.

She released another grunt as her body folded into my arms.

"*Shhh,*" I whispered. "You're fine."

I settled her into a cradled position against my chest, grit my teeth, and pushed away my own pain—something I'd gotten very good at over the last handful of years.

"Breathe." I told her. And to myself.

An exhale against my chest.

"Another. Slow."

Inhale, exhale.

"Good. I'm going to start walking now. Hang on or don't, whatever's most comfortable. I've got you."

Her body remained as stiff as a board until we hit the halfway mark and her weight finally released against my hold. It felt like a small victory. Her head rested against my chest.

Good girl, I thought.

A breeze caught her hair, sending spirals of silky ebony against my cheek and wafts of that same coconut smell as when I'd tackled her at the park. The scent had me visualizing the sun resting on the ocean's horizon and waves crashing against my toes.

How long had it been since I'd taken a vacation?

Hell, how long since I'd taken a single day off work?

... How long since the scent of a woman's hair had me considering it?

We were halfway to the town's square when the hum of an engine pulled my attention behind us. Shifting Sunny's weight so my left arm could grab my gun if needed, I refocused my senses to my peripheral. The car slowed. I glanced over my shoulder just as Darby drove by, rubbernecking from the driver's seat of his patrol car like a damn spider monkey.

Christ.

There I was, cradling Sunny Harper like a new bride.

Of all the freaking times for this kid to take an interest in the safety of Main Street. Our eyes met for a brief second before he disappeared downhill, and I had no doubt the entire station would know about Sunny's "ride" by morning.

So be it.

The night was just beginning to lighten by the time we reached the park. I wasn't sure if Sunny had fallen asleep, so I gave my best guess on where she'd parked. I knew it wasn't where Colson and I had entered, and I remembered her saying she was about a mile into her jog before the attack, so my best bet was the north entrance. I pivoted and stepped onto a shortcut through the woods where I picked up the jogging trail a few yards in. I didn't like that my gun hand wasn't free. Keeping my head on a swivel, I scanned the woods as we passed through. The lampposts did a shit job of illuminating more than a few feet, and, Sunny was right, there were pitch-black spots in-between. Dark enough to shade anyone's face. There was also enough underbrush for a damn elephant to hide. I recalled the debate years earlier between the cowboys and local conservationists—aka hippies—about clearing the shrubbery in City Park. The hippies didn't want "man" to touch the nature. The cowboys wanted it cleaned up. In the end, the hippies won after a three-day protest.

I replayed Sunny's description of the attack in my head. There was no question someone could hide along the trail, so that part added up. But why was the pastor's kid hanging out at the park at midnight? Why attack a lone jogger? Why Sunny? Or, had he followed her? Did the pastor's son have something against Sunny? And who *the hell* was this third person? It couldn't have been an accomplice of Julian

Griggs, because why would his accomplice shoot him in the face?

Assuming Sunny's story was true, of course.

The crime scene photos from her attack in Dallas flashed through my head. Holes in the walls. Bruises on her face. Clumps of her hair along the blood-speckled sink.

My grip tightened around her. She pressed deeper against the squeeze, and that same damn protectiveness that I felt when seeing the photos for the first time came over me again. Intense. Raw. Visceral. What I imagine a father feeling over his daughter.

Or, a husband over his wife.

Another breeze, another puff of hair across my neck. I looked down at the beautiful curls, my gaze skirting from each strand wondering which ones had been ripped from her head. Wondering how long it had taken for the hair to grow back. Wondering if she'd been embarrassed. If she'd felt shame? Wore hats? Or maybe she cut it all off so she didn't have to look at it.

Each strand had grown back. Healed. Long, beautiful. Resilient. Strong.

Like Sunny.

Sunny with her stygian, wild locks of armor.

I stepped into the north parking lot and stopped cold. I could almost hear the guitar riff in the background as I stared at the only vehicle in the parking lot—a freaking gleaming, glistening, sparkling, cherry red 1972 Chevy Cheyenne with white running stripes down the side.

Holy. *Dream car.*

No *freaking* way did this badass beast belong to a woman named Sunny. I almost popped a boner. I'm not even kidding.

"Please tell me that's your truck," I said, not caring if I woke her.

Her head lifted from my chest. "It runs. I promise."

"Runs through my blood like a goddamn shot of espresso. She. Is. *Beautiful.*" *I whistled.*

"Thanks." I felt her smile.

My jaw literally slacked as I crossed the lot. I was madly, head-over-heels in love. With the truck.

"Keys?"

"In my pants."

"In that case..." I released one of my hands.

She slapped my wrist and looked up at me with a mixture of humor and *did-you-seriously-just-say-that?*

My thoughts exactly.

"Alright, I'm going to set you down now—"

"Without digging in my pants?"

I cocked my head, eyeing the truck. "Weeeeell..."

She rolled her eyes. "Set me down."

"You ready?"

She nodded against my chest, that lax weight suddenly tense again.

"Here we go." Bending at the knees, I slowly lowered her to the ground. Once I was sure she was steady, I let go.

She didn't make eye contact. Despite the woman's badass exterior, she was embarrassed that I carried her. It was a fleeting moment of insecurity confirming the layers and layers that made up Sunny Harper.

She pulled a key—an actual key, not a key fob—from one of the hundred hidden pockets in her pants. Modern marvels those things are.

She unlocked the truck. I pulled open the door and offered my hand. She declined and climbed into the cab, which, also, ironically, had a tropical smell of sorts. The interior was upholstered in shiny leather, cherry red, like the paint.

Like those lips.

"All in?" I asked.

"In."

Standing between the door and the driver's seat, I placed my palms on the top of the truck. "Long drive to your house?"

"No."

We stared at each other a moment before I stepped back.

"Stay safe, Miss Harper. Call me if you need anything."

I started to close the door, but she strong-armed it.

"Thank you," she whispered, her eyes never reaching mine.

I dipped my chin, stepped back, and tried to ignore the ball squeezing my stomach as two badass taillights faded into the darkness.

13

JAGG

"*W*here's my daughter?"

Halfway up the station steps, I paused and looked over my shoulder. A pudgy, short man in a golf cap, a blinding neon-blue paisley golf shirt, and corduroy pants—despite the heat—slammed the door to a black Porsche. I glanced at my wristwatch—4:34 a.m.

I was *so close* to being home.

So *damn* close.

I looked back at the station doors, willing them to slide open and someone—any-freaking-one else—to walk out the door and deal with whatever the hell this asshole had going on.

"You," he said.

I cocked a brow. Not in the fucking mood. Especially for a rich, sports-car driving prick. I was imagining my fist connecting with Porsche-guy's nose when—

"Where's my daughter?" He demanded.

Daughter, Porsche, money...

It had to be Arlo Harper. Sunny's millionaire real estate mogul father.

I turned fully to him as he stomped his stubby, gnome-legs across the parking lot. My first thought was how someone who looked like Sunny came from this man's DNA. She looked nothing like him, and based on the six-figure sports car, Rolex around his wrist, black wingtips (not loafers and definitely no tassels)—at four in the freaking morning—looks weren't the only thing they didn't have in common. As if the woman didn't intrigue me enough.

"I won't ask again, Mr.—"

"Detective. I just escorted your daughter to her truck, where she just left the park."

"What?"

What?

"I thought she was here." Arlo said, a line of confusion running down his forehead.

"No. She just left."

My confusion now matched his.

He closed his eyes and blew out a breath. "That *girl.*"

I blinked, surprised that his first comment wasn't asking if she was okay. I was also surprised at the whiff of soap coming off his skin. He'd taken time to shower before coming to the station to check on his beloved daughter.

"Where was she going?" He asked.

"Can't tell you that, sir."

"What the hell do you mean you can't tell me that?"

"Because I don't know where she was going."

"Well," he grumbled. "I want to talk to whoever's in charge of the case."

I took an inward deep breath. I wanted *home.*

"You're looking at him."

"Oh. You're..." The man scanned me from head to toe like I was a college dropout applying for a loan.

"Detective Max Jagger."

"Arlo Harper. Harper Construction."

Okay. That did it. The man attached his company to his introduction and I officially couldn't stand him.

"Sunny Harper's father." He continued, 'father' being the lesser of the two titles, apparently. "I want to know what happened tonight."

"I'm sure Sunny gave you all the details when she called you."

"I haven't talked to her."

Wait. What?

"How did you hear about the incident, then?" I asked.

"Hazel De Ville called me."

"Hazel De Ville, from Mystic Maven's?" The same art shop where Seagrave had been found with six bullets in the chest? What were the freaking odds here?

"Yes. She called, saying old man Erickson called her looking for my contact info."

"How do you know Erickson?"

"Bought some land from me years ago. Good man."

"How do you know Hazel?"

"We've been friends for decades. She supplies the art for a few local apartment complexes I own."

"Sunny didn't call you from the station? I assumed she contacted you with the call she was offered."

"You assumed wrong."

So Arlo was an asshole and Sunny had daddy issues.

"I thought you lived in Dallas?"

"I do. I'm here on business. Got a project going on south of town. A new resort going up. Is this a game of twenty questions, Detective?"

Just then—

"Mr. Harper."

I turned to see none other than Chief McCord's puffed

chest striding out the front door.

Fucking fuck fuck.

Chief Fuck-face breezed past me as if I weren't even there. The two men, friendly apparently, shook hands and I couldn't help but notice the resemblance. Two gruff bastards pushing sixty, desperately clinging onto their thinning hair while replacing dreams of six-pack abs with Budweiser and Netflix. Both single, a while based on the lack of tan lines on Harper's left finger. One, plenty in the bank, the other, plenty in his ex-wife's banks. Yep. Two peas in a mid-life-crisis pod.

Arlo addressed the chief. "I want to know everything that happened here tonight, and then I want it cleared up immediately. I don't need this shit tarnishing the Harper name."

You have got to be fucking kidding me was all I could think.

"I understand, sir," the chief replied quickly, his lips puckered for Arlo's ass. Hairy, I'd bet my life on it, by the way. Really hairy.

"Why wasn't I called immediately, McCord?"

It was the first time McCord graced me with a look—a disapproving sidelong glance before focusing back on Pudgeo.

"Come on in, Arlo. We just put some fresh coffee on."

Fresh. *Ha.*

"Jagger." The chief conveniently left out my title as he turned to me. "You can head on home for the night."

I ignored him and turned to Arlo. "I'd like to speak with you sometime today, if you don't mind, Mr. Harper of Harper's Construction."

"I'll handle it, Jagger," The chief growled.

"Mr. Harper, your daughter waived her right for an attorney this evening. Do you know why?"

"Not surprised. She's had enough experience with those blood suckers, although I'm sure you know all about that by now." His gaze narrowed. "And I've done a lot to keep the incident in Dallas under wraps and I expect the same discretion here."

Incident.

"Do you know of anyone who would want to hurt your daughter?"

"No, but I wouldn't."

"Why's that?"

"She and I aren't close."

"What about anyone who maybe wanted to get to you?"

"Are you saying my daughter was attacked because of me?"

"Detective—" McCord snapped.

"Ah, good morning boys..." In his ever-perfect timing, Colson rushed down the steps.

He focused on me, his eyes laced with warning.

"Detective, you've got a call. Tanya's forwarding it to your cell phone. I'll update Mr. Harper on the evening's events. Feel free to head home."

My ringing cell phone cut off the words on the tip of my tongue that surely would have gotten my badge pulled right then and there. Grinding my teeth, I handed my card to chubs.

"Call me if you think of anything that could be helpful in understanding why your daughter was attacked tonight. I'll be in touch with you later today."

He slid the card into his pocket as the chief pulled him up the steps.

As I watched Colson, McCord and Arlo disappear into the station, I added another to-do to my morning. To figure out what the hell was going on between Sunny and her dad.

14

JAGG

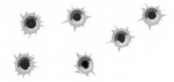

*T*he night had faded into a crystal clear morning without a cloud in the sky. A thin fog swayed above wilted grass, the evening's cooler temperatures burning away with what the radio just told me was already eighty percent humidity. Could've guessed that, though, because even with the wind whipping around my Jeep, my ass was sweating against the leather seat. I really needed to get the AC fixed. Ass sweat at seven-thirty in the morning never lended itself to a good day. The summer air was thick and cloying. Another three-figure day on its way.

And a full moon coming.

I pulled into the town's square, already a bustle of activity. Donna Jo was watering flowers outside her hair salon, Tad was wiping down the rocking chairs in front of his tool shop. A wave of bicyclists passed by, getting in a quick workout during the coolest part of the day. A few cowboys on horseback trotted past, going to and from their business. Subarus topped with kayaks on their way to Otter Lake. And then, there was Donny's Diner, not a parking spot open, not a booth unfilled.

Not a single person talking about anything other than the *Slaying in the Park.*

I had no doubt word had already gotten out about the evening's events and it was only a matter of time before the citizens of Berry Springs found out the victim was the pastor's son. I had a feeling they wouldn't care too much about the other victim. Survivors had a way of being forgotten faster than the dead. It was something that always bothered me.

I ground my teeth as I drove by the diner. Cowboy hats topped the red booths. The legendary waitress, Ms. Booth, who knew everyone and their dogs, leaned over a table, filling coffee and spreading the gossip. Two people waited in line at the front door.

I made a mental note to stop in later that morning and get the bead on what the gossips were saying. I'd solved more than a few cases just by sitting in the corner booth for an hour. Amazing what people said when they thought no one was listening.

I stopped at the only stoplight in town, in the center of the square, where a Wrangler-wearing Stetson was nailing something into a tree next to the fountain. I squinted, leaned forward.

City council meeting 6pm tonight -
CANCEL Moon Magic Festival!
Keep our town safe!

My eyes rolled into the back of my head. They were at it again. The cowboys versus the hippies in yet another undoubtedly hot debate about canceling the annual festival. Every year, half the courthouse filled with cowboy hats, the other half beads and braids arguing about free speech. The cowboys didn't want Berry Springs to be a part of anything that suggested promotion of witchcraft. The hippies told them to go fuck themselves. Every year, the meeting ended with a call to the cops and no resolution.

The tagline 'Keep our town safe,' suggested this year was going to be different. Two homicides leading up to the festival might just give the cowboys enough ammunition to get the thing shut down. Fear is a powerful thing.

Regardless what came out of the meeting, one thing was for sure—it would be the shitshow of all shitshows and I wanted to stay as far away from it as possible.

I hung a right off Main Street onto a narrow road lined with quaint shops, restaurants, bars, and bakeries that catered to the tourists. The shops were ornate buildings, nestled between the trees that lined the road. The cul-d-sac ended at the edge of the woods that surrounded the city park. The street was the most recognizable area in Berry Springs, second only to Donny's Diner. The locals had dubbed it, "Tourist Row."

It also happened to be the location of Seagrave's murder and the Cedonia Scroll heist.

I rolled to a stop next to an old, weathered sign that read *Mystic Maven's*. I didn't bother locking my Jeep as I slammed the door and stepped onto the sidewalk. I dipped my chin at the pair of Goldendoodles walking their owner.

"Mornin' Detective."

"Morning, Ms. Addington."

I quickly pivoted onto the pebbled pathway that cut between the buildings to avoid small talk that would start with "I heard..."

I yanked at the collar of my T-shirt, cursing the sweat already beginning to bead. Damn humidity. In response to Colson's advice to "button-up," I'd gone above and beyond my usual uniform and chosen my thinnest grey T-shirt with pit-stains, ripped khaki tactical pants, and my most scuffed pair of ATAC boots. He'd be proud.

I slowed, scanning the ground, the edge of the buildings, the rooftops. Although I'd been to the spot countless times since the shooting, my gut told me I was missing something. To look deeper. And I always listened to my gut, aside from when it told me to get some rest.

It had only been three hours since I'd left the station, and as you may have guessed, I didn't take Colson's advice to get a solid night's sleep. I'd gone home, reviewed case notes over a double whiskey, caught the scores on ESPN, followed by an ice-cold shower to bring me back to life. The sun was beginning to come up when I forced myself to lay down on the couch sometime after five-thirty. I might have slept, although I'm not sure. It was that weird state of either dreaming or thinking. Finally, I got up at six-thirty and started the coffee.

A mosquito the size of a taxi buzzed around my face as I kneeled down. Blood-stained rocks still colored the ditch where Lieutenant Jack Seagrave took his last breath, although fewer than the day before. Probably some sick teenagers wanting a piece of memorabilia from a cop killing. I picked up one of the rocks and turned it over between my fingers, my mind racing.

How did it connect? The Black Bandit, the cursed scrolls, the blue sedan, the Voodoo Tree? Sunny Harper?

Lieutenant Seagrave had been shot six times.

Six.

I'd seen plenty of gunshot wounds over the course of my

life, the majority were one, maybe two hits. Rarely had I seen six.

One or two suggested desperation, fear of getting caught, or a simple, quick kill. More than two suggested emotions. That it was personal. That it was no coincidence.

I had Darby pull the list of cases Seagrave had worked during the last year of his life, and, as suspected, that list would take days to comb through.

Could it have been a revenge killing?

But *who?*

The Black Bandit. Everything looped back to the Black Bandit, I was sure of it.

I ran my fingers through my hair and sat back on my haunches.

Something was in the air, aside from biting gnats. I could feel it in my bones.

I glanced over my shoulder where Ms. Hoffman's bird-watching camera had recorded the video of the Black Bandit, along with the moment Seagrave had fallen to the ground. A few more damn inches and the camera would have caught the whole show. Unfortunately, we only got his foot. His scuffed, brown loafer sagging after life left his body.

Too early.

Way too damn early.

"Well, mornin' there, Detective."

I turned to see Hazel De Ville padding down the pathway. Beams of sunlight sparkled through her long, dreadlocked silver hair. She wore a brown skirt to her ankles with rope sandals to match, and a tie-dye T-shirt that read *Stay Weird.*

"Morning." I pushed to a stance, my knees popping in protest. When the hell did my knees start popping?

"Sure early for you to be out here, isn't it?"

"Sure early for you to be spreading gossip, Ms. De Ville."

A silver brow slowly cocked. "Ah, so you know I called Arlo Harper last night." She snorted. "Of course you do." She stopped next to the bloodied rocks. "I've known the Harpers for decades, back when Arlo bought his first property here. Good people. I come from a time where neighbors still reach out to neighbors. Erickson reached out to me, I reached out to Arlo."

"And I come from a time where neighbors leave homicides to the authorities."

"Well, maybe if the kids of your generation still believed in actual human to human communication instead of texting or sitting behind video games all day, there wouldn't be so many homicides to investigate, Detective."

"Not arguing with you there, ma'am."

"Smart boy. Well, I knew you'd have some more questions for me." A smile cracked her lips. "Come on in for some coffee, son. You look worn."

Worn.

I followed Hazel up the pathway contemplating, for the umpteenth time over the last few weeks it seemed, if I was getting old.

Old.

Hazel pulled a massive keyring from her woven purse and unlocked the thick wooden door. Burned incense—something called Patchouli, I think—lingered in the air from the day before. The early morning light sparkled through the windows, pooling on a gleaming hardwood floor.

Despite the dated appearance of the rock building, the inside had been completely renovated. Stark white paint and little gold lights highlighted the art on the walls, this in contrast to dark wood Hazel had chosen for the floors. Wind chimes and sun catchers hung from the ceiling, catching the light and sparkling off the walls. Glass cases speckled the main floor, housing everything from handmade jewelry, "healing" crystals, glass-blown knick knacks, ashtrays, to pipes. The room was spotless.

"You always keep it this clean in here?"

She laughed, flicking a few light switches from behind the cash register. "I'll assume you meant to add 'no offense' to the end of that question. Yes, I always keep it this clean. Wasn't sure if the kid who dusted for fingerprints after the scroll was stolen was pleased or pissed."

When it came to scanning for evidence, cleanliness had its advantages and disadvantages. Advantage was that it allowed for finding trace evidence easier, as well as recovering prints or tracks. Disadvantage was that, in more cases than not, the scene had been cleaned prior to the authorities searching it. Hotel rooms were an investigator's worst nightmare. They'd either been cleaned by housekeeping five times over before authorities showed up, or, filled with so many prints and human DNA that it made it almost impossible to nail down a suspect.

Hazel glanced up from the computer she'd just powered on. "Anything turn up yet? With my stolen scroll or with the Lieutenant's shooting?"

"Not yet." Not that I'd tell her, anyway. "I was hoping you might have remembered something else, anything else, over the last few days."

"This leads me to believe you've been chasing your tail over the last few days."

"Part of the job."

"Let me get that coffee going, then we'll talk. Caffeine is good for the brain."

So is Baileys, but I bit my tongue.

As Hazel disappeared into the kitchen in the back, I made my way to the corner of the room where the fourth Cedonia scroll had hung before the Black Bandit swiped it. Now in its place hung a painting of a tree, its electric green leaves glowing in the beam of sunlight shining on it. I cocked my head.

The colorful tree was in contrast to a dark blue background, its long branches growing away from the trunk like snakes. The roots ran deep underground in a kaleidoscope of colors, the ends disappearing off the canvas.

I knew this tree.

I squinted and leaned closer, my eyes tracing each one of the branches.

"Beautiful, isn't it?" Hazel snuck up behind me.

"What tree is this?"

She handed me one of the rainbow-colored ceramic mugs in her hands. "Not sure."

"Thanks." I took the coffee but didn't sip, still staring at those branches. Thick at the bottom, crowded at the top. The perfect climbing tree. Then it hit me—the Voodoo Tree.

"This is the tree from City Park."

"There's many trees in the park."

"No, I mean..." My mind started to race. "Who painted this?"

"It was donated."

I turned. "Seriously?"

"Believe it or not, Detective, there are a lot of people who paint for love, not money."

I snorted, then refocused back on the painting. "Who donated it?"

"A woman traveling through town. A painter. We traded a few pieces of art, and this is one I got from her. The others have sold. It's a popular tree, you know. Lots of people have painted it."

"What was her name?"

Hazel shrugged. "I don't remember. The woman was a gypsy. Had her whole life packed up in her car."

"Wasn't a blue sedan, was it?"

"No. Bright yellow Volkswagen with a peace sign on the door." She grinned.

"When was this?"

"That I received this painting?"

I nodded.

"Oh, dear." She cocked her head, her gaze shifting to the ceiling, a little bell on the bottom of one of her dreadlocks jingling. "Years ago."

"And you just put it out?"

"No. It was over there," she nodded to the opposite corner. "But no one ever noticed it. Not like you are, that's for sure."

A moment clicked by as I searched the painting, the wall around it, then back to the painting. I imagined the Black Bandit standing exactly where I was. My eyes drifted from branch to branch in the exact path I'd climbed the real tree the night before.

"What do you see, Detective?"

"Witchcraft," I mumbled.

A soft *hmm* escaped her lips. "Look closer."

I leaned in, almost nose to nose with the painting.

"Now tell me again, what do you see?"

"A clue."

Hazel leaned in. "I see magic."

I straightened, took a step back and focused on her. "Why don't you say whatever it is you're dancing around."

She eyed me for a minute. "Fine. I don't want you idiots to shut down the Moon Magic Festival this weekend."

"Why?"

"Well, for one, I'll make three months' worth of revenue in two days. Two, because I'm sick of the divisiveness in this town. I'm sick of the narrow-minded, short-sighted rednecks exploiting stereotypes and spreading fear and propaganda about a religion that is not rooted in evil."

"You're talking about Wicca?"

"Yes, I am," her chin lifted with defensiveness. "Berry Springs should welcome all people, from all walks of life, not just those who ride horses, chew tobacco, and tuck their balls into the left side of their Wranglers."

"One, thanks for the visual, two, who's embracing stereotypes now, Ms. De Ville?"

"This is serious, Detective. This is exactly how wars start, how civilizations fall. If we all worked together, respected each other, embraced our differences, and *learned* from each other, the world would be a much better place. Festivals like Moon Magic don't only bring money into the town, but they also build a sense of community." She stomped her foot like a child. "You *cannot* cancel the festival. I will *not* have it. It will lay a dangerous precedent. Our town will shrivel up and die if we don't embrace others."

"It will shrivel up and die if someone starts a fire during this burn ban."

She rolled her eyes. "Because everyone's going to be smoking *doobies,* is that right?"

"I'll see what I can do." I sipped my coffee—piping hot, fresh. "But I want something in return."

"Of course you do."

"Tell me about the Harpers."

"What in particular do you want to know?"

"You said you've known Arlo for decades."

"Yes, before he made all his money. I was friendly with his wife."

"His wife is deceased, correct?"

"That's right."

"How?"

"Cancer. Such a shame. Her name was Betsy. She used to come into my shop from time to time. Bought a few pieces from me, then looped me in with her husband once he started building. That's how we got to know each other. Betsy could *see* the art, if you know what I mean."

"When did she die?"

"Around two years ago."

"What do you know about Sunny?"

"That she wouldn't kill the pastor's son."

"Where did you hear it was the pastor's son?"

"Old man Erickson is the one who called me for Arlo's number, remember?"

I was stupid to think the entire town didn't already know that the victim was Julian Griggs. One thing they didn't know, though, was Sunny's story that *she* didn't kill him. That someone else did. A phantom, in the wind.

"Why so sure she wouldn't have done it?"

Hazel shook her head, letting out a little *tsk, tsk.* "You agree with me. I know you do. Don't play that game with me. That girl wouldn't shoot someone in the face. You know it as well as I do."

"When was the last time you saw her?"

"It's been awhile. When Arlo's company started to grow, they moved to Dallas, but kept some properties here. Rumor is Arlo goes back and forth a lot. Easy, with the thirty minute flight and all."

"Sunny too?"

"Until she moved here about a year ago."

"Where does she live?"

"Bought a place by the river."

"What river?"

"Shadow River. East of town. Her house is the only one down county road 3228. Her Daddy owns the land around it. Leases it for hunting."

"What brought Sunny back to Berry Springs? Do you know?"

"You'll have to ask her."

I let the conversation linger a moment, wondering if Hazel knew about Sunny's attack in Dallas.

"She single?"

Hazel cocked her brow. "You interested?"

"I'm interested in finding who attacked her."

"You'll have to ask her."

A moment settled between us.

"You know…" Hazel scanned the shop with squinted eyes. "Doesn't it strike you as odd that the only thing stolen from my shop that night was the Cedonia scroll? I have a few pieces of jewelry in this shop worth a thousand bucks. The Black Bandit didn't want it. That scroll was all they wanted."

"Meaning—not Seagrave. Is that where you're going with this?"

"Exactly. Just my two cents, son. I don't think the Cedonia thief shot your lieutenant. Just sayin'."

I felt a headache settling between my temples. Way too early for a headache.

"Has anyone else asked you about the Cedonia scroll?"

"Yes. Yesterday. A busty little blonde came in asking some questions."

"Who?"

Hazel held up her index finger, then sauntered back to the cash register and dug out a card.

"Briana Morgan, with Harold and Associates."

I took the card, my brows arching. "An art investigator."

Hazel nodded. "Got the vibe that whoever the scrolls were originally stolen from hired her firm to get them back."

Speaking with this Morgan chick just jumped to the top of my to-do list.

The phone rang.

Hazel glanced at the clock. "Nope. No sir," she said addressing the ringing phone. "Not eight o'clock yet." She looked at me. "I do need to get moving, though. Need to put out a few new pieces before I open."

She let the call go to voicemail.

"Thank you for your time," I lifted my mug. "And the coffee."

"Thank you in advance for doing whatever you can to keep the Moon Magic festival running this year."

I nodded. "Before I leave. Is there anything else you remember from that night?"

She shook her head. "Wish I did, son. I'll let you know if I do."

"Let me know if the busty art investigator stops by again."

She grinned. "Will do."

My hand was on the door knob, when—

"Detective?"

I paused and turned.

"Leave the scrolls alone."

"No stone unturned, Ms. De Ville. That's how it works."

"Even when the scrolls are said to be cursed?"

"Especially with cursed scrolls."

She shifted her gaze to the painting on the wall. "Just be careful you're not barking up the wrong tree."

I dipped my chin. "Ma'am."

A black bird called out from the tree above as I stepped outside into a single beam of sunlight already burning the sidewalk. I didn't have time to worry about curses, witchcraft, or supernatural powers, or the fact that Hazel was the second person including Colson to tell me to leave the scrolls alone.

I might've had a to-do list for the day that was as long as my dick, I decided to add one more stop to that list.

15

JAGG

*I*t was eight-thirty in the morning by the time I reached the "only house" down County Road 3228, north of Shadow River. A bit early for an unannounced drop in, but like I said, that damn list. I'd already called the art investigator, Briana Morgan, twice, and left two voicemails. I decided to wait again until after lunchtime. Mainly because my battery was already low.

The road to Sunny's house was long and lonely, desolate, surrounded by miles and miles of dense forest, wilted under the heat. It was tough to imagine a woman living out there alone. Assuming she did, anyway. I had no idea what, or who, I was going to find at her house. I prepared myself for another man, and daydreamed about another woman. Wouldn't be the first time I'd walked up on that. I had the video to prove it.

I braked at a rusted mailbox at the end of a rock driveway flanked by wooden fences. New fencing, I noted, and wondered who'd built it. Then I wondered why I immediately assumed she hadn't. The woman was capable of holding me off in a physical altercation. Building a fence was something she could likely do in her sleep.

I squinted at the house a hundred feet from the mailbox.

I'd expected a sprawling "Harper Construction" mansion, or given its location, maybe fancy ranch house of sorts. What I got was a small, weathered, A-frame cabin with a wraparound porch and picnic table out front. The cabin was a freshly-painted evergreen color, with deep red shutters. I thought of Sunny's lips. The paint color matched the soaring cedar trees that enclosed it. Barely a yard. All trees.

It was cute. Quaint. No way in hell an heiress to a real estate fortune's house.

Hesitating, I glanced in my rearview mirror, then back at the little house. The underbrush had been trimmed, but much like the drive to it, endless woods surrounded the cabin. No fields, no rolling hills. Just trees that sloped down to Shadow River somewhere behind the house.

I flicked my turn signal, then laughed at myself and flicked it off, then turned into the driveway. As I inched closer to the house, a blazing red caught my eye, where my dream car from the night before, a 1972 Chevy Cheyenne, was parked under the cedars.

Yep, the old A-frame, teeny-tiny cabin belonged to Sunny Harper.

Add it to my list of shockers.

I parked next to a blooming lilac bush, careful not to graze the purple petals. Always liked lilac bushes. The sweet scent carried like a perfume as I climbed out of my Jeep. The woods were vibrant with energy. Birds singing overhead, grasshoppers chirping, and in the distance, the sound of river water rushing over rocks. A magnificent blue butterfly flittered past my face. I couldn't explain why, but a sudden feeling of warmth ran over me, more than the beams of sun shooting through the cedars.

It was peaceful.

Real country.

Then, I noticed the lack of human noise. No voices, televisions, radios, microwaves buzzing in the background. Nothing.

A warm breeze whispered through the trees as I crossed the driveway and stepped onto the porch. A scent of vanilla wafted out of the open windows and screen door. My brow cocked. The woman jogged with a nine millimeter in her pants but left her windows and door open in the middle of the woods.

The porch was small, enclosing the cabin, with a few slats recently replaced. Two rocking chairs sat to the side and based on the wearing beneath the legs, were used frequently.

Two chairs.

Two.

I skimmed the ground for cigarette butts, ashtrays, pipes, empty beer or soda cans. None.

Potted begonias lined the porch, their red and pink petals overflowing in a hodgepodge of brightly-painted clay vases that seemed to go together despite their obvious mismatch. Enormous citronella plants sat at the edges of the porch, and hanging from the corner, the biggest electric bug zapper I had ever seen. Thing could fry a squirrel.

Now *that's* the girl I knew.

I glanced into the trees, lingering a moment on the wind chimes.

I looked in the front window. Lights off. Dark inside. I knocked on the door. The screen wobbled on its hinges. No answer. I searched for a doorbell with no luck.

"Hello?" My voice sounded deep and gruff against the stillness of nature. Old. Like I didn't belong there. Like no one did.

"Miss Harper?" My tone raised an octave, now sounding like a high school kid calling out for approval.

When she didn't grace me with her presence, I did another quick rapping on the door before pulling it open.

Vanilla enveloped me. Vanilla—and leather.

The place could have been a post card for 'cozy log cabins,' or 'smallest houses on the planet.' It was one, large room with a loft overhead. The A-frame ceiling had gleaming, exposed beams running along the top. A rustic chandelier hung from the center. Box fans hummed in the windows, pulling in the fresh summer air, which somehow felt cool under the shade of the house. Did the rich kid not have air-conditioning? Or did she choose to keep it off? A night without air-conditioning in the dead of a southern summer was almost unbearable, so I assumed the latter. Either way, my Jeep was in good company.

The main living room—otherwise known as the only room—was separated by a U-shaped brown leather couch over a Navajo rug facing a rock fireplace. At least a dozen plants—real, not fake—lined the walls, their leaves turned to the sweeping windows that overlooked a deck with more blooming flowers.

I noticed a few handcrafted wooden statues that I'd seen in Mystic Maven's, making me wonder if the two were closer than Hazel had led me to believe. One was kneeling in prayer, another in some sort of meditation position, and the third had a distended belly and was holding a small child that kind of looked like an alien.

Weird.

The kitchen was to the right. Tiny and spotless as if it were never used. Sunny didn't cook. One strike against her.

To the left, a small door that I guessed led to the only bathroom/laundry room. I lifted my gaze to the loft, where a four-poster king bed centered the small space, a deep crimson comforter against the dark wood walls. The bed was made, and based on the immaculate cleanliness of the rest of the house, I'd be willing to bet my next paycheck on hospital corners.

The decor was minimal, bordering on masculine if not for the oil diffusers, candles, and stack of Cosmopolitans on the coffee table. You know, the sex advice magazines.

Interesting.

Once I pushed away the image of Sunny rolling around naked in those crimson sheets, I stepped back outside and made my way to the back of the house. Nothing interesting to note back there. No lawn care equipment, tools, shed, no sign of a man. I began down a narrow, pebbled trail that led through the woods. The path wasn't manicured, but someone had done the arduous, back-breaking task of cutting through the underbrush and leveling the trail, and hauling up river gravel.

Sunny?

Beams of early morning sunlight shot through the thick canopy of trees where birds took notice of my presence, squawking loudly as if announcing the unannounced visitor. Happy or annoyed, I wasn't sure.

The sound of rushing water grew closer. I was halfway through a bend in the trail when I stopped cold. Call it that finely tuned instinct from decades running special ops, but I knew I wasn't alone anymore. As my hand drifted to the gun on my belt, a growl so low vibrated behind me—inches, if I had to guess—that every hair on the back of my neck stood up. A list of wild animals flashed through my head. Bear? Mountain lion? Rabid coyote?

I froze and weighed my options, my hand inches from my gun. The animal had gotten the drop on me, no doubt about that. The next move was my own. The growl intensified, along with a scraping against the dirt floor. Definitely not a bear. I ran down my Boy Scouts list of what to do when you cross paths with a mountain lion. Number one, do not run. Running from a mountain lion is like playing hard to get. It triggers the mountain lion's instinct to chase and attack. Two, do not crouch or bend over. No problem there as I wasn't in the habit of bending over for anyone. And three, hold your ground.

"Whoa, there now, buddy, calm down," I said emphasizing my southern drawl as if that somehow made me less of a threat. Holding my breath, I decided to face my fate, the snarling now accompanied by a viciously snapping jaw.

I turned like a ballerina on a spindle and my eyes locked on the jagged teeth of the largest—and most pissed— German Shepherd I'd ever seen in my life. It's paws, twelve inches from my boots, it's snapping jaws six inches from my dick.

That alone was enough to make a grown man piss his pants, but it was the pistol pointed directly between my eyes that really got my blood pumping.

16

JAGG

A mane of dark curls cascaded behind the gun pointed at my head. The steadiness of the barrel told me it was locked, loaded, and ready—and wasn't the first time it had surprised an unannounced visitor.

"Miss Harper, lovely to see you. I'm going to need you to lower that gun."

"Detective, lovely to see you as well. I'm going to need you to tell me what you're doing on my land."

"I'll tell you once you pull Cujo away from the marbles that were once my ball sack." My gaze slid up to hers. "Which, by the way, is one millionth of their original size."

Sunny said something to the dog that wasn't "hey, this guy's funny," and instantly the barking ceased and the beast backed up, settling next to its master's feet but keeping his beady, black devil-eyes on me.

I snarled back. Damn dogs. All of them.

The gun dropped from my face, revealing an emerald gaze just as intense.

"You can lower your hands now."

I dropped my arms along with the inch of pride the woman had just peeled off of me.

It had only been five hours since I'd seen her, but the knot below her eye had gone down and was replaced by speckles of purple bruising. The scratches on her neck and arms were an angry red. A white bandage covered the stitches on her arm. If her ribs were sore, her stance wasn't showing it. If she were in any kind of pain, or if she was emotionally shaken, she wasn't showing it. In fact, she seemed to wear her injuries like a badge of honor.

Victory, for the second time.

My heart gave a little kick.

She wore a black tank top—no nipples visible this time, much to my dismay—and faded jeans revealing hints of tanned skin through holes at the knees. Her feet were covered in a pair of strappy sports sandals. Her toenails, a cherry red as electric as her eyes. And that damn hair, dancing on the summer breeze, a rogue strand tickling across red, shimmering lips pressed into a thin line of scrutiny.

The woman was gorgeous.

My thoughts short circuited between the rabid dog at her feet and the stunning natural beauty in front of me. I didn't like how only her presence seemed to spin my thoughts like a blender. Sunny Harper had a way of knocking me off my game, and I didn't like it.

I squared my shoulders and said the first thing that came to mind.

"You got a permit for that cannon, Miss Harper?"

"You got a warrant to be on my land?"

"Don't need a warrant to chat."

She shoved the nine millimeter into the band of her pants with an ease that verified her comfort level with it.

Considering her other nine millimeter was in custody at BSPD, I wondered how I missed her arsenal of weapons in that shoebox cabin.

Maybe in a safe under the bed? Next to her vibrators? One, or two prongs?

Dammit.

"How's your arm?"

"Fine."

"Ribs?"

"Fine. Did you call?" She asked, although it wasn't a question as much as a thinly veiled message that she didn't like me showing up unannounced. Got it.

"Are you busy?" I responded.

She stared at me with a pair of slitted eyes and for a moment, I thought she was really going to ask me to leave and not come back without a warrant. Finally—

"Settle," Sunny demanded in an authoritative voice that had me automatically easing my stance. I realized she wasn't talking to me when my peripheral caught movement to my right side, then, on my left side. Two more massive dogs emerged from the brush. Three pairs of black irises now eyeing me like a T-bone steak.

Three dogs had been stalking me, not just one.

I'd been played beyond played. Tricky, tricky bastards.

My gaze shifted between the dogs, then back to the fourth skeptical pair of eyes burning holes through my soul.

The lack of security in her house suddenly made sense.

"Fine." She said, the single word followed by a jerk of her chin—my cue to follow.

She snapped her fingers, addressing the biggest GSD. "Whoa, there now, buddy, calm down," her tone a sweet, southern drawl.

The woman was *mocking me.*

Her lip curved as she breezed passed me, an extra sway of attitude in those hips.

Little. Smartass.

The three dogs eyed me as they passed by, then fell into step behind the flowing hair of their master. I waited a beat, watching the Captain and her army descend down the pathway, each soldier at her beck and call. The woman knew how to make people fall in line and how to get what she wanted.

Sunny Harper was no man's fool.

She was the leader of the pack.

An alpha female.

No...

A Queen among servants.

I fell into step behind her.

"Any trip wires or land mines I need to be aware of?"

"Not on the trail."

My brows arched as I glanced into the surrounding woods.

We walked in silence until a curve in the trail opened up to the riverbank, a full-blown K9 training center. Damn impressive. Speckled along the rocky bank was an intricate obstacle course consisting of ramps, stacked barrels, tubes, balls, hurdles, hoops, and a pair of full-sized boxing dummies with chunks of rubber missing from their forearms. One missing half his cheek.

Tough go for that one.

A group of cages sat in the distance where another dog, as black as midnight, watched me from behind a muzzled snout.

I turned back to the obstacle course.

"Impressive."

A wet snout nudged the back of my hand. The biggest

dog had taken a more subtle interest in me. Its sable hair was now flat against its back, so I considered that progress. I flicked my wrist at the snotty nose then wiped my hand on my pants.

"Hup," Sunny snapped at another dog, who promptly leapt through the air, landing nimbly on one of the platforms. I watched the furball bolt through the course, quick, agile, flawless.

"Impressive," I repeated, referring now to the dog instead of the course.

"It's easy to train a willing mind."

"And those who aren't willing?"

"Hard work and pointed effort."

"Precious commodities."

"More like deficiencies these days."

I couldn't agree more.

She continued, "It's not just time and effort, its perseverance. Not giving up on them. That's the tipping point. That what makes a good or bad dog, great. Or anyone, for that matter."

We watched the dog finish the course, then jog up, its tongue hanging out of a big toothy smile. She kneeled down and ruffled its ears, smiling and praising with full attention.

I watched her, in awe of the different woman I was seeing from the night before. Not five hours earlier, Sunny Harper had been holding a nine milliliter over a dead body. Now, there was a hint of softness to her. A loving, nurturing side. A contentment, with her dogs, in the middle of the woods.

Her sanctuary, I guessed.

I zeroed in on the bandage on her arm again, my stomach clenching. As I reached out to help her up, the dog lunged at me.

"Christ," I jumped back, flashing my palms.

"Enough." She scolded the dog, sending its tail between its legs, and me making a mental note to pack an extra pair of boxers for my next visit. Sunny nodded to the river in some nonverbal cue and the dogs took off like bullets into the water.

"Thank God you don't need in-home care."

"Sorry about that. They're protective."

"Understatement of the century." I reached out my hand again. "Let me..." I helped her to a stance. I was shocked that she let me touch her. That's when I realized Sunny Harper's attitude, or resistance, I should say, was very impacted by her environment. I wondered if her house was the only place she let her guard down.

"How are you really doing?"

She took a deep breath. "I'm fine."

"That wince you gave when you inhaled says otherwise."

She looked at me, her eyes squinting in suspicion as if to figure me out.

That makes two of us.

"So. You said you wanted to chat?"

"If you don't mind."

She nodded. "I expected it. But I expected a call, not a drop in."

"You seem just as territorial about your place as your dogs."

"I'll take that as a compliment."

"You need to lock your doors and windows."

"Did you go into my house?"

"Never. I'd never set foot inside a stranger's house without a warrant."

"Your reputation says otherwise."

"I'll take that as a compliment."

We fell into step together down the riverbank, the dogs running circles around our feet.

"You're supposed to be taking it easy." I said.

"I am."

"Training three monsters isn't taking it easy."

"Are you scared of my dogs, Detective?"

"Of those hundred-plus pound trained assassins? You're damn straight I am."

She smirked and I found myself staring to get the full picture of it. It wasn't a smile, but the first time I'd seen something close to it.

Breathtaking.

"Well, too bad you're scared because I was looking for someone to help with attack commands."

"Based on their display in the woods back there, I'd say they already had their first lesson of the day."

"No, an *actual* attack. Attacking another human on command."

"You know I'm a cop, right?"

"On someone with a *bite sleeve,* not just some random passerby, crazy. But, you know," she shrugged, "I get that they're intimidating and all..."

"And I get that you're good at goading people."

Her lip twitched. That little grin again.

"I also get that you don't like people telling you what to do, but I'd like you to make an exception for a medically trained professional. I know Buckley told you to rest. I also know that bruised ribs hurt like a son. We can either sit here for our chat, or head back up to those rocking chairs I saw on your front porch."

"If you've truly had bruised ribs then you know that it actually helps to walk."

I did know that. Despite my doctor's orders, I'd run six

miles the day after a roadside IED blew me six feet into the air. Cried the entire way. Sunny was tough. I respected it but I didn't like knowing she was in pain.

"When's your next check-up?"

"I get the stitches out in ten days."

"Did I do that? When I tackled you?" The question blurted out before I could catch myself.

"No. It happened when I was pushed to the ground."

I nodded and released the breath I didn't realize I was holding.

"How's it feeling, really?"

"Like someone poured liquid acid on my skin."

"Thanks for being honest." I said and meant it.

"Thanks for carrying me to my truck last night." She looked down.

"It was no big deal. Like I said, I've had bruised ribs before."

She slapped me.

"Just joking." I winked. "You weigh half as much as your smallest dog."

My phone rang. I pulled it from my pocket, read the caller ID—*Mom*. I silenced it and slid it back in my pocket with a curl of my lip.

A spray of sprinkles rained against my back.

"Tango, *no*."

"Tango?" I wiped the speckles of mud off my pants. Wasn't like they'd been washed in a month, anyway.

"That one is Tango and the black one is," she slid me the side-eye. "Max."

"*Max?*" I couldn't help but laugh. The dog that stealthily stalked me from the side had the same name as me. "Never been so proud to have a dog named after me."

"*After* you? Maybe I should have named him Zeus after your ego."

I chuckled again.

"The third one is—"

"Wait. Hold up. I want to know more about this Max. Where does Max sleep?"

"In my bed."

"Oh, *really?*"

"Yes. Really. Anyway, as I was saying—"

"At the foot of the bed or under the covers?"

She rolled her eyes. "At the *foot.*"

"I'll have to work on that."

She shook her head, the grin morphing into a full-blown smile. I wondered if it was the same smile she'd flashed at the judge to get out of her latest ticket. It was mesmerizing... and almost enough for me to ignore the fact that she allowed dogs in her sheets.

Almost.

No cooking, strike one. Dogs in bed, *major* strike two.

"Any other pervy innuendos, Detective?"

"Just gathering pieces to the puzzle."

"Well gather them somewhere other than my sheets."

I opened my mouth—

"*Anyway...*" She cut me off. Probably for the best. "The third 'monster' is Athena, a German Shepherd/Collie mix. She's nine years old. The alpha of the crew." She pointed to the monster that almost attacked me on the trail.

"*Athena?* You mean to tell me the dog that almost ate my dick for breakfast is a gir—"

She held up a finger. "Might want to rethink that sentence unless you want to lose those balls you speak so fondly of. Although I think the exact verbiage was marbles."

She held up her hand and closed her thumb and index finger together. "Small."

"Anything is small compared to Tango's over there."

"Why are men so fascinated with balls?"

"Clearly you haven't been with the right men."

"Are you always this charming with women?"

"'Fraid so."

"Now I know why there's no ring on your finger."

"Says the gun-toting dog-lady."

"Dogs mind better than men."

"Dogs *break* quicker."

Her brow cocked as she seemed to ponder this insightful comment for a moment.

"Anyway," I said, before she returned the favor and began psychoanalyzing me. "You mean to tell me the dog that shrunk a pair of wrecking balls..." I paused to drill home the last two words. "...is a *girl?*"

"You think that just because Athena has a vagina and not a pair of stinky, hairy balls, she's less lethal than a man?"

Nerve hit—and note to self that Sunny had terrible taste in men. Sunny Harper had a touch of feminism in her. Strike three.... four, five, and six. Between her aversion to the kitchen, the dog hair in bed, and advocacy of women's rights, I was beginning to question my sanity for feeling so damn protective over the woman. Maybe I just needed to get laid. *Or* maybe she was an evil sorceress as Officer Haddix had suggested.

"I didn't say that, exactly." I corrected.

"Athena is just as lethal as her male counterparts. Trust me. She's smarter too."

"Now look who's cocky."

A shrug.

"Why'd you name her Athena?"

"Goddess of wisdom and war."

"A contradiction by all counts."

"Not really."

"Wisdom is to avoid confrontation at all costs. Kind of like that part of Krav Maga you slept through."

"War teaches you how to handle it. And look who's begun, what I believe detectives call, *leading* questions."

"Because I was about to ask you to tell me why your entire life revolves around self-defense?"

Her face snapped to me, fire replacing the lighthearted flirty banter we'd fallen into.

"Don't patronize me, Detective Jagger. You know exactly why I've taught myself self-defense. I have no doubt you pulled my records last night and know about my attack in Dallas. Assuming you read through the entire thing without falling asleep, you know everything that everyone else does. I have nothing to add and don't want to talk about it again. If you've come here to talk about what happened in Dallas, you're wasting your time. End of discussion." These final words were punctuated by her pulling ahead of me a few steps.

I caught up and we walked a few seconds in silence along the riverbank, her eyes locked on the rushing water.

"Okay. No questions about Dallas. But I would like to know if you remember anything else about your attack last night. Sometimes stepping away helps the fog to clear a bit."

She took a deep breath as if to calm the anger that had arisen from me bringing up the Dallas incident, then nodded. "I do remember something else. I was going to call you later this morning, actually. I remember a car pulling into that small lot across the park—you know, the one with that mobile drive-through coffee shop—as I pulled into the park at midnight."

"Was it following you?"

She blew out a breath, suggesting she'd exhausted the question herself. "I don't know. I really don't."

"Did it turn around, or park?"

"I'm not sure, but I remember thinking it was weird because the coffee shop obviously wasn't open."

A tingle started at the bottom of my spine.

"Do you remember what kind of car it was?"

"No."

Dammit.

"But I remember what it looked like."

I stilled, as if already knowing what was coming...

"It was a blue, four-door sedan."

That tingle flew up to my neck. It was the first thing linking Lieutenant Seagrave's death to Sunny's attack, verifying my instinct the incidents were connected.

"You're sure?"

"Yes. Trust me. I notice things like that. Now, anyway."

My mind started to race. A blue four-door sedan placed the Black Bandit at both Seagrave's murder and Sunny's attack. But I knew that Julian Griggs wasn't the Bandit because his black truck was parked at the trailhead, and based on my research, the kid did not also own a blue sedan.

"Could it have been Julian Griggs' car? The pastor's son?" She asked, sadness washing over her face.

"No. And where'd you hear that name?"

"My father came by this morning."

Father. Not Dad.

"Interesting man, he is."

"You met my father?" Her eyes rounded in both shock and horror.

"After I dropped you at your truck, he came to the station looking for you."

"Oh." She looked away.

"Why didn't you call him from the station?"

She shrugged, scratched her head. An uncomfortable tick. Yep, daddy issues for sure.

"Soooo... I'm picking up on vibes that you two might not be that close."

She snorted. "Nice work, Detective."

I ignored her quip. "Why? Why aren't you close to your dad?"

"Did you come here to ask me about my father?"

"I'd like to know why the man took the time to shower before coming to his daughter's aide."

Her jaw twitched. She swooped down, picked up a rock and hurled it across the water, skipping it eight times before disappearing under.

We walked a few more steps in silence.

"It's years of family stuff, Detective."

"I'd have you call me Max, but to avoid any confusion with your current bed partner, you can call me Jagg. Everyone else does."

"I know everyone calls you Jagg."

"What else have you heard about me?"

"That you're aggressive and rude. And a womanizer."

"Phew," I swiped my forehead. "Thought you might insult me for a minute."

She snorted. I didn't bother to defend myself. Never had. ... ... And, the labels weren't entirely inaccurate, let's be honest.

"Back to you." I said. "It's my understanding you recently left Dallas and moved here. Why?"

"Needed a change of scenery."

"Now I expected better than a cliché from you, Sunny."

"I'll take that as a compliment." She smirked, then took a deep breath. "My mom recently passed, and... I needed a change of scenery."

The fact that she referred to her mother as mom, instead of *mother,* suggested the two were close. Closer than her *father,* for sure.

"This still doesn't explain why you're not close to your father."

"We're just not close, and that's that. No big story there."

The old Sunny from the night before was back in full force. Locked up tighter than a dime bag in a hooker's cooch. Then, true to form, she changed the subject.

"Anyway. Any idea who's blue sedan it was?"

"Undetermined at this time. Have you seen the car anywhere else?"

"Not that I remember."

"Spend some more time thinking about it, and let me know, alright? If you see it again, call me. If it comes up your driveway, call me. Don't go to the door."

"I'm not stupid."

"Do I need to remind you that your damn door was unlocked, Sunny? Your windows wide open?"

"Do I need to remind you of your welcoming committee? These dogs would smell someone in my house before I even made it halfway up the hill."

"And what? You're just gonna go all Yosemite Sam and double-barrel their ass? Pop 'em with that gun you keep strapped onto your hip?"

"Don't discount my dogs, Detective—"

"Jagg."

"Jagg," she emphasized with attitude. "My dogs are professionally trained guard dogs. I am a professional. Do

you even have the slightest clue what these animals are capable of?"

"Enlighten me, professional one."

"A trained guard dog can be better than a security system, which, I might add, are often faulty. Don't get me started on technology."

I smirked. She continued.

"Over sixty-five percent of convicted felons admit that an intimidating dog would have scared them away, *not* a security system. If trained well, a good dog alerts when a stranger enters their territory and will attack on command, either giving their owner time to get away, or get in a damn good shot. Your welcoming committee back there was capable of inflicting seventeen hundred and fifty pounds of pressure on your marble-sized scrotum sack."

I'm really glad that caught on.

She continued, her passion palpable—for the dogs, not my scrotum sack. "The dogs I work with are bred for this, Jagg. It's literally in their bloodline. Two of my dogs have served as police dogs, and one of them, Max, helped solve a case of a missing teen."

"A detection dog?"

"You're familiar?"

"Very. One sniffed out an IED during my last tour in Afghanistan."

Saved my life, not his. But she didn't need to know that. Bottom line I was very aware a dog's ability to sniff out narcotics, explosives, or cadavers.

Sunny opened her mouth to ask a question, but I cut it off. I rarely spoke about those days. Especially not to a woman.

"So Max is a certified detection dog?" I asked.

"Yes. He's fully trained, certified, and very good. You

know his sense of smell is ten-thousand times more accurate than a human's? *Ten thousand.* In the case of the missing teen, Max sniffed the girl's clothing and picked up her scent in the woods. Led police right to her. The girl had wandered away from her family's campsite and got lost."

I thought for a moment. "Do you think he could sniff out our missing third person from your attack? The guy pushed you away and killed Julian?"

Her eyes rounded with excitement. "Yes... yes! He absolutely could. That's a great idea. What do you need from him? From me? From us?"

"Well, I guess he'd just need to smell the clothes Julian Griggs was wearing when he attacked you and was shot. According to your statement, this third person physically engaged Julian, right?"

"That's right."

"Then the third person's scent will be on Julian's clothes."

"That's right. And maybe Max can confirm who that person was if you get a list of names and bring someone in."

Or, if that person comes to your house, I thought, but didn't say it. This was just as much a security measure for Sunny as an asset to the case.

"Let's do it. What do you need from me?" She asked again, a child-like hope sparking in her green eyes. Sunny was no fool. She knew BSPD doubted her story about a third person and would have no problem calling her a liar and throwing her under the bus just to move the case along.

"You'll have to bring Max up to the station, along with his papers, certification, and anything else you have on him. Griggs' autopsy is scheduled to begin tomorrow afternoon. The chief is putting a rush on it considering the effect it's going to have on the community. After that, we'll have access to the clothes he wore last night. Give it a day for me to run it through the bullshit red-tape paperwork. Bring him to the station the day after tomorrow."

"Done." She nodded, then stopped, turned away from me and stared mindlessly into the water. She shook her head, and as if speaking to no one in particular, whispered, "I don't get it. I've never even met Julian. I don't get why he attacked me."

I stepped next to her. "Do you think it was random, Sunny?"

She looked at me, cocked her head with sarcasm. "That the pastor's kid was lurking in the park woods at midnight and decided to attack me? Doesn't feel random, does it?" She blew out a breath. *"God,"* She scrubbed her hands over her face. "I just feel *so*—"

Sunny dropped her hands, turned away from the water and walked over to the cages. Dismissing me, the subject. I kept my eye on the dog locked inside, an inky-black pit bull with silver eyes that seemed to glow in the daylight. A beast. I guessed the dog weighed close to ninety pounds, thick, proud, and all muscle. I couldn't begin to imagine the wrath he could inflict on someone, especially a young child. It was the type of dog that made people cross the street or turn the other way. The type of dog I'd seen in more than one drug raid.

The pit's silver eyes were fixed on me.

"What's his story?"

"This is Brutus. A rescue."

"A rescue from what?"

Her gaze slid to mine. "I'll give you one guess."

"He was a fight dog."

She kneeled in front of the cage. While she'd coddled her other mutts like babies, she approached this one with caution. Slowly, with ease as one might approach a ticking bomb. Felt familiar.

Sunny flattened her hand against the cage and began speaking in a low, soft voice.

The dog's eyes never left mine.

"I got him six weeks ago," she said softly. "He'd been raised by a reputable breeder, who'd taken care of him. The bastard who bought him thought he could turn an adult dog into a fight dog overnight. Put him through absolute—" Her voice cracked. "He's been through a lot. Literal torture. He's a bit of a loose cannon." She stuck a finger inside the cage, then another, slowly rubbing the dog's nose. "He has a neck and shoulder injury that didn't heal correctly." She glanced over her shoulder, anger sparking in her eyes. "An injury he didn't have when the breeder sold him."

"Is that why he's not moving around much?"

"Yes. He's mobile and can do everything any other dog can do, but I think he's in constant pain and he tires out easily."

Ticking time bomb, loose cannon, chronic pain... a cage. Hell, it was like looking in the mirror.

She continued, "He'll have to have surgery but not until I can break him. It's slow moving with this guy. He moves at his own pace. Walks to the beat of his own drum, you could say." She exhaled deeply. "But he's going to be okay. We'll get him taken care of. I'm not giving up on him. He's going to be just fine. Aren't you Brutus? You're my good baby. That's it, good boy."

What would it be like to have someone have that much faith in you, I wondered. To have that kind of commitment.

"Why do you keep him caged?"

"He's penned because he's not fully trained yet. This is Brutus's daytime home until I can break him. It's for the safety of my other dogs, not mine. He wouldn't hurt me, I'm sure of it."

"Hell of a gamble."

"Hell of an instinct. You of all people should understand the power of human instinct."

I did and it was telling me there was more to this story. Kind of like all her stories.

"How exactly did you get Brutus from his abusive owner?"

"I ... loaded him up in my truck."

"With or *without* the owner's help?"

She shot me another look, that strong defiance from the night before. "Without. I found out Brutus had been sold when I'd gone to the breeders a few months ago. In casual conversation the breeder shared her concern over his new owner. Guess she had an instinct about the guy too, but money talks. She felt guilty, I could tell. Anyway, I couldn't get it off my mind. Literally, for a week I couldn't sleep, thinking about it. So I did something about it. I tracked the bastard down, went to his house and saw the conditions Brutus was living in. The bastard had put Brutus in a box, a cage not much bigger than his body. They'd put blades in the top and sides. If he moved, he'd get sliced. It's was a tactic to break him mentally."

It sounded a lot like what I'd been through in SERE training.

"He was muzzled, starved, dehydrated and in so much pain from his shoulder injury, which I can only assume is blunt force trauma..." She stopped talking, her face turning to granite. "When I saw him... Jagg, I'll never forget it," her voice was as soft as a whisper. "He spotted me in the woods where I had snuck up. We communicated nonverbally. Me and the dog. I have no doubt in my *soul* that Brutus knew I was there to save him. ... I swear he cried when I released him." She sniffed, then squared her shoulders, swallowing back the emotions. I got the feeling she did that a lot. I took a step back to give her a moment, and if I'm being honest, to give myself one, too. The story was real. The emotions were real. Her sadness was palpable and dammit if I didn't feel some sort of feelings for that mutt, too. I'd seen my fair share of animal abuse but imagining it happening to this pit, staring into my damn soul my long lost brother, churned my stomach.

"And then what happened? You just walked up to the front door and said, 'hey, let me take that dog off your hands.' And the drug addict said, 'okey dokey, here you go'?"

"More or less."

"Less, as in, you stole Brutus from the guy in the middle of the night."

Her lack of response was response enough.

"You know the guy reported a dog thief the next day at BSPD."

Her eyes rounded. "He did?"

"Yep. I remember it. Well, I should say I remember him. Kenny Shultz. Everyone at BSPD knows his name. Came in whining that someone stole his dog, a black pit with grey eyes."

"I'm surprised he cared enough to report it."

"As you said, money talks. The dog was worth something to him."

"Humph," was all I got.

"You know, I could technically arrest you right now, Miss Harper."

She pushed to a stance, turned to me and jerked her chin up, those red lips pressed into a thin line.

"Do it."

We stared at each other a moment, both daring each other to make a move. Two stubborn, bull-headed type A's.

Ol' Brutus couldn't be in better hands. If anyone was going to break him, it would be her. I wondered how many proud men Sunny Harper had house broken over her life.

"I'll tell you what," I said. "Just bring Max up to the station the day after tomorrow to sniff Griggs' clothes and we'll call it even."

"Done." She glanced at her watch. An appointment? Or done with me? "Well, it was good speaking with you, Detective."

Done with me.

"Call me Jagg, for the tenth time. And keep your eye out for a blue sedan."

I took another glance at my soul-brother.

"Have a good day, Miss Harper." I turned into three pairs of beady eyes and three wagging tails. I dipped my chin. "Tango. Athena. Max."

I felt Sunny's eyes boring into my back as I started down the river bank.

I turned, catching her stare.

"Hey, Sunny?"

Her brows arched.

"You might want to move those wind chimes you've got hanging above your truck. Hate to have anything happen to that beauty. And that reminds me, I have one more question to ask you. What church do you go to?"

I watched her wheels start to turn. "Religion isn't confined between four walls."

"Or within the three knots of the triquetra symbols you've got hanging from those chimes."

"You're observant, Detective."

"Jagg. Eleven. And it's the job. What's with the triquetra?"

"Why don't you just come out and ask me if I'm a witch?"

"Are you a witch, Miss Harper?"

"Sunny. And no."

"Do you practice Wicca?"

"What does this have to do with anything?"

"Gathering facts."

"The triquetra symbol represents life, death, and rebirth —and protection."

"It also represents the Wiccan Triple Goddess and the interconnected parts of human existence, as practiced in witchcraft."

She narrowed her eyes in a way that reminded me of the moment after I tackled her in the park.

I smiled. "Just looking out for that Chevy. Love to take it for a spin sometime."

"I'll bet you would. Good day, Detective."

I turned, her obedient soldiers watching my every step.

The rest of the morning was spent visiting used car dealerships inquiring about blue, four-door sedans, leaving three more voicemails with Briana Morgan of Harold and Associates, leaving two with Arlo Harper, who was also avoiding my calls, and then working my other cases I'd let drop over the last twenty-four hours. This last fact emphasized by the nineteen voicemails I had when I finally got back to the station, at three in the afternoon. The temperature had hit a sweltering ninety-five by noon, and the feels-like temp well past one-hundred. As suspected, air conditioners were breaking all over town, causing a spike in nine-one-one calls and two fist fights at the local HVAC company. Tempers were running short.

I yanked at my wrinkled collar as I slid behind my desk. Ignoring the phone, I pulled out the black and white images I had of the Black Bandit, then checked Griggs' height and weight from his case file. Then, I pulled up a few full-length images and videos of him from social media. I went back and forth between both sets of pictures for what felt like a full ten minutes. The weight was undoubtedly different. The

Bandit was leaner than Griggs, narrower shoulders. The way they walked, moved, all different. There was also no sign of a limp on Griggs' left hip. I'd asked the ME to confirm this as well during the autopsy. Not that I needed the information after comparing the photos. Combining all this with the fact that his truck had been parked at the trail-head while Sunny had spotted the blue sedan across the street confirmed that Julian Griggs was definitely not the Black Bandit.

I ran my hands through my hair and leaned back, feeling a headache brewing along with the ache in my back.

I was mid-reach for my pain pills when a rap of knuckles sounded at the door.

I grunted.

"Hot as balls out there, ain't it?" Lieutenant Colson sauntered in and Sunny's remark about the male obsession with nuts ran through my head.

"You get the AC fixed in your Jeep?" He asked.

"Not yet."

"You can use the station's loner if you need to." He grinned.

The Gray Ghost was a fifteen year old black impala with shoddy wheel alignment, a cracked windshield, and a pair of stains in the backseat that no one claimed to know how they got there.

"I'll pass."

He sank into the seat across from me.

"How's the wife?" I asked, noticing the bags under his eyes.

"Insomnia. *Pregnancy insomnia,*" he emphasized each word as if pronouncing the rarest disease known to man.

"Can't you sleep on the couch?"

"She walks. Paces. Circles. Hums sometimes. Through

the *entire house.* Last night she hummed Sweet Caroline while pacing the kitchen for two hours. Guess that's the name. Anyway, I woke up this morning to an empty jar of peanut butter in the oven, a jug of milk in the pantry, and three guns disassembled on the kitchen table."

I grinned. Lieutenant Colson was hell on wheels in the office, but it was no secret that when it came to his wife, all bets were off. Bobbi wore the pants in the relationship. Very stretchy pants.

"How much longer do you have to go?"

"Three weeks."

"You can hold out three weeks."

Colson shook his head, giving me a look of pity not unlike how Sunny had looked at Brutus. "You really need to get a woman in your life, Jagg."

"So I can get no sleep?"

"You don't sleep anyway."

He got me there.

"No," he continued, "because if you had one, you'd at least know that when the baby comes, sleep will be even more elusive than with an emotional insomniac."

"And that's exactly why I don't have a woman. Or a baby."

"There's more to life than a job, you know. What's going to happen if you lose this one? What are you left with? A box television and a window AC unit that smells like asshole?"

"You come in here to give me a life lesson, Colson?"

"No." He leaned forward on his elbows, his gaze sharpening. "I came here as a partner, a co-worker. A friend. You know how I feel about you dropping either Seagrave's case or the Harper case, regardless if you think they're connected. *Hear me,* Jagg. You need to take a step back. Your little attitude with Sunny's dad and the chief last night did nothing for you. I'm looking out for you, man, same as you would for me."

"I don't need it."

"You need this job. Or a life. Both, preferably."

"Noted." Heat began to rise up my neck. I wasn't in the mood.

"Fine." He leaned back. "I've said my piece. Anyway, I wanted to tell you Bobbi's brother, Wesley Cross, is going to take a look at the bullet casings from Seagrave's scene sometime today. Hoping he'll be able to determine the model of gun that was used. He's not making any promises, though."

"And he also knows to compare them to the one found at Sunny's scene?"

Colson nodded.

"Let me know when you hear something."

There were three big things this information would give us: One, if the casings found at Seagrave's matched the ones found at Sunny's, then it would be undisputed that the cases were linked. Two, if both those casings matched the gun Sunny carried the night of her attack, then she was in a world of trouble. Third, if the casings did not match, and the bullet used to kill Julian did not come from Sunny's gun, then she was telling the truth and we'd need to buckle down and find this third mystery person.

Colson leaned back in the chair. "Town's already gotten wind of it. Church is in an uproar, demanding answers, wanting someone's head. Whispers of witches returning with the full moon is already spreading like wildfire through town. Pun unintended."

"Well, they're going to have to keep their stakes at home."

"No, they're going to need answers before this thing gets

out of hand. People are picketing on the square to cancel the Moon Magic Festival this weekend. It's a fucking mess, dude. The longer this thing—"

"I get it. I know."

Colson crossed his ankle over his knee and stared at me a minute. "How is she?"

"Who?"

"Miss Harper."

I shrugged, keeping my eyes on my computer while taking notice of the defensiveness that sparked at the mere mention of her name. Like she was mine. Only mine. *My* business.

Not his.

"She must be in a boatload of pain today."

I narrowed my eyes and looked up. "Say it."

"You could have given her a ride or called me to take her to her car. You didn't have to carry the woman down Main Street in the middle of the damn night."

I'd debated on telling Colson about my visit to Sunny earlier that morning, but that just sealed the deal.

"Why didn't you take her to her car last night, Colson?"

"Why are you so defensive about her?"

A knock at the door paused the pissing match. It also had me unclenching the fist that had curled into a ball under the desk.

Darby poked his head in. "Oh. Sorry. Am I interr—"

"No. Come in."

Colson pushed out of the chair, dipped his chin. "Keep me updated." *Yeah, right.*

"Same." *Yeah, right.*

Darby stepped inside. "How you doing?"

"Shut the door."

I didn't wait for the door to click closed before going in.

"Next time you decide to run your mouth to everyone like a gossipy little girl, consider it the last you ever work with me, you got that kid?"

Darby's Adam's apple bobbed. "I only told them that I saw you helping Sunny to her car last night. That's all, I promise."

I surged out of my chair, a sharp pain adding to the fire brewing inside me. "You lie to me again, I'll have your badge pulled. You saw an opportunity to share information —*gossip*—and pounced on it in a bullshit effort to make yourself seem important. The fact that I carried Miss Harper to her car has no bearing on the case other than that the woman could barely walk. Gossip doesn't look good on anyone, kid. Especially a rookie cop. Don't fucking forget that."

"Yes, sir."

"Now that we've got that out of the way. Why are you here?"

"Two things. Sir."

I lowered into my chair. Fucking back.

"Sit, Darby. Relax. Just don't ever gossip about me again."

"Yes, sir."

The rookie sank into the chair Colson had just vacated and placed a folder on my desk.

"You asked me to look into Sunny's ex-boyfriend. The one who attacked her in Dallas years ago."

And almost *killed her.*

I picked up the folder and began flipping through.

"Like I told you last night, the guy, Kenzo Rees, got six years in state prison for the attack and previous transgressions. But get this, he got two more added on once inside."

"Why?"

"Beat a fellow inmate within an inch of his life."

My gaze slid up to his.

"Incident report says Rees stole a meat mallet from the kitchen. Cornered the guy in a cell and beat him until he almost died, but not before torturing him first. Started with breaking his fingers, knee caps, collar bone. Then, wrapped the guy's head in a sheet, busted his teeth out, his nose, his face to a pulp. Then started on his skull."

"How did it get that far? Did the guy not scream?"

Darby nodded to the report. "You'll read in there that Rees gained quite the following in prison. Had his buddies stage a fist fight in the rec room while he beat the guy. Rees spent two weeks in the hole."

"What was the fight about?"

"My DPD contact thinks some sort of show of power. Leadership."

I skimmed Rees's latest mental health assessment where the psychiatrist diagnosed him with BPD, or Borderline Personality Disorder, with emphasis on something called Borderline Rage, described as inappropriate, intense anger or difficulty controlling anger. The doctor noted that this impulsivity appeared to increase with his time in imprisonment. The doctor suggested antidepressants, on-going therapy, as well as a full medical evaluation and DNA analysis.

Goosebumps flew over my skin as I stared down at the image of Kenzo Rees taken after the incident of him beating an inmate. Short, buzzed hair highlighted a blotchy, scarred scalp and a two inch row of stitches above his right ear. He had narrow, beady eyes, a sharp nose and jawline. Tattoos colored his neck, a few extending onto his jaw. I knew his type. I'd arrested his type.

I'd kicked his type's ass.

A flurry of thoughts shot through my head, including Rees ripping Sunny's hair from the roots. Throwing her down the stairs, beating her head against a mirror. Then, my thoughts switched to images of her kissing him. Having sex with him. Her being *his*.

My pulse skyrocketed.

I zeroed in on a small, circular tattoo just below his left eye.

"Was Rees in a prison gang?"

"It was the assumption. The Collars, they called themselves. The crowd he ran with was no stranger to solitary confinement, let's just say that."

"The tattoo under his eye appears to be new. See if he got it in prison."

Darby shook his head. "Tattoos are illegal in prison. In the US, anyway."

"It's amazing what you can do with a confiscated ballpoint pen."

I couldn't tear my eyes away from Rees's picture. Dark, slitted eyes with wide pupils, the irises as black as the ink below. There was a swirly look to them, feral. Crazy.

And Sunny had *dated him?*

My headache turned into a meat mallet pounding my brain. The fact that rich-girl Sunny had dated such a loser was another thing about the woman that didn't add up.

What the hell was she thinking?

Sunny didn't lock her doors, didn't listen to me, her doctor, and dated gang members?

What had she seen in him? I knew he'd been her high school boyfriend, but even if the guy had drastically changed over the years, I knew from experience, that someone who had the capability to beat another human unconscious showed signs years before the attack, sometimes as early as childhood. What had a beautiful, smart, well-kept millionaire's daughter seen in Kenzo Rees?

I contemplated that for a minute, then realized I couldn't see her with the captain of the football team, either. I couldn't see Sunny with anyone. Nothing, or no one, seemed to fit the badass loner.

I visioned her from the visit that morning. The softness I'd seen in her, the nurturing care and love she put into her dogs. The dedication she put into training and rehabilitating animals.

"It's not just time and effort, its perseverance. Not giving up on them." Her words suddenly hit me like a ton of bricks.

Sunny Harper was loyal. She was the type of woman who didn't give up on someone. She put in the work. Didn't back down. Didn't run when the cards weren't in her favor.

Sunny Harper was a freaking saint.

She'd probably stood by Kenzo Rees, trying to pull him back when he strayed to the dark side. My dad had been the same way. Loyal to a fault. And look where that got him.

The thought made my skin crawl for so many different reasons. And, for what seemed like the hundredth time since I'd met Sunny, I suspected there was more to the story.

I wanted to know more about their relationship. I also wanted to confirm that I wasn't being fooled by her like every other man that crossed her path.

"Talk to the warden there," I said to Darby, finally tearing my eyes away from the monster in my hands. I slid the picture into the folder and shut it. "See what other information you can get from him about our boy here. Figure out when Rees is up for parole next."

"Yes, sir."

18

JAGG

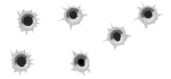

*I*t had been a hell of a day and when the clock on my office wall clicked to eight-thirty, I decided to take a break with only one thing on my mind. ... Fine, two.

A beer would have to do.

I rolled to a stop next to a browning pine tree and cut the engine, a blanket of humidity replacing the breeze from the drive. The air was still, stifling. Heavy. The flickering neon light of Frank's Bar flashed off the trees. Laughter followed by a fiddle from a country song floated through the air. A million stars twinkled around an almost-full moon.

Damn full moons.

It felt like everything was aligning for something big.

I could feel it in my bones.

My aching, creaking, popping bones.

Halfway across the parking lot, I decided on a whiskey instead of that beer.

I pushed through the front door. There was a different scent lingering in the air that night—chemicals and vanilla. Aqua-Net and cheap perfume.

It was Karaoke night at Frank's Bar. Less known as Berry

Springs's Single's Night. The place was packed. Funny how quickly people forgot about a slain cop.

I ignored a few cat calls as I made my way through the Stetsons and Old Spice, beelining it to the only open seat at the end of the bar—my seat.

"Howdy do, Detective?" Frank called out from behind the taps, a sweat of sheen across his brow, a fresh tattoo down his forearm. "The usual?"

"A double."

"You got it. Be just a minute. Damn full moon."

Good to know I wasn't the only one who believed in ill decisions at the turn of the tides.

As if on cue, the juke box switched to an old Bobby Bare song called *Marie Laveau*. Took me a second to realize the song was about an ugly witch from the Louisiana bayous. Took me even less than that to register the giggles and chiding at the other end of the bar. Something piqued in me, a sixth sense if you will. I leaned back on my stool, zeroing in on the notorious Aldridge twins. Two wild, twenty-something southern spitfires who thought they ran the town and every man in it. Their blonde, over-teased hair sat like helmets over pointy shoulders, barely-there tank tops, and wranglers that gave new meaning to the word camel toe.

As quickly as I noticed them, my gaze shifted to the strands of dark curly hair peeking out from the center of a group of big-bellied cowboys next to the twins.

Sunny.

The volume on the jukebox was turned up...

. . .

Down in Louisiana, where the black trees grow, lives a voodoo lady named Marie Laveau with a black cat's tooth and Mojo bone...

... followed by the bullies' pitched voices like nails on a chalkboard...

"Never knew skin could be that pale or rip that easy. Bitch is a walking commercial for vaccines."

"Didn't know herpes could spread to your arms."

"Gross. Probably fell off her broom on her way to hospice. Bitch has got stage-five something fo sho."

"Careful, she'll turn us into a frog."

"No, this one'll shoot you through the eye..."

Fire popped through my veins like an explosion. I surged to my feet, knocking the bar stool behind me onto the ground. I crossed the room with tunnel vision.

Sunny Harper stood facing the bar top, that strong, straight back as she was bullied from behind. Her slitted eyes remained forward, her jaw locked in a way that almost contorted her face. Flush covered her cheeks, her hands curled to fists at her side. Restraint.

Shocking restraint.

No, *practiced* restraint.

The cowboys to her right were leaning inches from her, sensing blood, their anger fed from a day of gossip about the death of the pastor's son. The Aldridge twins were chiding her from the back. A pack of dogs around the injured deer.

My entire body lit with rage.

"You like to target Christians, Voodoo Bitch?" The fat

redneck to her right leaned forward. *"Why don't you come to my house next time? I've got a stake in my back yard I'd like to show you..."*

His buddy picked up a strand of Sunny's curls. *"Bet these kinky, black pubes light up real quick."*

The redneck grinned a nasty, yellow-stained grin. *"Bet it smells about the same, too. Let's see..."*

My hand clamped down on the fat bastard's forearm as his hand reached for the switchblade on his belt. My other hand grabbed his buddy's wrist, twisting it until he dropped the curl and his head slammed onto the bar top. A pitcher of beer toppled over, a handful of bottles shattered on the hardwood floors.

Chaos erupted.

I flipped open the knife I'd swiped from fat boy's belt and leaned into his buddy's ear. "You ever touch one strand of hair on that woman's head again and your fingers won't be the only nubs I'll cut from your body. You understand me, cowboy?"

I dipped as a fist whizzed through the air next to me— less than three inches from Sunny's face.

That was it.

I snapped.

I spun Sunny's body away from the center of the chaos and slammed my fist into the redneck's face.

The two-hundred-fifty pound bastard locked up like a plank, flipping a table on its side as his body hit the floor. The crowd scattered like ants. I grabbed Sunny's hand and addressed the blonde bitches now gaping at the carnage on the floor.

"Bite your tongues next time, ladies, or I'll make sure every person in Berry Springs knows about all the dicks you two dirty cunts have sucked in that bathroom." I nodded to the camera above the bathrooms. "Now, unless you want to spend the rest of the evening in a cage for the dime bag you've got in your purses, I suggest you begin your walk home." I held out the hand that wasn't gripping Sunny's. Freshly manicured nails trembled as they set their glittery keychains in my palm. "You can pick these up at the station after signing up for community service. I can promise you the dick is just as accommodating in the jailhouse bathroom."

Then, behind me—

"*Shit.* Sorry about that Detective, I didn't realize what was going—"

I turned to Frank, his eyes wide, broken glass in his hands.

"If you don't get a better handle on your bar, Frank, I'll make sure the doors get closed up and you never see this place again."

Frank's eyes narrowed to slits.

"Let's go." I pulled Sunny away from the bar top and yanked her close to me. If someone—*anyone*—else laid a finger on her, I was going to lose my shit. More than I had, anyway.

Hand in hand, I led Sunny through the now-silent bar, every pair of bloodshot eyes locked on us. Not a single word was spoken, not a single drop drunk, not a muscle moved as we maneuvered through the tables.

Sunny didn't jerk away, didn't try to push me away. Good thing because I didn't know how I'd react if she did at that moment. The woman knew to shut her mouth, mind me, and leave me the fuck alone.

Good girl.

The whispers started the moment we pushed out the

front door and a flash of coherence sobered me up real quick—

I'd just gone to bat for Sunny. Publicly. Nothing else mattered to me the moment I saw her get bullied. Not my friends, not my reputation, not my fucking badge. It was as if a switch had flipped in me, with Sunny's finger on the trigger.

That was the first time a little warning bell ticked off in my head.

Evil witch or not, Sunny Harper had some sort of spell over me.

And I needed to be careful.

DARBY

I lifted my beer mug to my lips, hiding half my face as Jagg blew past me with Sunny's hand in his. I wasn't sure if he'd seen me, but I was stupid to think he hadn't. It probably didn't matter that I'd taken extra care to slip in through the back door and sneak into the corner where, lucky me, a pitcher of beer had been abandoned.

Going to Frank's Bar had been a gamble, but when Jagg hadn't left the station until past eight that night, I knew there was only one place he'd go aside from home. The guy loved his evening whiskey. Double. Always neat.

So, I took a shortcut while Jagg had taken the long way, probably hoping to come across a blue, four-door sedan.

I'd rehearsed my speech in the parking lot in case Jagg confronted me, although I'd forgotten it by then. Something about meeting an old friend traveling through town for a beer, who just so happened to be running late. But, turned out, I didn't need the story after all because Jagg never approached me. Jagg didn't even look in my direction because he was too busy putting the final nail in his career in the most blatant knight-in-shining-armor way I'd ever seen. I almost took notes, if I'm being honest. Not that I could pull off something as Fabio as that. Hell, I'da probably tripped on the way over to save Sunny. Hopefully right into the Aldridge twin's chests, who, thanks to Jagg, I learned used the bathrooms at Frank's Bar for more than just applying lipstick. And by "the bathrooms at Frank's Bar," I mean, my new 24/7 hangout.

I watched it all go down while sipping a mug of flat, warm beer that tasted like piss. Jagg had noticed Sunny almost immediately. I watched his shoulders square, his chest puff at the men around her. The man was tunnel-visioned. Hypnotized.

Bewitched.

Jagg had beelined to Sunny. Laser focused on *her* and nothing else around him. I watched as he went all Incredible Hulk, dismantling two boozed-up cowboys with a lightning quick precision that confirmed it wasn't his first bar brawl. Difference here, though, was his actions were nothing short of excessive force and something that could get him a misconduct review with his boss—and possibly his badge pulled.

For *her*.

What the hell was so special about Sunny Harper?

Why her?

Having arrived at Frank's ahead of Jagg, I was able to observe Sunny for a good ten minutes before her savior showed up. The moment she'd stepped into the bar, heads turned. I thought this was because of her beauty initially, but the stares quickly turned to whispers. I heard a few choice words, including, "killer," "murderer," "witch," "devil worshipper," and the grand finale of them all, "white-trash bitch." The last one from the Aldridge twins. Damn those girls were hot.

Sunny didn't respond, simply stepped up to the bar, asked for the takeout she'd ordered and waited patiently.

Taunting everyone with just her presence.

Then, I'd watched the beguiling Sunny Harper, a wicked enchantress, stand there and let Jagg kick the cowboy's asses. Let him risk his career for her.

Fuck that.

Fuck that kind of woman.

Don't get me wrong, the woman was hot. A showstopper, no doubt about that. But in a creepy, Addams Family kind of way. Maybe Jagg had a secret thing for emo. Whatever worked.

I shoved aside the beer that tasted like old man's piss, pulled out my phone and opened a new text message.

Me: *He just left with her.*
Lieutenant Colson: *Where to?*
Me: *Not sure.*
Lieutenant Colson: *Follow them.*
Me: *Yes, sir.*
Lieutenant Colson: *Keep me updated and keep your head on a swivel.*

A zing of excitement shot through me as I chugged the rest of the beer and jogged out the back door. It was like my own little James Bond movie. I slipped into my truck, turned the engine and waited for the taillights of Jagg's Jeep.

I was not going to screw this up.

Because, after all, my life was also on the line.

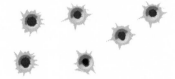

*T*he front door of Frank's slapped shut as I pulled Sunny into the parking lot. The bugs roared over the heat waving over my already-boiling skin.

"Jagg. You're hurting me." Sunny's calm voice pulled me from my rage.

I softened my grip on her hand but didn't let go.

"Where's your truck?"

"Under the oak tree over there." She nodded to the far side of building.

"What the hell are you doing parking in the shadows? Don't you know by now to park under a street light or lamppost? And if there isn't one, find somewhere else to fucking go."

Goddamn this woman's fearlessness.

The woman was *me.*

I heard the front door open and slam shut behind us, and for a moment, I actually wished someone would come up on me. I needed another fist fight to release the truckload of adrenaline flooding my veins. I looked over my shoulder to see a couple beelining to their

Can-am Roadster as if they'd seen a ghost. Damn tourists.

We rounded the building and I stopped cold. Sunny jerked against my hold.

"What?"

"I'm assuming those weren't there when you got here."

Her jaw dropped as she followed my gaze where the moonlight illuminated two long, thin scratches running down the entire length of her 1972 Chevy Cheyenne.

"Oh *my*..." her voice faded in a breathless whisper as she jogged to her truck and ran her finger down the scratches. She kneeled down, examining the damage. "I've been here literally *ten* minutes. Who could've... *why?*"

Sunny had not only been publicly bullied, someone had also keyed her truck.

Oh, *hell no.*

I pulled the gun from my belt and spun around.

"*Stop.*" Sunny surged to her feet and grabbed my arm with both hands. I literally dragged her through the dirt.

"Jagger, *stop*. Please." She dug her heels in, dropping her weight against my pull. "Stop you idiot, macho-male maniac. *Stop!*" She dropped my arm—more like flung it down. "Do *not* go back in there, Jagg. It's not worth it."

I stopped, pivoted. "Someone keyed your truck. You're goddamn right it's worth it."

I started to turn but she yanked me back.

"It's *not* worth it Jagger. Who cares about my damn truck?" She stood toe to toe with me. "And what are you going to do, anyway? Beat up the entire bar? You think my car will be in one piece after that?"

That gave me pause. Going back in there and cracking skulls in Sunny's name would only make it worse for her.

She was right.

"Just... calm down, Jagg."

I stared at the front door of the bar, gun in one hand, Sunny on the other.

Sunny's focus remained on the side of my face. She took a deep breath, then another, until finally, I found myself releasing an exhale.

"Good. Thank you. Come on." This time, she pulled me across the parking lot.

Once at her truck, she fisted her hands on her hips. "Well... *shit.*"

I forced my focus to switch from kicking ass to solving the problem at hand. "A buddy of mine can fix the paint first thing in the morning."

"I don't need you to handle it."

"I know." I grabbed her hand and pulled her with me. "Let's go."

She jerked her hand back. We squared off like two sumo wrestlers, right there under the fluorescent lights of Frank's.

"Where?"

"I'm driving you home. I'll have my buddy come get the truck."

"What? No."

"Dammit, Sunny." I dropped her hand and began pacing, stalking back and forth like a madman, flexing and unflexing my fists with each step.

Sunny stood motionless, watching me like someone might a recoiling snake. Her hair danced around her face in the breeze, strands of ebony against her lips. God those lips.

I planted my feet and turned to her. "What the hell are you doing here, anyway?" I demanded.

"Not that it's any of your business, but getting dinner. I don't cook." She squinted. "Why are *you* here?"

"I come here all the time. The stool at the end of the bar is molded to my ass. I can handle my shit here."

"What the hell's that supposed to mean?"

"It means a beautiful woman with a target on her back should have better judgment than to swing by a dive-bar on the way home. *Especially* alone."

"I'll have you know I've been here dozens of times since I moved here."

"Trolling for men?"

"Fuck you."

My hands fisted at my side.

"Don't talk to me like that," she continued. "And you think a single woman can't handle her shit?"

"Based on what I was looking at when I walked in, no, I don't think you were handling your shit."

"What would you have had me do? Bust a bottle over the redneck's head? Break those pretty little blonde's noses? Put a damn spell on the place?" Her voice cracked with the last one, and of all the insults that had been hurled in her direction, that one apparently stung the worst.

"Listen, Sunny. This is a small town, with all the small-town clichés, right in the middle of the Bible Belt. When a pastor's son's face gets blown off in the city park, people are going to talk. They're going to want answers. And I get that, Sunny." I shot her a look. "My entire job is to get answers. The entire town is already looking at *you*. Questioning you, your every move. And when your stubborn ass saunters into the one bar frequented only by locals, you're asking for it. Whether you like it or not, people are blaming you."

Heat flared behind those green eyes. "You think I don't know that?"

"*Exactly.* That's my point. You know that, so why did you come here? You need to lay low until this thing blows over."

"If you're so desperate for this thing to blow over, why don't you and the Lieutenant tell everyone I shot Griggs in self-defense and move on? Close the case?"

"Did you kill Griggs, Sunny?"

"*No.* I've told you a hundred—"

"Then someone else did and I'm not going to let you roll over for this. I wouldn't be doing my job if I did that. Your attack wasn't random. And I know you believe that, too, which is why you shouldn't have gone to Frank's tonight."

"I was *hungry*. There wasn't much more thought to it than that."

"Then, regardless, you should have walked out when they started chastising you. I guarantee you someone would have eaten the three pieces of lettuce you ordered."

She glared at me.

"I'm not doing this with you anymore, Sunny. I'm not arguing like a fucking child and I'm sure as hell not going to put up with your arrogant, fearless, defiant behavior."

"Who asked you to put up with me? Who asked you to even help me?"

"Cut the bullshit, Sunny. You need to drop that damn armor you wear."

"Fine. I'll drop it right here." She spun on her heels and stalked away from me.

Hell. No.

I grabbed her elbow, spun her around.

"You walk away from me again and I will hog tie you, throw you over my shoulder and carry your ass home."

Her nostrils flared as she stood strong against my hold, staring me down as I was her.

God, I was frustrated. Beyond normal, anyway.

I dropped her arm. "*Jesus,* Sunny, you claim to be an

expert at Krav Maga, right? You should have walked the heck away. Diffused the situation."

"Really? That's what you would have preferred I'd done, huh? Run from the bastards? Let them win?"

"*Yes.*"

She slammed her fists on her hips. "Is that what you would tell your son or your daughter? To tuck tail and run no matter what the situation?"

I opened my mouth to respond but no words came out. I pictured the junior high autistic boy getting beat up by the governor's son. On his back, but still fighting. I respected him. Truth was, standing up for yourself and others was something I built my life on. I *never* backed down. Not once. Even when I was the tall, skinny kid being bullied in junior high, I fought back.

And had plenty of broken bones to show it.

Sunny was the same damn way. She didn't back down either. Against all odds, despite her past, despite getting the shit kicked out of her at the park.

I respected the hell out of her for it.

"Exactly," she said, reading my thoughts. "I'm done here. Do you mind if I turn my back and walk away from you now, Detective Jagger?" The sarcasm seethed from her lips.

She turned on her heel and stomped to her truck.

I followed Sunny home that night. Without her knowledge, of course. Someone had to watch out for the woman. I'd waited until she was safe inside her cabin to reverse down the road and begin tackling the evening's to-do list.

One, figure out which of the bar rats had keyed Sunny's truck.

And two, figure out why the hell Officer Darby was following me.

21

SUNNY

*M*y hand shook as I poured a glass of wine.
I hadn't planned on this.

I hadn't planned on *him*.

I hadn't planned on my carefully crafted world getting turned upside down the moment—the *freaking moment*—I had finally found peace.

Happiness.

Content solitude.

Leaving everything off except for a dim light in the kitchen, I left a trail of flip flops through the living room and sank onto the couch. I stared out the window. The night was young, the moon low in the sky, hiding just below the tree-tops in the distance. Slashes of black branches swayed against the glowing spotlight. A cool breeze blew in through the open window.

Athena pulled herself off the floor, padded over and licked my hand. Tango and Max were out on their nightly bathroom breaks before coming in for the night. Brutus was still by the river.

Athena never left my side.

I stroked the course, sable fur on the top of her head. "Good girl, baby," I cooed, to calm myself just as much as to soothe her. "Good girl."

Athena and I had been through a lot together. New jobs, new houses, new men, new me. Therapists, nights on the bathroom floor, days not leaving the bed. Tears until there were no more. Fear until there was no more.

My stomach rolled at the thought it could be happening all over again. Maybe not in the exact way, but an attack was an attack. Abuse was abuse. Physically and mentally. I'd experienced both in the last twenty four hours. At the City Park, of all places, and then the local watering hole. Attacked physically, then mentally. For the second damn time in my life.

Was it happening again?

Could it all happen again?

I'd spent the last eight years picking up the broken pieces of a life changed forever. Putting one foot in front of the other while realizing the woman I once knew was no more, and having no idea who that new woman was. All I knew was my soul, the very core of me, had changed the instant Kenzo Rees slammed his fist into my jaw.

Funny how life can change in an instant.

There's no going back after you wake up in ICU and remember you were put there by the hand of someone you loved. Someone you'd given your heart to.

Someone you *trusted*.

That was what hurt the most, believe it or not. Looking back, it was the shattered trust that did me in. Of all the scars I'd gotten that night, that was the one that never quite healed back correctly. That shattered trust had not only made me question every word and motive out of every man's mouth from that day forward, it made me question myself. That was the worst. I not only lost trust in other people, but in myself as well. And that's—*that's*—the dangerous part. Once you lose faith in yourself, everything else is like a slow burning ember, gradually fading away over time until it eventually turns to dust. My confidence, gone. My self-worth obliterated.

I remember looking in the mirror a few months after the attack and feeling like my actual *face* had changed. Physically. My skin, bone structure, everything had changed. How crazy is that?

I didn't even recognize the woman I'd become. I just knew that a dark hole had formed somewhere in my body, stealing that childhood light that used to shine from me. The darkness was always there, every day, for better or worse.

For better or worse.

It wasn't until six years after the attack, a year after my mom died—followed by the downward spiral of my father —that I'd decided I was going to turn that worse into better.

I remember the moment like it was yesterday. I woke up on the kitchen floor with a bottle of vodka in my hand, an empty pizza box at my feet, and my first blinding migraine. Ever had a migraine before? Hell on earth. Damn close, anyway. I peeled my torso off the tile and vomited on my lap. When Athena lapped it up, I decided I'd had enough.

I'd gained thirty-seven pounds since the attack. Thirty-*freaking*-seven pounds, and no, those lbs. didn't come with a pair of strapping young boys to dote on. It was all booze, pizza, and double-stuffed Oreos. Double, because regular whipped diabetes just wasn't enough. I'd stopped working out, wearing makeup, feeling pretty—ever. I didn't date because I didn't trust men. Didn't have friends because I didn't trust anyone. I lived off my father's money, working part-time at a vet clinic, interacting with as few humans as possible.

I was done wallowing in misery, the disgusting self-loathing that had become as routine to me as the anti-depressants I'd popped throughout the day. I was done accepting the pain, accepting the life mine had turned into.

I made the decision that day, sitting on my kitchen floor covered in half-eaten vomit, that if something can change me, for better or worse, then something can certainly change me back. This time, though, that change was going to be by my own hand, not at the mercy of someone else's. I was going to be in control of whatever new woman I was going to be.

After throwing away the vodka and pizza box, I shredded dear Daddy's credit cards, then burned them after I'd taped them back together a split-second later while sobbing uncontrollably. That was the first time I realized the real power of money. Of greed. The false comfort it provided. But you couldn't be an independent woman while relying on a man to pay your bills, now could you? I joined a gym, made an appointment with a therapist, signed up for self-defense classes, signed-up for firearm training, applied for my concealed carry license, and adopted Max from a rescue facility that took in retired police dogs.

It was just me, Athena and Max, rebuilding a new world together, whatever the hell that looked like.

The days slowly morphed into carefully constructed routines and schedules, down to the minute. I learned this type of structure eased my anxiety and helped bring back that control I felt like I'd lost. I also learned that self-defense, guns, dog training, and martial arts came easily to me. I loved all of it.

But losing the damn weight? That's another story. Not unlike finding the perfect vibrator—something I'd also realized the power of. The first step is overcoming the mental block, being open to the new adventure. Pun unintended. Then, it takes time, effort, perseverance, and a few unfortunate bruises along the way, but in the end, complete, total satisfaction. Losing the thirty-seven pounds took me six damn months that included a detox off gluten, dairy, sugar, salt, and a wicked case of food poisoning from an organic, vegan by-product called *Miso Thorny*. I do not recommend the last part, or any health food named after a sexual innuendo from the eighties. Nineties is probably cool. Eighties, no.

It was slow going, but eventually, I began to feel better. Physically first, then mentally. And finally, emotionally. I brought back the full-length mirror I'd once removed from my bedroom, returned the scale to my closet. Flushed the bottles of antidepressants down the toilet and replaced the goblet that I drank my evening martinis in with a much more socially acceptable shorter glass that read *Let that Shit Go*. Ratted T-shirts and sweatpants were replaced with, well, *less* ratty T-shirts and sweatpants... turned out the new Sunny had as much interest in fashion as the old one.

Oh well. Can't win 'em all.

Physically, the old Sunny was back. But in the place of the once naive, rose-colored-glasses girl was an independent, lethally trained, paranoid perfectionist. A deadly combination in any man's book.

My safe-zone, my comfort zone, was my house, so I started my own business where I could work from home, combining the only two things I trusted—self-defense tactics and dogs. I ate, drank, slept and worked behind the walls I'd built around myself, only leaving when it was absolutely necessary. You know, to get gas, booze, and food.

I was healthy, happy.

Unstoppable.

It wasn't long before the looks and attention I'd gotten from men before I let myself go, came back. But instead of smiling and giggling at the attention, this new, improved, *smarter* Sunny decided to use this to my advantage. Unfortunately, I couldn't avoid civilization all together, so I learned how to get in and out with what I needed, more often than not, at the assistance of man. You see, I might have built myself into Sunny 2.0, but the scars still remained. All men needed to die, in my humble opinion. Men could not be trusted. I did not let men into my space, into my head, into my bed. It had been six years since I'd had sex, and while most might cringe at that thought, I wore the record proudly as some sort of badge of honor proving my independence. I didn't need anyone. Celibacy gave me control over every part of my body, and for me, that was an easy adjustment. Well, that and the fact that vibrators had come a long way. Pun definitely intended. In my book, men were stupid, ignorant, easy to seduce and easier to tame. Men were helpful, then disposable.

Forgettable.

Enter Detective Max Jagger and his two-hundred and fifty pounds of pent up rage tackling me like a gorilla in City Park. The moment he'd appeared at the scene of the "Slaying at the Park,"—a title that made me want to run into oncoming traffic, by the way—he'd caught my eye. Controlled my focus. Not because of the gun in his hand, or his six-foot-four beastly frame, or the rugged sexiness that came as effortlessly to him as his disdain for manscaping.

Or anything that involved self-care, obviously. But because of the authority that oozed from him. The detective owned the room instantly, so to speak. He was the one I needed to keep my eye on.

The brash, unapologetic detective inserted himself into my life despite my every attempt to keep him at arm's length.

Jagg was everything I didn't like in a man. A cocky, controlling, bulldozing alpha male. Jacked-up testosterone on the brink of self-destruction.

He was nothing I'd known before... and everything I never knew I needed.

From the moment he'd pinned me to the grass in the park, I'd felt *something.* Drawn to him in a way I didn't understand. Although his grip around my wrists had loosened and eventually released, it was like the touch never left my skin. The heat and tenacity of the hold tightening every time I saw him. Every time I heard his voice. Every damn time he looked at me in that way.

And then he had to go and be my knight in shining armor.

Forget the attack, forget my keyed truck, Max Jagger was like an EF5 tornado, blowing into my life and turning everything I'd so meticulously placed onto its head.

I was mentally prepared for an attack, prepared for the violation of my privacy. I'd lived through it once, I'd do it again. But Max Jagger? No, I wasn't prepared for him.

I wasn't prepared for the way he had me questioning if I could trust a man. Or even let one into my life again.

I wasn't prepared for the guilt I felt for deceiving a man with as many trust issues as I had. If Detective Max Jagger knew the secrets in my closet, there'd be no going back.

For either of us.

I pushed off the couch and stepped onto the deck, into the cool evening air.

I took a deep breath, then another. While my thoughts were as muddled as a Mojito, I knew two things for certain: One, I had a decision to make.

And two, I wasn't ready.

22

JAGG

$\mathcal{I}$ walked through the front door into a wall of air-conditioned air scented with fresh bacon, coffee, and a cloud of discount perfume strong enough to singe nose hairs. It was Wednesday night in the south, otherwise known as church night. Donny's Diner was packed to the gills with men and women wearing their Wednesday night best, pretending to be meditating on the daily word, when in fact, they were gobbling up the daily gossip as fast as Ms. Booth's fresh apple pie. A plate of steaming flapjacks passed me by sending my stomach growling. There were many things I loved about the south, but top of the list was the fact that coffee, bacon, and waffles were an acceptable meal no matter what time of day.

I glanced at the clock on the wall, a ridiculous black and white cartoon cat.

8:07 p.m.

Typically, Donny's closed its doors promptly at nine o'clock, whether you were finished with your meal or not.

But, as with every other small business in town, Donny's was staying open later to cater to the influx of tourists flocking to the Moon Magic Festival. Two days away and the town was already overflowing with tourists. Calls to the station had gone up more than fifty percent. Everyone was hyped up, on edge, fueling an energy flowing through the sleepy town like nuclear vibrations. The current heatwave and impending full moon only added to it.

I was operating on exactly forty-eight minutes of sleep, thanks to a pain pill that had kicked in somewhere after three in the morning. I'd gone to sleep with visions of Sunny Harper in my head, dreamt of her legs around my waist, her curls bouncing on my shoulders, and woken up with a raging boner that was embarrassingly easy to remedy.

After following Sunny to her house, I'd gone back to Frank's and was as welcomed as a bad rash. Not surprisingly, though, my little display had unnerved people enough that I was able to get a confession in under five minutes. According to Sandy, the waitress, the fat redneck was the asshole behind keying Sunny's truck, and I was a bigger asshole for never calling her back after taking her home a few weeks earlier. After that slap in the face, I drove to the redneck's house where I pulled him out of bed by his hair and slapped him with a misdemeanor and five-hundred dollar fine. Because the broken nose I'd given him when I slammed his face against the counter just wasn't enough.

I was quickly becoming the least popular guy in town.

An old shoe. Without the tassel.

After that, I'd gone home, dreamt of Sunny, beat off, and was behind my desk with a cup of coffee before the sun came up. I'd spent the morning catching up, and the after-noon watching Julian Griggs' autopsy. The temperature had hit a sweltering ninety-eight by noon, making the dress shirt

I'd changed into before the autopsy feel like a strait jacket. Funerals and autopsies were the only two times I wore button-ups. It was my ridiculous way of showing respect. Although I'd unbuttoned my top button and rolled up my sleeves sometime during the Y-incision down Griggs' torso, no amount of extra air helped the constant state of damp I'd been in all day.

I'd attended countless autopsies through the years and while nothing was worse than a child's, attending one where the victim's face had been blown off had a way of setting the tone for the day. True to form, Jessica Heathrow, the medical examiner, hadn't shielded the audience from the gore. Helps light a fire under the investigation, she always said. Jessica didn't believe in sugar-coating shit—one of my favorite things about her.

The autopsy hadn't revealed much more than we already knew. Julian Griggs died of a gunshot wound to the head. Several scratches and bruising on his torso suggested a physical altercation, backing Sunny's story that he'd attacked her. Unfortunately, it did nothing to confirm the part of her story that a mystery third person had emerged from the woods, engaged Julian, and in the end, was the one to pull the trigger.

We were still waiting on ballistics to confirm if the pin markings of the casing found at the scene matched Sunny's gun.

The Cedonia Scroll art investigator, Briana Morgan, still hadn't called me back, nor had Sunny's dad, Arlo Harper, or the warden of the prison where Kenzo Rees was caged. I felt like my hands were tied behind my back. To top all that off, I was no closer to finding the damn Black Bandit.

It had been a hell of a day and the last thing I wanted to

do was listen to more gossip about voodoo, witches, or the Slaying in the Park.

Unfortunately, that was exactly what I got.

I'd just made it to the corner of the counter when—

"Detective Max Jagger." The southern accent was as thick and slow as the syrup on the plate next to me. I turned into the wart on ol' Mrs. Berkovich's face.

"Ma'am."

"Don't *ma'am* me now, son. What're you and the other police boys doin' to keep these hippies under control? Saw two of 'em sleeping on the square last night. Right there against the fountain. Probably smoking dope and conjurin' up some spell for another Slayin' in the Park. I spent this mornin' cleaning my shotguns." She squinted. "Unrelated. Anyway. I want them out of here. The whole goddamn town smells like patchouli."

My gaze flickered to the gold cross around her neck. A forgiving God, indeed.

"Are they bothering you personally, Mrs. Berkovich?"

She lifted her eye brows with an attitudinal shrug. "All I know is ever since these beatniks came to town, something's been eating the flowers on my front porch. All my plants, close to death."

"You think the hippies are eating your front porch flowers?"

She scoffed. "They eat all sorts of natural shit."

"So do deer, Mrs. Berkovich."

"Well, in that case, I'll shoot to kill next—"

"Hold on there, Annie Oakley. I'll drive by your house the next few evenings. Keep your sawed-off shotgun away from the windows and under your pillow where it belongs."

She lifted her chin and nodded. "Thank you, son. By the way, I ran into Patricia yesterday."

I stilled, no way on earth had I heard that correctly. I turned fully.

"You say Patricia?"

"Yes, sir."

"My *mother?*"

"You got more than one, son? Hell, wouldn't surprise me these days."

"What was she doing in town?"

"*Ahhh,* guess you didn't know." Mrs. Berkovich's eyes sparked, sensing gossip like stink on pig. "Said she was lookin' for houses."

God himself could have walked through the door and I wouldn't have been more surprised.

"Looking for houses? *Here?*" I asked, although the voice in my head was telling me to shut the hell up.

"Yep. Mentioned she tried to call you a few times, no answer. Asked how you've been doin.' I figured she'd paid you a visit after that."

No, Patricia Jagger knew better than to knock on my front door. Although, I realized then that her increased— unanswered—calls must have been because of her pending visit.

Should've changed my damn number.

"Well, lock up your husband." I said. "Have a good evening, Mrs. Berkovich."

I turned back to the counter, feeling the woman's eyes burning a hole into my back. Jagger family drama. Add it to the list of shit I had to deal with that day.

A shoulder nudged into my arm. I took a step back, cocked a brow and watched ol' Louis Smith, the town's plumber, shoot me a glance sharp enough to cut glass. Or, steel pipes, I guess.

What the hell?

Food. I just wanted fucking food.

Christ, just get me some damn food.

I maneuvered my way to the only open stool in the middle of the counter.

"Seat's taken."

I tilted my head to the side, my patience officially obliterated.

"Is it?"

"That's right," Bob Powell, a local farmer, sipped his coffee without gracing me a glance.

"By who, Mr. Powell?"

"Ain't none of your business, *Detective.*"

I stepped forward, nudging two truckers out of the way.

"You got something to say to me, Bobby?"

"Yeah, son, I do." The old man turned on his stool, coffee in one hand, the other sliding to his lap. I kept my eye on it. "I got a problem with you busting Cowboy Billy's nose last night at Frank's."

"Do ya now? You're gonna have a bigger problem than that if one fingernail touches the gun you've got on your belt."

He sneered, pulled his hand away. "Billy wasn't causin' no harm, Jagg."

"He was drunk off his ass bullying an innocent bystander."

"Innocent bystander? Is that right? Was innocent bystanding what that white witch was doing when she put a bullet in Pastor Griggs' son's face?"

I leaned forward. "Bite your tongue old man."

"Ah, look who's finally decided to respect women." He laughed an asshole laugh. "Figured after what your mama—"

I lunged forward the moment two arms wrapped around

my waist and heaved me off my feet.

Colson's deep voice vibrated in my ear. "Say one more word, Jagg, and I'll throw you through these fucking windows. I'm not fucking kidding."

I was pulled through the front door, where a crowd had gathered on the sidewalk.

Fuck.

Colson grabbed my elbow and yanked me to the side of the building. I jerked my arm away.

"What the hell is wrong with you?" He threw his hands up. "I can't. I can't do this right now. I've got a pregnant insomniac at home waiting for her biscuits and sausage, blueberry double stack, cheese grits, T-bone steak, and fucking large chocolate milkshake. I don't have time or patience to deal with your antics or try to figure out why you're so hellbent on sabotaging your career. Or what the hell is going through your head right now, but God help me, I will—"

Saved by my ringing phone. I yanked it from my pocket, glanced at the name, then looked at Colson. "Then, I'll get the hell out of your way, then. Enjoy your double-stack. And your pancakes."

He muttered something as I pushed past him, ignoring the stares from the windows. The assholes should thank me for giving them something else to talk about for the evening.

I answered the call as I jumped into my Jeep.

"Thanks for calling me back." I fired up the engine.

"Sorry it took a while. Had a financial review to prepare for."

"Prisons get enough of tax payers' money."

"Warden's don't. Anyway, what can I do for ya?"

"Kenzo Rees. Does that name ring a bell?"

"Does botulism make you vomit?"

"More pain than vomit, actually."

"You've had botulism?"

"Mongolia isn't known for its sanitation standards."

"Damn, dude. I sometimes forget you were a SEAL." Wish I could. "Anyway, yeah, what's got you hunting down Rees?"

"I've got a case that Rees is loosely linked to. His former girlfriend was recently attacked in a city park. Does the name Sunny Harper ring a bell?"

"Sure does. Rees wrote her a few letters the first few weeks of his sentence."

"Letters? You mean, mail?"

"Yep. We still check all the incoming and outgoing mail. Some prisons don't. We do."

"What did they say?"

"Short of it, he was going to kill her. Finish the job when he got out. Blamed her for *making* him hit her and for getting thrown in jail."

My pulse kick-started. "Did she see them? The letters?"

"Hell no. I'll have to check, but I think it was only two letters total. We showed the prosecutor, addressed it with Rees, and it stopped. Guy was crazy the first few months of going in. The letters are still in his file."

"I want to see them. I'd like anything you can give me on him."

I pulled onto Main Street, noting the Moon Magic Festival protesters had doubled in the last thirty minutes.

"No problem, whatever you need as long as it doesn't involve that satan spawn coming back here."

I swerved off of Main Street, hit the brakes. "What do you mean, coming back here?"

A brief pause, then, "Sorry, guess I thought that's why you were calling. Kenzo Rees was released eight days ago."

23

JAGG

*F*ifteen minutes later, I hovered over the desk in my living room, flipping through the reports I'd printed from the email the warden had just sent.

Eight days ago.

My mind spun with possibilities.

Kenzo Rees had been released from prison exactly three days before the Cedonia Scroll heist that ended with Seagrave's murder. Days later, Sunny was attacked in the park. Coincidence? No shot in hell.

I compared Rees's height and weight to what I believed was the Black Bandit's, and while definitely fuzzy, it was plausible.

Was Kenzo Rees the Black Bandit?

Over the phone, the warden told me Rees had been a problem inmate from the first day, threatening and goading guards and other inmates. Rees's first physical altercation happened within eight hours of his sentence. The guy walked in with something to prove. By week two, Rees had joined forces with a small group suspected of gang affiliations—after his cell mate had died of what was recorded to be a heart attack. Even the warden didn't believe that. And so began a tumultuous stay at the state prison. I'd pulled more pictures of Rees from his file, printed each, and with a magnifying glass, searched over each one of his visible tattoos. A snake slithered up his left forearm, a trio of demons clawing out of his other one. No gang tattoos other than the one under his eye, backing my assumption he'd joined "The Collars," in prison. No Wiccan or Pagan tattoos. I'd asked if Rees had taken any interest in art, painting, history, the Bible, or cursed Wiccan scrolls, to which the warden laughed. Kenzo Rees hadn't taken any interest in prison other than pumping iron and hand to hand combat.

Aside from several visits from a sleazy lawyer they called "Stilts," Rees didn't receive a single visitor while behind bars, including Sunny. I'm not proud to say I audibly exhaled when I heard that. I hoped to God Sunny wasn't one of those women who blamed herself and pitied her abuser. Hell no, she wasn't. She was the type to enroll in Krav Maga and befriend massive German Shepherds.

I'd already called Darby, informed him of the news and given him a new task—find Kenzo Rees. Regardless of whatever the kid had up his sleeve, I needed all hands on deck because Sunny's safety was in question. I'd also pulled in the infamous billionaire Steele brothers, of Steele Shadows Security, to use their endless resources as well. I didn't have many people in my life, but the Steele brothers and I had one bond in common, we'd spent our glory days running special ops for the military. They were good guys, my unofficial brothers, hell, my unofficial family, and considering they had more money than God, were good to know in a pickle.

Gunner Steele was going to hit up the car dealerships around the prison to see if Rees had purchased a blue four-door sedan. If anyone could intimidate information out of a car salesman, it was him. Axel and their head of security, Max Blackwell, was going to use their hacking skills to see if they could track Rees using the last cell phone number in his name before going in. Gage was going to do what that hotheaded bastard did best, look for the guy boots-on-ground style. Old school.

I already had three calls into Rees's parole officer, with no response yet. Not that I expected too much from that call because, if I knew anything from being a detective, it was that those mandated check-ins didn't mean shit. I'd also left two more voicemails on Briana Morgan's cell phone, followed by a call to Harold and Associates to confirm that the woman was indeed investigating the Cedonia scroll heist. I didn't know why the woman was so hellbent on not calling me back, but I intended to find out.

Above all else, though, I needed to check on Sunny.

24

JAGG

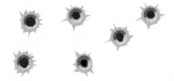

*I*t was just past nine o'clock in the evening when I turned onto county road 3228. A pair of glowing taillights in the distance caught my attention. The vehicle appeared to be stopped, halfway in the ditch. Considering only Sunny lived down that road, the stranded motorist was either her, Kenzo Rees himself, or someone looking for her. Either way, a win/win for me. I lowered my right hand to my lap, resting inches from my gun, wanting nothing more than to come face to face with the gang-banging bastard sitting behind the steering wheel of a blue sedan.

My headlights bounced off the bumper of a 1972 Chevy.

I rolled to a stop and climbed out of my Jeep, my headlights illuminating Sunny, and all her wild hair, twisting her neck to see who was coming. She was flat on her back, half her body under the front of her truck, her head next to a flat tire.

I walked up, glanced at the tire, then took a moment to soak in the view. Wearing a pair of cut-off jean shorts and a V-neck T-shirt that ironically read *Girl Power,* Sunny avoided eye contact and continued doing whatever the hell she was doing. Her hair was a frizzed mess around her head, speckled with grass and dead leaves. I was pretty sure something was crawling in it, but considering I could practically *feel* her vile mood, I decided to keep that to myself. A smattering of dirt stuck to her sweaty forehead, making me wonder how long she'd been stranded. Regardless, one thing was obvious, Sunny Harper had absolutely no clue what she was doing. I'd be amused if not for the fact that I was pissed she obviously hadn't stayed at home as I'd instructed her the evening before.

"What seems to be the problem here, Miss Harper?" Pissed or not, I couldn't help the smartass dig.

I could feel her eye roll more than I could see it.

"Oh, you know, just decided have a quick looksee under my truck." She huffed out a breath. "I'm trying to change my damn tire. *Obviously.*"

"Are you? Because by the looks of it, you're trying to change the axel."

Her body stilled.

A moment ticked by and I would have paid my next paycheck—you know, all hundred dollars of it—to see the expression on her face.

"What were you doing leaving your house?" I demanded.

"Getting a salad."

"I told you not to go out. Where did you go?"

"Gino's."

I grit my teeth and shook my head. Right in the middle of damn town. The woman didn't listen and was going to get herself hurt. Again.

"Three things, Sunny." I seethed. "Three things I have an

issue with right now. One, who leaves their house for a *salad?* Two, I told you to stay out of public and away from people until everything blows over, and on top of that, the doctor told you to be resting. And three, how is that screwdriver in your hand going to help you change your damn tire?"

She looked at the screwdriver, a second passed, then released a hefty sigh. She set the tool on the ground, craned her neck to get a better view of me and met my gaze with a fire of her own.

"One, have you ever had Gino's Flaming Farro salad? It's nothing short of Italian perfection. Artichokes, peppers, onions, cherry tomatoes, cucumbers over a bed of farro—a gluten free Italian grain for your information, because I'm assuming your fridge holds nothing more than boxes of bacon and cases of beer. PBR if I had to guess..."

Ouch.

"And," she continued, "Gino's does curbside delivery so I didn't even have to get out of my truck. Two, I don't take orders. From you, or anyone. When are you going to get that through your head? And my ribs are a lot better today. I'm fine. And three, I thought I grabbed the wrench, thank you very much."

"Liar."

"I don't lie."

"Liar."

"Fine. I only lie about hand tools."

"Ever consider just learning how to cook?"

"No offense, but I get the feeling you're not whipping up three course meals on your own, Jagg."

"Hey, a breakfast burrito takes multiple steps."

"That's your idea of gourmet?"

"Honey, it's every man's idea of gourmet."

"Whatever. Look, do you mind? I'm kinda busy here."

"Scoot over. Better yet, get out of my way."

"Are you always this demanding?"

"It's part of my charm. We've already been over this. Scoot."

"No. Just tell me what to do."

"I just did. Scoot. Get out of my way."

"You're unbelievable, you know that? They should bottle your testosterone."

"If you don't get off your back, I'll give you a free sample."

That got her up... and I don't know if I was pleased or offended.

I watched her shimmy out from under the fender—absolutely no clue what she was doing under there—her boobs jiggling and hips swaying in a way that had my pants tightening. I helped her up. Based on her smooth movements, she hadn't been lying that her ribs were better, but she still should have been resting. I took a moment to look at the injury on her arm. It was clean, with a new bandage. The swelling was gone.

Good.

I rolled up my shirtsleeves and squatted down. She handed me the flashlight.

I looked the tire over, searching for a nail or whatever had pierced the rubber. I got nothing.

"Looks like you've got a faulty valve."

"What? No. I just bought these tires."

"How long ago?"

"Two months."

My gaze shifted to the rest of the tires, each of which

were low. The bottom left would be flat by morning. I pushed off the ground.

"You got four new tires?"

"Yes." Her eyes locked on the back left tire. "That one's almost flat, too, isn't it?"

"New or used?"

"New." Her brow furrowed as she looked at me, and although I already knew what I was going to find, I circled the truck, examining each tire with Sunny quiet on my heels.

"What's going on?" She asked, concern evident in her voice. "Why are all the tires low?"

"Someone tampered with your tires."

"What?" Her eyes rounded. "What the hell? This is *ridiculous.* I didn't kill the pastor's son. You mean to tell me that redneck from Frank's Bar keyed my car and ruined my new tires? Unbelievable. He's got another thing coming because I'm not going to put up with—"

"Sunny, this wasn't done last night."

"What—how do you know that?"

I leaned in closer, to triple-confirm. "Each tire valve has been punctured. Same spot, every one. The tires have been losing air for days."

"Days?"

"That's my best guess."

"But I haven't been anywhere long enough for someone to do it."

Aside from your house, I thought, but didn't say it. My mind was racing.

"Leave your truck here. Don't touch anything. I'll get it towed and taken care of."

"No way. I live just a few more miles down the road. I can—"

"*Leave it.* It'll be taken care of. I need to make a call. Get in my Jeep."

"No, I—"

"Sunny. I'm not doing this. *Get. In.*"

Two minutes later, I slid behind the wheel. "Buckle up."

I fired up the engine, took one last look at the truck, then pulled onto the dirt road. My call wasn't to the station, or to Colson, it was to Phoenix Steele, oldest brother and CEO of Steele Shadows Security—someone I trusted with my life, because right now, I didn't know who to trust. Colson wanted me locked in a padded room, Darby was following me for reasons I had yet to figure out, and the Chief of Police wanted my badge. My list of people to call for favors was running short.

Phoenix promised to have one of his mechanic buddies pick up her truck within the hour and have new tires on it by morning, no questions asked. New paint would be another story though. He'd also promised to wear gloves, avoid each valve as much as he could, and bag up all four tires so I could have them scanned for Kenzo Rees's fingertips first thing in the morning.

Mother fucker.

The evening air whipped around the open Jeep as we drove deeper into the woods. I looked over at Sunny, who hadn't moved, or uttered a single word since we'd left her truck on the side of the road. Her curls danced around her face, flickering strands of ebony against her lips. God, those lips. Her jaw was set, eyes narrowed, her thoughts racing. She wasn't sad, or scared, the woman was pissed.

And it pissed me off.

My hands squeezed around the steering wheel. I didn't want her to be fearless. I wanted her to be scared. Fear was a good thing. It kept people from making stupid, irrational decisions. I assumed Sunny didn't know her former boyfriend had been recently released from prison because she would have connected those dots like I had.

It was him. I knew it in my gut.

I just had to figure out the right time to tell her.

I was about to get that chance.

25

JAGG

*S*hadows from the almost-full moon danced along the rutted dirt road that led to Sunny's cabin. The air was warm, pungent with the smell of river water as we neared her drive. The winds had picked up. The environment was primed for wildfires.

I thought of Sunny making that drive daily, or at the very least, multiple times a week. Alone. Sunny truly lived "in the sticks." While her dad owned multiple housing tracts and apartment complexes in the surrounding towns, she chose to live out in the middle of nowhere. Away from people, society.

Away from danger.

There was no doubt Sunny was a loner. Her family was her dogs, her home, her sanctuary. Her safe place.

The thought didn't only concern me, it terrified me. I didn't like her so far away from civilization and first responders.

So far away from me.

We pulled into the driveway, the headlights bouncing off the trees until pooling onto the A-frame cabin.

My first indication that something was off was when I noticed the picnic table had been moved from where it sat earlier that morning. And then I saw the black spray paint splashed across it.

I looked at Sunny and watched the shock—the horror—slide over her face.

She flung herself out of the Jeep before I could stop.

"Sunny," I hollered, slamming the brakes and shoving the Jeep into park.

"God*dammit.*" I grabbed my gun and jumped out.

Sunny sprinted across the yard to her house, materializing a gun from her belt that I hadn't even noticed was there. She passed by the picnic table, spray painted with the word *witch, with barely a glance.*

I raised my own gun and scanned the woods as I jogged onto the front porch.

Shattered flower pots, shredded shrubbery, sliced screened windows, and graffiti covered the front of her freshly painted home.

Bitch.

Whore.

Slut.

Cunt.

A pentagram splashed the door with bright red paint.

"No," I grabbed her shirt and pulled her away from the door. She fought, but I got in first and swept the room.

"My dogs, Jagg! My dogs, where are they?" She blew past me, waving her gun like a damn magic wand. Tears shimmered through the wild panic in her eyes.

I grabbed her arm, pried the gun from her fingertips and set it on the windowsill.

"Where were they when you left?" I asked, simultaneously scanning the house that was absolutely trashed.

Pictures were shattered, the furniture was overturned and sliced to shreds, spray paint covered the walls, her comforter. The dishes and cookware in her kitchen lay in a million little pieces on the floor. Not that she probably cared much about that. *Witch,* in large, block letters, across the fireplace.

"I left them in the house." She frantically looked around. "I always leave them in the house when I'm gone." She jogged out the back door, onto the deck, which was in the same shape as the front.

"Athena!" Sunny cupped her hands and yelled, the panicked tone sending a chill up my spine. *"Theeeena! Tango! Max!"*

I spun on my heel at the pop of the screen door behind me, gun raised, finger over the trigger. Three furry, snarling masses shot like a cannon through the dark living room, laser focused on me.

"No!" Sunny lunged in front of my gun. "No! *Settle!* Settle!"

The speed of the charge slowed, the barking did not.

"Put your gun down, Jagg!"

I lowered my Glock as she dropped to her knees in front of me.

"Settle." She soothed, opening her arms to her dogs. "Settle, babies, *shhh,* calm. Come here. *Shhh."*

The dogs immediately relaxed, either remembering me, or sensing the sudden calmness in their master. Probably a little of both. The barking slowed to whimpers as she stroked them.

"That's it. *Shhh.* Good babies." Her voice cracked, followed by a sniff.

My fucking heart broke. Her sanctuary—her family—had been violated.

Rage boiled up my system like acid.

Sunny surged off the floor, her eyes popping. "Brutus."

"Where is he?"

"By the river. I don't bring him up to the house until bedtime." She ran out the door. *"Come."*

I wasn't sure if the command was for me or the dogs, but I followed. There were immediate things that needed to be done in that house, like search for trace evidence, but at that moment, the most important thing to Sunny was her dogs—and shockingly, I cared, too.

We jogged down the trail, Sunny leading her pack while I hung back a few steps, double-gripping my gun, tuning my senses to the woods around us. The moonlight led the way, bright enough that we didn't need flashlights. A breeze blew at my back, a few withered leaves flittering down from the trees, sending me jumping at each one.

Sunny's pace quickened as the musty smell of the river grew closer. I could practically hear her heartbeat on the breeze.

The trail opened to rushing water and the sound of her feet pounding the river rocks. This time, I pushed to a sprint and pulled ahead of her. If something had happened to Brutus, I wanted to be the first to see it. I wanted to shield her as much as I could. I wanted to be there for her the moment her world shattered. My first zing of panic came when the dog didn't bark as we barreled down the river. I focused on the black silhouette in the cage.

Move.

Bark.

Do something, you idiot.

As I neared the cage, two silver eyes sparkled in the moonlight. Brutus stood, wide neck, thick chest, muscular legs, all in one piece. His eyes locked on mine as Sunny threw open the cage door. Relief washed over me. He was okay. I found my gaze drifting to his injured shoulder, hoping it was okay, too.

I blocked Athena, Max and Tango from getting any closer.

"Brutus baby, are you okay? It's okay. Settle, baby."

Sunny slowly reached out her palm and dropped to her knees in one fluid movement. "Good boy. Good baby."

The dog finally moved, backing up while keeping those electric eyes on me. I don't think I've ever seen hair darker than Sunny's, until seeing his. Brutus would be almost invisible in a pitch-black night.

The other dogs hung back, respecting the pit. Or fearing it, perhaps.

Once I was sure everything was okay, I stepped back and made the call to the station, where Tanya promised to have someone there within ten minutes. I took note of the time, then shoved my phone into my pocket.

Sunny pushed to a stance, waiting to exhale until she was fully upright. She turned to me, not with fear or anger in her eyes, but gratitude. Thankfulness. She had her babies. Her dogs were okay.

Her face softened and a soft smile crossed it.

In a time that anyone else would be riddled with panic, fear, or rage, Sunny Harper smiled. Her car had been keyed, her home destroyed, but in that moment, Sunny found the light. She found the one reason to be thankful and clung onto it with such grace and beauty.

I stepped forward, cupped her face in my hands and kissed her. Right there, under the moonlight, next to the rushing river, I kissed her. She went limp beneath me and kissed me back. Something that resembled butterflies filled my stomach, warm goosebumps prickling my skin.

Sunny.

An unfamiliar adrenaline flooded my veins as I wrapped my hand around the back of her head, fisting that beautiful black hair.

Mine.

Her hands found my stomach. Her fingers ran over my abs, and just when I thought she was going to lift my T-shirt, she pulled away and looked up at me.

Her green irises twinkled with heat under the moonlight.

"What was that for?" she whispered softly, blinking, her chest rising and falling heavily.

My mouth opened but nothing came out. I took a step back.

"I don't know," I whispered back, staring into her eyes.

I took another step, the warm night cooler than the heat bouncing between us.

She broke the stare first.

I forced myself to take another step back.

Holy. *Shit.*

26

JAGG

*M*oonlight shimmered off her hair as she nervously ran fingers through it, looking everywhere but my face. Unexpected? Uh, yeah, agreed. Although her expression had drawn a blank, the flush in her cheeks gave her away.

She felt it too.

Whatever the hell had just happened between us was mutual. I knew it in my bones.

A second passed as I debated a flurry of half-formed actions through my head. One, grabbing her, pulling her into my arms and kissing her again. Two, tearing off that stupid, plain white T-shirt that she somehow made sexy. And three, ripping off those teeny shorts and burying myself inside her. No panties, because in my dreams she didn't wear any. Ever. Along with these erotic thoughts, I felt the unprecedented desire to ask her if what had just happened was okay. Should I apologize? Had I gone too far? Was she going to turn me in for inappropriate behavior?

Fuck, was all I could think.

Fuck, fuck, fuck.

The world around me slowly began to register again. The rushing water, the evening breeze, the break-in at her house. I inhaled and broke the silence by getting back on track with the reason we were standing on the riverbank in the first place, a reason that somehow seemed less impactful than what just happened between us.

"You have no other dogs on your property, right?" I asked.

"Right." She replied quickly, thankful for the change of subject. Apparently I wasn't the only one thrown off. Good. That made me feel better.

"Okay, here's what's gonna happen now. We're going to go back up to the house and I want you to go directly into my Jeep. The police will be here soon. Don't enter the house, don't touch anything. Get in the Jeep and stay there. Do you understand?"

"Yes," she responded without a fight, much to my surprise. "But my dogs..."

I looked at the cages and opened my mouth—

"*No.* Jagg, I'm not leaving them down here. If you want to put them in the cages, I stay with them. Or, they come with me. Those are your two options."

There she was. That hot-headed, stubborn Sunny I knew. Damn it all to hell.

"Fine. They can come up too, but they don't go into the house either. Understand?"

"Yes."

"Will they stay with you? By your side? I repeat, they *cannot* go in the house."

"Yes. I promise." She grabbed a handful of leashes from a box hanging on the side of the cage. "I'll tie them up next to your Jeep, next to me."

"Are you sure because I don't want to have to deal with—"

"I *got* it." She snapped, squaring her shoulders.

"Okay." It was then that I realized that Sunny was more of a partner than a victim at that moment. I could count on her to do as I said, not fall apart, not cause extra strain and stress on a crime scene.

The respect, tripled.

The sexual attraction, ten-fold.

"Alright. Let's go."

I started down the riverbank but when I didn't hear steps behind me, I stopped and turned back. Sunny was staring at Brutus.

"What's wrong?"

She looked at me," I... ah..." then back at the pit. "I don't know what to do here."

"With what? What?" My patience dissolving.

"I don't let Brutus run with the pack. Like I said, he's a loose cannon, and if he attacked—"

"Game over."

She nodded. "Exactly. Not even Thena could hold her own against his weight and jaws, especially at her age. Although she'd put up a hell of a fight."

"I don't doubt that."

We stared at the mutt, his gaze locking on mine as it always seemed to when I was close.

"I'll take him." I said.

"You'll what?"

"I'll let you guys go ahead and we'll come up a minute later."

"I... *no.*"

"You think I can't hold my own against those jaws?"

"I have no doubt you can't."

"Well. Challenge accepted then." I focused on the dog, but didn't stretch out my hand. We were about to find out if two alpha males could make it up a hill together.

"No, Jagg, listen. It's not time to be all macho male. If anything happened…"

"Don't worry. I won't sue you."

"Gee, thanks, but that's not what I meant." She heaved out a breath. *"Fine."*

"Good." I handed her my gun. "Take this."

"I don't need it."

"Take it or this isn't happening. We left yours in the house. As long as you don't wield it like a damn sword this time, take it."

She rolled her eyes, then stuffed it into her waistband. "You'll have to be slower with Brutus. His shoulder wears quickly."

"We'll be fine. I'll be less than ten seconds behind you. If you see anyone, shoot. This is your land, your home, your dogs. Protect it."

Her eyes narrowed into steely strength. She nodded.

My heart kicked.

Fuck, this woman. That moment, something else, a foreign feeling, mixed with the pride I felt for her. Little did I know that feeling was going to turn my entire world upside down.

"Go." I said, despite all the things on the tip of my tongue. "Go."

She stepped past me, commanding Athena, Tango, and Max to follow. I scanned the woods ahead of her, wanting to be by her side but knowing she wouldn't leave Brutus alone. She had her gun and her guard dogs. She was going to make it up that hill.

I turned to Brutus, still standing in his cage and doing what he did best, staring into my goddamn soul.

"Okay. Brutus. My name is Max—actually, Jagg. Here's what's going to happen."

The dog slowly blinked, unimpressed.

"You're going to follow me up the hill, calmly, nicely, staying at least two feet away from my nuts and my jugular. In that order. Got it?"

He glanced at Sunny in the distance, then back at me.

"I might not have a mouth full of fangs but I've got some jujitsu moves that will wrap your balls around your thick-ass neck quicker than you can say the word neuter." I was selling myself to a *dog*. And what the hell was my obsession with balls?

I looked at Sunny's silhouette fading into the tree line.

"Alright, kid, it's go time." I unlocked the gate and pushed it open. "I don't know Sunny's commands, but... come. Follow. Whatever. Don't eat me."

I turned my back on him in a ridiculous act to prove my fearlessness, then started walking. After a few steps, I glanced back and almost jumped when I realized the thing was right on my heels. I hadn't even heard his paws against the rocks. The dog truly was like a phantom ghost.

We started up the hill, my head on a swivel, my focus ahead of me where Sunny was making her way up. My boot caught a root and I stumbled, causing a blow of pain through my back. I glanced back at Brutus, now three feet behind me, his head hanging low, a slight limp in his step.

I kept moving.

"Fight through it." I grit my teeth, addressing the dog as much as myself. "Fight through the pain."

I glanced back again. His limp was worse.

"We don't do pain, Brutus. Push it aside and keep

moving. Pain is for pussies. You're no pussy. I'm no pussy. Fight it."

I swear he snarled as he lifted his head, but I'll be damned if his pace didn't quicken. My lip curled up. I slowed, though, scanning the woods from side to side so he wouldn't think I was doing it for him. A few seconds later, he caught up and was by my side again.

"I've decided I'm going to call you Brute." I looked down at him.

"Why, you ask? Because two syllable names are for pussies, too. You're not a pussy. Max, Jagg, Brute. One syllable. Strong. Manly." We walked a moment. "Don't tell Sunny about that two syllable comment."

His limping had deepened and I had to fight from kneeling down to check him out, or hell, scooping him into my arms. There would be time for that later—the checking, not the scooping.

We crested the hill and stepped out of the woods, where Sunny was staring up at the word *CUNT* sprayed-painted across her back windows.

She glanced over her shoulder as we approached.

My damn heart broke at the pain in her eyes.

Together, we stood silent, gazing up at her vandalized home, four dogs at our feet.

"Who would do this?" She whispered in disbelief.

I chose my next words carefully. It was time.

"You said you left the dogs in the house, right? When you went to Gino's to pick up dinner, you left them inside your house?"

"Yes. I always leave them in when I go anywhere. Excluding Brutus, during the daytime only. Like I said, he stays in the cage and I bring him up before bed."

I let her comment linger, wondering if she'd come to the same conclusion I had.

She did. Smart woman.

"Oh my God."

I didn't say anything, wanting to hear it from her own mouth. Honestly, a part of me hoped she'd have a different conclusion, a different opinion. But I knew in my gut, there was only one. And it unnerved the hell out of me.

"The inside of my house was vandalized. My dogs would have attacked anyone who stepped foot past my front door." She gasped, looking back at the house, then to me, her eyes round with fear. "Jagg. At least one of my dogs knew whoever did this."

I looked at her, that knife in my gut twisting deeper.

I nodded.

"It's time to talk about your attack in Dallas, Sunny. It's time to tell me about your ex-boyfriend."

"Why?"

"Because Kenzo Rees was just released from prison."

27

JAGG

*T*he blood drained from Sunny's face leaving a pale, pasty white skin glowing against the darkness. Her expression confirmed that she wasn't aware that her former boyfriend-slash-woman beater had just been released from prison. The tremble in her body told me she was terrified.

The way I responded shook me to my core.

"Nothing is going to happen to you." I grabbed her shoulders, turned her fully to me. "You've got me. I won't let anyone hurt you again. Do you understand me? Nothing is going to happen to you. Nothing."

She stared at me, full shock freezing her face.

"When?" The single word came out in a breathy whisper.

"Eight days ago."

Her jaw dropped.

I nodded, letting her know I agreed with her racing thoughts. *Yes, it is a very real possibility that Kenzo Rees destroyed your home and was somehow involved in your attack.*

The ice-cold fear in her eyes sent a blast of that protectiveness through me. I squeezed her shoulders.

"He won't hurt you again, Sunny." I pulled her to me. "He won't hurt you again."

She fell into my body. I wrapped my arms around her. The sweet coconut smell of her hair enveloped me. I kissed her forehead and looked up at her house, that blast turning into a raging fire. It was as if everything else faded into the background and only one thing remained. One target in my sights.

Kenzo Fucking Rees.

Blue and red lights bounced off the trees, the sound of tires against gravel following seconds later. A chorus of growls came next.

"*Stay.*" Sunny pushed away from me and kneeled down next to the dogs.

I looked at my watch. It had been exactly six minutes since I'd called dispatch.

"Go straight to my Jeep and take the dogs. Don't move, don't go anywhere. Let me handle this."

Sunny nodded, gripping the leashes, her face still white as a sheet.

I cupped her cheeks. "Let *me* handle this. This is *my* job."

She nodded.

"Don't say anything to Darby. Just get up the hill, to the Jeep."

She looked at the headlights cutting through the yard. "How do you know it's Darby?"

"Just guessin'. Straight to the Jeep. Not a word, got it?"

She stared at the patrol car.

"Okay? Sunny. You okay?"

"Yes."

"Say it again."

She inhaled deeply. "Yes. I'm okay," a little stronger this time.

"Good. Let's go."

I slid my hand into hers and guided her up the hill while she muttered commands to her dogs the entire way. We split off at the driveway. I met Darby in front of his patrol car. He wore a Grateful Dead T-shirt, wrinkled, and damp with sweat. Khaki shorts and flip flops completed the incapable look. He shut his car door, gaping at the graffiti on the house.

"Damn."

"Nice response time."

"I was nearby."

"I'll bet you were."

His gaze flickered to mine, then quickly back at the house.

"You find Kenzo Rees yet?"

His eyebrows raised. "It hasn't been an hour since you called me and told me he was out of jail."

"Hour's a long time."

"... No, sir. I haven't found him yet."

A moment ticked by.

"Did she get a look at who did this?" He glanced at Sunny climbing into my Jeep, her army obediently at the tires.

"No. Pulled up to it like this."

"Do you know when it happened?" He pulled his notebook from his pocket.

"Within the last hour."

"Was she home?"

"No. She'd gone into town to pick up dinner at Gino's."

He kept his gaze on the graffiti, and off of me. A full ten

seconds passed as I gave him the opportunity to tell me why he'd been following me. When he didn't, I decided to go along with it and see how he played the thing out. Make him sweat, then get the full confession because my gut was telling me there was a lot more to the story than Darby's interest in shadowing me. I also decided to keep my theory that Sunny knew her intruder to myself. I needed to flush out that theory before my spy ran back and told Colson. I didn't trust Darby, plain and simple. Besides, at the moment, I had one focus and one focus only—to turn Sunny's house upside down, find a trace of Kenzo Rees, and get the mother fucker locked back up. Barney Fife's clandestine mission could wait.

"She was gone about thirty minutes total. Last night, her truck was keyed at Frank's. Cowboy Billy admitted to it. She didn't call it in." I paused and looked at him, knowing he'd been there. He stared ahead. Kid would break. Took time. I continued, "I want you to go back to the bar and see if anyone knows or heard about who could have done this tonight. Check the security cameras. Go to Cowboy Billy's house and verify his whereabouts tonight. Do the same for the Aldridge whores. Tell them both I'll see them in the morning."

My gut told me this had nothing to do with Cowboy Billy and everything to do with Kenzo Rees, but it would be nice to officially check off that box.

"Before that, though," I continued, "I want this entire house photographed, inside and out. We need to get it swiped for fingerprints and check for trace evidence. Need to write this down, Darby?"

He flipped open his notepad. "Did Miss Harper call you?"

I cocked my head, staring bullets into the side of his

face. It was the first time I wondered if he was recording the damn thing.

"She got a flat tire on the way home from Gino's. I gave her a ride."

Sweat beaded on his forehead. He swiped it away. He didn't ask anything else about it, which I noted. A normal person would ask how I knew that, or where the truck was exactly, or if the tires had been slashed, perhaps. Or what the heck I was doing on the road behind her. Not Darby. And I wasn't going to share the information about the valves being tampered with. Not with him.

"Did you see her truck on your way in?" I asked.

"No." He shook his head.

Phoenix had already towed it. The man worked fast. Not that I was surprised.

Darby nodded to the front door. "Busted locks?"

"Nothing obvious." We stepped onto the porch. "Could have used a pick or credit card. The cabin is old and isn't exactly Fort Knox."

He kneeled down at the front door, searching for footprints.

"I'll get someone out here from the state crime scene unit, but it will be awhile."

"I've got nothing better to do."

I didn't doubt that. "Stay out of the way and pay attention. You might learn a thing or two."

Darby nodded, a moment passing before he looked up at me and finally addressed the elephant in the room. "Do you think Rees did this?"

"That's what we need to find out, kid. Get at it. We've got a long night ahead of us."

. . .

Three hours, and jack *shit* later, I watched Darby back down the driveway, on his way to Frank's to interview and pull security footage. Aside from confirming that a switchblade had been used to pop the bullshit apparatus Sunny considered a lock, the crime scene techs found nothing. The doorknob was covered in prints, presumably Sunny's, but regardless, they lifted what they could on the off chance Rees was stupid enough not to wear gloves. There were no prints on the edges of the furniture—where he would have had to handle it in order to toss it over—or on the dishes he'd shattered, or appliances he'd tossed around. No empty spray paint cans in the trash, cigarette butts on the grounds, nothing. Between Sunny's hair and her dog's, it was impossible to search for any of his. My Jeep had trampled any tire tracks, so that was no use either. And of course, Sunny didn't have security cameras, something I was going to have remedied immediately by my own two hands. Fort Knox would have nothing on Sunny's place by the time I got done with it.

As suspected, Darby didn't even ask how the intruder could have gotten past her dogs—a huge clue in narrowing the pool of suspects and finding the fucker. Although I already knew it was Rees. I knew it in my gut. Revenge, the oldest motive in the book, and the hardest to shake.

Darby still had a lot to learn, including sharpening his instincts. It was something I knew took time, but because we didn't have time, I was going to personally, and secretly, handle everything I asked of the kid, because, well, if you want something done right, you've got to do it yourself.

As Darby's headlights faded into the darkness, Sunny released the dogs and climbed out of my Jeep, vibrating with as much anxious energy as her mutts.

"What did you find? Anything? Prints? Anything? What—"

"No. Nothing."

Her shoulders slumped. "There's got to be something."

"There's *always* something. I promise you, I'll find it."

"It's him. I know it. He called me a cunt that night in Dallas, over and over. I remember." She looked at me, eyes wide with adrenaline. "You think it's him, too, don't you?"

"Yes. I do."

She nodded. "Good. We agree, then. It is. I know it." She looked back at the wreckage of her once beautiful home. "Oh my God, where to begin..."

"Tomorrow. We'll start on it tomorrow."

She slowly nodded. A moment slid by before she turned to me. "Thank you," she said softly. "Thank you, Jagg. Thank you for everything."

"I'm not leaving you tonight, Sunny."

"No. Please. It's fine. You've done enough."

I turned fully to her. "I said, I'm not leaving you tonight."

"Jagger... we can't..." she whispered and looked down.

I lifted her chin. "I am not leaving you, Sunny."

She stared at me, pain, fear, desire, confusion, all wrapped up in shimmering green eyes that told me she'd had enough for the evening.

"But the furniture is shredded, the couches, the bed... everything..."

"I've got a place we can go."

She blinked.

"You're not staying here tonight. We're not staying here."

She looked at the house, then back at me. "What about the dogs?"

"I'll take care of it. I'll take care of them, too."

"You hate dogs."

"Now where would you get an idea like that?"

"Call it woman's instinct."

"Does that instinct tell you that I'm going to take care of you tonight? Of everything?"

"... Yes."

"Good."

"Jagg, I—"

"I'll take care of it. That's it."

She bit her lip, looked back at her house, then finally nodded. "Okay. Let me pack a bag."

"You have three minutes."

JAGG

*G*ritting my teeth, I adjusted—for the tenth time—in the driver's seat, trying to put some space between me and the cold, wet, snotty nose blasting stinking, hot breath against my neck. My shirt collar was already damp with drool. Dog hair spun around the interior of the Jeep, one landing on my lip every few seconds.

Damn Max. The dog's head was practically resting on my shoulder. In the backseat next to him sat Athena and Tango, quivering messes of excitement to be riding in a vehicle with no top.

To my right, Sunny, with ninety-pounds of Brute on her lap.

We were a freaking motley crew of beasts driving down a narrow dirt road in the middle of the night. Every bump in the road was followed by squeaking leather, an announcement of the punctures their nails were surely making in my leather seats.

I started to itch. Literally—itch.

"You okay?" Sunny's face poked out from behind Brute, who's expression resembled something like constipation.

"Yep. Dandy." I spat out a clump of hair.

"I'll clean your Jeep tonight."

"Don't worry about it." Dog smell didn't go away.

"Where are we going, anyway?" She asked.

"Don't worry about it."

I took a slow and steady left turn onto an even narrower dirt road. After another five minutes, the woods opened up to acres of manicured fields in front of soaring mountains in the distance. Although it was almost midnight, the woods were flooded with light as bright as twilight.

The full moon was almost complete.

I stopped at a newly constructed iron gate just off the road and jumped out.

"No." I snapped to the dogs, although Sunny was already controlling them.

After being denied on the first passcode entry, I tried another, then other, until finally hitting the jackpot. I shook my head as I walked back to my truck. After locking the fence behind us, we drove slowly through the field. Fireflies sparked above the silver grass. I picked up the gravel road and took a curve around the mountain, where I spotted him.

Mounted on horseback, my brother skillfully weaved back and forth behind his head of cattle, herding them across the field. A cattle dog was on his left, one on the right, and one barking feverishly at a calf who'd broken loose.

I accelerated, rolling to a stop along the fence.

"Stay here. Might be a minute. I'll be back." I pulled a stack of mail from the console, then jumped out and jogged over to the chaos.

"Take Duke," Ryder said, nodding to the horse next to him as he slid off his own. No "well, hey there," or, "good evening," or "good timing, bro." Pleasantries and small talk weren't my brother's thing.

I jumped on Duke, a gorgeous tan quarter horse with a white mane.

Wearing his usual cowboy hat, T-shirt, faded jeans and cowboy boots, Ryder jogged over to the calf, stealthy, arms out, reminding me of the skilled soldiers I used to run with. Although my brother was no soldier. Not in the traditional sense anyway.

While I kept the herd moving, Ryder approached the calf from the side as the thing bucked and leapt with excitement, showing no interest in rejoining the herd. The cattle dogs were going ape shit. The cows were starting to veer off the path I knew had taken my brother hours to establish.

"Get it done, bro," I hollered out.

This was met with the middle finger.

I watched my brother and the calf dance, Ryder nimble on his toes, waiting for the right time to strike. The calf was a five-hundred pound cluster fuck of stomps and snorts.

Patience, my brother had that in spades. It was one of the biggest differences between us.

Finally, Ryder pulled the rope from his belt, slung the loop in the air as smooth as a true American cowboy and snagged the calf by the neck on the first throw. I pulled Duke's bridle and met him at the edge of the herd.

"I'll tie her up," he said. "Then you take her to the field and close her in. Make sure to close the gate."

"Which field?"

"Skywalker."

"You got it."

Twenty minutes and a bucket of sweat later, the calf was locked in the pen. Duke and I met Ryder back at the herd.

I tossed him a water I'd snagged from the mini fridge in the stable. He sipped, slid his into the saddle bag while I chugged mine.

"When'd you change the passcode?" I asked, wiping the sweat from my brow.

"Yesterday."

"Thanks for the heads up."

A grunt.

"Figured you chose something more creative than our football numbers."

Ryder pulled the bridle and changed course, his focus singularly on his herd. I did the same and took a second to look my younger brother over.

Dark circles faded a pair of aqua-blue eyes that once sparkled with energy. His face, his neck and arms were a deep bronze from spending all his time outdoors. His brown hair was unkempt and shaggy, curling just below his ears. He'd trimmed his beard since I'd seen him last, but if I had to guess, it wasn't in an attempt to lose the uni-bomber appearance. It was to let his face breath during this insane heatwave blasting through the mountains. New scrapes and cuts streaked his arms, probably from mending fences all day.

Ryder was a full-time rancher, full-time hermit, and full-time avoider of any human contact. Ten years in federal prison tended to have that effect on people. I'd done my best when he'd gotten out. Visited every day, tried to drag him to the bar, suggested a vacation, all I could think to do. No dice. Ryder was nothing like the brother I once knew. Not that I would know, really, because he never spoke about his time behind bars or about what had put him there in the first place.

Never spoke about much anymore.

I pulled the bound stack of mail from the waistband of my pants.

"Mail."

He caught it midair, stuffed it into his saddle bag without so much of a glance. Understandable, considering all the guy got was solicitations. Two days after Ryder had been released, he'd purchased a massive ranch on the outskirts of town, confirming my suspicion that he'd amassed a hefty savings account before his life was turned upside down. The guy never left his ranch. Every Friday morning, I made the twenty country-mile drive to deliver his mail, although he knew just as much as I did that it was to check on him more than anything else. That night, though, I had another reason to visit.

"Missed you at Lieutenant Seagrave's funeral."

"I was busy."

I glanced around the fields. "I can see that."

A second slid past.

"I need a favor."

"You? Or the woman you've got sitting in your Jeep?"

My brow cocked. Never underestimate the eye of my brother.

"Do you still own that cabin on the lake?"

"Yeah."

"I need it."

"You got it."

Relief washed over me. Ryder had changed so much in the last year, I wasn't sure if the best friend I used to have would be willing to help me out. Good to know loyalty never dies.

"Is this on the books, or off?" He asked.

"Off. Don't tell anyone we're there."

A quick nod. "Keys are in the house, blue keychain. There's no running water or electricity on right now. I can call tomorrow—"

"No. I don't want anyone knowing we're there. There's

something else, though. I need to leave her dogs with you for a while if that's alright? You still have the kennels?"

He nodded. "How many?"

"Four."

"There's room."

"You don't mind?"

"No. They need to be separated?"

"Nope. Just fed and watered. And brushed, and bathed, and neutered..."

He grinned. "You never did like dogs. She must be something."

"That about sums it up. Sure you don't mind?"

"I said I don't mind."

"Thanks."

"Put them in the pens at the east of the property, under the trees. I'll get the food and water."

"I owe you."

"I've got a spare generator in the garage if you think you'll need it in the cabin. If not, candles and bug spray are in the storage room. Food, water in the pantry. Books in the library—"

"Books?"

"Yeah, you know, printed work consisting of glued pages bound by a cover?"

I smirked. Loyalty wasn't the only thing that didn't die.

"I didn't know you read."

He didn't say anything. I wondered if reading was how this "new man" passed the lonely time on the ranch.

He continued, "Get fresh sheets. There's some in the laundry room. Extra guns in the cabinet. Condoms in the drawer."

Wasn't sure if I'd need the last two items, but better safe than sorry.

"Thanks, bro." I maneuvered behind a wandering cow.

"Go. Dump the dogs and be on your way. I've got this."

"I don't mind to stay."

"I know. She might."

I glanced back at the Jeep.

"Go," he said again. "I've almost got them in. Not my first rodeo."

29

JAGG

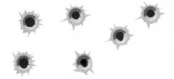

*I*t was one in the morning by the time we drove down the long, winding dirt road that led to the fishing cabin on the lake that Ryder had purchased a few weeks after getting released from prison. It would be my first time there. Guy wasn't big on invitations.

A canopy of trees blocked the moonlight from the two dirt ruts my bother considered a driveway. The underbrush was gnarly and thick, scratching the sides of my Jeep. I was looking for a clearing ahead when the road abruptly stopped and my headlights bounced off the edge of an iron gate, barely noticeable through the bushes. I stopped the Jeep and looked in my rearview. Guess backing out was the only option.

"We're here... I think."

Still no cabin in view, I turned off the engine, grabbed Sunny's bag from the back and got out while Sunny did the same. It had been easier than expected to convince Sunny to leave her dogs with Ryder, making me realize exactly how much she feared her former boyfriend. And how much she was beginning to trust me. Emphasis on beginning.

The moldy smell of lakeshore was pungent in the humid night air, the roar of the cicadas deafening as I flipped the latch and pushed open the black gate. Sunny swatted a mosquito from her face as I pushed aside an aggressive swath of blooming forsythia branches that was blocking our way.

I froze. Sunny did too.

A small log cabin blended seamlessly into the trees around it as if sprouted from the earth itself. The house would be invisible to anyone not looking for it. It was perfect for what we needed. A wraparound porch encircled the front, with untrimmed bushes invading the small space. The log walls had been stained dark. The roof replaced with clay tiles, giving it an island bungalow feel. I didn't realize why until we stepped inside. Moonlight pooled onto the floor through sweeping windows that overlooked a bridged walkway that led to a dock on stilts above the lake. The reflection of the almost-full moon stretched across the black water, fading into the waves lazily pushing along the shoreline. A million stars twinkled in a sky that somehow looked miles larger than it had an hour earlier. It was an unbelievable view. An oasis.

A secret oasis on the lake.

The strong sent of freshly chopped lumber told me Ryder was actively renovating the space.

"My God," Sunny whispered behind me, gaping at the view. "It's beautiful."

I went to flick the light switch then remembered we had no electricity. A step ahead of me, Sunny pulled a candle and lighter from the bag and seconds later, the dancing flame bounced off a room the size of a shed. A luxury shed, but it was tiny nonetheless. Gleaming hardwood floors matched the logged walls and beams running across the ceiling. A half-wall separated the space from the kitchen, which consisted of a counter, sink, gas stovetop, a duo of coolers in place of a fridge and a battery-powered coffee pot. On the far side of the room was a small door which I assumed was the bathroom, that I prayed included a shower.

Two folding chairs sat in front of the window.

That was it. The bungalow was spotless, though, thank God for that. Ryder always was a clean freak.

Both our gazes landed on the bare, single bed against the wall. Not a king-size. Not a queen. A double.

A *double.*

One fucking foot larger than a twin.

Her gaze flickered to mine, then quickly to anywhere else but the bed, as mine did the same.

"I'll sleep on the deck," I said.

"No." She shot to her feet, the unlit candle she was holding tumbling to the ground. "You're here because of me. You're doing this for me. *I* will sleep on the deck."

"Listen. I might not be mister charming—" I stopped when she snorted a laugh. "But I've got better manners than that. You'll take the bed. This conversation is over."

"I'll be fine." She lit the candle and set it on the fireplace mantel.

"No you won't. No amount of bug spray is going to keep those mosquitos from swarming you all night, so unless you want to become some science experiment for whatever undiscovered deadly virus they're currently carrying, you'll stay inside. I'm not going to say it again."

She released a small huff reminding me of a little girl throwing a temper tantrum, but said nothing else about it as she kneeled down and began unpacking more candles. I won that battle.

Slowly, candles were lit and a warm glow blanketed the room. Thankfully, a steady breeze from the lake blew in through the windows, making the temperature bearable. Almost comfortable, even. It wouldn't keep up though. The moment the air stilled, the small space would feel like a sauna, not to mention when the sun came up. This had me wondering what kind of clothes Sunny had packed. Then, picturing her in a bikini, and then, a slinky negligee. I watched her for a moment, moving around the room, strategically placing the candles. Making herself useful. She had an elegance, a grace to her that I never noticed before.

"Sorry there's no electricity and water."

"It's no big deal." She smiled, the candle in her hand reflecting in her eyes. "It's like a little adventure. As long as you've got bug spray I'm good. And coffee..." Horror froze her expression. "Dear *God* in Heaven, tell me you got instant coffee?"

Note to self the woman liked—*needed*—her morning coffee. We were definitely alike there. I pulled a can from the bag that was looped around my shoulder.

She blew out an exhale. "I love you."

"That didn't take long."

She rolled her eyes.

"Are you hungry?"

She paused, shrugged. "Not really."

Sunny had tossed her "perfect" Farro salad from Gino's in the trash at her house, confirming she'd been at that flat tire for a good handful of hours before I'd shown up.

I walked over to the cooler and flipped it open.

Hamburger patties, hot dogs, salsa, a bag of chips, carton of eggs, bacon, a half-case of beer, a liter of whiskey—and a box of Twinkies. An *entire* box.

Our options were protein, protein, protein, more protein, and a diabetic coma.

And booze.

Booze for the win.

I bypassed the hard stuff and grabbed an ice-cold beer. I needed to keep my wits about me.

"Beer?" I asked?

She turned away from the fireplace mantel, now glittering with candles. She'd pulled her hair into a knot on the top of her head, a few curls cascading around her face. The light danced across a long, slender porcelain neck with just a sheen of sweat. I'd never seen her with her hair up before, away from that face. I licked my lips.

The woman was *stunning*. It was almost as if I were seeing her for the first time.

"What did you say?" She asked, her head tilting to the side.

I blinked, momentarily forgetting the question I'd just asked her.

"Beer. I asked. Would you like a beer?"

"That actually sounds great."

I grabbed another one and popped the tops on the edge of the counter. She was next to the cooler when I looked up.

"Thank you." Sunny took the beer from my hand, tipped it up and sipped, then rested the cool glass to her chest. She closed her eyes and released an exhale.

My dick pulsed in my jeans.

She turned away and stepped into the main room and stared out to the water. She fell silent. I knew she needed a second. A bit of time to digest the realization that the man who once tried to kill her was quite possibly stalking her now. My heart broke as I stared at her, her elegant silhouette washed in moonlight.

"My cabin is just around that bend, you know," she finally said. "I recognize it."

I already knew that. I looked at the outline of the mountain in the distance where a few twinkling lights speckled the top, on a clearing above a cliff known as Devil's Cove, the location for the annual Moon Magic Festival.

"I live less than a half mile from Devil's Cove. There's been so much traffic lately. Trucks, trailers, everyone setting up for the festival. The dogs have been so hyped up."

"It's supposed to be the biggest one in years."

"It's the full moon."

We both shifted our gaze to the moon.

Yes, something was in the air. We both could feel it.

A few moments passed in silence before Sunny slid open the back door and stepped onto the deck. The moonlight caught her stygian hair, outlining her body like a mystical nymph beaconing to me. Like one of her dogs, I crossed the room, following her. The woman had a way of hypnotizing people, creatures, into hanging onto her every word, following her every move. It was like a special power.

And my kryptonite, apparently.

30

JAGG

I followed Sunny down the bridgeway to the small dock at the end. Aside from the beam of moonlight down the center, the lake was as black as ink. The air had cooled, a million stars twinkling in a cloudless night.

I watched her walk, slowly, her gaze fixed straight ahead.

I would have followed her into the water if she jumped. The woman was like a drug to me. More than pills or booze had ever been.

"It's beautiful out here."

"Yes," I said, my eyes locked on hers as I met her at the end.

The water danced below us, lapping against the posts.

She sipped her beer, then rested her elbows on the railing and looked into the water below. Sadness, the weight of the evening, washed over her face.

"I'm sorry about your house," I said.

"I'll repaint. The furniture can be replaced. I'll fix it back." *Like I always do.* She didn't say it, but I knew that's what she was thinking.

"I'll help."

She looked at me. "I don't understand why you're helping me so much."

I looked away. I knew exactly why I was helping her so much, but God help me, I didn't want to acknowledge it. I wasn't ready. Wasn't fucking ready.

"Do you go this far with every one of your cases?" Her question was loaded.

"You think me kissing you was part of the investigation?"

She shrugged, looked out to the water.

I lightly grabbed her chin and turned her face to me.

"Would that have bothered you?" Loaded, perhaps more so than hers.

"Why don't you just call me a liar about the third person so everyone can move on? Say that I killed the pastor's son in self-defense and close the case. The town can move on..." Her eyes locked on mine, her chin lifted. "And so can you."

"Listen, Sunny, I kissed you because I wanted to. Was it smart? No. Do I regret it? No. But I want to make one thing clear. I wasn't manipulating you and don't insinuate otherwise. If you don't want me to do it again, tell me. Tell me." My fingertips tightened around her chin. "Tell me not to do it again."

She stared at me, searching my face with wide eyes.

"Tell me," I ground my teeth. "Goddammit tell me not to touch you again."

"I'm not worth it, Jagg," she whispered.

Colson's warning about losing my job echoed through my head, followed by Haddix's warning about her powers of seduction to get what she wanted. The way I seemed to stumble since the day I met her. Yet while I should have been reminding myself that my past experiences told me that *no* woman was worth it, I found myself wondering why she thought she wasn't.

Sunny had more emotional baggage than she led on.

Possibly more than I did.

She jerked her chin away, her face suddenly hard like granite.

"I want to cut the bullshit, Jagg. I want to know what you know about my attack, exactly what you know about Kenzo and why you've taken it upon yourself to be my bodyguard."

"I will once you tell me about what happened in Dallas. It's time to talk, Sunny. Tell me about Kenzo Rees."

A minute ticked by before, finally, she began.

"We started dating in high school. Kenzo was popular, the definition of a jock. Football, basketball, baseball, he did it all. A popular guy. A bit of a bad boy. We went through the trials and tribulations of any young relationship, on and off, on and off. ... Looking back, he showed signs of aggression back then."

"Like what?"

"He started getting in regular fistfights, things like that. Started falling behind in school and sports. I remember he was really possessive of me. Abnormally so. I also remember he was really hard on his family dog... it's silly that I remember that, but I do. He was mean to the poor thing. It was like he was showing his dominance to something that couldn't fight back. I broke up with him over it once. Should've never gone back." She looked down.

"Don't dwell on that. That kind of thinking is unproductive."

"I know. You're right." She took a deep breath. "Anyway, after graduation, we went to the same college and that's when things started to really change."

"What changed?"

"Kenzo."

"How?"

"Drugs. He started hanging out with the wrong crowd, so to speak. I tried to pull him away from them which just made him cling tighter it seemed. I did everything I could, but he just got... darker and darker. It happened so slowly that I kept thinking it was just a phase. It wasn't. We started drifting. I almost broke up with him two days before it happened." Her hand trembled as she took a shallow sip of beer. I didn't ask any questions. Just listened.

"It was my twenty-first birthday. We were at a party at one of my friend's houses. His 'new' friends showed up and it started to get wild. He left the party for a bit. I know now that it was to get high."

Kid had taken enough coke to kill a horse, but she didn't need to know that I knew that from reading the report.

"When he came back, he accused someone of flirting with me. He pushed the guy around but was eventually pulled off of him. I remember the feeling I got then, the churning in my stomach. Looking back, it was almost as if my body was telling me to run. That things were about to get really bad. I told him I wanted to go home. We caught a ride to my townhouse, where the argument got worse." She looked down and began picking at a thread on her shorts. "I'll never forget the moment he hit me. The *shock* of it. I was stunned. It was funny, I didn't feel the pain or blood running down my chin. I was just so shocked. I didn't fight back." She looked at me, self-disgust evident on her face. "Can you believe that?"

"I can. Most women who experience their first physical abuse don't fight back, for the very reason you just said. The shock of it."

"I remember the look in his eyes after he hit me. It was

like they flared, bulged out of his head. Like he liked it. Like a switch was flipped... and that *look* made me more scared than the fact that he'd hit me."

Blood lust. My grip around my beer tightened as my pulse skyrocketed. I squeezed my other hand into a fist and curled my toes in an effort to dispel the rage bubbling up. This wasn't about me, or the fact that I wanted nothing more than to sprint to my car, find the fucker and slam his head into the fender until the thing cracked open.

This was about her.

I needed to be there for *her*.

"After that, everything became a blur. He punched me, over and over. I remember hearing the pop as my nose broke. I tried to run then, I guess finally getting some balls. And that's when he pushed me into the bathroom and bounced my head off the mirror, and then..."

She went silent, still, every muscle in her body tense.

Fuck. I was not good with this shit. I didn't know what to do or what to say to make it better. I unfisted my hand and placed it over hers. Although she was doing exactly what I'd asked of her, I wanted her to stop. I didn't want to be the cause of any more of her pain.

"Sunny. It's okay. You don't have to—"

She pull her hand away and sniffed. "No. I want to get this done. And then I don't ever want to talk about it again."

"Sunny—"

"And then he ripped out my fucking hair, Jagg. Chunk after chunk, he pinned my head against the sink and started ripping it out screaming racist bullshit and telling me he always hated my kinky hair. I remember that pain more than anything else. The *fire* when the strands ripped from my head. The throbbing pain after. It felt like someone had poured acid on my scalp and lit a match. That's when I started crying. He hadn't only beaten me but was defiling me as well. Ripping out my dignity. Then, he threw me down the stairs like I was worth nothing more than a rag doll. I fucking *hate him,* Jagg. I fucking hate him." She turned to me, eyes wild, her jaw twitching with rage. "Do you know where he is?"

"I'm working on it. *I'm* working on it, Sunny."

I knew that look. I'd seen it many times in my career. The need for justice and revenge, the beginning of a vigilante mission that, more often than not, landed the person in the morgue.

That would not be Sunny.

I would not allow it.

"He was at my house tonight. He is the one who destroyed my home. It makes too much sense with the dogs. He knew Athena and she's the leader of the pack. The other dogs would follow her reaction to anyone. Hell, he was there when I adopted Athena from the vet two years before it happened." She blew out a breath and shook her head. "My question is, why? Why come after me again?"

"Revenge. He blames you for everything."

"How do you know this?"

I told her about the letters Rees had written in prison that the warden had told me about. The letters that never got sent. She wasn't surprised.

"Why not just kill me, then? Wait for me to get home and put a bullet in my head? Or, hell, burn the house down? Kill the dogs?"

"Fear. He gets off on it. He got out of jail, wants you to know it. Wants you to know that he knows where you live and is watching you. Wants you to know he's coming for you. He wants you to fear him."

"But how does this play into my attack at the park? We

obviously know Kenzo wasn't my attacker, because that was the pastor's son. And it's safe to assume he wasn't the third person who ran up and saved my life and killed Griggs. Because why would he do that?"

"Truth?"

"Truth."

"I don't know, Sunny. But it's no coincidence Rees was released from jail only a few days before you were attacked in the park. He's been watching you, following you, knew you were at the park. He's involved in your attack, there's no question in my mind."

I just had to find the damn connection between the pastor's son and mother fucker. It was there, I felt in my gut.

"I know you think this all links with the Lieutenant's death. Why?"

"You know that blue, four-door sedan you noticed parked across the street the night of your attack? It was also on camera at Lieutenant Seagrave's shooting."

"At Mystic Maven's Art Shop."

"Right. Whoever stole the Cedonia scrolls is the answer to all this."

"The person people call the Black Bandit."

"Where'd you hear that?"

She flashed me a *seriously* look. "You can't step foot anywhere in this town without hearing the name."

Fucking gossip. "The question is..." I ran my hand over my chin. "Is Kenzo Rees the Black Bandit."

A moment slid by as we watched the water.

"Do you think the Black Bandit killed Seagrave?"

"Only one way to find out."

"And when you find him?"

"He'll wish he'd never been born."

She popped her fist against the dock railing. "I *hate* him.

I want to find him. Now. I want to end all this." She looked at me, a new kind of fire blazing over those eyes now. "He's got another thing coming, Jagger."

"He does. But not by you." I set down my beer and turned fully toward her. "You've got to promise me you're not going to try to handle him yourself."

She looked away.

"*Sunny.*" I jerked her chin toward me with a bit too much force, but I couldn't help it. A sudden desperation clawed at me. "Guys like him don't back down. It's a pride thing. You push him too hard, he'll kill you, Sunny. He'll call it revenge, but it will be to prove to himself that he's better than you are. I want you to look at me in my eyes, right now, and tell me you're not going to be a sitting duck for him. Be the strong woman I know you are. Avoid the fight."

She stared at me a moment, her face loaded with emotions.

"Back to my original question, Jagg. Cut the bullshit. I want to know why you're doing all this for me. Tell me. Tell me why—"

"You want to cut the bullshit, Sunny? Fine. *Fine.* Here's the truth. It's taking every ounce of my energy not to throw you on the dock right now, rip that stupid T-shirt from your body, destroy those tiny-ass shorts that I'd never let another man see you in again, lick the sweat from your neck and fuck you until you can't remember your own name. How's that, Sunny? How's that for cutting the bullshit? Truth is, you've hypnotized me, stolen every one of my goddamn thoughts, my common-fucking-sense since the second I laid eyes on you. Truth? I fucking hate it. Got that? I hate you can do that to me. Why? Because I don't trust you. Is that what you wanted to hear?"

I lifted her chin and crushed my lips against hers. When

she opened her mouth, when she accepted me, I devoured her under the moonlight.

Under her spell.

31

JAGG

Streaks of dawn were just beginning to crest the mountains as I jogged up the station steps, ignoring the knot in my back, getting worse by the minute. I inwardly laughed at myself—not in a funny way, in a *you're-so-damn-pathetic way*. During my door kicking days, I considered it a good night to sleep anywhere that didn't involve scorpions the size of your fist. It's amazing how quickly you can go soft... in more ways than one.

Damn Sunny Harper.

I hadn't slept a wink since sharing a beer with Sunny.

Most men wouldn't after a kiss like that. It had taken every bit of restraint I had not to make a move. Sunny shared the darkest moments of her life with me. She'd opened up, which I knew was no easy feat. And while I knew there were many more layers to strip, it was a start. Something deep in me cared, felt proud. It meant something to me that she trusted me when I knew, in Sunny's book, men were as valued as her kitchen.

It had been sexual restraint due to respect. Something, I

can say with complete confidence, I'd never experienced before.

Me, on the other hand?

Uneasy—that's the best word I can think to describe the way I was feeling. While Sunny seemed to be making strides against her distrust in men, I was questioning my own sanity. Every decision I was making, every instinct, every damn flutter in my stomach. One month ago, I would have never kissed a woman involved in one of my cases, smoking hot or not. Hell, I never kissed a woman without the end goal being the condom rolling off. But I'd kissed Sunny— twice now—because something in me couldn't hold back. My thoughts, my actions, just seemed to be cloudy since I'd met the woman, and I couldn't fight the feeling I was missing something.

Colson was questioning me, the town was questioning me, and I'll be damned if I hadn't started questioning myself. I *never* did that. Maybe the pain in my body was finally wearing me down, but I felt like I was slipping.

Something was just *different.*

After the tears and *that kiss,* Sunny and I stayed on the deck for another hour, sipping our drinks, watching the moon rise while listening to the waves crash against the lakeshore. It was a comfortable silence, one that I'd never experienced with another woman. Then, after demanding that I call Ryder and check on her dogs, Sunny made her way back to the bungalow. I'd followed, as was becoming suit and certainly nothing I was proud of. There'd been no argument about who got the bed. Sunny was all cashed out on arguing and emotions.

I'd given her space to use the bathroom, waiting out on the deck for what seemed like an exceptional amount of time to use a six-by-six space that didn't have running water.

I finally gave up and settled onto the deck and closed my eyes. Two minutes later, Sunny exited the bathroom, indicating that she'd been waiting until I stopped pacing and laid down to come out. Was Sunny modest?

Through the open windows, I listened to the bed creak and groan as she climbed into it. I waited until I was sure she'd fallen asleep before sneaking back inside where I grabbed another beer, perched myself on the windowsill and watched her sleep.

This was a first for me. I'd never watched a woman sleep in my life.

Sometime after the third or fourth beer, the restraint I'd been practicing all night tripled, with me having to dig my toes into the floor to keep from crawling into bed with her.

I listened to the sounds of the night, the nocturnal creatures skittering about, the heat bugs screaming, the waves crashing outside. The breeze rustling through the trees. No white noise of the local news running on loop in the background, no cell phone beeping at me, emails dinging, cars racing by, no buzz of an old window air conditioning unit. Nothing.

I realized how long it had been since I'd heard nothing.

My mind had drifted to thoughts of what it would be like to take a vacation with Sunny. The beach, a tropical jungle, maybe even a trek through the desert. Anywhere that involved a string bikini. I thought of all the places I wanted to take her, to watch her smile, relax, let that guard down. To take away an ounce of that weight she carried on her shoulders. I wondered what it would be like to date her, be her man.

And her to be mine.

Mine.

As I watched the steady rise and fall of her chest and the

moonlight sparkle off her hair, something ignited inside me, so intense, so passionately, that I'd made a decision right then and there.

I'd take a bullet for Sunny Harper. She'd been through enough. I'd take a damn bullet for her.

With that unsettling realization, my thoughts shifted to the case, which carried me through the rest of the night spent laying on the floor next to her.

After the nocturnals had gone quiet and the birds began their early morning rounds, I'd gotten up, brushed my teeth using a bottle of water, changed clothes, and waited until I heard the hum of a truck making its way down the driveway. At exactly five a.m.—because a Steele brother was never late —Phoenix delivered Sunny's truck with four, gleaming new tires. No news of Rees's whereabouts—yet. I transferred her old tires to my Jeep, driven Phoenix back to his place, then made my way into town, leaving Sunny asleep in bed, with a note and an extra gun by her side.

The station was quiet that morning, people still sleeping off the energy they'd used from gossiping about my outburst at Donny's the night before, and the break-in at the "witch's" house.

I beelined it to the break room for a cup of coffee.

Three cups and one bag of beef jerky later, the sun had risen along with the noise in the station.

I'd just left another message for Briana Morgan, the elusive art investigator, when a pair of knuckles rapped at my door, followed by Colson stepping inside, phone to his ear. After barking a few orders, he clicked it off and slid it back into his pocket.

He sank into the seat, combing his fingers through his hair.

I nodded to the Styrofoam cup on my desk. "Coffee?"

"Baileys?"

"Not yet."

He grinned. "No thanks. I've had a gallon already. Coffee, not Bailey's."

"Of course. Busy morning?"

"We've got every volunteer officer and firefighter on standby tonight. The Moon Magic Festival is officially double what it was last year. Hotels are sold out within a sixty mile radius. The campgrounds," he laughed a humorless laugh, "we've already responded to five calls between the four of them." He shook his head. "I gotta tell you, something's in the air, man."

I couldn't agree more.

"Listen…" He said. "About Donny's last night—"

"I get it. I shouldn't have gone off like that. I know. You don't need to say it."

Colson nodded. "Okay, good. That's your second public outburst in two days, Frank's, now Donny's. I'm gonna choose to believe it's not gonna happen again, 'cause, Jagg, I'm not putting my neck out for you anymore, got it? I've got too much to lose right now. A wife, a baby. I need my job. I've got too much to lose."

"Clear."

"Okay." He waved his hand in the air to dismiss that topic. "So, I came by to tell you two things. One, the switchblade found at the Slaying in the Park belongs to Julian Griggs. His prints are all over it. No one else's."

"He had it pulled then, when he attacked her."

Colson nodded. "Seems plausible."

"What else?"

"Jessica just forwarded me the toxicology report on him. Seems like the ol' pastor's kid had been dancing with the devil, so to speak."

"How so?"

"Kid was as high as a kite on coke."

Cocaine.

My spine straightened. "You sure? Coke?"

"Feel free to question Jessica, but I wouldn't. Woman did me a favor by pushing this through so quickly."

My head started to spin. Julian Griggs had been high on coke when he attacked Sunny—and who was once known as the biggest coke dealer in the area? Kenzo Rees. There was my connection. Loose, but it was there. Somewhere along the line, Julian Griggs had crossed over to the dark side, right into the clutches of Rees. I just had to figure out a way to confirm this connection, and more importantly, why Griggs attacked Rees's ex-girlfriend.

"What did the Pastor have to say about it?"

"Shocked. Fell to his knees and began praying."

"So he was surprised? There were no signs of drug abuse or violent behavior before this?"

Colson shook his head. "Not that he was ready to admit, anyway."

"You know The Collars are notorious coke dealers." I opted to leave Kenzo Rees's name out specifically to avoid another Sunny showdown with the Lieutenant.

Colson nodded. "Checking into them is on my to-do list today. The gang is notoriously tight lipped, though. Hell, the only reason I know what I know about them is because I arrested a new recruit a few years ago. Kid has just been released from prison, broke into someone's house without realizing the house belonged to a retired colonel in the army. Kid walked right into the barrel of a shotgun where he pissed himself and obediently waited until the cops showed up. He had a new tattoo on his arm, still red around the edges. The symbol for The Collars."

"What did you get out of him?"

"Not much. Said breaking into the house had been a mistake. Said he got addresses mixed up or some shit. Basically, I was able to put together that new Collar members go through an initiation phase, kinda like a fraternity. Somehow, his B&E was related. But like I said, he didn't divulge this information. I slapped him with a few charges, destruction of private property, public intox."

I felt like I'd just taken a shot of espresso. I was practically buzzing with this new information. Had Sunny's attack been Julian Griggs' initiation to The Collars? Rees ordered him to do it? It made sense. It added up. I just had to figure out how to prove it.

"Anything back from ballistics? Either the casings from Seagrave's scene or Sunny's?"

"Not yet. I've got Darby following up. So..." Colson said, moving on from that conversation. "How are you doing? Heard about the break-in at Harper's." His gaze sharpened.

"What did you hear exactly?"

"That the crime scene unit found jack shit."

"Then you heard correctly."

"You think it's connected to her attack?"

"Among other things, yeah."

"Could be a pissed-off church goer. One of Pastor Griggs' most beloved followers."

"I wouldn't think 'bitch, whore, slut, and cunt are part of his beloved followers' vocabulary."

"Givers on Sundays, sinners on Mondays. You know how it goes."

I nodded, wrapped my hand around the back of my neck. When did my neck start hurting?

"I drove by her place on my way home last night hoping to catch you guys. See if you needed anything. You and

Darby had already left... and Miss Harper wasn't there either."

I met his gaze, my eyes narrowing to slits.

He continued. "You don't happen to know where she went off to, do you?"

We stared at each other for a minute, the tension in the room going from casual to heated in under two seconds flat.

"She went to a friend's house," I lied. "I advised her it wasn't safe to stay in her cabin until we found who vandalized it."

"A friend's house? *Bullshit.*" He slapped his palm against my desk. "This woman has got you under her fucking spell, Jagger. You're letting it happen. You're thinking with your dick instead of your brain, and I gotta tell ya, I've never seen you like this before. You've lost your focus. You've got too many balls in the air. You're missing the obvious. I don't like it. I don't like *her.* Maybe you should pay a bit more attention to the writing on her cabin walls. Because right now, witch—"

I surged to my feet. "You say another fucking word, Colson—"

He surged to his and cut me off. "You know the Chief's got me hunting down those fucking rednecks you roughed up at Frank's last night? Wants me to convince them to press charges. To come in and give formal statements about your use of excessive force. What the fuck were you thinking? McCord aims to have your badge pulled by the end of the week. People here are noticing. You're becoming a joke, do you understand that? A lovestruck puppy. Sunny Harper is going to make you lose the only thing you've got in your life. I hope to fuck she's worth it."

My desk phone buzzed.

Again, three, four...

I slammed down the button. *"What?"*

"There's a Miss Harper here to see you, Detective."

Colson barked a laugh and threw his hands in the air.

"Tell her I'll be right out." I clicked off. "This conversation is over, Colson. Get out of my office."

"I'll see you in the fucking unemployment line, kid."

With that final warning, the door slammed closed.

32

JAGG

I pushed out the front doors of the station and into the blazing sun. It was only eleven in the morning and the humidity was already stifling.

Damn this heat.

Damn Colson.

Squinting from the rays of a sun that seemed to be sitting on the treetops, my gaze landed on the show-stop-ping beauty leaning against the fender of a red and white Chevy Cheyenne. One dog in the back, one in the front. Her arms were crossed over her chest. Sexiest damn thing I'd ever seen.

A small smile spread as our eyes locked.

My stomach dipped, and for the first time, I realized why they called that butterflies.

God, the woman was gorgeous. Tunnel-visioned, I crossed the scorching asphalt, sweat beginning to bead on my forehead, although I was sure it wasn't because of the heat.

She was wearing those damn cut-off jean shorts again and a plain V-neck T-shirt that, despite its loose fit, draped over her curves like satin. A worn pair of Birkenstocks, that should have been trashed a year ago, covered her feet. Why did it turn me on that she was wearing them to their last days? She'd pulled her hair back, a river of curls down her spine, and a faded purple baseball cap that read "Life is Good," on her head.

The T-shirt shirt rippled in the breeze, just enough to hint at an erect nipple that I knew wasn't because she was cold.

Was she thinking about the kiss, too?

I had to fight from swiping the sweat on my brow as I walked up. I didn't want her to know the effect she had on me, although, based on the widening grin, she did.

Max paced back and forth in the bed, tail wagging, a long red tongue panting against the heat. I swear the dog actually smiled when he saw me. Brute was in the passenger seat, a flash of silver irises sparkling in the sun. The pit eyed me as I walked up, but the single flick of his long, thin tail gave him away. I figured that was the closest thing to a smile I was going to get from that one. Again, progress.

It was a weird moment. Very... relationshipy. My woman, my dogs, coming to see me at work.

In my dreams, anyway.

"What a motley crew."

With a mind of its own, my hand drifted forward and tucked a wayward strand of curls behind her ear. It took everything I had not to lean down and kiss those lips, sparkling with a gloss, that I knew from last night, was sweet and minty. I noticed she'd put on some makeup and I couldn't help but wonder if it was for me. I hoped so.

"Thank you for the new tires. How much do I owe you?"

"Twenty-thousand dollars."

She grinned. "Wow. Five thousand a piece, huh?"

"Yep. Those rims aren't silver, they're platinum. Only the best for you and those stinky mutts."

"Well, in that case, put it on my tab, then."

"It's racking up." I grinned, flicked another strand of her hair. A flirty move. I was a damn high school kid again.

She cocked her head and met my grin. "All that instant coffee, beef jerky and processed meat from the cooler really ticking up the total, huh?"

"It's all organic."

She laughed. "You wouldn't know organic food if it slapped you in the face."

"This coming from the Takeout Queen herself."

"You've really gripped onto that, haven't you?"

"I want you to stay put, Sunny. No take out, or curbside whatever. How many times do I have to tell you? Stay out of public until this thing blows over."

She stepped forward, closing the inches between us, a flash of desire in those eyes.

I licked my lips.

"I want you to be less demanding," she responded, in a low, sultry whisper. "More asking, less telling." Her finger ran down my chest, blazing a trail of heat under her fingertip.

If the front door to the station hadn't opened, I would have kissed her right there.

We both cleared our throats and took a step back as Tanya sauntered to her car, eyeing us the entire way.

"Did you get my note?" I asked.

"I did and it only took two cups of coffee to decipher the script. You write like a kindergartner."

"I was doing long division in kindergarten."

"But not learning dangling participles, apparently."

"No, what's that? A type of ambiguous grammatical

construct where a misplaced modifier could be misinterpreted as a word other than the one intended? No, I have no idea what a dangling participle is."

"Show off. Anyway, yes, I got the note that read, 'Gun on counter. No home. Ryder expecting you. Ten o'clock, station.'"

"Never claimed to be a poet. You didn't go to your house, did you?"

"Technically, no."

My eyes narrowed. "I don't do technically."

"I drove by."

"You didn't stop? Didn't go in?"

"No. I *promise.*"

"Good girl. Anything new?"

"No, thank God. Just total destruction with the word 'witch' gleaming in the sunlight. At least it hadn't been burned down."

"We'll get it fixed. One step at a time, beginning with Max." I ruffled the dog's ears, fur disbanding into the sunlight. "Is he ready for his big morning of sniffing Julian Griggs' clothes and hopefully leading us to his killer, otherwise known as this mystery third person from your attack?"

"He sure is. We've already practiced a bit."

"Good. How was Ryder when you stopped by?"

"I don't know."

"What do you mean? He wasn't there?"

"He was there. On a horse in the field."

"He didn't greet you?"

"No, and that's fine. I drove to the cages, played with the dogs for a while, leashed-up Max and Brutus and then was on my way."

I made a mental note to chide him for not at least saying hi. And when did I become big on manners?

"Alright, well, get in. We'll drive around to the back." I opened the passenger door to her truck.

"Uhhh, *no,* you get in."

"No ma'am. I've been wanting to drive this beauty since I first laid eyes on her."

"She might disappoint you, Jagg." Sunny pinned me with a gaze anything but playful, and oh, so loaded.

"Doubt it." I winked. "Get in."

Brute eyed me as I settled behind the shiny, wood steering wheel, then took his place between us. I fired up the engine, a smooth, low rumble and promptly popped a boner in my pants. She was definitely no disappointment.

"Max good?" I glanced in the rearview.

Sunny rolled her eyes.

Of course the genius dog was good. I slowly started through the parking lot and rounded the brick building.

"Why did Brute come along for the ride?"

"He has a vet appointment after this. Might get some steroids for his shoulder. Seems to be bothering him more lately."

I glanced down at the dog, who bowed his head, embarrassed by the conversation. I understood that feeling.

"So," Sunny said, glancing over her shoulder at Max. "How do you want to do this?"

My head cleared, my dick relaxed.

"We'll take him to the picnic tables in the back. I'll bring Griggs' clothes outside and let him do his sniffing thing."

"Sounds easy enough."

Easy enough. Ha. I thought of Colson and how many prying eyes would be watching us from the window.

My next thought surprisingly was... *fucking bring it.*

With Sunny and crew waiting patiently outside, I checked Griggs' clothes out of evidence, logging the time, date, and purpose, and leaving a blood sample and rights to my unborn child—just joking—then, I met Sunny and Max under a shaded, grassy area behind the station. While Max was a bouncing ball of energy, Brute stayed at Sunny's feet, never leaving her heels. I stepped back and watched Sunny do her thing with Max. The process was interesting. She'd hidden several bags among the trees and shrubbery, each holding various articles of clothing. The bag holding Griggs' clothes was placed next to a budding sapling. Sunny guided Max to each bag muttering commands, giving him a treat each time they reached Griggs' bag. After a few rounds of this, Brute tired and meandered over to me where he sat an inch from my boot. I kneeled down, scratched behind his ears, then gently rubbed his shoulder. A massage always helped me. The dog practically melted into my touch as we watched our master work.

"Whose clothes are in the other bags?" I asked.

"Mine in one, one of your T-shirt's in another, a leash from your brother's kennel in one, and the rest filled with clothes I got from the thrift store on the way in. Lots of different scents."

"Good to know the Jagger brothers are covered."

"We'll see," she winked.

I watched her work, fascinated. "Explain this to me."

"It's really not that complicated. Just takes a lot of repetition. Once Max sniffs Griggs' clothes, I take him around to each bag. When we come to Griggs', I praise him and cue him to bark, then take him to the next bag where I don't. And on and on we go, until he eventually goes directly to Griggs' bag after sniffing something with Griggs' scent. He should be able to pick up every person's scent on the clothes and will bark when he comes into contact with that person." She glanced over her shoulder. "Hopefully, the third person from my attack."

If that person came within ten feet of Sunny, he or she was as good as exposed—and very likely soon to be missing a pair of balls. It was a long shot, but at that moment, I was willing to try anything to get a break in a case that seemed to get fuzzier with every passing hour. On that note...

"Hey, what do you think about Max hanging out with me today?" I asked. "While you take Brute to the vet?"

"No. And it's Brutus."

"Not between me and him."

"Oh you guys are BFFs now?" She looked over her shoulder.

"Only women use the term BFFs."

She looked back at Max who was still moving from bag to bag, having a blast with this new, little game.

"I don't know... Why do you want to 'hang out' with him?"

Max suddenly barked, leaping and pawing at the bag of clothes holding Griggs'.

"That's why. I'll be making a lot of rounds today, following up on leads regarding your case and Seagrave's. Who knows what this guy could pick up."

"Meaning, you think you might cross paths with the third person?"

"Never know." I nodded to the beast. "Max could be my partner for the day. You know, like Turner and Hooch."

"You're old."

"Thanks."

She looked back and forth between me and her son.

"I don't know... He's a lot to handle, Jagg."

"Comes with the name." I winked, this earning me another eye roll. "Sunny, how's he going to help at my brother's house? What's there? Let the old boy stretch his legs. Learn how to be a real man for a day."

"Because the fact that his owner is a woman makes him less of a man?"

"Yes."

She fisted her hands on her hips. "That's chauvinistic."

"No, it's the truth. Men can do things women can't, and vice versa. There's certain things men have that women don't, and vice versa. For example..." I unbuttoned my pants and started with the zipper—

She slapped a hand over her eyes. "Okay, okay, *geez,* point taken."

I chuckled, zipped up.

She uncovered her eyes. "*Fine.* You can take Max for the day and teach him how to pee standing up."

"He'll be in good hands."

"I hope so. Just remember, he'll listen to you, Jagg. Just be firm. Strong. You know, like a woman."

"If you were any other woman than yourself, I'd take that as an insult."

"Thanks... I think."

Max jogged over, his entire backside shaking with his tail.

"See? He's excited. We'll have fun, do man things."

"Like go to the titty bar? Chop some wood, maybe compare ball size after a burping contest?"

"We'll throw lunch in there, too."

"Well, that's something I can help with." She reached into the bed of her truck and lifted a cooler from the bungalow. "Lunch."

My brow furrowed with shock and confusion as to what was happening.

"What?"

"Lunch."

"... Why?"

"Are you familiar with how lunch works?"

"Not someone bringing it to me."

"Well, brace yourself then, because this one involves a blanket and three courses."

My jaw literally slacked as my gaze shifted back and forth from the cooler to the woman holding it. Never, in my life, had anyone brought me lunch.

"I mean, why?" I asked like a blubbering Neanderthal.

She swallowed deeply, quickly, as if nerves had suddenly flustered her. "It's just my way to say thank you. For the tires, for helping take care of my dogs, for finding me a place to stay... Dammit, for *taking care of me*."

The words, so uncomfortable to her, so consuming to me.

"Okay, then. Lunch sounds good. Where should we sit?"

She smiled, appreciating the drop of emotions. I liked

that she wasn't all emotional. It was becoming one of my favorite things about her.

"There's a really pretty tree just outside of City Park with a small clearing under it. Just about a football field from here."

I grinned and bit my tongue at her use of measurement.

"Grab the blanket and leashes and help Brutus. Please."

My grin widened at her obvious effort. She'd put thought into not only the lunch, but her behavior.

Damn the woman.

After replacing Griggs' clothes, we took off across the grass, a picnic basket, blanket, and two dogs in tow.

Five minutes later, Sunny spread the blanket under the one and only Voodoo Tree. That's right—the tree that had once been encased in candles and voodoo dolls was now the site of our picnic.

Irony.

Or was it?

The tree looked completely different in the light of day. Almost magical, like a tree you'd see in Lord of the Rings, with long, outstretched branches covered in lush, green leaves. A blue and black butterfly flittered from branch to branch next to us.

I smoothed out the blanket while Sunny tied the dogs to the tree trunk and gave them water from a portable bowl thing.

Handy.

"Sit." This to me, not the dogs. I did, feeling immediate release in my back as I took the weight off my feet. A breeze swept past, cooler under the thick shade of the tree. Surrounded by woods, we were out of view of the public, and I wondered if that was done on purpose. Was she embarrassed to be seen with me? Or did she know I was being chastised for being seen with her? My gut told me the latter.

Sunny settled next to me and slapped my hand away as I attempted to help unpack the cooler.

I took a sip of the tea she'd given me—sweetened to perfection.

"Bon Appetit."

I looked down at the bowl she'd placed in front of me. "Uh... what's this?"

"Gino's Flaming Farro salad. Try it and you'll know why it's worth leaving your house for."

I glanced at Brute, who snorted. I grinned. She didn't.

I took another sip, reminding myself I'd eaten *way* worse overseas. With an inward thump on the chest, I dug in while she did the same with her matching weird-ass salad. I'll be a son of bitch if the thing wasn't delicious. Cool, flavorful, light but filling.

"Eh?"

"Not bad." I mumbled around another bite.

Sunny broke her breadstick in half and tossed the pieces to the dogs. No gluten. I did the same.

"Do you come here a lot?" I asked.

"The park, yes. Well I used to, anyway. Sometimes after a jog I'd walk through the woods and this tree catches my eye every time."

"You're not the only one." I told her about the shrine, the candles, the voodoo dolls that had covered its branches earlier that week.

"Well," she shrugged as if were no big deal. "Good someone's putting its beauty to use."

"You think using this tree as a Wiccan shrine is putting it to good use?"

"Why not?"

"Because it's vandalism."

She laughed—*at me.* "Oh give me a break. Sounds like someone was peacefully honoring whatever God they choose to."

"Exactly."

"You're kind of narrow-minded, you know that?"

Not lately, I thought. My decisions had been anything but on-track.

"Well, that stuff doesn't fly in this town. Especially that it was constructed the day of Lieutenant Seagrave's funeral."

"You think the tree's somehow connected?"

I surprised myself at my hesitation. "I'm trying to figure that out. That, and what feels like a million different things."

"Well, forget it all for now. Eat. Relax. Enjoy the beauty and shade this marvelous voodoo-tree gives us."

A few moments passed while we ate, watching the squirrels, birds, swatting at the flies.

"Can I ask you something?"

"Sure." She said.

"What were you like in high school?"

"You mean, why did I date someone like Kenzo?"

"Yeah."

"Well," she sipped her tea. "You know how I told you that Kenzo was popular, athletic, a jock?"

"Yeah."

"I was none of the above."

"I refuse to believe that the daughter of a millionaire didn't have a group of friends."

She looked at me, cocked her head. "Do you think money makes people more valuable?"

"Without question."

"That's a very short-sided, cynical way to look at the world."

"You obviously came from a lot of it."

"You didn't."

"No."

When I didn't expand on the subject, she pried. "What were *you* like in high school?"

I almost laughed at the image that popped into my head.

"I was a tall, gangly, unathletic kid with braces, who also happened to be the captain of the math club *and* the science club. I was smart, which made me a nerd. And I was dirt poor which made me a target."

"Ah," she said. "Therefore shaping your jaded view about money."

"Absolutely. I won't deny that. Money makes life easier, opens doors, creates opportunities I never had."

"I think you opened your own door, Jagg. Your reputation from your time in the Navy precedes you. Rumors are you were the youngest officer to ever be named chief. And after you moved back here, you were promoted to detective after only a year working the beat. People fear you. Respect you... Why did you leave?"

"Leave what?" I knew what she was asking, and God help me I didn't want to get into it.

"Leave the military. The teams."

I swallowed deeply, wiped my mouth. "I was deemed unfit for active duty."

"Why?"

I shifted. "My back. Got hurt during a mission that went sideways. Suicide vest, ten feet from me."

She stilled, blinked. "I'm so sorry."

"Don't be. I'm one of many, trust me on that. And in most cases, in better shape."

"I don't consider carrying a bottle of pills in your pocket every day, better shape."

I looked down at my pocket, where, sure enough, the outline of a pill bottle was visible. "How did you notice that?"

"You've had a bottle in your pocket every time I've seen you."

I blinked, realizing she was right. Every morning when I left the house, I slid the bottle into my pocket... how many days had I'd done this? When was the last day I hadn't taken a pain pill?

I glanced up, into her eyes, those green irises saying so much with nothing at all.

She looked away.

Message received.

Like a fucking nuclear bomb.

She must've read me like a book because she switched conversations. She'd made her point, and she was ready to move on.

"Try the cheese," she said.

I attempted to focus on my salad while my thoughts raced trying to nail down a day that I hadn't taken a pain pill.

"The cheese, I said, try it. The little white balls. They're marinated mozzarella balls. Best I've ever had. ... And drop it."

Drop it. *Drop it, Jagg, drop it.*

I shoved a white ball in my mouth—amazing.

She smiled. I smiled back.

"Alright, Dr. Drew Pinsky, let's get back to you. So you weren't popular, despite the rich dad."

She laughed. "In spite of it, you could say. My father kept his thumb on me. Restrictions, curfews. He'd check my phone, my social media. I was told what to do and how to do it. Every day of my life. I had zero independence."

"And you rebelled?"

"I'd say that's an understatement."

"Is that why you live the way you do?"

"And what way is that?"

"Minimally and ridiculously independently."

"Yes. I didn't want his money. I still don't." She looked at me thoughtfully. "Funny, huh? While you look at money as a gift, I look at it as a restriction full of strings attached."

"How did you rebel?"

"The tattoo was first."

My brows shot up along with a tingle straight to the tip of my dick. "You have a tattoo?'

She grinned, widely this time. "Yes."

"Where?"

"Nowhere you'll ever see."

"Challenge accepted."

She grinned.

"How else did you rebel?"

"Well, I started running with the wrong crowd."

"Kenzo?"

"Yes. Remember I told you he was a bit of a bad boy. It was gradual, really. Parties here and there, after football games. That turned into drinking. Other things."

"Drugs?"

"A bit. Yes."

"Do you still do drugs?"

"Not since my twenty-first birthday."

"The night it happened."

Her face darkened as she nodded.

"Did you do coke?" I asked. It was none of my business, but for some reason I cared. I had to know.

"No. Pot only. I tried mushrooms once. An experience I would never wish on any type A personality."

"Oh I've seen it, trust me."

"I bet. Anyway, my biggest rebellion, really, was leaving Dallas and moving here last year."

"Why did you leave your dad?"

She shifted, another flicker of nerves on her face. She didn't like talking about her dad.

"Tell me, Sunny."

"After my mom died, my father... went off the deep end. First time I noticed his grief was going beyond 'normal,' was when he started having whiskey with his morning eggs." She wrinkled her nose. *"Whiskey.* Can you imagine?"

I shrugged. "Worse things to have with breakfast."

She laughed. "Guess so. Anyway, after his second DUI, I talked to him, told him I was worried. We got in a big fight, nothing changed. It got worse. I started staying the night at his house some. Some nights he wouldn't come home at all. I started watching him. Even followed him a few times."

"Why?"

"Why what?"

"Why not just let him be? People grieve their own way."

"That's not how I work, Jagg. I'll never forget how he and mom took care of me after the incident with Kenzo. Despite our strained relationship, my father was there for me. He was the one who took me to the doctor, to the police. Sat by my side. My mom took care of me physically, but my father took care of all the legal crap. He even amped up the home security system to make me feel safe."

"The number one thing dads are supposed to do is protect their daughters."

Her soft smile was brief, quickly fading.

"But it's so obvious there's tension between you two. So, again, why did you leave Dallas? All the years later?"

She chewed on her lower lip. "I just needed to let things

go. My father just wasn't my father anymore. I left."

"Something happened."

She looked down.

"Tell me, Sunny." I wasn't proud of the desperation in my tone. I wanted to know. I wanted to know everything about her.

"He just started making bad decisions, that's all." She shook her head, wanting to end the conversation. "He'll find his way. Redemption is real."

Her neck was flushed almost purple, a physical reaction to her discomfort in the conversation.

So I backed off. The woman had made me a picnic and I wasn't going to ruin it for her by pressing any more than I already had. I made a mental note to follow up on the conversation at a more appropriate time.

"So," she said. "Those are my Daddy issues. Now, tell me why you've ignored two of your mom's calls that I've noticed."

My brows raised. "Wow. Note to self about your eagle eyes."

"I consider it a gift. I can read a cell phone from a mile away."

"A man's worst nightmare."

"Stop deflecting."

I sighed. "Fine. My mom and I aren't close either. And that's that."

"Why?"

I shoved a forkful of salad in my mouth. "Because she's a whore, Sunny."

"Holy *smokes,* Jagger."

"Too much?"

"Yes."

"Well, it's true."

"Is it? *Really?*"

"My mom walked out on me, my brother and my dad when I was fifteen, for another man. Found out later, she'd had two affairs before that. Three dudes. My mom took the oath of marriage with my dad and then banged three dudes while she was married to him."

"Okay... that's tough. I'll give you that. How long since you two have talked?"

"Since the day I came home to my dad surrounded by empty beer cans and a note telling him she was gone."

"And she's tried to contact you?"

"Countless times. Not at first, really. But when she found out I enlisted she started reaching out. More so over the last few years, especially." I ripped a handful of grass from the ground and ran the blades through my fingers. "She even sent me something, a gift I guess, a few weeks ago."

"What?"

"Nothing. It's stupid."

"What did she send you?"

"Oh, this stupid compass. A replica of an old one. When I was a little boy, I was always wandering the woods around our house. A regular Boy Scout. Shocking, huh? Anyway, on my eighth birthday, she gave me a gold compass with my initials on the front. On the back, an etching of our house with an arrow pointing to it. Under that, the words, home is where the heart is."

"Wow. That's sweet... and thoughtful."

I snorted. "It's funny. I actually got mad at her when she gave it to me because we were so poor, I didn't want her spending so much money on me."

"Did you use it?"

"Took it everywhere with me. Worked like a charm."

"Where is it now?"

"Lost it. My last mission in Iraq. The suicide bomber that fucked up my life."

"You carried it with you all those years?"

"Guess so. Like I said, it was quality."

"And *quality* was the only reason you held onto it?"

"Yes."

"And she recently sent you a replica. How did she know you lost it?"

"Hell if I know. Dad mighta told her. They talked from time to time. Before he died."

"Where is it?"

"I pawned it." The words came out sharper than intended. "The day of Seagrave's funeral. It paid my electric bill. That was nice."

A few moments passed and I could feel her disapproval. Or maybe it was my own.

"Jagger... How old are you?"

"Thirty-nine."

"So you haven't talked to your mom in twenty-four years?"

"No ma'am."

"Jagger. Call her. Call her back."

"No." I cut her a warning glare. "Don't."

"I'm just saying twenty-four years of a grudge has a way of shaping someone."

"Do you have a psychology degree I'm unaware of?"

"Are you aware that your issues with your mom has totally shaped your personality? Especially with women?"

I tossed the blades of grass and picked up my drink, wishing it was from Long Island.

"It's obvious you don't trust women, or hell, even respect them as you should. One might even call you a bit sexist, Detective."

"Now just a minute there, Susan D. Anthony. That's one hell of a label."

"It's B."

"What?"

"B. Susan B. Anthony."

"Oh."

"When was your last real relationship?"

"Define real."

"Real, as in, I am her boyfriend, and she is my girlfriend, and we are committed and even thinking about moving into together."

"Never."

"And the last time you took a woman on a real date? Flowers, food that doesn't involve processed meat, opened the car door for her, walked her to her door after, the works?"

"Never."

"When was the last time you bought a woman a real gift?"

I opened my mouth to respond, but she cut me off.

"Something that didn't involve batteries or cuffs. Something thoughtful."

The compass flashed through my head. Truth was, I'd never given anyone a gift that thoughtful. And I didn't like where this conversation was going.

"I'm just saying," she continued. "Don't write off every woman because of a few mistakes your mom made. Ones, that, if I had to guess, she's spent the last two decades regretting."

"My mom does *not* regret leaving my dad."

"Maybe not, but based on her repeated calls and gifts, she regrets the dissolution of her relationship with her sons. Family's important, no matter how flawed they are. There's a loyalty with blood. It's not something to discount." She turned fully to me. "Do you write off everyone for their mistakes?"

"Depends on the severity of the mistake."

"Would you write me off?"

I leaned back on my elbows, suddenly needing distance for some reason. My eyes locked on hers, assessing, assessing, assessing.

"I don't know, Sunny. I don't know. To be honest, I feel like I don't know much of anything lately."

She stared at me a moment, then shifted her gaze to the treetops, swaying in the warm breeze.

A heavy moment passed between us.

"Well, on that note, lets finish up." She said. "I should get Brutus to his appointment."

Fifteen minutes later, Max hopped into the back of my Jeep while Sunny helped Brute into the cab.

"Let me know what the vet says." I said, and shockingly meant it.

"I will."

"You good?" I asked, my eyes squinting.

A quick dip of her chin.

"About everything?"

Her eyes dropped to my lips, then trailed back up to my eyes. "I hope so," she whispered.

"Me, too," I whispered back. I inched closer and trailed my fingertip along her jawline. "Take Brute to the vet, then straight back to the bungalow. I've got an appointment but will be home in a bit."

Home.

She nodded, her face tilting into my hand.

"I'm sorry I can't spend the day with you."

"It's okay. I'd rather you be doing exactly what you're doing."

And then what? I wondered. What was going to happen when I caught Kenzo Rees, this crazy mystery third person, and closed the case on Sunny Harper? We'd just go our separate ways? The feeling had my gut clenching.

Her gaze flickered over my shoulder to the station. I followed it, zeroing in on the silhouettes behind the windows. One tall and as thick as an ox, and one short, pudgy and balding. Colson and Chief McCord. No doubt about it. Tanya was peeping out of the other, if I had to guess, gearing up to spread the gossip of my romantic picnic in the park.

Fuckers... and Miss Fucker. ...See? Already started respecting women more.

I turned back to Sunny, shifting my stance to block her view from them. Or, theirs from hers, rather, in an overprotective move I hadn't felt for any woman other than Sunny.

Fuck the warnings, fuck the small-minded gossipers, the stares at my back.

A hot breeze swept through her hair. I wrapped my hand around the back of her head, pulled her to me and kissed her.

Passionately.

Possessively.

Right there in front of *everyone*. Marking my territory —*mine*—and daring anyone in that fucking building to challenge me on it.

Was Sunny Harper worth it?

I sure as fuck hoped so, because I just jumped in with both feet.

JAGG

"*A*fternoon, Detective."

Darby stepped into the room, dark circles under puffy, bloodshot eyes. His hair, usually combed perfectly to the side, was mussed, his skin pale. I observed him closely as he crossed the office, tapping a yellow manila folder against the palm of his hand. He looked tired, but he was definitely amped up about something.

After officially removing my balls and staking claim on Sunny Harper by laying a minute-long kiss on her in front of the entire station, I assumed his drop-in had something to do with that. Or, perhaps he was going to come clean about following me. Or maybe he was going to ask about the German Shepherd that was currently tied to my Jeep, snoozing in the shade.

I was wrong on all three counts.

He didn't sit. "I've got a few things for you."

"Make it quick. I've got a meeting in ten minutes."

"With who?"

"What've you got for me, Darby?"

"I just got off the phone with Wesley Cross about the

ballistics analysis. The gun used to kill Julian Griggs, the pastor's son, was a Glock nineteen."

I could practically feel the relief washing over me. "So, not Sunny's, then. Sunny's gun was a Ruger."

"Right."

I continued, verbalizing my thoughts so that the rookie would have something to my benefit to spread around the office that afternoon. "So, according to Wesley's analysis, this verifies Sunny Harper's story that she did not kill Julian Griggs. That someone else did. Most likely this mystery third person from her attack, which also verifies she wasn't lying about that. What about the casings from the Cedonia Scroll heist and Seagrave's murder?"

"Also shot with a Glock nineteen."

My eyebrows popped up. Sunny was all but cleared from both shootings.

"Does he know if the same Glock was used at both scenes?" If so, that information would be huge and suggest the same person had killed both Griggs and Seagrave.

"He hasn't confirmed that yet."

I rubbed my chin. The gun that shot both Seagrave and Griggs was still at large, whether it was the same gun, or different was to be determined. Either way, the news was huge for Sunny.

"Okay, what else do you have?"

Darby stepped forward. "I think I found a link..." The rookie's voice lowered, for either dramatic effect or because he hadn't shared what he was about to say with anyone else. Either way, I asked him to close the door.

"What link?"

"A link between Seagrave's murder and Sunny's attack. It's Kenzo Rees."

A shot of excitement surged through my veins. "Explain."

"Lieutenant Jack Seagrave was the cop who found and arrested Rees after he beat the shit out of Miss Harper in Dallas."

I stopped breathing, my shock too great to form a sentence.

Darby continued. "Rees fled Texas the moment Harper's dad took her to the cops. Dallas PD put out a BOLO and multi-state warrant for his arrest. Days later, someone here in Berry Springs called in someone sleeping in their car on the side of the road. It was Seagrave who responded. He recognized Rees and arrested him on the spot. Rees was extradited back to Texas where he was charged with first degree battery and sent to jail."

My heart was a steady pounding by the time Darby finished.

Revenge.

Kenzo Rees was going down the damn list of people who'd been part of putting him in jail.

Rees killed Seagrave.

Rees had Julian attack Sunny as initiation into his gang, The Collars. Maybe a scare tactic, or a failed kidnapping.

Kenzo Rees was my fucking Black Bandit.

"How do you know this?" I asked.

"I spent last night going over Sunny's—"

"Miss Harper."

"Sorry. Miss Harper's file from her attack. Like you said, the fact that Rees had just been released and all of a sudden she's attacked and her home vandalized seemed like too much a coincidence."

How the hell had I missed Seagrave's name in the

report? *You've lost your focus... too many balls in the air...* Colson's words slapped me in the face.

Darby continued. "I tried to find any link to Rees and witchcraft, or interest in the Cedonia Scrolls but found nothing. That's the only thing that still seems odd. I'm going to research the gang he's associated with more this morning. See if they're connected to buying and selling pagan art. Never know. I'm also gonna see if I can track down one of their members and ask if they know the Black Bandit."

"Why don't you leave that part to me, Darby?"

"You think I can't handle it?"

"I didn't say that. But when you start poking around gang members, you best know what you're doing."

"I do."

"You don't. And I'm telling you to back off The Collars. We need to place Rees at both scenes. We've got means and motive, for both Sunny and Seagrave, and now we need opportunity. We need Rees to be linked to that damn blue sedan. It's his, I know. If we can verify the link, that puts him at both Seagrave's and Sunny's scene. That's where I need your focus. I need you to leave The Collars alone and follow up with the dealerships again. Find where the hell he got the car. Extend the search."

Darby's lips pressed into a thin line, displeased with my orders. Bottom line, the kid wasn't experienced enough to interview ex-cons or gang members. Gotta crawl before you walk. All of us had. I just happened to walk a bit sooner than most.

"What about—"

"No, Darby. Dealerships. Focus on that damn car. Go. I'll find Rees."

I glanced at the clock, then gathered my phone and keys and started out the door.

"Keep me updated, Darby.

I didn't wait for a response because I had an appointment to get to.

"*I'll find Rees.*"

I grit my teeth as Jagg's words echoed in my head.

No, Detective Max Jagger, *I'll* find Rees.

While Jagg had been busy doing what he did best—playing knight in shining armor with Sunny, *Miss* Harper, *my ass*—he should have been tracking down the lead I uncovered earlier in the day while doing the long list of to-do's he'd given me. One of the many leads the perfect, infallible Detective Jagger had missed. That's right, me, the rookie, the nobody, the loser, the pissant, had spent the morning casing a trailer park on the outskirts of town where it was rumored that Kenzo Rees was temporarily living. I'd gotten the information by spending the afternoon the day before getting an oil change—that I didn't need—at an off-the-books garage run by former inmates. Thought it was a good bet. Gave it a shot.

I'd worn my most wrinkled Grateful Dead shirt, holey jeans and flip flops, and offered them fifty bucks for service. Once my truck was in the bay, I slipped on my headphones to make them think I was lost in my own Franklin's Tower, but instead, I listened to the chatter while they worked. I caught bits and pieces, including Sunny's name—no *Miss Harper* there, trust me—Griggs' name, and finally, "trailer number eight-forty-three."

Bingo. A lead. One that Jagg should have hunted down.

You see, while brute strength and intimidation might be Jagg's asset, mine was that I went unnoticed. I was just a regular, boring, normal nerd who could sneak through the shadows without so much of a glance.

As I'd already proven in spades.

Jagg was slipping.

And I was going to be there to pick up the pieces... and his badge.

36

JAGG

I set a paper bowl of water next to the edge of the patio outside of a coffee shop named *Deja Brew,* then settled into a corner table shaded by a massive maple tree. Max lapped up the water, leaving a trail of slobber across my boot as he plopped down next to my chair.

Fuck, it was hot.

I'd felt like an idiot ordering a bowl of water with my cup of coffee, but what was I supposed to do? I could only assume wearing a coat of fur in this blistering heat was nothing short of torture. That, and Sunny would have my ass if the dog got dehydrated while under my care. She probably had a test for it or something.

I looked down at the furball at my feet, his long tongue hanging out of his mouth, drooling with short pants of breath. He looked up at me and his tail thumped against the chair. I ruffled his ears and wondered how Brute's vet appointment was going.

After wiping my palm on my pants, I picked up my phone to check if I had any missed calls or texts from Sunny. I didn't. I pulled up an image of Kenzo Rees. My jaw clenched. I clicked into my videos and watched the grainy black and white video of the Black Bandit sneaking out the back door of Mystic Maven's Art Shop. I flipped back and forth between Rees's image and the video, then rewound the video ten times watching the smooth movements of the heist, the speed, the single focus of the Cedonia Scroll, then the jog down the steps—and that damn limp.

The left hip...

The left hip...

Mind racing, I slid my phone into my pocket then took a sip of my eight-dollar coffee, the heat of the paper cup less than the temperature outside. Everyone ahead of me had ordered some sort of frozen or iced concoction, half of which I couldn't even pronounce. Never was a fan of fancy drinks, or iced-anything for that matter. I liked my coffee black, strong and piping hot. No matter what the weather.

I'd chosen the outdoor patio for two reasons, one, I didn't want to leave Max in the Jeep. God forbid PETA show up at my doorstep, and two, I wanted privacy for the meeting I was about to have.

I was scrolling through my unread emails when clicks on the hardwood told me my company had arrived. I looked up to see a striking blonde in a grey skirt-suit thing and black heels that added four-inches to her already tall frame. Her hair was pulled back in a tight little bun, a pair of thick, black, trendy glasses over blue eyes. I don't know what I expected when I'd scheduled a meeting with an art investigator, but that wasn't it. Add red lipstick and a loose tie and this chick could have walked straight out of a Poison video. And, yet, my dick had no response. Not a single salute.

Sunny. Sorcery. There was no other explanation to it.

I stood and thrust out my hand.

"Agent Morgan."

"Briana." We shook hands, hers strong and commanding as if to let me know that although she was one of the few women in an industry dominated by men, she was no fool. Briana had an air of confidence about her as pungent as her spicy perfume. I knew her type, and I knew exactly how to do this dance.

"Cute dog." She kneeled down and pet Max's head, to which he responded with a groan of satisfaction instead of a growl of warning that a stranger was getting too close. The dog didn't care about my safety. Sunny was his only master. Got it.

I motioned to the chair across from me. "Please. Sit." As she did, I said, "Sorry about the choice of seating, but—"

"Discretion. I get it." She set her designer purse on the chair next to her. Business must be good.

"Would you like some coffee?" I asked, already knowing the answer. Briana had learned long ago that the best way to work with her male counterparts was to keep meetings short, sweet and direct. No coffee. No drinks.

"No, thank you," she politely responded.

"You're a tough gal to get ahold of."

"I'm busy."

And important, I get it.

"Well, thanks for squeezing me in," my ill attempt to sound impressed leaked through. "As I said when we spoke earlier, I wanted to talk to you about the Cedonia Scrolls your company insured and your investigation surrounding the heist of the pieces."

"You want to talk about Lieutenant Jack Seagrave's murder."

Briana came to play.

Good.

I leaned forward. "Miss Morgan, the piece you're investigating is currently tied to a local homicide. Your cooperation here is not only appreciated but expected."

"Do you have a warrant for my notes on the case?"

Okay. Miss Morgan was not only no man's fool, but smart too, and therefore, damn good at her job, I imagined, which made me even more eager to learn what she'd uncovered so far.

"Alright," I narrowed my eyes. "Let's just cut through the bullshit here, then. I want you to help me find the Black Bandit."

"And what do I get in return?"

"Not to be charged with obstruction of justice."

Her perfectly plucked brow arched. "Or, I could turn you in for threatening a potential informant. I believe they call that police misconduct. I'm sure your boss and Chief McCord would love to hear about this little meeting."

Apparently the Cedonia Scrolls weren't the only thing Briana had investigated before calling me back.

"Have you ever lost a loved one, Briana?"

The flicker in her blue eyes told me yes.

"Me, too." I said. "Most whose cases have been shifted into the freezer—gone cold, in case you didn't catch that. And you're right. I technically need a warrant for information you might have to help me solve a murder. And I'll get it, you can bet those diamond studs you've got in your ears on that. But I'd rather not spend the rest of the day cutting through red tape. So, Miss Morgan, to answer your question—what do you get if you help me out right now? A solid fucking night's sleep after knowing you did everything you could to bring a slain officer justice."

Her stare was loaded with calculated calmness.

"How did you know I was the one working the Cedonia Scroll case?"

"How did you know McCord wants my badge?"

A moment ticked by before she finally nodded, deciding to grace me with a little give and take.

"I'll help you. Under one circumstance."

"Name it."

"I want to be credited for helping find the Lieutenant's murderer."

It shouldn't have surprised me. The woman wore her career goals as blatantly as the label on her purse.

"Done."

"What do you want to know?"

"There are four Cedonia Scrolls total. Were all four scrolls stolen from the same man?"

"Yes."

"You've uncovered three so far. I want to know how."

"The scrolls were stolen together, but then sold off piece by piece. Each scroll was worth more separately than all four together. I recovered the first three before they even touched their buyer's hands."

"Impressive."

"I like to think so."

"How did you do it?"

She shook her head. "I don't reveal my sources, surely you understand that. Besides, this isn't about the first three scrolls, this is about the fourth, stolen from Mystic Maven's Art Shop."

"Why has the fourth been so hard to track down?"

"It was the most valuable of the group. It's changed hands several times since it was stolen."

"How did you recover the first three so easily?"

"By a little quid pro quo."

"Seems to be the theme in your career."

"Didn't get here by the color of my hair, no matter what you think."

"I don't doubt that, Miss Morgan. I can spot a snake when I see one. And I respect it. Now, tell me, all four scrolls are connected to the same underground buyer, aren't they?"

She stared back at me, blankly. That answer was yes.

I continued. "Being able to recover three pieces of stolen art so quickly suggests you had inside knowledge of this buyer. You're working with someone to recover the scrolls. Who?"

Her head tilted to the side as she took a moment to respond. *Bingo.* Briana Morgan was working with someone.

"Who?" I repeated.

"Someone with a lot to lose," she said, finally.

"Like going back to prison?"

Her lips pressed into a thin line.

"Your informant is the Black Bandit, isn't it?"

No response.

I continued. "The Black Bandit is stealing the scrolls *for you,* isn't he? Because, as you said, he's got a lot to lose, and it's tied to those scrolls."

A slow blink. This definitely wasn't her first rodeo with law enforcement.

"Give me the name, Morgan."

"I wish I could."

"What the hell's that supposed to mean?"

"I don't know it. My informant communicates with me through a burner phone. A new number every few days."

"Give me the latest number."

"Sure, but it won't do you any good. All of a sudden this person has clammed up. Won't return my calls, texts. It's as if they've vanished into thin air."

"But you've met the person. Tell me what they look like."

"No, you're assuming. I didn't technically meet the person. We arranged a drop for swapping information. I staked out the place for two days before."

"So you *think* you saw who it was?"

"I believe so, yes."

"Describe the person. Tell me what you know."

"I won't, Detective, because I'm not one-hundred percent sure that who I think it is, is it."

"Bullshit."

Her brow slowly cocked. She was playing me now. She'd met with the Bandit. I knew it in my bones. But she wasn't going to share this with me. *Why?*

"Is Kenzo Rees the Black Bandit?"

"I can't confirm or deny that, Detective."

"Well, for your sake, I hope it isn't, Morgan, because if so, you've struck a deal with the devil and I'd keep one eye open if I were you."

We stared at each other for a minute. It was like looking in the damn mirror. The woman was not going to break.

"What about Julian Griggs? Does that name ring a bell to you?"

"The victim in the Slaying in the Park?"

So fucking glad that had caught on.

"I don't know him personally," she said. "Just heard the gossip."

"What about a blue four-door sedan? Ever seen one of those at your clandestine meetings with the Bandit?"

She flipped over her palm and shook her head. "Not that I've noticed."

My patience cashed out. I popped my fist against the table, sending my coffee toppling over. Max skittered to the corner. Briana Morgan didn't flinch.

"The Black Bandit is either the person who killed Lieutenant Seagrave, or is the key to finding out who did it. I also believe they're involved in the Slaying in Park. I'm going to ask you again, Miss Morgan, tell me what you know about the Bandit. Tell me what you know about Kenzo Rees."

"The Black Bandit..." she tilted her head thoughtfully to the side, her voice as calm and maddening as the flippant look on her face. "Who picked that name, anyway?"

"An *anonymous witness* to one of those heists, but I'm willing to bet money it's you. You did."

"Interesting." She stood, grabbed her purse and gaze down at me. "Look closer, Detective."

"What the hell is that supposed to mean?"

She turned away and sauntered across the patio.

Look closer.

"Hey, Morgan?"

She paused at the door but didn't grace me with a glance.

"I'll have the warrant in your hands by this evening."

"I have no doubt you will, Detective. Good day."

37

JAGG

*M*ax whimpered in the back seat as my Jeep bottomed-out in a pot hole. My grip tightened around the steering wheel as I barreled down the dirt road, a cloud of dust spinning up from my tires and melting into air that seemed as still as a rock. Dusk was on the horizon, a ball of fire resting on the mountain peaks.

The full moon and the Moon Magic Festival was tonight, and so far the stars were aligning for a major shitshow.

My pulse hadn't slowed since I'd left *Deja Brew,* and in fact, had only gotten faster as I'd tried to dance around the red tape to get a warrant for Briana Morgan's files. I'd left a voicemail with the judge, who'd called the chief, who then called my boss and had me stonewalled, engaging in a pissing match about who should submit the warrant. McCord was trying to delay it, to spite me.

He wanted me off the case. He wanted me out of a job.

Well, the mother fucker had another thing coming.

Despite him, I'd gone by the judge's house myself, where his wife assured that he would get back to me as soon as possible, then asked me to never come by with business again, punctuated by a slamming door in my face.

The Jagger popularity streak was hitting new highs.

It wasn't until I got pulled over after leaving the judge's house, for doing seventy in a forty-five, that I decided to get the hell out of dodge for a bit.

To top *all that* off, I hadn't taken a pain pill all day. Every time my hand slid to my pocket, I'd look at Max and think of Sunny and her subtle way of suggesting I was addicted.

My back was knots, new pains in my hips that I hadn't felt before.

God, the woman and the effect she was having on me.

My Jeep seemed to drive itself in one direction.

Not Frank's Bar.

Not the gym, or my apartment.

Not to my brother's.

To the bungalow where Sunny Harper was waiting for me.

I didn't think, just drove. Just a few minutes with Sunny, a reprieve from my shit afternoon, then I'd take Max back to my brother's and then head back into town and sit in the Chief's office until he pushed through the damn warrant.

The meeting with Briana Morgan hadn't been a total bust. I learned that the Black Bandit had something to lose. Something that made him cut a deal.

A weakness.

I was damn good at exploiting weaknesses.

Two things bugged me, though. One, why didn't she just come out and confirm that Kenzo Rees was the Black Bandit? Why so protective of him? Two, most importantly, what was she hiding?

Why?

I made a mental note to spend the evening looking into

Miss Morgan, her social media, public records, where she went to school, hell, anything to find a link that could lead to the Black Bandit, which could lead me to Kenzo Rees.

I needed to find the son of a bitch.

I needed food.

I needed a shower.

I needed a freaking pain pill.

I needed... *something.*

A reflection in the rearview mirror caught my attention. My gaze narrowed as the bumper of a truck edged around a corner behind me, disappearing as I took another corner.

I was almost half way to the bungalow and hadn't passed a single car since turning off the highway. No one lived down that road, and aside from the occasional hunter or wandering stoner, no one drove down that road.

I shifted my focus back and forth between the rearview mirror and the road ahead of me.

I slowed.

Look closer... Briana's words echoed in my ear.

I peered in the mirror.

Look closer...

And then I saw it, the dented hood of Darby's truck.

Son of a *bitch.*

I gassed it, sending Max stumbling backward, clawing at the seat. I pulled a U-turn, my tires spinning out as I skidded back onto the road and hit the gas. Beams of the setting sun blurred the truck just ahead of me. My jaw clenched as I accelerated, lining up for a perfect head-on collision. A cloud of dust burst into the sky suggesting Darby had slammed his brakes. A horn blasted through the air.

I kept on the gas, faster, faster, until finally slamming the brakes and skidding to a stop an inch from Darby's hood.

"Stay," I growled at Max as dust blurred everything around the Jeep.

I climbed out, my heart pounding. I pulled my gun from my holster as I hurled myself onto the hood of his truck and threw myself over because there wasn't enough room between the vehicles.

"Out."

Dust swirled around us.

When the door didn't budge, I reached through the open window, grabbed Darby's shirt collar and dragged his ass onto the dirt road. I dropped him, sending him stumbling away from me.

I slammed the truck door and squared off with him, gun in hand.

"What the fuck are you doing, son?"

Beads of sweat rolled down the side of my face, but that was nothing compared to the flush of heat on the rookie's cheeks.

"I... uh..." His gaze remained fixed on my gun. "Put down the gun, dude."

"Not until you tell me why you've been following me."

The rookie ran his fingers through his oily hair, muttering something under his breath.

"You have two fucking seconds, Darby."

"I was told to, alright?" He blurted. "Colson asked me to keep an eye on you."

"Why?"

"Because he thinks you've gone over the edge. A loose cannon. Wanted me to keep a bead on you, that's all."

Loose cannon.

"I promise," he stammered. "That's all."

I holstered my gun. "Well, you failed him, kid. I saw you

the moment I walked into Frank's the other night. Seen your every move since."

"*Shit.*" Darby began pacing. "Freaking *shit.*" His steps were quick, erratically changing positions. I narrowed my eyes and watched him. I wasn't the only man on the edge.

A breeze swept past, clearing the dust and sending a flurry of sable fur shooting out of the Jeep like a cannon, sharp, quick barks.

Familiar barks.

Darby froze, eyes rounded in terror as the dog barreled toward him, stopping inches from his untied shoe. Max bounced, pawed, his nose in the air, sniffing, sniffing, sniffing. Exactly as he had done earlier while Sunny was training him to sniff out the third person from the night of her attack. The frantic sniffing was nothing like when he'd met Darby at Sunny's house the night of the vandalism. This was different.

This was the turning point.

My eyes narrowed as my hand slid back to my gun. I stepped closer.

"Max." The dog didn't hear me, didn't budge. "Max, *settle!*"

The dog stopped instantly, recoiled, and joined me at my heels.

Darby gaped at me.

My pulse roared in my ears.

"What did you do after photographing the Voodoo Tree in the woods?" I pulled the gun from my belt, kept it low, but it kept it loud.

The flush drained from the kid's cheeks.

"The evening of Seagrave's funeral," I repeated, seething. "The night of Sunny Harper's attack in the park. The night some mystery person ran out of the woods and shot a hole through Julian Griggs' face. Answer me, Darby, what did you do after meeting me at the shrine?"

"I..." his gaze drifted to my gun.

"*Where*. Did you. *Go?*"

I inched closer. Max growled at my hip.

"I did it!" His scream exploded out of a pale face, bulging eyes, wild with adrenaline. "Okay? I did it! I killed Julian Griggs. Pastor Griggs' son. I *freaking* did it."

The confession poured from his lips like an inmate on death row.

I fisted his uniform collar and pulled him off the ground.

"Did you fucking hurt Sunny?" With my other hand, I lifted the gun to his face. "Did you fucking hurt Sunny?"

"No." His answer was barely audible. "No... I promise... no... I pushed her to the ground to get her away from Julian. I saved her life. No... Jagg..."

My body shook with rage. "I'm going to ask you again and I swear to God I will put a bullet in your head if you don't tell me the truth. Did you hurt Sunny?"

He tried to shake his head against my choke hold. His feet kicked back and forth, dangling above my own.

I released my hand and watched him crumble to the ground gasping for breath.

And began sobbing. Like a little freaking girl, sobbing.

I holstered the gun for the second time, took a few steps back and gave him a second to catch the breath I'd stolen from him. Finally, he shifted onto his ass, pulled his knees to his chest and looked up at me.

The kid was absolutely terrified.

"Did you vandalize her home, Darby?"

"No." He swiped the tears from his cheek. "No. I promise. I was only close by that night because I was following you."

I heaved out a breath, dragged my fingers through my own hair.

I squatted down in front of him.

"Okay, calm down and tell me, Darby. Tell me everything. And I'm not in the mood for bullshit or beating around the bush, so tell it how it is. Nothing more, nothing less. What happened that night?"

It took a solid ten damn minutes for the kid to get his full story out. It went something like this:

After photographing the shrine at the Voodoo Tree, Darby had taken it upon himself to search the surrounding woods for more signs of witchery. What he got was someone bolting out of the woods and attacking Sunny Harper. He claims he hesitated, not sure what to do, but once the man —we know now to be Griggs—started beating Sunny, Darby took action. An honorable act and one that saved Sunny's life. Once Griggs engaged Darby in hand to hand, Darby pulled his gun and shot. Twice. After realizing he'd blown the kid's face off—and seeing his first dead body, by his own hand—Darby lost his shit and bolted while Sunny was dragging herself up from the ground. He said he watched old man Erickson pull up. The man never even saw him.

"Hang on a minute. Your uniform was clean, though, when you responded to dispatch ten minutes later and showed up at the scene."

He nodded. "I had a spare shirt in my patrol car. I ran back to the car, and by the time I was getting there, Tanya was radioing me to the scene. I threw up, changed my shirt, and went back. I had blood on my pants and I was sure you'd notice. But you didn't."

I didn't notice. *Christ,* I didn't notice blood all over the rookie's pants. Holy shit. Sunny had distracted me from second *one.*

312 | AMANDA MCKINNEY

"Why didn't you come clean? Why didn't you tell us?"

"Seriously?" Darby's voice pitched. "I am *brand new* to the job, Jagg, and I shot someone in the face. The *pastor's son*. I recognized Griggs instantly. We're around the same age. The freaking *pastor's* son," he emphasized. "I know how this story goes. I'm not stupid. Even though it was justified, I'd be put through the freaking ringer, then pushed to desk duty until the Chief got a reason to fire me. This shit doesn't fly in small towns. I'd lose everything I worked for." Tears swam in his eyes. "This job is the first time I've ever felt *worth* something. Like I was doing something that mattered. Like people respected me. First time since I was a stupid, nerdy, little kid."

"You had multiple times you could have come clean to me."

"Bullshit. You've had your head so far up Sunny's ass, I felt like I couldn't say anything that wouldn't set you off. And besides, every second that passed, I felt like I was in too far. Then when I saw how everyone was questioning you? About your decisions? The great, mighty Max Jagger? Hell, I was asked to follow you, for Christ's sake. And you didn't even shoot a kid in the face." He shook his head. "I'd be out the door and bullied out of town. I'd never get another law enforcement job in my life."

It was true. Every bit of it. ... Including my head being up Sunny's ass.

I couldn't help but pity the poor kid.

Fuck.

My hands fisted at my sides. It suddenly felt like my world was spinning out of control.

"Get up."

Darby's face tilted upward.

"Get off the ground. Grab your balls; get up."

The rookie pulled himself off the ground, his uniform covered in dirt, streaks of dried tears down his cheeks.

"Wipe your face."

He swiped the back of his hand over his cheeks.

I crossed my arms over my chest. "Well. What are we going to do now?"

He blinked. "We?"

"Gotta come up with something, right?"

Hope sparked in his swollen eyes. "Anything. Tell me what to do, and I'll do it, Jagg. Anything."

"First. Grow up. Man up. If you're going to be in this job, you need to hold your head up, square your shoulders, and remind yourself every damn day that it's *your* town. Stop taking orders, stop following me around. Carve your *own* path. And start with the damn gym."

He blinked again.

"Every single day, I want you to start your morning in the gym. Put on some muscle, kid. That way, the next time someone engages you in hand to hand combat, you won't have to blow their face off." I turned, walked back to my Jeep, pulled a plastic container from the back and hurled it at him. "Protein. Tastes like shit, but drink it. Bulk up. Become someone you're proud of. Someone people don't want to mess with. You'll be the rookie for a while and they'll treat you like one, but that doesn't mean you have to accept it. Prove them wrong. Be the first in the gym every morning, be the first in the office every day. Work your ass off, above and beyond. Do something to make them respect you. It's time to man up, Darby."

He took a deep, shaky breath. "Okay. Okay. Man up. Got it."

"Good. Here's what's going to happen now. You're not

going to say a *word* about this to anyone. Not a word. You got that? Not a single one."

He nodded, eyes wide.

I continued, "You're going to go home, stay home, stay out of this for a while. Tell Colson you're still following me, whatever you need to do to appease him, but stay low until I find the Black Bandit. You got that?"

"We can pin it on him." Darby's eyes flared with excitement. "On Kenzo Rees, the Bandit. We can pin it on him. He shot Seagrave, then Griggs... while trying to get to Sunny, perhaps? It makes sense. It fits. We can pin it on him."

"We can't pin it on him until we find him, can we?"

He nodded, color beginning to return to his cheeks. "Okay. Yes."

"Now, get home. Mouth shut. Man up."

"Yes, sir."

I turned to head back to the Jeep when—

"Jagg?"

"Yeah?"

"Thank you."

"Thank me when it's over."

Something in my gut told me the end was coming soon, but only if I wasn't too blind to see it. I climbed into my Jeep, ordered Max in the back, and watched Darby—the mystery third person from Sunny's attack—reverse down the road.

My stomach rolled.

I couldn't believe I hadn't seen it. The man who killed Julian Griggs was not only right under my nose, but was helping on the fucking case.

Why hadn't I seen it? Why hadn't I put that piece of the puzzle together? The kid had blood on his pants, for Christ's sake, and I missed that. I didn't even consider the very obvious fact that Darby fit perfectly into the timeframe and location to be the mystery third person.

I didn't miss shit like this. Hell, my entire career—my reputation—was built on noticing the smallest clues that everyone else overlooked. It's what made me good at my job.

I was one mistake away from being told to turn in my badge. My life. The only fucking thing I knew. Why, all of a sudden, wasn't that my primary focus? My primary concern? Why wasn't I doing everything in my power to keep my job, instead of sabotaging it?

There was only one explanation for my sudden insanity.

Sunny Harper. The beguiling fallen angel as enchanting and hypnotizing as a siren, sending men to their knees with a single sparkle of those green eyes.

Hell, she'd said herself that she wasn't good for me.

She was right.

She was blinding me.

How many details had I missed since laying eyes on the enchantress?

The thought made me want to slam my fist through the windshield.

I was embarrassed.

I *was* slipping. Colson was right.

I was slipping.

And I knew why.

... And I knew exactly what I had to do.

38

JAGG

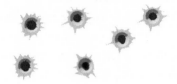

The last of the sun's rays painted a blazing sky as I rolled to a stop behind Sunny's truck.

I clicked off the phone and stared at the bungalow.

A minute passed.

I watched the bushes and trees sway in the evening breeze, a static white noise against the heat bugs. Fireflies danced around the blooming forsythias, pops of yellow gold against the growing shadows of dusk.

Max bulleted out of the Jeep the moment we stopped, a wagging tail fading into the long trunks of pine. Me on the other hand? I couldn't seem to move.

Part of me wanted to shove the Jeep into reverse, drive back to my rat-hole apartment and focus only on work. Forget about Sunny. Another part of me—the most alarming part—wanted to pack a bag, head for the border, and forget *everything*. Maybe become a bartender in a small town where no one knew my name. Or, maybe just never work another day in my life. Rot on the beach somewhere until my time came to face all the demons I'd been pushing away.

I stared at the sliver of the window I could see through the yellow bushes. It was dark in the bungalow and I wondered what Sunny was doing. If she was watching me.

If she'd hate me after tonight.

Of course she would.

But it was something I had to do.

With that thought, a weird trickle of nerves had me pulling the keys from the ignition. I'd be okay. I'd always been alone. I wasn't good in relationships, or anything to do with women, let's be honest. This was for the best. I had nothing to offer a woman, or a family. Hell, I'd be doing Sunny a favor by cutting ties with her. Regardless of what my brother had said—or hadn't said, for that matter.

After Darby's taillights had faded in the distance, I'd called Ryder. When I asked him if he could do me another favor, he'd said no problem. When I told him that favor was to put Sunny up in one of his spare rooms and be her body-guard until I found Rees, then escort her back home, where I'd never see her again, he'd said, "You sure?"

You sure?

You sure?

With those two little words my mute-brother had sent off a bomb in my heart. Although Ryder's contact with human civilization was shoddy at best, he'd obviously picked up on something—with me, with her.

Was I sure?

Fuck.

I stuffed my phone and keys in my pocket and got out, leaving everything else behind.

Two squirrels skittered across the iron gate, the roar of the heat bugs nearly drowning out the waves crashing in the distance. The forest was buzzing with activity. With energy. Anxiety.

The full moon effect, no doubt about it.

I was exhausted, pissed-off, hungry and in pain. And nervous. I was a freaking nervous wreck as I pushed through the front door.

The bungalow was dark, the sweeping windows glowing with the setting sun. A candle was lit on the fireplace mantel, the bed was made, and Sunny's bag was tucked neatly in the corner.

But no Sunny.

Her scent lingered in the air. Something soft, clean, floral.

I made my way across the room, noting the open bathroom door and glancing into the vacant kitchen. Knew she wouldn't be there. I stepped onto the deck, the scent of charred wood catching my attention. I zeroed in on movement at the end of the pier. The water was still, pitch-black, except for the reflection of the setting sun across it. Sunny swam down the middle of the blazing color, smooth strokes of her long, slender arms, a *V* of waves following behind her body. Her long hair flowing against shimmering colors of fuchsia. I watched the waves ripple past her, growing bigger and bigger, until fading into the shoreline. A perfect metaphor for the ripple effect this single, small woman had on the world around her.

I slowly walked down the bridgeway to the dock.

I don't know how long I watched her. I don't know at what point exactly my thoughts had faded and my pulse had slowed just watching the waves around her.

Truly hypnotic.

Healing.

She stopped, spun in the water, her hair spreading around a pool of sparkling tangerine light.

A smile caught me as our eyes met and although I could barely make out her face, I knew she smiled too.

She ducked under the water, then bobbed back up and began swimming back. About ten feet from the dock, she dove under again... and was gone. A few seconds passed, a minute. My brows pulled with concern while I forgot all else. My shirt was off and belt halfway undone when I heard a giggle behind me.

I turned and looked over the railing where Sunny lurked along the side of the dock.

"Gotcha." A blinding smile cut through the darkening night.

"Another minute and you would have had an entirely new snake to worry about." I re-buckled my belt, her gaze drifting to my bare chest.

I pulled on my shirt. "Come on. Get out of there. This place is crawling with cotton mouths. I don't feel like having to amputate a leg tonight."

She swam around. "For some reason I don't think it'd be your first."

I opened my mouth to respond but my brain short-circuited, little bombs going off, stealing my ability to move or form a single sentence as Sunny pulled herself out of the water wearing nothing but one of my long, white T-shirts.

Dear God and everything Holy.

Like a slow motion scene from the latest James Bond flick, water shimmered over her body, a silhouette against the orange of dusk.

Her wet, shimmering hair ran down her back, droplets of water pouring off the ends. A few strands cascaded around her plump, round breasts and the pink nipples that were blinding me like a fucking deer in headlights. The thin fabric clung to her feminine curves and the most perfect pair of tits I'd ever seen in my life. A pair of red panties were just barely visible through the white, this somehow sexier than if she'd been fully naked under the shirt.

She flashed me a sheepish grin as she breezed past me and grabbed a towel.

"Sorry. I didn't pack a suit, and... it's just too damn hot to not go for a swim."

Hot? *Hot?* Yeah, the temperature had just tripled in the last five seconds. I was staring at every high school boy's fantasy. I was literally in the middle of my own wet T-shirt contest. Although it was no contest. Not a single woman could hold a candle to the vision I just laid my eyes on.

Sunny Harper was the most beautiful woman I'd ever seen in my life. No makeup, no frills, dripping wet, in a baggy T-shirt. The woman was *stunning.*

She wrapped the towel around her torso, miraculously holding it in place by tucking a corner at the top under her armpit. How women did that, I had no clue. This new look morphed into an entirely different kind of a sexy—a nerdy, awkward burrito hiding every curve of her body, only making me want to see them again.

"I wasn't sure when you'd be back," she said, making it clear that her erotic swim hadn't been intended for my eyes. "How did the rest of your afternoon go?"

"Fine." I stared down at her, her skin like butter under the orange light. Flawless. Beautiful.

"Saw you brought Max back with you... are you planning on going back out?"

It was the perfect opportunity to tell her, but my mouth simply wouldn't form the words *Yes, I'm dropping you and Max at my brother's and never seeing you again.*

"You don't want to talk about anything. Okay." She cut

off my thoughts and smiled. A twinkle of excitement flashed in her eyes. "But are you hungry?"

My gaze shifted to a cooler at the edge of the dock—that I hadn't even noticed when I'd walked up. Another missed clue for the par.

"What's this?"

"Dinner."

My brows arched. "Lunch, and now dinner?"

She shrugged, that little change in demeanor I'd seen when she'd lifted the picnic basket from the back of her truck earlier. Shy and a bit uncomfortable with anything involving real emotions. Dammit it was cute. Endearing. Whether true or not, I felt like it was a side only I got to see.

I didn't know what to do, to say, didn't know how to bring up the fact that I planned to never see her again.

… But I knew I was hungry, and I couldn't stand there like an idiot.

I took the plaid blanket from her hands. It was the same one we'd used at lunch.

"Thought maybe we could eat and watch the sun set," she said while gathering everything else.

It sounded… perfect. *Perfection.*

I laid the blanket on the edge of the dock while Sunny lit a circle of Citronella candles around us, then set a can of bug spray on the end for good measure. A few pillows were set out, plates, napkins.

A twilight dinner on the lake.

"Sit," she demanded.

Per usual, I did. I smoothed the edges of the blanket because I didn't know what else to do. Not unlike lunch, Sunny had everything, every detail, planned out. The fact she'd put so much thought and effort into it made me a little happy, and a little nervous.

She settled in next to me, poured red wine into two paper cups and handed one to me.

I sipped. Like damn liquid joy down my throat. Good wine.

"How's Brute?"

Concern pulled her face. "Vet said he needs to have surgery."

Words I'd heard more than a few times.

"You going to do it?"

She nodded. "Anything to take his pain away."

I was glad to hear it. That damn dog had squirmed its way into my heart.

Sunny opened the thermal bag and began unloading the contents. The smell of salsa, cheese and bacon filled the air, but it wasn't until she unwrapped a burrito the size of a mini-submarine and placed it on my plate that my stomach growled. Loud.

In awe, I shook my head and looked at her. "Don't tell me it's a breakfast burrito."

"Sausage, egg, cheese, jalapeños, peppers, and bacon. Lots of bacon. You seem like a bacon kind of guy."

"You seem like my dream woman."

She smiled, continued, "Chips and salsa are in the bag, next to the roll of Tums for later."

"Definitely. Dream woman."

She laughed.

I looked at her spread—scrambled eggs, peppers, and red potatoes smothered in cheese. A mouth-watering gluten-free hash in a plastic bowl from Ryder's kitchen.

"Hang on... Where did you get all this?"

She continued stirring her hash, avoiding eye contact and a response.

"Sunny. Where did you get this food?"

She huffed out a breath, looked at me. "Well, I was going to wait until you took a bite and didn't keel over and die, before I told you I cooked it. I made it."

My jaw literally dropped.

"Oh well, thanks." She rolled her eyes

I slammed it shut. "Sorry. I mean, *you* cooked this? Everything? I thought you didn't cook."

"You're the one who said I should learn, right?"

"Well... yeah... but..."

"You didn't expect me to listen?"

"Not really."

"Well I did, and don't get too excited until you try it."

"Where did you get the food?"

"Farmer's market. On the way back from the vet this afternoon."

"Okay, but how did you make it? The kitchen isn't even working."

"Well, turns out your brother has a fire pit with this grill-grate-looking thing over it..."

I bit my tongue.

"... So I gathered some hickory wood—"

"How did you know what trees are hickory?"

"Now, that insults me. I know my trees. I have a hickory tree in my backyard. Anyway, I cooked the bacon, eggs, onions, peppers and potatoes in this heavy black skillet thing I found buried in the cabinets. It wasn't so hard. I'm sure I overcooked the bacon, but I didn't want to spend the evening puking. I'll get it down. The salsa on the other hand?" She shook her head. "Holy cow. *Not* easy."

"This is *homemade* salsa?"

She raised her palms. "Made by these two hands, chopped up by a hunting knife I found hanging in the back."

My eyes rounded.

"I washed it, don't worry. Anyway, it's got fresh, chopped tomatoes—*obviously*—and onions, cilantro, garlic that took me thirty minutes to dice, lime... and what else? Oh..." Her eyes widened with fear or concern, I wasn't sure which. "And jalapeños... I, uh... hope you like hot stuff. I... didn't exactly take the seeds out. I guess you're supposed to take the seeds out?"

"Sunny, I'd snort jalapeño seeds for breakfast. You're definitely good there. You understand there's nothing more delicious than homemade salsa, right?"

"Aside of breakfast burritos?"

"Of course."

She smiled proudly. So damn cute. "Good cause the only things here that weren't made by these two hands are the chips and the wraps. Your wraps, cause—"

"Gluten free, I remember."

She winked. "Okay, dive in. Here we go. Good luck."

We clanked forks.

Her entire body tensed as I dipped the burrito in the salsa and took a bite.

It was *freaking* delicious.

"Oh my..." I smiled around a full bite, a piece of egg tumbling out of my mouth. "Good. Sunny, *good.*"

Her face lit with a child-like excitement.

With salsa smattered on my lips and eggs on my chin, I leaned forward, wrapped my spare hand around her head and pulled her in for a kiss.

She yanked back, licking her lips and laughing.

"Sorry, lady, that's what you get. This is *damn* good."

"Good. Bon Appetit," she said, but instead of digging into her own food, she crawled to the edge of the blanket and began undoing my boots.

I froze. Legit, froze.

I watched her unthread each lace and gently pull off each boot. The evening breeze swept over my hot skin like silk. I wiggled my toes. God, it felt good.

She looked up and smiled.

It was my second, total, cat-got-your-tongue, shocking moment in the last ten minutes.

A woman taking care of her man.

Sunny crawled back up and settled beside me. I stared at her a solid ten seconds.

"Sunny. Thank—"

"*Shhh...* eat. Dinner's always more relaxing with shoes off... and those boots look miserable. No offense."

I looked back at my feet, bare against the darkness, the comfort of it. Little thing. So big.

"Eat," she repeated. "Relax."

"Yes, ma'am."

We ate like two starving POWs, watching the last ray of sun dip below the horizon. The lake faded into one black mass in front of us, waves rippling in the breeze. Stars began to twinkle around the biggest full moon I'd ever seen in my life. Fireflies sparkled around us. They seemed to gravitate toward Sunny.

I understood how that could happen.

The best part, though? The easy, casual conversation we fell into. No death, no murder, no brutal attacks, just light, fun conversation. We talked about cooking, gardening. We talked about the Moon Magic Festival happening that night, and all the traffic and hodgepodge of people that had invaded the small, sleepy town. I was so glad I wasn't out there. Hell, there was nowhere else I'd rather be at that moment.

Max had sauntered up sometime in the middle of our

conversation, covered in burrs and Lord knew what else. He scored a few pieces of bacon then disappeared back into the woods. I don't think he liked the dock. It was the first time, since I could remember, that I'd forgotten about my cases. Murder hadn't crept up and stolen the few moments of peace I was allowing myself.

I'd relaxed.

Enjoyed myself.

And wasn't that something?

I leaned back on my palms and took a deep breath, wondering if this was what vacation felt like.

"All good?" She looked at me, her eyes bright with satisfaction. She enjoyed pleasing me, and that was definitely something I could get used to.

"Better than good." I wiggled my toes again.

"Good. There's one more thing." She pushed off the blanket, disappeared to the corner of the dock, then returned with a small, brown box wrapped with a gold bow that sparkled under the moonlight.

I sat up straight.

She handed it to me.

"No." I shook my head. "A gift?"

"Yes. A gift."

"No, Sunny. You can't..."

"Just open it. Come on. You're making me nervous."

I stared at her.

"Open it, Jagg."

Shaking my head, I pulled the gold ribbon and opened the box. Tucked among red velvet was a gold, vintage compass.

My jaw dropped for the second time that night. "It's not..."

She smiled.

I turned the compass over in my hands—*MAJ* etched across the back. It was the compass my mother had sent me two weeks earlier. The replica she'd had made to replace the one I'd lost in Iraq.

"Where did you get this?"

"I made some calls."

"Some calls? I pawned this."

She shrugged as if it were no big deal.

"How did you know where I pawned it?"

"There's only one pawn shop in town."

"And it was still there?"

She shook her head. "No. The owner told me someone had purchased it pretty quick."

"And they just gave you the name of the buyer?"

"No, unfortunately, they wouldn't give me the name."

"Must've been a woman."

She winked.

"So how did you get it?"

"You know that little art shop in town? Mystic Maven's?"

The image of Seagrave's bloodied body popped into my head. "I know that place very well."

"I stopped by. Hazel, the owner, and I go way back. I asked her if she had any idea who would buy an old compass from the pawn shop. Turns out, she knows a man who collects vintage compasses in town. I tracked him down. Bada bing bada boom. Got the compass."

I turned the compass over in my hands, memories flooding me. Happy memories. When times were easier, when my mom and dad were still together and in love and the biggest problems I had was finding sticks straight enough to whittle into a sword. When I had no constant pain in my body. It was as if I was seeing the compass in an entirely new light.

"Why did you do this?"

She looked down a moment. "You know, it broke my heart, the story about you and your mom."

I set down the compass and turned fully to her. "Thank you, but there's a lot of history there, Sunny."

"I get it." She picked up the compass, turned it over in her palms. "But it's *family,* Jagg... You know, just because someone loses their way, it doesn't mean you should toss them out of your life. Cast them aside."

"My mom made that decision. Decided that for me."

"People make mistakes." She handed back the compass. "It sounds like your mom has gone above and beyond to try to rekindle things with you. I'm sure she didn't mean to hurt you."

"So." I stared down at the compass. "You think I should call her back. Meet with her?"

"Forgive her."

I trailed my finger over the top of the gold. "Why do I feel like there's more to this? More than just forgiving my mother?"

She looked away.

I turned her face toward mine.

"What's going on, Sunny?"

Tears welled in her eyes, her bottom lip quivered.

"Don't leave me, Jagg," she whispered, sucking the air out of the world around me.

"... Don't hurt me, Sunny," I whispered back.

We grabbed for each other, giving in, releasing to whatever this undeniable thing was happening between us. We kissed, long, slow kisses, under the stars, under the moonlight. I threaded my fingers through her silky, black mane. A desperation I'd never felt before guiding my body, my head, my heart.

Sunny wasn't good for me. I wasn't good for her. I didn't care.

The only thing I knew was that I didn't want to lose her.

I was *not* going to lose her.

I was going to *trust* her.

As I laid her down on the blanket, the compass tumbled onto the dock, the gold reflecting in the full moon—the arrow pointing directly at Sunny.

At us.

JAGG

*H*er hair fanned over the plaid blanket, the twinkle of the full moon in her green eyes. I cupped the back of her head, the energy, the anticipation vibrating between like the waves washing on the lakeshore.

I waited. I waited...

Finally, her chin dipped, ever so slightly—*Yes, she invited.*

I crushed my lips to hers as she wrapped her arms around me, her nails gliding down my back.

Surrender. She'd finally surrendered to me.

We, to each other.

The blood funneled between my legs in a firestorm of excitement and torment of needing to be inside her immediately. To finally feel what had stolen my thoughts, my dreams. Myself.

To have her fully. To mark her as mine.

My. Own.

Her nails dug deeper as the desperation in our kiss intensified, releasing our pent-up sexual tension in that one kiss. She needed it, too, as badly as I did. Goosebumps ran over my skin under her touch, my senses already overstimulated by an animalistic hunger overtaking us.

I tugged up her shirt, reveling in the warmth of her bare skin against mine and pulled it off. I leaned up, stripped my own off.

"Everything," she demanded quickly.

From her place on the ground, her gaze drifted over my body as I stood and slid out of my pants and boxer briefs. Her eyes glittered as she took in my cock, her body beginning to squirm against the blanket.

My Sunny. Waiting for me.

She mesmerized me. Her lips full and puffy from the kiss, the heat sparking from her eyes, the way her breasts moved as she stretched her arms over her head, offering herself to me like a lamb before a sacrifice. The moonlight reflected against her milky pale skin, almost otherworldly, as if she was something more than us mere mortals on earth. And she was. And she was mine.

I straddled her and took her nipple in my mouth, my pulse skyrocketing as my tongue circled the puckered skin, suckling like a baby that couldn't get enough. She fisted my hair, the sting of the pull going right to my dick that was already a raging hard-on.

I worked my way down her stomach, her perfect, little navel, to that little crease of her inner thighs.

Those red lace panties.

Licking, kissing, I peeled them off her, trailing them down her legs next to my tongue. Her breath picked up, the movement of her hands over me becoming faster, more frantic. We locked eyes as she spread open for me, bending her knees and widening herself to me. Opening fully.

She smelled like vanilla. Warm, wet vanilla. And then I spotted the tattoo, a vibrant blue butterfly on her inner hip.

Resurrection.

I trailed my finger over the beautiful wings and looked into her eyes. A small smile spread over her lips.

My butterfly.

Keeping my eyes on hers, I lowered into the pink folds. I could feel the heat pulsing off her skin against my mouth. Slowly, softly, I licked the crease of her thighs, teasing her, making her beg for it. She did. Her knees opened wider, her ass lifting off the floor all but shoving herself to me.

God, she was beautiful.

I slid my hands under her ass and squeezed as I buried my face into her pussy. I melted against the warmth, the scent of her, the slickness as I ran my mouth over the folds separating them with the tip of my tongue.

"Jagger..." her whisper barely audible as she dragged her fingers through my hair.

She grew wetter, swelling around my mouth. I knew she was throbbing as much as I was, and I hadn't even touched the Holy Grail. I squeezed her ass cheeks and trailed my tongue to her clit. Her breath hitched, her body jolted instantly at the touch. I wanted to fucking devour it, eat it, press it in my mouth until it became a part me. I circled the tiny, swollen bud, suckling madly, sending her into quick pants as she pulled my hair.

"Oh my..."

One finger, then two, plunged into her warm wetness, sliding in and out with each circle of my tongue, the pressure increasing with each thrust of my hand. Licking, lapping, sucking that clit as I repositioned my other hand, slid my thumb between her ass cheek and pressed.

She screamed my name as she came, the most beautiful sound I'd ever heard in my life.

I lapped up that sweet juice, trailing my wet fingertips down her thighs as I watched her come back to life.

Her eyes met mine.

"Come here," she whispered, her hands grabbing at me.

I crawled over her, my cock, painfully hard, dangling above her stomach.

She was so beautiful, sated, satisfied under the moonlight.

I'd done that.

And I would do it every day for the rest of my life if she'd let me.

I lowered down...

"Wait."

I pulled back.

"Wait..." she whispered.

"What?"

Her tongue darted over her lips, her brows crinkled in a look that resembled concern. You want to know the crazy thing? At that moment, my response wasn't disappointment or anger that she was possibly pulling the plug on sex, it was that I was so damn glad I'd already satisfied her, if we were done.

Mind-blowing, that was.

"It's okay. What? You can tell me anything." I whispered. "Say it. What?"

"It's been... It's been awhile."

I blinked.

"... Since I've had sex."

"How long?"

"Six years."

My brows popped.

She snorted. "Thanks."

"No... no, I didn't mean... it's just surprising."

"I know."

"We don't have to..."

"No, Jagg," she threaded her fingers through my hair. "There's nothing more that I want right now. Please. I want you. Just... be slow."

"Are you sure?"

"Yes." She gripped my hair. "Fuck me, Jagg. Take me."

I lowered down, repositioning my tip against her opening.

"Tell me if I hurt you," I whispered. "I'll stop."

She nodded, closed her eyes and wrapped her arms around me.

"Take me..."

The heat of her almost took my breath away as my head separated her folds. The touch like a blast of lightning against my already-throbbing head. I closed my eyes and tilted my head up, savoring the moment, knowing that if just the tip of her was that good, I wanted to draw it out as much as possible. Something I'd never done before.

I slowly slid inside, a wave of lightheadedness gripping me as a sheath of hot, slick sweetness squeezed around my cock. She was so tight, a vise sucking me in, pulling me deeper and deeper into the rapture that was Sunny Harper.

Soaking into her, I leaned next to her ear. "Are you okay?"

"Yes." This whisper was marked with her legs wrapping around me, her hips thrusting upward.

Fuck.

We kissed as I began to slide in and out, slowly establishing a rhythm, moving together under the moonlight like the water next to us. Each thrust deeper than the last until her pussy sucked in my entire cock.

It was true ecstasy. Better than any adrenaline rush, any

drink, any pill. My thoughts, concerns, fears, everything evaporated in a cloud of mist around us as we kissed, kissed, kissed and moved together.

I was on the brink of coming when she pulled away from my kiss, fire sparking in those eyes.

"You okay?"

She didn't speak. The heat in her eyes was enough. She pushed me off her and onto my back with a force rivaling the one she'd used to fight me off her in the park.

Holy *shit.*

"I'm going to fuck you, Jagg. I'm going to fuck you the way I've wanted to since the moment I saw you and I'm going to watch you watch me come again."

That was my Sunny. Unbridled passion, taking what she wanted, exactly as she wanted it. So fucking hot.

Take me was all I could think. Never let me go.

She crawled on top of me, straddled me, wrapped her hand around my cock and guided my tip inside her, jacking me off at the base while she slowly worked her way down.

I thought I was in ecstasy before.

I gripped her tiny waist, helping to guide the movement. I could actually feel her stretching around me.

"That's it, baby. That's it."

She closed her eyes and bit her lip, her face squeezing with each inch she traveled lower, lower and lower.

I was about to explode.

She finally was able to settle onto me, my cock fully enveloped in her vise, her clit pressing against my hair. She braced her palms, her weight, on my chest and began the ride, those breasts swaying under the moonlight.

It was the sexiest thing I'd ever seen.

"My God," she exhaled sliding up and down, grinding her clit against me with each drop. My grip around her waist tightened as her speed increased. Faster, faster. Sweat slicked our bodies as I bounced her hips against mine. She *fucked* me faster, faster, her hair bouncing on her shoulders as she tilted her chin up to the sky, exposing that long, pale neck to me. She began to moan, pant.

I couldn't take it anymore.

I slid one hand at the base of my cock and thumbed that slick, swollen clit, sliding over it as she rode me. I pressed hard, fast, her breath escaping her, mine lodging in my throat. Tingles ran over my skin as goosebumps spread over her own. Her pussy tightened around me, little squeezes telling me she was close.

"Sunny," I said through ground teeth.

She opened her eyes, a strand of hair bouncing down the center of her face.

"Look at me. Sunny. Look at me."

Our eyes locked. "I love you, Jagg. I love you."

With a guttural groan I poured myself inside her as she screamed my name one more time.

40

JAGG

The moon had risen further in the sky when we'd finally pulled away from each other. The words she'd yelled out while she came had wrapped around us in a warm blanket, something I never wanted to let go. It wasn't awkward or weird, it was just a release. An acknowledgment of something we both knew to be as true as our beating hearts.

I didn't say it back.

I didn't know why.

She didn't seem to care, though, as was Sunny. She knew what she'd done to me when she said it.

Dissolved me.

I watched her blow out the candles, the thin, white T-shirt stopped just below her butt cheeks, revealing that sexy tuck when she moved just the right way. I wanted to be there again, in that exact spot, and I got the feeling that desire wouldn't leave me for the rest of my life.

I'd had Sunny Harper.

There was no going back.

I gathered the blanket, bag, the cooler and followed her up the hill.

My phone had started blowing up sometime between her orgasms and in a move nothing short of impressive, I'd silenced it without her noticing. The entire town could be in flames at the hand of the devil himself and I wouldn't have cared.

I buckled my pants, slipped into my boots and slung my T-shirt over my shoulder. Sunny hadn't bothered to replace her panties. In fact, I don't even think we knew where they were.

With the full moon guiding our way, I watched Sunny walk up the hill, those long, lean legs. The way the T-shirt outlined her perfect ass with each step. The way her hips swayed back and forth...

That sway...

That... *sway*...

... ...

I squinted, tilting my head to the side, a little explosive, red alarm bursting somewhere deep in my psyche.

"Hey, Sunny?"

"Yeah?"

"You okay?"

"Why?" She asked over her shoulder, her wild hair blowing in the breeze.

"You've got a gangsta limp all the sudden. Straight out of a rap video. I think they call that swagger, or something."

She laughed. "No, I think it's to keep their pants up."

"You're not wearing pants... Seriously, did I hurt you?"

"Oh, no, no, no. It's just my hip. I fell out of a treehouse when I was a kid. My left hip gets a little wonky from time to time."

I stopped cold, my veins turning to ice.

"My left hip."

41

JAGG

*a*nd that was the final shock of what would be the evening that changed my life forever.

I couldn't move. I was rooted to the ground with invisible strings while my brain started spinning. My stomach plummeted to the ground.

Briana Morgan's words echoed in my ear.

"The Black Bandit... Who picked that name, anyway?"

"... Look closer..."

I zeroed in on Sunny's long, *black* curly hair.

The Black Bandit.

Sunny Harper was the fucking Black Bandit.

Briana had named her partner in crime, her informant, after her pitch black hair.

And I had *fucking* missed it. The Bandit had been right there in front of me the entire time.

I'd *missed* it.

I can't explain the emotions that pummeled through my body at that moment. Shock, anger, gut-wrenching *embarrassment*. All this quickly replaced with a racing heart and a rage like fire over my skin. I'd been lied to. Played like a fucking fiddle.

Sunny Harper was the *Black Bandit a*nd I hadn't even seen it.

Never. Again.

Never fucking again.

"Sunny."

She stopped instantly at the tone in my voice, and even through the growing darkness, I could see her entire body tense. She knew. At that moment, she knew she'd let it slip.

She didn't turn, as if she knew what was coming.

A second went by with us standing ten feet apart on the trail that led through the woods to the bungalow.

Max whimpered.

And then she was gone.

Like a flash of lightning, the woman took off into the woods.

The cooler and bags tumbled to the ground as I spun on my heel and sprinted after her, laser focused on the black hair zipping through the trees like a goddamn deer. The woman was freakishly fast. Beams of moonlight shot through the canopy above, silver spotlights dappling the forest floor below. It was like a damn light show, flashes and swaying shadows in the breeze.

Twigs slapped my face, a few slicing the skin on my bare chest. The pain like gasoline to the fire that was raging through me.

I'd been played.

Played.

A flash of black and brown emerged from the side, Max, chasing after her, sensing something in the air.

The trees enclosed around us, stealing most of the light.

I had a feeling Sunny would fade away as soon as darkness fully engulfed us.

I wasn't going to let that happen.

Gritting my teeth, I surged forward, pressing into a fast sprint, ignoring the pain shooting up my back, the branches slicing my skin, the rocks, the gangly roots threatening to trip me with every step.

I took a risk and switched paths, running around the boulders she was struggling to maneuver through.

Almost...

I could smell the coconut in her hair as I jumped onto a rock and leapt through the air like a cheetah. My body slammed into hers. I wrapped my arms around her, flung her bodyweight and we hit the ground, tumbling three rotations before my back slammed against a rock. I pinned her wrists above her head and straddled her torso before the woman could even blink.

Moonlight slashed her face as she gasped for breath and struggled against my hold. Her now-shoeless bare legs flailed at my back, her T-shirt somewhere around her waist.

How had this woman fooled me? How had I been stupid enough to be inside this woman only moments ago, handing her my fucking heart?

Idiot.

A chorus of snarls and barks screamed around me.

"Settle!" I yelled over the noise as I glared down at Sunny, my pulse roaring in my ears.

The barks faded into low whimpers as Max paced anxiously back and forth next to us, unsure what to do. My body trembled as I leaned into her face—her lying, deceiving, hypnotic face.

"Did you kill Seagrave?" The voice that came out of me

was something I'd never heard before, so low, so deep, I was surprised she even heard it.

"No." Her chest heaved. *"No."*

My phone started buzzing—for the tenth time—but I didn't dare release her wrists. I ground my hips deeper against her ribcage. She sucked in a ragged breath, gasping for air. I realized then that I didn't have handcuffs, a gun, not even a damn shirt to gag the woman. A series of beeps followed the incessant calls. Voicemails, texts messages, the pitched sounds setting me even more on edge.

"I'm going to ask you again, and God help me if you lie to me this time... Did you shoot Seagrave after you stole the Cedonia Scroll?"

"No!" She blurted out, the single word taking all the breath she had in her.

"Why didn't you tell me?" I screamed, the sound roaring through the woods. "Why didn't you tell me you were the Black Bandit?"

She squeezed her eyes closed and turned her face away from the spittle coming out of my rage.

"Why?" I shook her wrists above her head like a rag doll.

"Stop it! Jagg, stop!"

"Why? Why the fuck didn't you tell me?"

"You don't understand, Jagg. Because I—"

"I don't *understand?* Because you're a lying, mother fucking *bitch."*

Her entire body stilled instantly. The words lingered heavy in the air, and fuck if I didn't regret them. The muscles in her jaw twitched as she slowly turned her face to mine, her eyes slitted with absolute fury.

"Tell me," I snapped.

"Fuck. *You."*

I stared at her, both of us still breathing heavily from the chase, the catch, the emotions. I spat inches from her face. She didn't flinch. I pressed her wrists into the rocks as I scoffed and pushed off of her.

She laid still, unmoving on the dirty ground where she belonged, that gaze shooting into mine with a rage almost matching my own.

Almost.

"You've cost me my fucking job," I loomed over her, spat again. "You cost me my fucking reputation. You made me a fucking fool—"

My phone rang again.

"*Fuck!* Jesus *Christ!*" I pulled the phone from my pocket. "*What?*"

A circus of background noise roared in my ears, then, "I need you down at Switchback Trailer Park immediately." Colson's voice crackled in and out, but there was no mistaking the sharpness of his tone.

"What the hell's going on?"

"Darby's been shot three times in the chest."

42

JAGG

I scrubbed my hands over my face as I paced back and forth in the waiting room, wishing I could scrub the smells away, too. Her smell. Vanilla and coconuts branded on my skin. The smell of the room around me. That damn cold, stinging antiseptic scent that was synonymous with every hospital waiting room on the planet.

At that moment I wasn't sure which scent I hated worse. Her's or the hospital's. Both, cloying and suffocating.

I looked at the clock for the millionth time and watched it click from 10:05 p.m. to 10:06 p.m..

Last time I'd looked it had been 10:03 p.m.. There had to be something wrong with the clock. Just like there was something wrong with the spitting window air-conditioning unit that did absolutely nothing to cool the small space. Kinda like mine at my apartment.

It stunk, too, come to think of it.

My gaze trailed the scuffed beige tiles on the floor. Half of which were from my own boots. Six mismatched chairs lined the walls, one with the outline of a stain that resembled a fist giving the middle finger. Someone had taken the time to scrub the stain, but given up somewhere around the knuckle. A stack of magazines sat on a coffee table in the center of the room, half of the covers ripped or colored on by undisciplined, stinky toddlers.

Kids stink. I don't care what you say.

God, I *hated* hospitals. Especially waiting rooms. Waiting rooms were the worst. If you were actually inside a hospital room it meant that something *had* happened or *was* happening. In my case, mostly, it meant that I was getting to meet with a victim for the first time, to begin the long path of getting them justice. Not that night.

It had been exactly an hour and twelve minutes since I'd left the trailer park where Darby had taken three rounds to the chest, courtesy of Kenzo Rees.

He'd gone to the trailer park after my pep talk in the woods where I confronted him for following me.

"Do something to make them respect you."...

The words slammed into my chest like a wrecking ball— for the hundredth time since I'd gotten the call. Darby had been shot because of me. Instead of going home and staying out of the case, like I'd told him to, he'd decided to man up right then. Followed up on a lead that I'd either missed, or hadn't had the good sense to pull out of the kid.

Something *else* I fucking missed.

I dragged my hands through my hair, the guilt twisting in my gut. My hand lowered to the bottle of pills in my pocket. A second passed, another, and another, and with a guttural groan I pulled my hand back up, reining in every bit of restraint I had to not punch a hole in the sheetrock.

Who the hell was I? Who had I become?

Years ago, none of this would have happened.

Years ago, I hadn't met Sunny Harper.

What the hell had *she* turned me into?

Do you want to know the most screwed up thing? After I left her there in the woods, half-naked, in nothing but my T-shirt—*my* T-shirt—I'd almost turned around and gone back to pick her up. While I knew Darby was bleeding to death from multiple gunshot wounds, I'd almost gone back to get the woman who'd lied to me and fucked me over like the chump I was. I contemplated going back the entire drive to the crime scene, jumbled thoughts paralyzing me from taking any action, to make a solid decision either way.

I wasn't this guy.

An irrational, indecisive, loose cannon.

Colson had been right, and when I'd arrived to the trailer park, it was obvious he wasn't the only one who'd thought so. I'd been cast out of most of the crime scene. Despite the fact the Moon Magic Festival was in full swing at Devil's Cove, it seemed like the entire town had shown up to the trailer park, bystanders allowed closer than I was. But even though I was restricted to the sidelines, it wasn't hard to miss the blue four-door sedan parked beside the shittiest trailer, or the excitement in Colson when he'd found Seagrave's gun in Rees's roach-infested hideout. Kenzo Rees had killed Seagrave for revenge, case closed. The credit fully owed to Officer Tommy Darby - the kid I'd sent into the mess in the first place.

According to a hyped-up medic, Rees's trailer had been like a scene in Scarface, with blocks of cocaine stacked in the corners, half of which were labeled with the symbol of an infamous South American gang, where Julian Griggs had just returned from his "mission trip." Yep, the kid had used the cover of God to monitor a drug-trafficking operation orchestrated by his new boss, Kenzo Rees, followed by an initiation that involved attacking Kenzo's former girlfriend.

The scum of the earth unite.

According to pictures found in the cell phone hidden in the trailer, Rees had been following both Seagrave and Sunny since he'd been released from prison. The night Sunny stole the Cedonia Scroll from Magic Maven's, Rees had been following her. The fact that Seagrave was the responding officer to the heist had been an opportunity too great for Rees to pass up. He'd shot Seagrave while Sunny escaped. Almost two birds with one stone.

Almost.

According to the first responder at the trailer park, someone had called nine-one-one after hearing gunshots. When the officer arrived at the scene, he found Darby surrounded by a pool of blood in the middle of the grass. The kid had been shot at close range, two in the shoulder, one dangerously close to the heart. He had a faint pulse when they strapped him onto the gurney, and that was literally all I knew at that moment, other than that it was all my fucking fault.

Rees had fled the scene moments before the cops arrived, by another car, or on foot, no one knew. The one place I knew he wouldn't go was the bungalow, though, because no one knew we were there. That had given me some sort of solace as I'd navigated my own nightmare.

Darby had been rushed to the hospital and was taken into surgery immediately. When I learned Darby's only next of kin lived across the country, I hauled ass up there. Someone needed to be there for the kid. Someone needed to be there if he pulled through.

It was the least I could do.

I looked at the clock again, then back to the tiles, then up at the clock one more time.

Sunny.

Over the last hour, I'd learned two things: There was

nothing like total silence to force you to examine the thoughts in your own head, and two, not even Sunny's betrayal could make me stop thinking about her. I was a fucking trainwreck of emotions ranging from extreme hatred for the woman, to extreme hatred for how I'd treated her after I found out she was the Bandit. I called her a bitch, spat at her face.

Spat. At her. *Face.*

I disgusted myself.

After I'd hung up the call with Colson, I'd taken one last look at Sunny and then left without another word, knowing I'd just destroyed everything between us.

Fucking par for the course.

A shadow on the wall caught my attention and I turned to see Dr. Buckley step into the room. He gave a quick glance around to ensure we were alone before refocusing on me.

"The surgeon is just finished up."

"Is he alive?"

"Barely, Jagg, I'm not gonna lie. Barely." Buckley's eyes were puffy, shaded, stressed. Whatever happened in that surgery room hadn't been good, or easy.

"How did it go?"

"As I'm sure you know, Darby was shot three times. Twice in the shoulder, and once in the chest. His shoulder is badly damaged and is going to need months of physical therapy, but the chest wound is what's critical. The bullet missed his heart and aorta by a millimeter. His lung was punctured, but he's lucky. Beyond lucky. He's running on machines and will stay in ICU for the foreseeable future. The next twenty-four hours are critical."

I scrubbed my hand over my mouth.

"They catch the bastard?" Buckley asked.

"Not yet."

"I hope you do. Poor kid. Too young to experience something like this."

Too young.

"Y'all contact next of kin?"

I nodded. "It will be tomorrow until they get here. I'm it for now. Can I see him?"

"No, I'm sorry. They're getting him situated now. No one will be allowed in the room for quite a while, and even then, he'll be knocked out for hours."

"I want you to call me with anything, any time. I want an update on his status every thirty minutes."

Buckley nodded. "I'll tell the nurse." His thick, calloused hand clamped over my shoulder. "You alright, Jagg?"

I stepped out of his hold. "Every thirty minutes. Got it?"

Buckley nodded, again, then glanced around the waiting room again. "I'll be here. We've already got our first overdose from the damn Moon Magic Festival. It's going to be a long night."

My gaze flickered out the window.

"Thanks, Buck. I'll talk to you in thirty minutes."

I didn't wait for a response as I strode out of the room. I might have been restricted from the crime scene, but that didn't mean I couldn't go hunting.

43

JAGG

The full moon was like a massive spotlight illuminating the town in silver glow almost as bright as day. A haunting purgatory, neither night or day, but somewhere in between. You could feel the electricity in the air. Although the festival was raging miles away at Devil's Cove, the town was a buzz of activity. Cars filled the two-lane roads that were normally vacant past nine o'clock. Store fronts glowed with life, staying open late to capitalize on the influx of boozy tourists. Loud music and laughter rang through the humid summer air. I passed a trio of young women in flowing skirts and tie-dye shirts, wearing crowns on their heads made of twigs and twinkling lights. Giggling, grabbing onto each other as they stumbled down Main Street. A duo of cowboys followed a few feet behind. I passed a patrol car, and another. BSPD was out in full swing, and unless I'd missed something—which at that point wouldn't surprise me—Darby's incident had been the only life-or-death emergency so far. There'd be plenty of DWI's, drunk and disorderly's, a few public intoxes, and probably a few indecent exposures but nothing they couldn't handle.

Little did I know what was coming.

I turned off Main Street onto "Tourist Road," the same strip where Kenzo Rees had shot Seagrave and where Sunny Harper had pulled off a heist right under my damn nose.

The strip was lined with people of all ages, each store front lit and decorated with moons and stars, tinkling chimes and hanging trinkets. I noted a few pentagrams, a few other Wiccan symbols. A band played at each end of the street next to food vendors flanked by long lines.

I slowed as I neared the end of the row of shops, imagining Sunny slinking through the shadows on her way to steal the final Cedonia Scroll. Then, I imagined Seagrave responding to a "suspicious person" call minutes later. The man had probably just tossed the foil from the ham and cheese sandwich he ate every night while on duty and chugged a Dr. Pepper from the pack he'd always kept stocked in the community fridge before jogging to his car. He shouldn't have died.

I slowed, visualizing where he'd parked, then, him getting out of the car, walking down the sidewalk, turning into the narrow alleyway that ran next to Mystic Maven's Art Shop.

I honked at a pair of teens stumbling across the road, then whipped my Jeep into the only open spot. I cut the engine, hopped out, and ignoring a few whistles, I stepped into the alley. A shadow from the building next door stretched across the asphalt, making it difficult to see. I looked around.

There were still many questions about that night. Why had Sunny stolen the scrolls in the first place? Why hadn't Briana Morgan given up Sunny's name? What was the connection, or loyalty, there?

I was still missing something right under my nose. I felt it in my gut.

A wave of sparkles across the bricks pulled my attention. I watched Hazel De Ville flick her *Open* sign to *Closed.*

I crossed the alley and rapped on the door. Hazel turned, cocked her head, then padded back and pulled open the glass door.

"Hurry, hurry, son, I'm trying to get out of here for the night."

She quickly closed the door behind me and turned off the lights to the main floor, leaving only a few dangling gold lights above the cash register in the back.

"Headed to the festival?" I followed her across the room.

"Every year. Good for business." She slid behind the counter and began shutting down her computer. "I make almost half my revenue during the Magic Moon."

I crossed my arms over my chest. "But you're not going only for business, Ms. De Ville."

She glanced up and followed my gaze to the hemp bag sitting next to her purse, a wooden voodoo doll peeking out of the top. Her eyes narrowed as she looked back at me.

"You going to arrest me, Detective?"

"Depends."

"On what?"

"How honest you are with the questions I'm about to ask you. One, how long have you been practicing witchcraft?"

"I don't practice witchcraft."

I nodded to the bag. "Your dolls say otherwise."

She huffed out an annoyed breath, neither impressed nor intimidated by my presence.

"I am Wiccan, Max Jagger. I practice Wicca. Is this illegal?"

"No. But I want to know why you erected a Wiccan shrine on the tree outside Lieutenant Seagrave's funeral."

She glanced back at the woven dolls, hesitated a minute, then met my gaze with slitted eyes.

"Fine. You got me. It was me. But the question shouldn't be why it was outside of the Lieutenant's funeral, it should be why it was at that tree."

"I'm not in the mood for riddles, Hazel."

"Or, for seeing clearly, apparently. The *altar—not* a shrine—had nothing to do with the Lieutenant, or his death, and everything to do with Lammas, the celebration tonight. But you wouldn't know that because you only saw what these small-town rednecks told you to see. Witches are evil. Therefore, the shrine must have to do with death. Right?" She pulled a doll from her bag. "This is not a voodoo doll, Jagg. It is not evil, or sinister, or black magic. Lammas is one of the four Greater Sabbats in the Wiccan religion. And this year, it just so happens to fall on a full moon. That's the reason this year's festival is so huge. Women and men who practice Wicca have flocked here to celebrate—*not* to curse." She huffed out a breath. "Listen up, because I'm only going to educate you once and hopefully at least one thing I say will get through that dense brain of yours. Lammas is a celebration of the first harvest of the year, a time to give thanks for the past and celebrate the future. It's the opposite of what you, and everyone else in this town has assumed, Jagg. These 'voodoo dolls' are actually called corn dollys and are used to honor the god Lugh, and in my case, those who have had a positive impact in my life over the last year. The altar in the park was a symbol of thanks and celebration, Jagg."

"Okay, fine, but why the park? Why there? Why not in your backyard?"

"Good question. That tree is sacred to me. It's where Earl asked me to marry him thirty-four years ago. It's not the first altar I constructed there—and not the first you've missed."

"Celebration aside, you'd be missing that tree if those candles you'd lit would have caught fire, Hazel. We're in the middle of a burn ban and one of the hottest heatwaves in history. The damn grass is like a tinderbox. It wasn't smart."

"I was feet away when you walked up. I watched you and Darby the entire time. When he blew out the candles, I left. I wouldn't have left them burning." She paused, staring at me in a way that made me feel like an insolent school kid. "What other questions can I clear up for you so that you don't *arrest* me?"

"The Black Bandit."

Something in her eyes flickered.

"You know exactly who the Black Bandit is."

"Do I?"

"Cut the bullshit, Hazel. You know Arlo and Sunny Harper better than I realized. Tell me why Sunny stole the Cedonia Scrolls."

"Jagger, *listen* to me. *Hear* me. Not everything is evil and nefarious with bad intentions. Not everything is bad and the reasons behind things are not always what they seem."

"Hazel, Sunny broke into your store and stole a very precious piece of art that could have made you a lot of money," I said, feeling like I needed to drill home the point that she didn't seem to care about.

"That she did." A grin tugged at the woman's lips. Not humor, but pride. "She's a pistol, that one."

I slid my palms onto the counter, leaned forward. "Why didn't you call it in? Why let her get away with it?"

"Why do you assume she's a *thief*, detective?"

I pushed off the counter, turned my back, my hands

balling to fists. I sucked in a deep breath and spun back around. "Hazel, I don't have time for this."

"Yes, you do, Jagg. Yes you do. Look closer..."

Look closer. Those fucking words again.

Briana Morgan and now Hazel De Ville.

Look closer...

"Why do you assume she's a thief?" Hazel repeated, emphasizing each word.

I suddenly stilled, my racing thoughts slamming into one seemingly-impossible concept like a brick wall.

No.

No *fucking* way.

A smile crossed Hazel's lips. "There you go. See? Once you stop assuming the worst in people, you see them for what they truly are."

I blinked, a solid ten seconds ticking by while I wrapped my mind around the earth-shattering thought.

"Say it out loud, Jagg. You know it now. Trust your gut. Say it."

"Sunny Harper is an art investigator." The words came out in a whisper, almost as if I was forcing it out.

"Good job, Detective. Damn, boy, thought I was going to have to spell it out for you. Took a while, but you got there and that's what counts."

My stomach *rolled.* "When? Why? ... How?"

Hazel put her hands on the counter and leaned in. "Normally, I wouldn't talk about someone else's business, well, someone that I respected, anyway. But despite your narrow-minded, cynical view of the world, I like you. And I like Sunny and I don't want you to screw this up. More than you have already, anyway, cause I'm guessin' you have." She pinned me with a disapproving look before continuing. "Yes,

Sunny Harper is a fine art investigator. She works under-cover. *Undercover,* Jagg. I didn't even know it was her who took the scroll until she came clean earlier today. She didn't want to involve me in the whole mess, bless her heart."

I ran my fingers through my hair and began pacing. It was *not* my day.

"How long has she been doing this?"

"When Arlo, her dad, lost his wife, the poor guy went off the deep end. Drinking, gambling, you name it. The guy's always been a bit eccentric and into art, but he started getting into the black market of stolen art. Buying one-of-a-kind pieces for his properties. You see, when people steal something valuable, they realize they don't know what to do with it because the authenticity of the art is dependent on the appraisal with it, a simple piece of paper that is rarely stolen with the object. Arlo, being the businessman he was, would knowingly purchase stolen art, forge the paperwork, then sell it for triple what it was worth, conning people out of thousands of dollars. This went on for a while, until Sunny found out someone from an insurance company was secretly investigating him. Arlo was one piece of art away from being arrested for larceny with intent to sell, a class B felony, with a sentence of more than a year in federal prison. The agent on the case had been gathering evidence against Arlo for months before Sunny entered the picture and secretly cut a deal to keep her dad out of prison."

"Let me guess, that agent is Briana Morgan."

"Yep. Deal was if Sunny recovered the stolen art, Briana would tear up her evidence on Arlo and close the case. Briana got the praise and money for recovering the scrolls and Arlo stayed out of jail. Sunny is the one, the Black Bandit, who recovered the first three Cedonia scrolls. Two weeks later, Briana offered her a job. Sunny's been an undercover agent for Harold and Associates almost a year now, her primary focus recovering the fourth scroll that I happened to stumble upon at a thrift store."

Holy.

Fucking.

Shit.

"Hold on." I held up my hand. "Sunny did all that for her dad? He's an asshole—forgive me. And they're not close. Hell, she doesn't even seem to like men at all. Why put her neck out there like that for him? Especially after what she went through?"

Hazel shook her head. "Boy, I'd slap you in the forehead if not for this counter between us. Don't you get it? Sunny put her neck on the line *because* of what she went through. She's fiercely loyal *because* of what she went through. Because she was betrayed so badly, Sunny will cling onto anyone she truly trusts with bloody fingernails. And I have a feeling she trusts you. Or trusted maybe."

My heart sank.

Hazel continued, "Sunny didn't leave Dallas until the deal with Briana was solid, and Arlo had sobered up and started therapy. To this day, Arlo doesn't even know what Sunny did for him. She is, without question, the most selfless and loyal woman you'll ever meet."

"When did she tell you all this?"

"This afternoon, when she came looking for that compass she gave you. Poor thing. I could see the torment written all over her face. She hated deceiving you. I'd never seen her like that. The look in her eyes when she spoke about you. It's deeper than just like or lust, Detective."

"If that's true, why the hell didn't she just tell me she was the Bandit?"

"Because you were so damn sure the Black Bandit murdered the Lieutenant. On top of that, she'd just been attacked, for the second time, and the entire town was calling her a murderer and a liar. She was scared. She didn't think you'd believe her that she had nothing to do with shooting that cop... hell, I genuinely think she thought you'd arrest her." Hazel tilted her head to the side. "You're not the kind of guy that exactly screams, 'hey, you can open up to me.'"

The guilt I was feeling was an iron fist in my stomach.

"Close your mouth dear..." I didn't even realize it was hanging open. "... and go get her. It's my guess you've got a lot of apologizing to do and I'm guessing—"

Her words were cut off by the sound of sirens blasting through the air.

That fist in my gut? Twisted ten times over, an instinct sending a chill up my spine.

Hazel's eyes widened.

Another siren, then another, a chorus of sirens wailing in the distance.

My phone rang.

"Jagger."

Shouts and screams filled the other end of the call. "It's Colson." His voice was panicked. He was running. I could hear the footsteps and the hitch of his breath.

"What's going on?"

"There's a fire at the festival. At Devil's Cove. The mountain is going up in flames." He jerked the phone away and shouted orders to someone before continuing. "The entire town will burn down if we don't get it under control. I'm calling in everyone I know. Trucks are headed to the festival, but the fire didn't originate there. We don't know where yet. I've got—"

Panic seized me as I shoved the phone into my pocket and sprinted out the door.

I knew exactly where the fire originated.

And I knew who started it.

44

JAGG

*C*louds of red smoke barreled into the night sky, fading into a black mass that blocked the moon. A line of blazing orange highlighted the mountain peaks in the distance. The forest was on fire.

I skidded around a corner, my tires sliding on loose rocks. Dust swelled around my Jeep as I dialed with one hand while gripping the wheel with the other.

"You alright?" My brother's voice was clipped. He already knew about the fire.

"Ryder, we need your help."

A horse whinnied in the background. "I'm on it."

"Is the fire close to your ranch?"

"Not yet and I'd like to keep it that way. I'm locking up the horses, the dogs."

"Are Sunny's dogs safe?"

"She came by a few hours ago. Got her dogs and left without a word."

My heart skipped in my chest. Sunny had left the bungalow and everything that kept her safe. It was my fault. My fucking fault.

"Where was she going?" My voice desperate. "Did she say where she was going?"

"No. Sorry, I—"

"*Shit.* I need you to get to her house. *Now.* I'm almost there but I have a feeling I'm going to need backup. Get every fire extinguisher from your house."

"Text me the address. I'm on my way, brother."

"Thanks."

"Hey, Jagg? Take a deep breath. Follow your instincts."

With that, we disconnected.

The normally desolate road to Sunny's cabin was filled with cars, trucks and SUVs packed with festival goers barely escaping the flames. While they were running from it, I was driving directly into it.

Trees blazed around me, flames spreading in waves across the parched dead grass on the mountainsides. Embers spun with the dust in the air that was blowing up from my tires.

I pressed the gas, my heart pounding like a sledge-hammer the deeper into the fire I drove. Sunny had left the bungalow and gone home, where Kenzo Rees had been waiting on her.

Fucking mother fucker.

I was shaking with rage by the time I turned down Sunny's driveway.

The pine trees were ablaze.

Half of her house was in flames.

I skidded to a stop and sprinted across the driveway, screaming her name as I jumped onto the porch. The heat from the flames coated my body like a stinging blanket. Sweat rolled down my temples.

"*Sunny?*"

I ripped off my shirt, wrapped it as a glove around my

hand and turned the doorknob, but the door wouldn't budge. I jumped back and slammed my boot against the wood. Again, again, until finally, against the heat and my weight, it buckled. I kicked open the door, the blast of fresh air sending a burst of flame above my head. Black smoke barreled out of the top of the doorway. I dropped to the ground and covered my nose and mouth with my shirt.

"Sunny!" I screamed, using my elbows to shimmy over the threshold on my stomach. Blinking away the tears, I scanned the room. The furniture was on fire, the rugs, the curtains. Black smoke prevented me from seeing into the loft, but from what I could see, there was no Sunny.

Movement had my head whipping to the side.

Athena, Tango and Max huddled in the corner, shaking like leaves.

"Come. *Come!*"

The dogs didn't move.

"Come, I said! Come on, you fucking crazy mutts!"

Athena moved slowly, clawing across the floor on her stomach much like I was. The other dogs followed suit.

I backed out the front door. Once the dogs crossed onto the porch, they went ballistic.

"Settle, *settle!*" I yelled, then turned back to the house.

Was Sunny in there? Burning to death? Listening to me scream for her but unable to respond?

I swear to God, right then and there, I had a mini heart attack. I looked down at the dogs, bouncing like monkeys and then it hit me—the dogs would have been by her side. If Sunny was in that house, they would have been huddled next to her. There was no doubt in my mind.

Trust your instincts...

I took one last look at the house. *"Dammit!"* I screamed, then turned back to the dogs. "Where is she? Take me to her.

Where's Sunny?" I frantically looked around for anything that carried her scent. I leapt off the porch, jogged to her truck and grabbed the purple baseball cap she'd been wearing at our lunch from the seat. I shoved it in Max's face. "Take me to Sunny. Search! *Go! Search!*"

The dog took off like a bullet, the others on his heels. Clutching Sunny's hat, I took off after them, sprinting through burning woods around me. Sweat poured like water down my face, my back, my skin so hot I kept looking down to see if it had ignited or not.

The thought that I was going to die actually entered my mind.

Then I'd die trying to save the woman I loved.

Swiping away the sweat from my face, I pressed on, blinking away the tears, trying to focus on that ball of sable fur sprinting through the woods.

Farther, farther, the dogs stretched ahead of me, until the smoke engulfed and they disappeared. They were too fast. My old, disabled ass couldn't keep up.

Fuck, fuck, fuck.

Distant screams had me planting my feet and whipping around. A group of teenagers wearing flowing dresses sprinted through the woods, ten feet from me, screaming and crying. More festival goers running from the flames.

"Wait!" I yelled. "Did you see anyone running this way? Dogs? Wait!" But my voice was lost in the hissing and crackling wood.

I turned back on course just as a branch engulfed in flames fell in front of me. I stumbled, the pain in my back crippling. Gritting my teeth, I straightened and pressed on, chest heaving, wheezing in and out. My vision began to waver. It wasn't the heat. It was the smoke. I couldn't damn breathe.

I'd lost the dogs, the trail.

I'd lost her.

I stumbled onto the tree next to me, covered my nose and mouth with my T-shirt and took several deep breaths. Embers rained around me, a few hitting my shoulders like little bee stings.

Keep going, Jagg. She needs you. Do not die here.

With my shirt over my mouth, I pressed on, running, stumbling, running, stumbling, aimlessly, until finally, I burst out of the trees onto the riverbank. I propelled myself into the water, the shock of cold nearly paralyzing me. I gulped, splashed it into my open eyes, snorting it to clear the smoke from my nose.

"Holy shit," I breathed.

When I pulled myself out of the water, I was face to face with a pair of silver eyes.

"Brute. Oh my God, Brutus." I fell to my knees, gripping the dog's head. He licked my nose. I looked over at the cages, his door on the hinges. Bastard had busted out. Hell yeah, he did.

"We need to find Sunny. I lost the other dogs. Did they come by here?" I realized I was talking to a dog. *"Shit... just...* Brute, I need you. Sunny needs you." I grabbed the baseball cap I'd chucked when diving into the water and shoved it against his nose. "Search. Go. Search." He didn't move. I pulled his face to my jeans where the dogs had jumped all over not five minutes earlier. "Follow their scent. Go. *Search!"*

Brute spun around and took off like the others, but because of his shoulder injury, his sprint was slow enough for me to keep up. There we were, two injured former fighters, with the world burning around us, risking their lives for their master.

"Thank you." I blurted out to him, so freaking grateful I could keep up with him.

We sprinted down the riverbank—best we could. I had no clue if we were going the right way, but I decided to trust Brute. He was all I had, and all I had was blind faith.

Trust your instincts...

"Faster, Brute!" Adrenaline burst through my veins. "Let's go. Faster. You can do it. I can do it. *Faster, Brute.*"

The creek grew narrower and narrower, the woods beginning to close in around us. I swiped the tears from my eyes and focused on the black fur just ahead of me. A line of flames outlined the top of the bluff that marked the end of the cove. The creek stopped, tall bluffs enclosed around us.

There was nowhere else to go.

We'd reached Devil's Cove.

Frantic barks came into ear shot.

Sunny.

Brute's speed suddenly tripled, as did mine.

The orange glow of the fire shimmered off the wet rocks of the bluff, illuminating three dogs at the base and a swath of black hair climbing midway, and about six feet below that, a bald, tattooed head.

Sunny and Kenzo Rees.

Fury hotter than the flame around me lit my veins. I didn't think, didn't plan, didn't consider the consequences or risks as I bolted to the bluff and began climbing. Hand, foot, hand, foot, my teeth grinding against each other with every inch. The rocks were wet and slick with moss, and although I didn't look down, I knew that a bed of jagged rocks lined the base. Sunny was high enough that if she fell, she'd be dead in an instant. Embers spun around Rees and his fucking white sneakers.

Dead. Dead. Dead. Those were the only words that penetrated through the all-consuming rage.

Dead. Dead. Dead. Kenzo Rees was a dead man.

My foot slipped, my body falling a few feet before I caught myself on another rock, ripping my fingernails off. Blood ran down my hand, my arm, the pain igniting a fresh blow of adrenaline.

Then, she screamed.

I looked up. Sunny dangled with one arm, her foot in the grasp of Kenzo's tattooed hand.

Her eyes met mine. Everything around me stopped.

There were no more options. I was staring Sunny's death in my face.

"Fight, Sunny!" I screamed. *"Fight!"* I tore my eyes away and climbed up the bluff with a carelessness like I had nothing to lose. Because if I lost her, I didn't care. Death, take me.

I could smell him. The sweat. The body odor.

I planted my foot, gripped a ledge, and using all my body weight, I propelled my arm above my head—and connected.

My bloody fingers gripped the bottom of Kenzo's jeans. I tugged, pulled, yanked, but the fucker didn't lose his grip.

I took one last look at Sunny, trying to kick out of his hold, fighting to the death. Tears streamed down her face.

My love.

The love of my life.

Our eyes met again.

I love you, I thought, *I love you.*

And with that final thought, I released my two-hundred-plus pound weight and dangled in the air with one hand around Rees' ankle. As planned, his grip slipped from Sunny.

We fell together, two bodies tumbling down the side of the cliff.

This is it, I remember thinking. I was going to die.

I desperately grasped at the rocks until my hand found the only root on the cliff. I still, to this day, don't know how I gripped onto the thing, or how it held my weight.

My body jerked to a stop as Kenzo's hands grabbed my foot. I planted my other foot and tightened my grip on the root.

I bent at the waist and wrapped my hand around his throat. I stared into his eyes as I squeezed with everything I had in me, staring into the soul of the devil himself, his eyes bulging, lips turning blue. Finally, his grip released and I watched his body shatter on the rocks below.

"Jagg!"

I don't remember the climb up to Sunny but I'll never forget her face when I'd finally made it.

"I love you, Sunny. I'm sorry. I didn't say it. But I do. I love you."

"I know."

I gripped the back of her head with my bloody hand and kissed her.

Just then, a rope bounced off the rocks next to us.

I looked up to see my brother's silhouette outlined against a pair of headlights.

"Better get a move on, bro!" He yelled down from the top of the bluff.

"She secure?" I yelled back, yanking the rope.

"Yep. *Go.*"

"Wait!" Sunny jerked away. "My dogs." Her eyes rounded in terror.

I looked down the bluff where four balls of fur paced back and forth.

"Swim!" I yelled down. "Get in the water! Swim!"

Brute faded into the shallow water, followed by the others.

"They'll stay there. They're smart. We'll come back for them. I promise. They'll be okay in the water. The rocks won't light. They'll be okay."

Sunny hesitated, tears filling her eyes.

I grabbed her chin. "Baby. Listen to me. You've got to get out of here. I'll climb back down and stay with them until help arrives. We'll be safe in the water—"

"No." Tears streamed down her face. "No. Nothing can happen to you. You're right. They're smart. We'll come back. God, promise me we'll come back."

"Yes. *Go,* Sunny." I shoved the rope to her. "No time to waste."

She gripped the rope and looked at me. "You saved my life."

"No." I kissed her head. "You saved mine."

45

JAGG

8 months later...

The afternoon sun was bright, the air fresh and cool, clinging onto spring although summer was only a month away. It was a glorious seventy-six degrees, with big, white clouds speckling an endless blue sky. I parked my Jeep between two jacked-up Chevys with American flags and tool boxes in the back.

I took a moment to look up at the thriving tree in front of me. I'd never seen a green so vibrant. So healthy. Squirrels zipped from branch to branch. There was even a blue bird, as bright as turquoise, sitting only a few feet above my Jeep. I can honestly say, it was the first time in my life, I took a second to appreciate a single tree.

I turned the ignition and climbed out of my Jeep. Yes, in case you're wondering, the same one. The same one I'd had when the world burned down around me. The same one with ripped seats and a busted air conditioner. I never got the thing fixed. I don't know why really, other than I'd come to like the fresh air. The Jeep's flaws were like a badge of honor, a weakness in the vehicle that I not only accepted, but embraced.

A metaphor, no doubt about that.

"Let's go, Brute."

Oh, and there was that. Nothing easier for hauling dogs around than a vehicle without doors.

Brute jumped out, tail wagging and took off into the woods, as he always did. A smile caught me as I watched him sniff like a bloodhound. Turns out, the pit was one hell of a detection dog. I watched him as he meandered through the new grass and seedlings, budding along the forest floor that eight months earlier had burned to the ground.

One thousand acres had burned during what was now dubbed as the Moon Magic Fire. It would have been a lot worse—catastrophic—if not for the river that helped contain the flames until the sky opened up six hours later and rained for almost an entire day. Autumn, followed by an icy winter, didn't allow for much regrowth, but so far, the season of new life was living up to its name.

Renewal.

Rebirth.

I straightened, stretching my spine, my hand almost instinctively going to my lower back.

The sound of tires on rocks had me looking over my shoulder at the black sedan slowly inching to a stop behind my Jeep.

"Hey, old man." Darby pushed out of the car.

"Hey, shorty."

He sauntered over, a new swagger I'd never seen in the kid. "How's the back?"

"What do you have behind yours?"

A shit-eating-grin crossed his face as he pulled a God-awful gold cane with an eagle head hand mount from behind his back. "Picked you up a cane."

"Thanks." I plucked it from his hand and hurled it into the woods, the sunlight glinting off the gold as it faded out of sight.

"*Hey!* That cost me seven dollars."

"More than those shoes, I'm guessing."

Darby kicked out the professional black loafers that had replaced his millennial white kicks. "At least they don't have holes anymore."

The kid had a point.

"How's the shoulder?" I asked.

He rolled his arm in a circle. "Good as new. Except when it rains. For some reason it aches when it rains."

"It'll keep you tough." I looked him over. Darby's blue button-up and khakis were freshly pressed with not a drip of syrup, ketchup or chocolate milk on them. Starched too, best I could tell. And not a speck of dirt. The kid had gained seventeen pounds of solid muscle since fully recovering from being shot three times. The added weight and ability to defy death gave him instant respect at the station. The scars from taking three rounds to the torso gave him a golden dick, apparently. Tommy Darby had become the most unexpected ladies' man in Berry Springs. I saw more than that, though. I saw confidence. And it looked damn good on him.

I lingered on the shiny badge on his hip for a moment, memories flooding me.

Times had changed. In eight months, my life had taken me down paths I'd never expected.

"Come on," I grabbed my bags from the back and

nodded to the trail through the woods that had been carved out of foot traffic over the last few months. Darby fell into step next to me.

"You know," he said, "That cane really would have gone with this new caveman look you've got on."

I ran my fingers through my hair, catching on a snag. That was a first. I couldn't remember a time that my hair was so long that it tangled. Went with the beard, though. I also couldn't remember ever having so many gray hairs. Only at the temples for now, but spreading nonetheless.

It felt good, believe it or not. The beard, the shaggy hair that curled just below my ears. Another inch and I'd be able to pull it back. I'd spent my life sporting crew cuts and smooth chins. Not anymore.

"So," Darby started, redirecting the conversation to the purpose of the announced visit. "I wanted to get your thoughts on this case I was just handed..."

Our conversation seamlessly switched to homicide, to me listening to Darby and doing my best to guide him in the right direction. I didn't know why the kid trusted me so much, but because he did, I wasn't going to let him down. He wasn't going to be the next *Dog,* he was going to be the next *Pit Bull.*

I was proud of him. He was the youngest cop to ever be promoted to detective.

As we took a curve in the woods, the sounds of nature faded to shouts, curse words, something about "your mama," tools banging, saws and drills. The fresh smell of lumber perked my senses—but that was nothing compared to seeing the woman standing at the edge of the woods.

Wearing a pair of khaki pants tight enough to hug that perfect ass, a pair of workman boots—although she'd kick my ass for calling them work*man* boots instead work*woman* boots—and a T-shirt that read *Goal Digger*, Sunny Harper stood with her hands fisted on her hips, her focus zeroed in on the project ahead of her. Her hair was down, flowing in the wind, just the way I liked it. The tool belt around her waist had my dick pulsing, the dirt smudged on her cheek had my heart kicking. Over the last eight months, I learned Sunny's loyalty and hard-working nature had no bounds.

She was the perfect woman.

And she was mine.

As if sensing me, she turned, a breeze catching those long curls as she met my gaze and smiled.

New beginnings.

Her attention dropped to the bags in my hands. Her eyes lit as we walked up.

"A picnic lunch?"

I lifted the brown sacks in one hand and a bag carrying our plaid blanket and bug spray in the other. Picnics had become a thing for us. Shoes off, every time.

"Breakfast burritos for my queen," I said.

"Oh, *gag.*" Darby rolled his eyes.

"I actually cook my woman breakfast in the mornings, Darby, not send them out the door with a bottle of prescription ointment."

"Dude, that was poison ivy, I promise."

We laughed.

"Well thanks for showing up, Sally." My gaze shifted to Gage Steele, sauntering across the field. In the distance, a dozen workers, including Gage's brothers, Axel, Gunner, and Phoenix, slinging hammers and pushing drills into the nearly finished frame for the lake house.

Our lake house.

Gage tossed me a hammer. "Added an extra grip around the handle, made special for fingernail-less nubs. I call it the Cripple's Clout."

I caught it mid-air and hurled it back. He doubled over, grabbing his groin.

"I think I like Ball Blaster better."

"Asshole," he squeaked out like a pre-pubescent boy.

Grinning, Phoenix Steele, the CEO of the project and a man of recovery in his own right, walked up, grinning at me. "Well, you've still got your aim at least."

"Big target," Gage ground out between clenched teeth.

Phoenix shook his head and refocused on me. "Rough plumbing and HVAC wiring should be done by Friday. We're ahead of schedule. Hopefully we'll start on the drywall within the next few weeks."

"Sounds like you could use a break, then." I jerked my chin to the trail that led to the Jeep. "I've two coolers filled with sandwiches, burgers, hot dogs. Water, beer, and three handles of Jack."

Phoenix grinned. "You had me at handle." He glanced back at the crew. "I'll let them know. Might even give them the afternoon off after. Your brother's connections are solid, man. We're way ahead of schedule."

I looked over Phoenix's shoulder to my brother, Ryder, straddling the center beam of the roof, high above the other workers. While everyone else worked in pairs, with occasional jovial banter back and forth, my brother worked solo. He was the first one at the site in the morning and the last to leave. His commitment to helping me out reminded me of the good ol' days when we used to be inseparable. Before his life had imploded and he'd turned into an agoraphobic mute. Sunny had tried to set him up with Briana Morgan, to which he denied with a quick change of subject and turn of his back. As I watched him hammer nail after nail, the sweat pouring off of the hard lines of his face, I wondered if I'd ever have that brother back. Until then—or if ever—I'd settle for someone, who regardless of his callous exterior, would take a bullet for me. That was more than enough, and I loved him for it.

"So, you ready for Monday?" Phoenix asked.

I pulled my gaze away from Ryder, a zing of excitement shooting through me at Phoenix's question.

"Hell, yeah." I nodded. "Brute and I will be there at eight, bells on."

Hell, yes, I was ready to get back to work. Two days after the fire, I sent my resignation to my boss and tossed my badge on Chief McCord's desk with a smile on my face, and Sunny waiting for me in my Jeep. Almost losing her, and Darby, for that matter, had jolted me more than any near-death experience had before. Life was short. It was time to change mine. To be a better person. To be a better man. To be like Sunny. And that started with ending my career as a homicide detective. I walked away from everything I knew, from the job that had become my life, from everything I ate, drank, and slept.

Although removing my badge from my belt had been like removing my right arm, it felt *right.*

It was time to slow down, switch paces.

I'd had too much death in my life. Too many lives taken, too many lives lost, too much pain, too all-consuming in what had become an unhealthy way of life for me.

Three weeks after that, on my fortieth birthday nonetheless, I'd gone in for back surgery, at Sunny's urging, to finally correct the problem that had been plaguing me for years. The recovery wasn't as bad as I'd expected, especially with Sunny as my sizzling-hot nurse—I even talked her into wearing one of those dirty nurse costumes—and Brute as my misery-loves-company partner. He'd gone in for doggy-shoulder surgery a week after mine. We'd recovered together, him and I, and the damn dog hadn't left my side since.

I'd been a fish out of water. No job, no strength, no plans. Totally lost. All this while detoxing off, what I realize now, was a very real addiction to pain pills. I haven't touched a pill since.

And it was the day I stopped trembling that I picked up the phone and called my mother, taking the first step in mending the crack from a two-decade-long grudge. She'd cried when I said simply, "hi." I cried when she told me she loved me.

It had stripped me raw, and Sunny had been my strength, my light. My path.

On Christmas morning, I'd taken Sunny to the tree in the park, once known as the Voodoo Tree, now known as the place where I dropped to my knees and asked her to marry me. She was my gift, my woman, my savior.

My own.

She said yes, and a week later, we'd begun designing our new lake house to sit on the scorched land we'd purchased from Sunny's dad. No handouts.

We had plans to rebuild the forest around our house, which was going to consist of a full-blown K9 training facility. After delivering the fourth Cedonia scroll to Briana, Sunny hung up her hat as an art investigator and decided to put her full focus on what truly made her happy, her business, Sunny's K9 Security. And me? I signed on to become

Steele Shadows Security's latest consultant. It would be less physical, less death, but still in the realm of what I knew. What I was good at, what I was born to do. And the pay was damn good, too.

Gage slung his arm around Darby's shoulder and the two began the ball-busting banter they established since I'd taken him to the Steele compound for hand-to-hand combat training a few months earlier.

Sunny beamed up at me, a smile brighter than the spring sun. "It's really coming along isn't it?"

I cupped her face in my hands and kissed her forehead. "I'd live in a matchbox with you."

"Been there, done that." She winked, then closed her eyes and inhaled, a sweet little habit she had when I kissed her face.

I took her left hand in mine and fingered the ring I gotten her. It was a band of diamonds, and in the center, three emerald stones to match her eyes. Unique, timeless, gorgeous. Just like her. I threaded my hand through hers and kissed her again, this time on the lips.

"Let's eat."

"Don't have to tell me twice."

As the construction crew disbanded, we settled onto the picnic blanket and fell into that carefree, comfortable, easy conversation I'd come to love almost as much as her ability to bend like a pretzel in bed.

For the first time, I felt happy. Free.

Light.

Looking back, it's funny how one single event can change a life so drastically. How it went, the paths you chose after, for better or worse—was your decision.

I chose better. Like Sunny had chosen.

And I wasn't ever going back.

~

Ready for Ryder's story?
Pre-order your copy today!

He's an ex-con who just wants to be left alone. She's stranded in the middle of a blizzard—a broken soul... an invitation to danger.

Photographer by day, Ben and Jerry's enthusiast by night, Louise Sloane isn't known for her organizational skills or obsession to detail. But when someone from her past goes missing, she makes it her mission to solve the case—especially when the mystery becomes linked to the notorious serial killer, the String Strangler.

During one of the worst snowstorms on record, Louise sets off to the small Southern town of Berry Springs, bulldozing her way not only into the investigation, but also into the home of a reclusive former inmate with eyes as cold as ice.

Ryder's one goal in life is to be left alone. A desire unacknowledged by the five-foot-two-inch train wreck who breaks into his house in the middle of the night. He wants nothing to do with her and all her curves—until she uncovers his secrets and unearths a link to the past that changed his life forever.

As boundaries are shattered and relationships are questioned, a body is found on Ryder's land, and it becomes apparent that the killer is closer than anyone realized. With his freedom on the line, Ryder must risk going back to prison or losing Louise forever.

Ryder (Steele Shadows Investigations)

★Hey book lovers, book bloggers, and bookstagrammers★ Want to participate in the promo event for Ryder? Just go to my website to sign up! Easy squeezy!

https://www.amandamckinneyauthor.com/contact

STEELE BROTHERS?

Want to read more about the badass, swoon-worthy Steele brothers? If you haven't read STEELE SHADOWS SECURITY, the complete series is available now!

CABIN 1
CABIN 2
CABIN 3

★ THE VIPER ★

Coming November 09

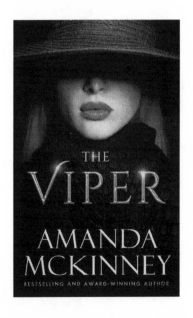

A brash DEA agent and a ruthless private detective collide

in this seductive small-town tale of revenge, murder, and the unbreakable bond between sisters.

"Revenge is an act of passion, vengeance is an act of justice." – Samuel Johnson

They say revenge is a dish best served cold. Apparently, they haven't met the Archer sisters.

Owner of Archer and Archer, Inc., a prestigious New York private investigative firm, Colette Archer embodies effortless perfection in her couture suits and trademark chignon. But this private investigator has a secret. When night falls, Colette slips on her wig and into the persona of a tequila-guzzling hustler who occasionally fancies two men instead of one. This double life comes as an unwelcome side effect of a horrific past that she and her sister, Jade, a bohemian martial-arts-instructing renegade, decide to settle once and for all—regardless of who they must destroy in the process.

Obstinate DEA agent James Black is one mistake away from spending his career crunching numbers in the confinement of his six-by-six cubicle. In a last-ditch effort to save his floundering career, James seeks the assistance of ice queen Colette Archer. Despite the spark of heat between them, she seems to despise him almost as much as poly-blend fabrics.

After following Colette and her sister to a sleepy small town in Montana, James learns of a devious and dangerous pact the sisters have made to avenge their past. Using Colette's weakness to his advantage, James tricks her into helping him uncover the whereabouts of a ruthless drug lord. But when Colette is brutally attacked, James realizes he has inadvertently set wheels in motion that might not only cost him his job, but also the woman who's stolen his heart.

Pre-order Today

♥ *And don't forget to sign up for my exclusive reader group and blogging team!* ♥

STEALS AND DEALS

★LIMITED TIME STEALS AND DEALS★

1. The Shadow (A Berry Springs Novel), **FREE**
2. Bestselling and award-nominated Cabin 1 (Steele Shadows Security), **FREE**
3. Devil's Gold (A Black Rose Mystery), only **$0.99**

(1) The Shadow (A Berry Springs Novel)

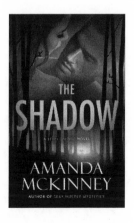

A gruesome murder linking to a famous painting sends FBI Criminal Profiler Eli Archer down a path of lies, deceit... and infatuation.

Get The Shadow for ★FREE★ today

(2) Cabin 1 (Steele Shadows Security)

★2020 National Readers' Choice Award Finalist, 2020 HOLT Medallion Finalist★

Hidden deep in the remote mountains of Berry Springs is a private security firm where some go to escape, and others find exactly what they've been looking for.

Welcome to Cabin 1, Cabin 2, Cabin 3...

Get Cabin 1 for ★FREE★ today

(3) Devil's Gold

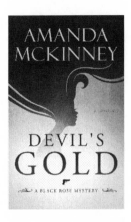

"With fast-paced action, steamy romance, and a good dose of mystery, Devil's Gold is a solid whodunit that will keep you surprised at every turn." -Siobhan Novelties

"...smart, full of energetic thrills and chills, it's one of the best novellas I've read in a very long time." -Booked J

Get Devil's Gold today for only $0.99

Sign up for my Newsletter so you don't miss out on more Steals and Deals! https://www.amandamckinneyauthor.com/contact

ABOUT THE AUTHOR

Amanda McKinney is the bestselling and multi-award-winning author of more than twenty romantic suspense and mystery novels. She wrote her debut novel in 2017 after walking away from her career to become a stay-at-home mom. Her books include the BERRY SPRINGS SERIES, STEELE SHADOWS SERIES, and the BLACK ROSE MYSTERY SERIES, with many more to come. Amanda lives in Arkansas with her handsome husband, two beautiful boys, and three obnoxious dogs.

Text **AMANDABOOKS to 66866** to sign up for Amanda's Newsletter and get the latest on new releases, promos, and freebies!

If you enjoyed Jagger, please write a review!

THE AWARD-WINNING BERRY SPRINGS SERIES

The Woods (A Berry Springs Novel)
The Lake (A Berry Springs Novel)
The Storm (A Berry Springs Novel)
The Fog (A Berry Springs Novel)
The Creek (A Berry Springs Novel)
The Shadow (A Berry Springs Novel)
The Cave (A Berry Springs Novel)

#1 BESTSELLING STEELE SHADOWS

Cabin 1 (Steele Shadows Security)
Cabin 2 (Steele Shadows Security)
Cabin 3 (Steele Shadows Security)
Phoenix (Steele Shadows Rising)
Jagger (Steele Shadows Investigations)
Ryder (Steele Shadows Investigations)

Rattlesnake Road

Redemption Road

★ *The Viper, Coming Fall 2021* ★

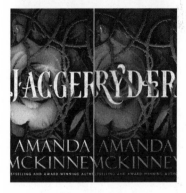

Like your sexy murder mysteries with a side of evil witch?
Check out THE BLACK ROSE MYSTERY SERIES about three
super-rich, independent, badass sisters who run a private
investigation company in a creepy, southern town...

Devil's Gold (A Black Rose Mystery, Book 1)
Hatchet Hollow (A Black Rose Mystery, Book 2)
Tomb's Tale (A Black Rose Mystery Book 3)
Evil Eye (A Black Rose Mystery Book 4)
Sinister Secrets (A Black Rose Mystery Book 5)

READING ORDER GUIDE

SMALL-TOWN MYSTERY ROMANCE

Steele Shadows Security Series:
Action-packed Romantic Suspense with swoon-worthy military heroes and smart, sassy heroines. Must be read in order. First-person POV.
#1 Cabin 1
#2 Cabin 2
#3 Cabin 3
#4 Phoenix (Steele Shadows Rising) - Can be read as a standalone.

Steele Shadows Investigations Series:
Action-packed Romantic Suspense/Crime Thriller. Each book is a standalone. First-person POV.
#1 Jagger
#2 Ryder

Broken Ridge Series:
Action-packed Romantic Suspense with swoon-worthy heroes

and smart, sassy heroines. Must be read in order.
First-person POV.

#1 *The Viper*

#2 *The Recluse*

Road Series:

Dark, emotional Romantic Suspense/Mystery. Each book is a standalone. First-person POV.

#1 *Rattlesnake Road*

#2 *Redemption Road*

Berry Springs Series:

Romantic Suspense/Mystery. Each book is a standalone. Third-person POV.

The Woods

The Lake

The Storm

The Fog

The Creek

The Shadow

The Cave

Black Rose Mysteries:

Romantic Suspense novellas. Must be read in order. Third-person POV.

#1 *Devil's Gold*

#2 *Hatchet Hollow*

#3 *Tomb's Tale*

#4 *Evil Eye*

#5 *Sinister Secrets*

Made in the USA
Middletown, DE
16 January 2022

58817366R00243